LIGHTEN UP

She Saw Her Pastor in a New Light.

Angela Ruth Strong

ENDURANCE PRESS

2012

ISBN 9780985674649 – Trade Paperback
ISBN 9780985674656 – Electronic book format

Cover Design by CSarton Design

Cover Photo used by Permission.

Printed in the United States of America

Letter from the Author

Dear Readers,

As a pastor's daughter myself, I've seen it all.

- My dad took over a church when the former pastor ran off with the secretary.
- My mom was a church secretary who discovered another pastor with a phone sex addiction.
- I met a pastor who confessed nine years of affairs to me but continued to hide it from his very large congregation because he said he didn't want to be responsible for any of them leaving the church. It happens. And it hurts lots of people.

In Lighten Up I focus on the daughter of a fallen pastor and the feelings of judgment that affect her. Others judge her, and she judges her father.

It's a story of how becoming a Christian doesn't make you perfect. You will still be tempted. And those temptations can be way too easily justified.

So this is my chance to warn readers that if you are looking for a sweet romance or sterilized view of Christianity, this probably isn't the book for you. It's going to be uncomfortably real at parts.

The novel became even more real for me the year after I finished writing it when my ex-husband left me for another woman. (You can read more about that journey on my blog: www.angelaruthstrong.blogspot.com.) The lesson Bethany learned through this story is one that I had to learn all over again.

"You, therefore, have no excuse, you who pass judgment on someone else, for at whatever point you judge the other, you are condemning yourself, because you who pass judgment do the same things." (Romans 2:1)

We are all susceptible to unfaithful desires. It's not enough to say, "I won't ever cheat on my spouse." You have to start with something like, "I won't ever have coffee alone with a member of the opposite sex." And then you have to create accountability.

For those of you who have had to (or will have to) deal with infidelity in some form, my prayer for you is that through it you learn to give and receive mercy like never before. For mercy is the only way to truly lighten up.

Sincerely,
Angela Ruth Strong

What readers are saying about

Lighten Up

"Lighten Up is one of the heaviest Christian novels I've ever read. It's also fun, smart, snappy, real, and convicting. Highly recommended for a reader who's looking for something different from the norm, with a lot of faith-challenging entertainment."

Christina Berry
Christy-nominated and Carol-winning author of
The Familiar Stranger

"Lighten Up is a powerful work of fiction. Strong's characters jump off the page and into the hearts of readers. Bethany's voice rings true with life and emotional traumas many will relate to. This is a book that makes you laugh and makes you think. It moved me. And I hated to see the story end, wondering what would happen to Bethany next."

Jill Williamson,
author of By Darkness Hid, Replication, and Captives

Dedication

To my parents Mike and Ginger McGrath
for being the most merciful people I know

Acknowledgments

Jim Strong
for making my dreams his dreams

J-Dog, Cat, and Mouse
for making me want to be a better person

Charla Leasure
for making the tragic entertaining

Christina Berry Tarabochia
for leading the way

Focus Seminars
for kicking me in the butt (in a good way)

Jeanette Light
for hiring me at her personal training
studio back when I was in better shape

Robert Sweesy
for giving me the opportunity
to work with Endurance Press

LIGHTEN UP

Chapter 1

"He's here!" I call over my shoulder, and immediately the electric charge of whispered hushes fill the room. Excitement grows within me like one of the birthday party balloons ready to pop.

I sneak one more glance out the window to mentally calculate the time before my brother Christian opens the front door. At the moment, he's climbing out of a fancy blue pickup that must belong to the buddy who took him golfing. Yeah, golf in November. I would have thought by this time of year all the "birdies" had migrated south for the winter.

The two men connect in front of the truck and head toward the house. Christian laughs at one of his own jokes, but his friend looks up at the window. He shoots me a grin before I'm able to drop the red toile curtain back into place.

I search my brain, trying to recall if Christian's wife Laurel mentioned the name of Christian's friend. I haven't met him before. If I had, I would have remembered that amused smile I just received. The guy is attractive, but even from a distance I could tell his appeal is from more than just appearance.

Giggles from an excited child interrupt my thoughts. The kid's mother tries to calm him down, reminding me of the anticipation I'd felt at Dad's fortieth birthday surprise party. At the age of ten, my Daddy had seemed perfect—I couldn't have been more wrong.

The front door swings open, bringing me back to the much more pleasant present.

"Surprise!" we all shout.

Christian grabs at his heart and staggers against the wall feigning a heart attack. The roar of laughter that erupts around me is exactly the response he was going for. It's as if he's been preparing for this party his whole life.

"Man, you'd think I was turning thirty or something!" he yells.

"Come here, old man." I wrap my arms around his thicker-than-I-remember middle. It's a good thing I talked my cousins into going in with me to buy him some exercise equipment for a gift. I wouldn't want his next heart attack to be for real.

Pulling away, I search for Christian's friend, expecting an introduction. But Laurel has other ideas. She drags me up the steps of her split-level home to help get the games going.

Laurel could have been a Stepford Wife. She's so perfect (meticulous, organized, um...mechanical) that I'm always a little uncomfortable around her. I mean, how did she ever get hooked up with my brother? He's the kind of guy who wouldn't hesitate to ask the President to pull his finger.

"Bethany." Laurel directs me, her blonde bob falling flawlessly around the fragile features on her face as she leans over a desk in the corner. "Will you pass out nametags?"

I take the sheets of computer printout labels from my sister-in-law. Now I'll find out the name of Christian's friend...or maybe not. I read a couple of the names. *Harrison Ford. E.T. Pinocchio.* I lift an eyebrow. "This is going to be an exciting party."

Laurel gives me an amused smile. "Turn around, Sweetie. I've got one for you."

"Oh!" I spin to give her my backside. I'm a little anxious to find out what kind of character Laurel would label me as. "Does it matter what name I put on who?"

Laurel rubs the little white strip onto my shirt then gives me a shoulder rub as well. "No. They'll all have to figure out their nametags by asking different people yes or no questions. But don't let them start yet."

I dutifully make my way around the room, explaining to people why I'm placing stickers on their backs. I don't know many of the faces—they're all from the hospital. I guess that is one thing Christian and Laurel have in common. They met because they both work in medicine. Laurel is an ultrasound technician—and definitely the kind to make you turn off your cell phone as is hospital policy. Christian is in pharmaceutical sales—a very successful salesman who never turns off his cell phone.

I head toward the kitchen. It's the one place I haven't yet labeled people. Christian's friend must be helping himself to a snack. I prepare my brightest smile as I round the corner, but it's wasted on my cousin. I try not to sound disappointed as I greet her. "Hi Dee Dee."

I look down at my list and pause at the *Pollyanna* nametag. Not long ago I would have thought it was perfect for her. Sighing, I peel off *Rachel Ray* instead.

"Hi." She smiles at me over her shoulder then arranges a fresh roll on a paper plate. "Try this."

I take the plate and bite into one end of the fresh Thai version of an egg roll. Its spicy sauce teases my taste buds. I'm addicted. "You made this?"

I'm not surprised because it's delicious, but because it's healthy. Dee Dee is usually all about comfort food—cheese, cream, and sugar.

"I thought it would add some variety." She smiles proudly at her display of chicken salad puffs, stuffed mushrooms, and tiny quiches.

That's more like it. Dee Dee's figure reflects her taste. No, she's not skinny, but I envy her curvy shape. She got her first bra when she was only nine. Mom always assured me that my time would come—she might as well have said the same thing to my brother.

Everything about Dee Dee is soft and inviting like a pillow. She's got full Angelina Jolie lips and big golden brown ringlets that flow to the middle of her back. Even her socks are soft looking—fuzzy and light blue.

I bet they're from the funky sock club we joined. It's more of a modern version chain letter where you send out one pair of socks and get thirty-six in return. I signed up both her and her adopted sister Star. Dee Dee doesn't know this because she's not talking to Star. In fact, Star isn't coming to the party because Dee Dee is here. But I'm not giving up on them. I'll get them back together somehow.

"Hey." Dee Dee motions past the snacks to the table full of presents. "How much do I owe you for Christian's gift?"

I think of the elliptical trainer still in the garage. Hopefully my brother will get a lot of use out of it. He's always hurting himself playing basketball and volleyball but hasn't quite figured out that if he conditioned between games he'd be less prone for injury. Did I mention he works in medicine?

"Fifty bucks."

Dee Dee scrunches up her face at me. "Really? I thought it was more expensive than that."

This is one of my plans to get her talking to her sister again—a little lame, but at least I'm trying. "Star went in on it as well."

Dee Dee's eyes narrow, and her soft lips press together into a hard line. She knows what I'm trying to do. She just doesn't know that Star has filled me in on what really happened between them. At first I'd assumed Dee Dee was mad at Star for getting pregnant before she was married. Once again I couldn't have been more wrong about a family member.

"Lookin' good!" Christian's booming voice interrupts. He grabs a stuffed mushroom from Dee Dee's display.

"It may look good..." I turn my attention to the tubby birthday boy and hold up my second fresh roll. "But these are actually good for you."

"Don't worry, sis." He says this around the fungi he just stuffed in his mouth. "I'm sure I'll eat plenty of those, too."

Shaking my head in mock disdain, I slap a label on his back. *Winnie-the-Pooh.* There. That will teach him.

I freeze with my hand on Christian's back as I realize he's not alone. His golf buddy is with him. My actions suddenly feel juvenile.

The buddy tilts his head when he sees what I'm doing. I follow his gaze and discover that my hand still covers the words on his sticker. He points and mouths the question, "Kick me?"

I laugh and step away from my brother. I can rejoice that at least I'm not *that* juvenile. "No. I haven't done that to him since he was…twenty-nine."

Christian leaves us to fill up his little plate to overflowing, so I'm finally alone with the guy I've been looking for. But what do I say? Glancing the sheet of labels in my hand I hold them up. "Here, I've got one for you."

The guy pivots obediently. "It's nice to meet you, too," he says over his shoulder.

I like his quiet sense of humor. And his rhomboids aren't bad, either.

Laurel claps her hands to get our attention.

"Yo!" Christian yells. "Listen to my wife."

The room quiets down after a few chuckles.

Laurel stands primly with her hands clasped in front of her. "I've planned an ice breaker game. You all have nametags on your back, and you have to figure out who you are. Yes or no questions only. One question per person, please. Go."

We all just stand there.

"Go!" yells Christian.

We go.

I give the new guy a look at my sticker. "Am I female?"

The guy's lips quirk up, and he doesn't say anything. I let out a huge hee-haw sounding laugh as I realize what I just asked. He chuckles.

"Yes, you are most definitely female."

I wipe imaginary perspiration from my brow. "You had me worried for a second."

"Am I male?" he asks in return.

I nod. No question there.

"Am I blonde?" I continue the game.

"Well..." The guy pauses. "You do act like it, but no."

I try to show offense at this, but I can't help smiling. "Your turn."

"You're breaking the rules, Blondie." Note: I'm part Filipino and nowhere near blonde. "We're supposed to only ask one question per person," he reprimands.

Visions of Laurel with her hands on her hips cause me to look timidly over my shoulder. She's not around, so bravely I reply, "But we're also supposed to get to know other people. How am I supposed to get to know you if this is the extent of our conversation?"

The stranger takes my argument in slowly. I wonder where Christian met him. I bet he's a doctor. He's got the all-American boy look to him. Clean cut, strong. Medium brown hair and light green eyes. Speaking of green..."You're green."

The man tilts his head slightly.

"You didn't ask another question, so I just told you. You're green."

He purses his lips together in thought. "I must be The Hulk. I get mistaken for him all the time. I don't know why."

I think back to the movie. "Do you rip your shirt off a lot?"

The guy nods thoughtfully. "That could be it."

I laugh so hard my abs start to burn. "Sorry, you're not the Hulk."

"Hmm..."

I don't know how he keeps a straight face.

"The Mask," he guesses.

I squint because he just lost me.

"That Jim Carrey movie always in the five dollar DVD bin."

"No," I groan. "This could take all night. I'm Bethany Light, Christian's sister. And you are?"

"Eric..."

I don't catch his last name over the conversations buzzing around me. I raise my voice. "How do you know Christian?"

"Church."

"Oh, yeah?" I like his answer. "I'll be there this Sunday. Christian wants me to visit. Well, and he also wants me to start counseling with the pastor." I blurt this out like I blurted out the am-I-female question. I roll my eyes to the ceiling. "That's probably not something I should tell a guy I just met."

Eric cracks a smile. "It's okay this time. I'm the pastor Christian wants you to meet with."

Well, bench press me and call me a dumbbell. "No." It can't be. "Christian was talking about a Pastor Austin." And I'm supposed to personal train his fiancée.

"My last name is Austin."

"Oh. My. Goodness." I stare at him for a moment then give the it's-a-small-world act. "Your fiancée made an appointment to start personal training at my studio."

"Yeah, she told me about you." He doesn't seem surprised at all. He should have been a poker player instead of a pastor. He certainly plays his cards close to his vestibule. "She wanted to come to Christian's party, but they're having a 'parents' night out' at her preschool."

"Right." I think Brooke mentioned that somewhere in her babbling on the telephone. Babbling Brooke. Ooh, I like that. "That's so funny!"

"What?"

I probably shouldn't tell him the nickname I just gave his fiancée. "Huh?"

"What's so funny?"

Think fast. "Um…if Brooke were here I would have given her the nametag Miss Piggy since you're Kermit the Frog." Argh—that wasn't any better than Babbling Brooke. *And* I gave away his nametag.

"You're telling me I'm Kermit the Frog?" Eric crosses muscular arms. "Then you should be Barry Bonds because you just cheated."

I laugh again. "I can't be Barry. You said I'm a girl, remember?"

I'm as giddy as a girl anyway. Why did this engaging man actually have to be engaged? And to one of my clients? I would be hanging out with the bride-to-be for the next twelve weeks. That's when their wedding is.

How could I have been attracted to an engaged pastor? My gut twists at the thought. I refuse to be as stupid as my dad.

Of course, Eric and Brooke aren't married yet...Bad Bethany! I mentally kick myself for watching too many romance movies. Who did I think I was? Jennifer Lopez in *The Wedding Planner*?

Eric steps away with a wave. "So, I'll see you on Sunday." He points to my nametag and ends our little game. "J. Lo."

Chapter 2

I pull my purple Jeep Wrangler into the parking lot of Grace Chapel. I'd parked here many times before, but never on a Sunday morning and never wearing a dress.

The building is a big box that used to read *Gold's Gym* above the door. It still has a big "G" in a circle, but now it stands for the name of the church. I wonder how it's changed since Gold's Gym built their new resort-like location closer to downtown Boise and left this pile of cement blocks behind.

I actually feel comfortable with the familiarity of the building even though it's a small church. I've been hiding out in large churches ever since my dad's confession.

Pulling open one of the glass double doors, I step into the warmth and am surprised to see how much the interior of the building has been redecorated. For one, it smells like coffee and spices rather than sweat and iron. Besides that, the juice bar has become an information center, the weight machines have been replaced by rows of chairs, and the steel grate stairs that used to lead up to a glass-enclosed aerobics studio is now crawling with children on their way to Sunday School.

I can't help wondering how women climb the stairs since you could easily see right up their skirts, not to mention the heels of their shoes slipping between the openings in the grate. It takes me a few moments to realize that I'm the only woman in a dress. I don't mind this revelation too much. I mean, I wear sweats to work, so Sunday is my day to dress up. It feels good to look like a lady for a change. And I won't be going up those stairs like the mothers and the teachers have to. I guess when you don't build your own church, you adapt to whatever building God blesses you with.

"Bethany!" Eric's fiancé Brooke surprises me from behind a potted plant. We met for the first time yesterday, but she greets me like I'm a long-lost sister.

"Hi, Brooke." I put my arm out to give her a half-hug, but she envelops me fully. "Nice to see you again." I hope she understands the words, with my voice being muffled by her shoulder and all.

"I'm so joyful that you came! Did you know I'm doing a solo today? I'm nervous, but it's a song that God's really laid on my heart. He's so good, isn't he?"

She says this all in my ear. I have to push away to respond. But how do you respond to that? "Yes." I don't know what exactly I'm saying yes to, but I don't think she heard me anyway.

"Do I have anything in my teeth?" She bares her teeth at me, and I half expect her to growl like Tony the Tiger. *It's grrrreat!*

"Nope."

"I just ate a poppy seed muffin, and I always get poppy seeds in my teeth. Don't you just hate that?"

"It's the worst." I'm actually thinking that those huge Costco muffins are probably the worst thing for her diet right now. She's a gorgeous woman with Kelly Ripa hair and skin that glows in a way I assumed was only possible in air brushed photographs. I may be the skinny one here, but I feel plain compared to her. Hey, the "Miss Piggy" name I gave her the other night actually fits.

Brooke giggles. "You're so funny."

Really? I know my thoughts are funny, but what is she laughing at?

"Oh my gosh. That reminds me of this incredibly funny comedy I was watching last night with that one comedian..." She laughs again.

I smile while looking over her shoulder for an escape. Christian and Laurel wave to me from a row of chairs. Sigh of relief.

"Excuse me, Brooke. I see my brother." "Oh yes. Now *he* could be a comedian. I bet he knows the movie I'm thinking of." She turns as if to escort me toward the "sanctuary" but ends up getting distracted by a shiny object. Okay, not really a shiny object, just another helpless victim. "Oh, Mick!"

The Mick guy looks up and gives a genuine smile. I wonder if he's ever talked to her (listened to her) before. Probably not, because he wouldn't be smiling if he had.

"Mick, this is Bethany, Christian's sister and my new personal trainer. Did you know I'm working out now? I've gotta get in shape for my wedding night."

Hackug. I choke on my own spit at her comment. Patting my chest, I try to play it off as a cough.

Mick stuffs his hands in his pockets and gives me an understanding wink. Okay, he has heard her talk before. He's just a nice guy, though you would never think it at first glance. His head is on the large side with dark hair greased back, and his skin is slightly pockmarked. I would scream if I ran into him in a dark alley.

"Nice to meet you," he says smoothly.

I think about staying to chat, but from the sound of things Brooke had just purchased Boardwalk and Park Place so she can have a monopoly on our conversation. "I used to wear a size four..."

I look to heaven and pray, *Please Lord, not the 'I used to look like a supermodel' speech.* It's unbelievable how often I hear that in my line of work. I interrupt. "It was nice to meet you, too, Mick. I've got to go join my brother now. I'll see you Monday, Brooke."

"Monday, oh right, I..."

Brooke's voice fades behind me as I join Christian and Laurel.

Christian slings an arm around my back as I sink into the chair. "I see you've made a new best friend."

I give a dry laugh. "She's a tad bit different than her fiancé." I glimpse Eric across the room welcoming another

19

newcomer. He's all ears. Maybe that's why their relationship works.

Laurel confirms my hypothesis. "They are a brick and a balloon. When Brooke starts to float away he holds her down, and when he starts to sink too low she lifts him up."

I think back to Paula Abdul's old song. *We come together 'cause opposites attract.* I'm pretty sure I still have one of her tapes in an old shoebox.

Laurel leans around Christian to speak more intimately. "Which reminds me, everybody in the church will be watching you because you spoke to Mick."

I lift my eyebrows.

Christian sees my expression. "He's being shunned."

"What?"

My brother says things for reaction. I shouldn't ever let his words surprise me.

Laurel elbows him in the gut. "Mick is our token single male, and we all want to see him happily settled down."

"Hmm…" I glance back at the gangster, as in fedora-wearing, black-and-white movie appearing, Tommy Gun-toting gangster. "Maybe he could do an internet dating thing and post somebody else's picture."

Laurel frowns. "He's…" Her words are drowned out as worship starts.

I stand to my feet and worship God with the congregation. It feels good. I can get lost in worship, focus on God, forget my problems. It's the sermon that shuts me down. I start picturing my dad behind the pulpit. I try to remember the sermons he gave when I was little and compare them to the sermons he gave during my high school years and beyond. I mean, how was he ever able to tell me to save myself for marriage? No wonder people think churches are filled with hypocrites.

I'm thinking this when Eric climbs onto the platform. I prepare to wrestle with my memories for the rest of the sermon a sermon I probably won't even hear.

"David was a man after God's own heart. Yet he committed adultery."

I snap to attention. I know the story, though I don't remember ever hearing my dad preach on it. Gee, I wonder why.

"How did this happen?"

Good question. One I haven't been able to answer. It's unfathomable to me. If you put God first in your life, and your spouse second, not to mention your children third, how does another woman fit into the picture?

Eric looks out at us in challenge. "I believe it was an innocent disaster."

Is there such a thing?

"The Bible says that David was out on his roof after sleeping during the day. His country was at war. This sounds like depression to me. He was probably trying to get away. He didn't go up there looking for Bathsheba. We've all been in that situation before, haven't we?"

My mind immediately rewinds back to the time I stayed the night at a friend's house in seventh grade, and her dad was watching a movie with some topless women in it. This was something that my own parents sheltered me from thank goodness, but nevertheless I saw it. Now it's burned in my memory.

"Even when we're innocent...especially when we think we're innocent...it can be hard to look away."

I had watched the movie in amazement.

Eric raised his hand in the air. "Am I the only guy ever tempted to buy one of those magazines behind the counter at the gas station?"

Now I watch Eric in amazement. Pastors aren't supposed to have those feelings. But what do I know? My dad ran off with the church secretary.

I look around to gauge the reaction of those around me. A few people are nodding. Others chuckle with nervousness. But nobody else has their mouth hanging open like I do. Not even Brooke. You'd think that after growing up with my brother I would be able to hide the expression of shock. I close my mouth and focus back on Eric.

He takes a deep breath. "It's a choice. David wasn't a Peeping Tom. Yet when he saw Bathsheba, he didn't choose to look away."

I close my eyes. Why couldn't my dad have looked away?

Eric's next words hit me hard. "This could happen to any one of us. Nobody is immune to temptation." I feel like he's looking right at me. I glance over at Christian. He's doodling on the bulletin. Of course, he's not the one having trouble forgiving Dad.

"So I encourage you to find an accountability partner. Let's practice confession of our thoughts, to keep them from becoming actions."

I think about this and wonder how many pastors commit big sins because they feel like they can't confess their little ones. God may not see the difference between sins, but I do. Big sins hurt more people.

"David confessed. He was forgiven. He learned a lesson, and so can we." Eric flips through his Bible. "I like how The Message translates Romans 8:5. *Those who think they can do it on their own end up obsessed with measuring their own moral muscle but never get around to exercising it in real life.*"

Huh. A scripture I can identify with. I'm a personal trainer. I'm in an abandoned gym. I'm listening to a verse about moral muscle. But still I feel like I'm missing something.

Eric makes a few more points then takes his seat. He doesn't really have a pulpit to step down from—just a headset microphone to untangle from his ear. I bite the inside of my cheek. I really liked what he had to say. I'd compared him to a poker player before, for being hard to read, but his honesty just made him transparent. I can trust him. I decide to talk to him after the service about getting together for counseling.

Brooke steps in front of the congregation and picks up a hand held mike. Oh yeah, the solo. Music starts to drift from the speakers and her singing joins in powerfully. For the first time, I enjoy listening to her. Her voice melts away any misgivings I'd had. I see Brooke as passionate for Jesus, and it's beautiful.

We're all guilty of the same things.
We think the thoughts whether or not we see them through.

The words I'll have to think about, though. It goes with the message, but I see a big difference in thinking about sin and actually committing the sin. I mean thinking about it is the same as being tempted, right? And Jesus was tempted, yet he never sinned.

Thunderous applause erupts when Brooke finishes, and I decide I like Grace Chapel. They've got spirit. I smile to myself at the mental picture of the two sides of the congregation chanting back and forth: "We've got the Holy Spirit, yes we do! We've got the Holy Spirit, how 'bout you?" Maybe if church were as exciting as a sporting event more people would come. Maybe it should be.

"Bethany?" Laurel turns to me as soon as the service ends. I bet she wants to invite me to dinner at their house—that's what perfect people do.

I look around for Eric, but respond to my sister-in-law. "Yeah?"

"Would you like to become accountability partners?"

Now I look at Laurel. "With you?" I'm pretty sure my shocked face is showing again.

Laurel nods. "Christian is always around when we're together. It might be nice for the two of us to get to know each other better without him."

It might be nice if Christian were always around. I remember an episode of Seinfeld where Elaine and George had nothing to say to each other when Jerry was gone. But I can't really tell this to Laurel. "I hadn't thought about it."

"Do you have an accountability partner already?"

The sermon had been a good lesson, but I didn't really want to act on it. "No. I don't."

"We can get together when Christian goes to city league basketball practice. Do you want to come over for dinner on Wednesday?"

"Wednesday..." I talk slowly, think quickly. Christian is already goofing off with a guy I'm guessing (from his afro and earrings) to be the youth group pastor, so he's no help.

Laurel sweetens her offer. "We could rent a romantic comedy to watch afterwards." Christian must have told her my weakness.

"I haven't seen the new Hugh Grant movie." I waver.

"Girls night it is." Laurel wins. "Six o'clock?"

"Alright," I say. And hopefully it will be.

Laurel turns to help out a mom juggling her toddler, so I head down the aisle to where I last saw Eric. He's picking up bulletins left on seats. What a servant. He looks up with an almost smile when he sees me coming.

"Was that sermon for me?" I ask.

Eric crosses his arms and squares his body toward mine. "I'm sure it was, though I didn't plan it that way."

Okay, it's my turn to be transparent. Flirting is much more fun, but I do need someone to be real with. My brother doesn't do serious, my sister is on the east coast—tracking down an Internet love interest, to put it nicely—and Mom moved to an island off the coast of Washington of all places.

I feel my face soften as I take off the "perky" mask. "I don't know how much my brother told you, but I'm really struggling with forgiving my dad for..." I falter.

Eric nods that he knows, (though who doesn't?) and I'm spared from speaking the words.

I roll my eyes toward heaven and give a helpless shake of my head. "The sermon was great. I just need a lot more of that. And some prayer. And maybe to vent a little. A punching bag would be good. Do you have a punching bag in your office?"

Eric's lips quirk up, but I see compassion in his eyes. "I think I'm the guy for you."

He means he's the guy for the job, but my heartbeat speeds up anyway for some silly reason. And believe me, it's silly because 1) I'm not getting married ever and 2) even if I were, I would never want to marry a pastor.

I smile back at my new counselor/pastor/client's fiancé. He's going to give me just what I need.

Chapter 3

Jade's unblinking eyes bore into my soul.

I take a step backwards. "No, I haven't gotten any packages for you. What are you expecting?"

Jade's shrug doesn't look very casual. Now that I think about it, I can't remember her ever relaxing. She lives life on the edge of her seat. "I ordered a Bosu Ball, but I had it delivered here so I could get the gym owner discount," she says.

Bosu Balls look like a stability ball chopped in half. They are great for improving balance and strengthening your core. I have the feeling that Jade takes her core work very seriously.

"Oh." I nod as if seeing the same urgency in the situation that she does. "I could call you when it gets here, but aren't you coming in tonight anyway?"

"Yes." Jade stands at attention. "Don't worry about it." She leaves Lighten Up without saying goodbye.

Jade is my part-time partner. I contracted her last spring to take over my accounting—the poor guy who did my taxes after the first year of business practically ordered me to. In exchange, Jade uses the studio at night to train clients of her own. This turned out to be a huge blessing for me because now I can't overwork. Before Jade, it wasn't unusual for me to train fourteen hours a day.

Jade isn't your typical accountant. She's a body builder—bigger than my brother and flatter than me. She brought pictures of herself posing to our booth at the Women's Fitness Celebration Show in September, but I turned the frame facedown whenever she wasn't around. She's buff, but most women don't want to look like her. Of course, I admire the dedication she has to pursue such a...sport. I just wish she would wrap her hair in a towel when she tanned so it wouldn't get so crispy looking.

The bell above the door jingles as Robbie the new UPS guy walks into Lighten Up. He's got a box under his arm the size of a Bosu Ball. Jade just missed him.

"Hey," I greet from my desk. The African-American guy is goooood looking. Two dimples frame his blinding smile and he kind of has this strut that reminds me of Will Smith.

Robbie looks around at all the equipment not in use. "Busy place."

I glance at my watch. "Well, I *am* expecting a client. She was ten minutes early last time, so maybe she'll be ten minutes late today." I have the feeling that Brooke is going to prove to be unpredictable. I should go over my cancellation policy with her again so she realizes that I still charge when clients don't show up.

"That gives me time to hang out with you." Robbie sets the box down on its side then takes a seat on top, propping his forearms on his thighs.

I'm kind of flattered because... "Aren't UPS guys supposed to work fast?"

Robbie's dimples flash again. And he's got this deep, smooth voice. "I'll just have to run later to get back on schedule."

I can't help it. "So that's how you keep in such good shape."

Robbie chuckles and his eyes twinkle. He opens his mouth to reply, but instead of some witty comeback I hear...

"Whew! Don't worry about me being late. I just got my warm-up jogging over here."

Guess who? Yep. She's out of breath, but that doesn't keep her from talking. And how does she look so cute after a jog? Her hair is twisted up, and she has big dangly hoops swinging from here ears.

Robbie stands up. "Gotta run," he says before jogging out.

My lips curl at the inside joke. Maybe *I* should order a Bosu Ball just to see my UPS guy again. It's a fun thought, but Brooke doesn't give me a chance to dwell on it.

"You're nails are beautiful. Where did you have them done?"
I glance at my hands in surprise.

Brooke continues babbling. "I love French manicures. I'll definitely want one for the wedding."

I turn my hand so she can get a better view, before stepping around her and pressing power on the recumbent bike. "I don't have a manicure."

"What?" She leans forward to get a closer look.

Between her and Jade I'm starting to feel claustrophobic. Now if Robbie had wanted to get that close...

"Wow! You just have really healthy nails."

I motion for her to take a seat. I don't trust her self-proclaimed warm-up. "We'll put you on some vitamins to get your nails looking this way, too. But if you want a manicure, my cousin has a spa right across the parking lot."

Dee Light's Day Spa. She was teased unmercifully as a kid, but now she's cashing in on her name.

"A spa!" Brooke sounds like she's doing another solo at church. "That's just what I need. I've heard a body wrap takes inches off your measurements." She hadn't been too happy after I took her measurements on Saturday.

"It can, but you also have to eat healthy for the results to last."

Brooke goes into her diet details from the entire weekend while I set equipment up. Having a small studio is nice, but my equipment has to be multifunctional. I can't have one machine just for the lat pull down like Gold's Gym has. I've got one machine that does it all. Lately, I've been able to buy more pieces of equipment, but I only have so much space. It's amazing what exercises I find to do with just a wooden box and a little creativity.

Brooke climbs from the bike and stretches her legs. I guide her to the leg press—one of my newer pieces of equipment. I'm able to squeeze in quick directions before she starts talking again.

"Wasn't church wonderful? Eric always has the best things to say. I love reading the Bible with him because he gets something different from the words than I do. He's so wise." She grunts this last part while finishing her reps.

I have trouble picturing Brooke listening to Eric. You'd think it would be the other way around. "Eric's message was good. Did he tell you that he's going to start counseling me on Tuesdays?"

She gasps, and I check to make sure she didn't just drop a weight on her foot or something. Nope.

"Tomorrow? That's wonderful! Counseling has helped me so much. Oh, did you see the earrings I'm wearing?"

I try to make the connection. Counseling to earrings. I guess they both could be…"Wonderful."

Brooke nods with the excitement of a puppy's tail. "I made them myself. I can make you some."

I demonstrate a glut lift for the boom-boom—as Star's daughter Jennica calls it. "Thanks, but my ears aren't pierced."

Brooke sits on her boom-boom instead. "You're kidding. You've never worn earrings?"

I grab her arm and pull her up. "I did a long time ago. My holes have grown back together."

Brooke gets the glut lift, but she can't grasp the earring concept. "Why don't you have them pierced again?"

I shrug. "I don't wear much jewelry at the gym."

"Well you looked so pretty at church. I loved your dress. I know. I'll make you some earrings to match it. Earrings can really pull a look together."

"Who am I trying to look good for?" I want to know.

Brooke stops lifting and clasps my hand. "For yourself."

I suddenly feel like a project—like Brittney Murphy on the movie *Clueless*. You know, the one who fell for Alicia Silverstone's man. I shake the thought away and smile at Brooke's enthusiasm. I'll get my ears pierced. Why not?

29

Chapter 4

Eric's secretary Rebecca shows me into his office. She's as old as my grandma, and just like my grandma she smells of vanilla. Too bad my dad didn't have a secretary like her. That would have kept him away from temptation.

In fact, Rebecca's presence outside the open door is a safety precaution for Eric when counseling me. I'm pretty sure it's standard procedure whenever Eric counsels a female, but it makes me feel untrustworthy. Like my father's reputation has preceded me.

"So, should I lie down on the couch?" I make a joke to cover up my anxiety. It's my first session of counseling—which means I'm a nutcase, right?

Eric moves from his desk to a loveseat. It matches the couch, but looks like a garage sale leftover. The sofa set in Dad's office had been from Ethan Allen—firm and plaid.

"Only if you're here for a nap."

I sit, cross my legs, cross my arms, and lean into the corner. I'm feeling shivery all of a sudden, like my teeth could chatter if I let them. So I keep my mouth busy with the verbal kind of chatter instead. "It's kind of funny that Christian wanted me to come to counseling though he's the one who won't talk about what happened."

Eric gives me his full attention, making me feel like a fish at an aquarium. He half shrugs. "That's probably why he wanted you to come—so you have somebody to talk to besides him."

I try to take the focus off me. "I just don't get how he could forgive Dad so easily. I mean, why hasn't this affected him more?"

Eric doesn't go there. "How has it affected *you?*"

Thinking about Dad makes my muscles tense as if they're preparing to throw things. But I don't. "I was shocked," I simply say. "My dad loved God. He loved us. He was such a good man—I can't even remember how many people he brought to the Lord, how many people he'd counseled just like you. But he had a nine-year affair. Nine years!"

"Maybe it was an innocent disaster," Eric suggests.

I huff. "Maybe the first time. But dear old Dad kept going back for more."

"The spirit is willing, but the flesh is weak." Eric argues my dad's side. Ugh. Why am I here again?

I think back to The *Scarlet Letter* by Nathaniel Hawthorn. It was a miserable book that I'd been forced to read for three different English teachers. (And then my mom accidentally read it when I told her how much I'd loved *The Scarlet Pimpernel*.) But basically it's about a single pastor in puritan times who gets a woman pregnant. The woman is punished by society though nobody knows who the father is. He ends up whipping himself in a closet because he feels so guilty. Lovely story, right?

I stood up in class the last time I had to read it and pronounced, "This isn't what Christianity should be about. It's about hope and forgiveness and restoration—not rules and guilt." My own words haunt me, now. Especially after Eric's next point.

"Nobody caught your dad. He chose to confess, didn't he?"

I teeter for a moment then tilt to the side of reason. "Well he had to—so he could run away with his mistress."

Eric sighs. "How do you feel about her?"

My stomach twists at the thought of Corrine. "She's a selfish, conniving whore." I didn't used to think so. I'd cried with her in ninth grade when her husband died of cancer. I ran a couple of 5Ks with her. When getting my degree in Exercise and Movement Science I'd started lecturing her on the candy dish she kept full on her desk outside Dad's office.

I remember this because Eric has a candy dish full of M & Ms on the side table. Usually I wouldn't even be tempted, but having studied nutrition I know the research behind the comforting effect of chocolate. I grab a handful and pop them in my mouth.

Eric rubs the back of his neck. "Do you consider Queen Bathsheba a whore?" Clearly he's thinking back to Sunday's sermon.

"No," I say while chewing. I swallow then clean my teeth with my tongue. "She was seduced by David. Just like Corrine seduced my dad."

Eric purses his lips before replying. "You can't forget that David was a man after God's own heart. Even good people make mistakes. People in ministry are constantly under spiritual attack."

"I know." I grab for some more candy. "But people in ministry should know right from wrong. If they mess up, they should be able to fix it, or at least stop sinning—not run away with the church secretary."

Eric's eyes are warm and wise. He looks at me in a way that I find almost as comforting as the chocolate. It's like he wishes he could fix it. "Tell me some good memories of your dad."

It's been a while since I've had good memories of my dad. I liked being a PK (pastor's kid). Everybody knew who I was, and there were always lots of activities planned. Now I avoid church activities because everybody knows who I am.

I take a deep breath and just start speaking whatever comes to mind. "Dad says that every time he shared a story about me in a sermon I would tell him it was a good message." I smile sheepishly because I'm sure it's true. "Um... he only reads books out loud. I remember his voice always reading to himself in the background as I played on Saturdays. And then if he read something he liked, he would call my mom in and preach it to her."

Eric listens quietly—nodding, encouraging. I wonder if he practices his sermons on Brooke. Or if he will when they're married. I picture him doing it while she sleeps because it's the only time she's not talking.

"Um..." Eric still isn't saying anything, so I dig deeper through my mental scrapbook. "He beat me at a church picnic pie-baking contest, but only because he put a banana smiley-face on his banana cream pie. Dad loved banana cream pie. We always made it for his birthday instead of cake...On my sixteenth birthday he took me to get my driver's license. He jokes that I totaled a car the first time I drove because the neighbor kid left his Hot Wheels in our driveway, and I ran over it."

I laugh at this. It brings back a memory of another time my dad really had me laughing. "Once--" I giggle. "--I was going with dad to deliver Meals On Wheels. I was probably about eight." I bite my lip and shake my head at how silly this is going to sound. "Dad accidentally put his sunglasses on upside down. He looked like a bug. I laughed at him, so he kept them on that way. And the whole ride home he acted like he was wearing a disguise so he wouldn't be recognized by bad guys who were after him."

I'd forgotten about that. I lean my head back and smile. Oh, to be a kid again.

"So he was a good dad?"

I grunt as newer memories take over. "He *was.*"

Eric rubs his hands together. "What would make him a good dad again?" ·

I roll my eyes toward the florescent lights above me. "A time machine."

Eric repeats the question as if I were a little kid. "What would make him a good dad again?"

"I don't know." I huff and look away. I'd rather feel sorry for myself than have to fix the problem. "Maybe if he moved back here. Or called more. Or if he begged me to forgive him and worked stuff out with Mom so we could all be together on holidays." I think of Thanksgiving the following week.

Eric reads my mind. "Is he coming for Thanksgiving?"

"No." I would like to leave it at that, but I know Eric is going to ask more questions if I don't extrapolate. "Mom's

33

coming for Thanksgiving. Dad will be here for Christmas. Without Corrine."

I think of the movie *Sleepless in Seattle* when Jonah calls into the radio station to announce, "My dad's kissing a ho!"

Eric leans forward. Good. Now he can talk. Maybe he'll offer to knock some sense into my dad—you know, pastor to pastor. "You can't change your dad."

This isn't what I want to hear.

"And I don't think waiting and hoping is going to help you much here, either."

Hmm....what would you call this? A lose-lose situation? Lucky me.

"You're a victim, Bethany. You didn't ask for this to happen. You didn't deserve for this to happen. But it happened anyway."

That's exactly how I feel!

"Everyone has been a victim sometime in their life."

I sit still. For a moment I thought Eric was going to join my pity party, but now he's comparing me to everyone else.

"It's up to you to choose if you want to stay in the victim role or if you want to move on to accountability."

There's his favorite word again. I prepare myself for another recap of Sunday's message.

"It's hard work but worth the effort. You have to move up the rungs on the victim ladder if you ever want to move on with your life."

Did I want to move on? I don't know where I'm going. I don't know what's ahead. But I'm tired of the way I feel right now. "Okay. I'm strong." I visualize kissing my bicep. "I can climb your ladder."

Eric scoots to the end of his seat as if he's been waiting for this moment since I entered the room. "First, there are four rungs of victimization. I'm guessing you started out at the bottom rung which is being unaware of or not accepting the problem."

"Well, yeah. It was a nightmare and I just wanted to wake up." Dad told us about the affair the afternoon before he

addressed Living Faith. It was unreal. It took me hours before I cried, but then the tears poured all night long.

Eric slowly continues, as if he's deep in thought, as well.
"The next rung is blaming others."

This catches me off guard. "Who else would I blame?"

"Okay, you're still there." Eric assesses me. "You're blaming
Corrine."

Duh.

Eric runs a hand over his face. "Real quick, before I go on...
The Bible says that we struggle not against flesh and blood, but
against principalities and darkness. Corrine isn't your enemy."

"Right. So the devil used her."

Eric's lips quirk a little. "We'll talk about forgiving Corrine
later. The next rung on the ladder is 'I can't.'"

"I do feel helpless." And hopeless sometimes.

"Then we move on to wait and hope—which we've already
discussed."

All of these rungs make sense to me. What more could
there be? Eric mentioned accountability, and I'm planning
to meet with Laurel tomorrow, but it's not like I'm going to
make the same mistake my dad did.

Eric explains. "The next four rungs are on the accountability side of the ladder. They are the opposites of the rungs I
just listed."

I think back trying to remember each of the steps. Eric
does it for me. "Acknowledge the problem, own it, find a
solution, and get on with it."

Deep breath. He lost me. "I'm aware now. But you just
said that I can't talk sense into my dad, so what else can I
do? And what am I supposed to own? What kind of solution
am I looking for?"

Eric studies me as he speaks. *"Do you believe the Bible verse
that says: All things work for good to those who love God and are
called according to His purpose?"*

"It's my favorite verse." Though I don't know where it's
found in the Bible--I'm not good with memorizing num-

bers. That's what a concordance is for.

"There are no accidents, Bethany." The way he says my name I believe him. "It wasn't God's will for your father to have an affair, but God allowed it. And He can use it for good. It's your job to find the good in all this. Find the value."

I shake my head and look up. What good can come out of an affair? All I see is bad. The church split. Instead of Living Faith, I now call it Dying Faith. Lots of people left never to return—possibly even my sister.

Eric speaks softly. "The value won't equal the victimization. And it might take you a very long time to find it. But it's there."

I rest my chin in my hands as I think about this. Maybe I don't want to climb the ladder. Maybe I just want to keep blaming Dad and Corrine.

Eric sees right through me once again. "Are you stuck on 'I can't'?"

"I am," I say, though I think I'm somehow stuck on all the victim rungs.

"That's okay." The understanding Eric reappears. Or I think he does until he adds, "For now."

"I've got a lot to think about," I say. Wow. It would be so much easier not to care.

"Are you still feeling strong?" Eric prods.

I feel like Eric just opened a lead box with kryptonite in it. "I don't know. But I've got you to spot me, right?"

Eric's eyes connect with mine and I can tell he gets the weight lifting analogy. "I'm here for you," he says. And as a personal trainer, I know exactly what he means.

Chapter 5

I groan and sink down onto my polka-dot couch the following evening. I wish I could put on my bathrobe and stay here all night, but I'm supposed to go to Laurel's for our first accountability meeting.

My 600-square-foot apartment is probably smaller than Laurel's garage, but it's all I need. The Civic Plaza high rise near BoDo (Boise Downtown) is a fun place to live. I've got a view of Bogus Basin, and I can just take the elevator to ground level and cross the street to attend a Stampede basketball game or buy fresh produce at the Farmer's Market in the summer. And if I do go out to eat, the restaurants near me are unique, not the chains like by the mall and in the suburbs of Meridian and Eagle.

I don't have a yard to take care of, and it's not like I do much entertaining, so it works. The only drawback is that my apartment is like a dorm with all the college students on my floor. I get called ma'am a lot.

I slide down to my side and curl up with a round throw pillow. The sun has already set—something that happens way too early for me in the fall and winter months. It makes me sleepy. I feel my eyes start to droop and I notice that Michael, my potted plant, is looking just as droopy.

I may not have a yard to take care of, but I do have one neglected fern. I'm actually amazed he's made it this long. Dee Dee lent him to me two years ago for the Sunday School lesson I was teaching about the sower and the seed. She didn't know the reason why she was lending him to me and kind of freaked out when I told her…I guess ferns don't have seeds. But the kids didn't know that and neither did I.

She's stopped asking for him back, most likely figuring I've killed him by now. The truth is, I want to keep him because the morning I used him for an illustration in Sunday School was the last week my family went to church together.

At Dying Faith we all wore nametags because Dad was really bad with names. (Though he said he did it for the congregation to be able to greet each other with familiarity.) And on that last fateful Sunday, Dad had taken his nametag off and randomly stuck it on the side of Dee Dee's potted plant after the sermon. That's how the fern got his name. I could never bring myself to remove the nametag after that, so the sticker has permanently pasted itself to the terracotta pot, all except for the curling corners. Nobody knows that I still have the last nametag Dad ever wore.

"What do you think, Michael?" I ask the plant. "Should I go meet with Laurel, now?"

He doesn't answer, of course, but the fact that I'm talking to a species of flora is answer enough.

I see that Christian's already left for basketball practice when I pull up to his house. I was hoping to ease into the one-on-one time with his wife, but at least I'll have lots to talk about thanks to Eric. Before I met with the pastor I was worried that Laurel and I would just sit and stare at each other uncomfortably.

Laurel greets me at the door wearing ballet slippers—actual ballet slippers, not flats designed to look like ballet slippers. She's adorable in them, but I still wonder what jokes Christian made.

"Hi, Twinkle Toes," I make my own joke.

Laurel smiles graciously. "Hi. You like my slippers?"

I step out of the way so she can close the door. "Are you taking up dance?" I ask. She does have the poise of a ballerina.

"No." Laurel leads me up the stairs. "I was complaining to Star about how our new wood laminate floors hurt to stand on after a while, so she gave me these. They really help."

I nod. How is it that even Laurel's problems make her appear more perfect?

"By the way, the label I gave you at Christian's party was an accident. I meant to put that one on Star if she came."

"Of course. A dancer for a dancer." Well that made much more sense. "Who was I supposed to be?"

"Mia Hamm."

Much better.

"I hope you're hungry. I found that awesome Olive Garden soup recipe online. I replaced the potatoes with cauliflower to cut down on carbs for you."

Pet peeve. I hate those low carb diets. According to Thermodynamic Law the only way to loose weight is to burn more calories than you consume. All those trendy diets that come out try to make weight loss complicated. You could honestly be on a Snickers candy bar diet and still lose weight, but that doesn't mean it's healthy. And potatoes are healthy.

I explained all this to Christian when he tried a diet that had him eating sausages instead of bananas. Argh. I guess he hasn't explained this to his wife. And I don't explain it to her either because I'm not comfortable being myself for some reason. With Christian I would give him another lecture then insist on making a salad. With Laurel I smile and sit humbly on a barstool.

"So how are you?" Laurel asks and I can't help feeling like she's making small talk and doesn't really care to hear my answer. Is this accountability thing going to work?

"Good." I smile and nod again. I try to think of something else to say as the hum of the refrigerator grows louder. "I'm meeting with Eric for counseling now."

Laurel stirs the soup and gives me an encouraging smile— as if I'm one of the pediatric patients at the hospital she's offering a lollipop. "He's very wise, isn't he?"

"He's stretching me," I allow.

Laurel dishes up the soup, and we head to the heavy, round farm table. Her decorating style is a little too country for my taste. Laurel says grace before I dig in. It's delicious, but I should expect nothing less from someone who aspires to be Martha Stewart.

"So I was thinking that for our accountability we should each share where we are in our lives personally, with God, and with others. Then we can pray."

"Okay." This might be more of a stretch than counseling.

"Do you want to begin?"

I slurp then wipe my chin with a napkin. "Okay," I say again. I'm off to a good start. "Personally...I'm getting my ears pierced."

Laurel's smile is overly sweet again. "Do you need prayer for that?"

I laugh uncomfortably. "No." I could ask her to pray for my relationship with the woman who prodded me into getting my ears pierced. But Brooke is soon going to be our pastor's wife, and I don't want Laurel to know that I have negative feelings where she is involved. "This is hard because my personal life, spiritual life, and social life are all connected," I give an excuse that sounds believable. Truthfully, I'd rather not separate the three and have to deal with each aspect on a deeper level. I'll just lay the big ones on her. "I'm struggling the most with forgiving Dad. And I also really want Star and Dee Dee to start acting like sisters again."

Laurel lays her hand on mine—which touches me in a way other than physically. "That's got to be tough."

I look down, and though I truly appreciate her gesture, I wish she would let go of me so I can eat some more soup. Her sympathy is starting to make me feel kind of pathetic. "It is."

She releases me and starts waving her hands around as she speaks. "Christian refuses to talk about it with me."

"Same here."

Laurel slaps her hand on the table causing my soup to slosh. "I'm not even sure of everything that happened. I wasn't at church when your Dad confessed. I've learned more through the gossip mill than I have from my own husband."

I chew on the inside of my cheek. "I wish I could forget it as easily."

Laurel meets my eyes. "I don't think it's been easy on Christian. It affects him more than he knows."

I lean forward slightly, expecting to hear news of a failing marriage or self-defeating behavior. Maybe Laurel's life isn't as perfect as she would like the world to believe.

She explains. "Everything is a joke to him."

I lean back. Tell me something I don't know.

"Even if I'm mad at him, he'll start teasing me until I'm laughing. He completely avoids any serious subjects, and it's got me really worried."

I take a bite of cauliflower and try to swallow the news. So, Miss Perfect's problem is that her husband is a funny guy. Life is rough. "Hmmm...what does Christian do to upset you?"

"I don't know." She shrugs. I wonder if she's hiding something or if Christian's infractions are really so minor that she can't even remember them. "He pops my toes."

Travesty! "He used to pop my toes, too. I loved it."

Laurel looks repulsed. "I hate it when anybody touches my feet."

Yet another reason I can't help thinking that my brother and his wife are mismatched. "Are you ticklish?"

Laurel looks surprised by the question. "No."

This conversation seems a little silly. "Okay. You pray for my ear piercing, and I'll pray for your toe popping."

Laurel gives a sheepish smile. "How about we pray over the effects of your father's sin and for wisdom in how to live our own lives?"

The prayer sounds like a good way to end our first attempt at accountability. I wonder if this is what Eric had in mind when he suggested we start meeting.

Chapter 6

The new Gold's Gym on Park Center has won awards for its design. Not only does it have a fountain cascading down a stone wall into the swimming pool, mahogany lockers, racket ball courts and a boxing ring, but it has three aerobics studios.

I head upstairs to Star's class in the main studio. I missed it on Tuesday because I met with Eric, so I really need my Thursday fix. Her dance aerobics class is a blast and you can burn up to 1200 calories. That's over half of what I consume in a day.

Yes, my life is routine. I work all day, head to Gold's in the evening then drop (literally) onto the sofa at night to watch a movie. It may be predictable, but it's a good life. And besides, I've got a cousin like Star to make things more interesting.

Today she is wearing a black halter tank, arm warmers, and a white fedora. Some people might think that her clothing style comes from her African-American background. (She's adopted, remember?) But I know that it's more of a dance-inspired thing. The fedora, for instance, adds to the flavor of the swing dancing she has planned. I picture her for a moment with Mafia Mick from church—in matching hats. But nah, she doesn't date. She says it's because her daughter is her true love, though I can't help wondering if Jennica takes second place to Star's love of dance.

My aunt and uncle did the evil-naming thing to her, too, and like Dee Dee she was also able to use it for business. After returning home from Hollywood as the pregnant/prodigal daughter she started Dance by Star Light out of her parent's garage. Now she's got a beautiful studio and teaches at the gym on the side.

42

The class is packed as usual. Star knows how to draw a crowd. Plus she's a local celebrity. She danced in a couple music videos before giving up her dream for parenthood. In fact, I think one of the backup singers in the last video she did is Jennica's father. Nobody has met the guy though.

Music fills the air and Star leads us in isolations before we really start to move. She's so fun to watch. She really gets into it and purses her lips with attitude. The rest of us look like a JV cheer squad compared to her.

The groove down leaves me swaying side to side—like when you climb off a trampoline and it's hard to walk normal. I don't look normal either. Christian would describe my sweaty, messy hairstyle as a "rat's nest."

"I'll walk down with you to get Jennica," I offer as Star takes her headset microphone off.

"Oh, thanks, but I'm staying late. I've got to learn this new routine and it's easier with Jennica in the childcare." Star pops a different CD into the stereo.

"Alright." I'm hesitant to leave.

I'm not one of those people who have lifelong friends. I love meeting new people, but I always end up losing touch. It's fun, but not very meaningful. I understand this more now after taking a personality quiz and finding out that I'm "Happy-Go-Lucky." Anyway, this personality flaw makes family very important to me. Star and Dee Dee are not just my cousins, they're my oldest friends. I see Dee Dee almost every day, but Star is always so busy. Must be the single mom thing.

"Hey, I'm going to get my ears pierced. Do you want to go to the mall with me tomorrow night?"

Star's expressive eyebrow arches high. (Only one of her eyebrows is expressive.) "Are you serious? Jennica has her ears pierced and you don't? Girl, I would expect you to be getting a belly button ring with those amazing abs of yours."

Star has an amazing body herself, all except for her abs. She's got these sculpted shoulders and longs legs that would make you think she was a Nike model, but underneath her sexy top is a belly that resembles a waterbed. She never lost all her pregnancy weight—probably because she and Jennica go out to eat every day. Jennica is practically a macaroni connoisseur.

Back to the bellybutton ring. "Who would see it?"

"Honey, if I go with you to get pierced, it's gonna be your bellybutton."

"Oh, so you can live vicariously through me?" I tease.

"You know it."

"Then I'll have to ask Dee Dee to come with me." I say this in a sing-song warning voice.

She gives me a look and cranks her music up. "See you next week," she says without any emotion, turning her back on me.

I look toward heaven. *God, what's it going to take to get those two back together?* "I'll be here," I holler over the tribal beat.

Out on the stairs I look down at the open weight room below, encircled by the second story balcony of cardio equipment. The people surrounding me vary from a guy in the wheelchair to a woman so large that she only wears dresses. A lot of times at Lighten Up I get clients with the misconception that you have to be in shape to work out at a gym. They come to me for personal training because they are too intimidated to step into a Gold's. The truth is that even I got intimidated when coming here for the first time, but there's something for everyone.

Speaking of everyone, I spy Jade in the distance bench-pressing a million pounds. I could say hi, but I head toward the juice bar instead. It'll be another hour before I get home, shower and make my favorite meatball minestrone out of ground turkey and whole wheat macaroni (the only kind of macaroni Jennica should be eating). I can't wait that long for nourishment. I plop onto a barstool and try to decide between the berry or the peach shakes both with names that make them sound a lot more exciting than just berry or peach.

I hear a male voice from behind me. "I'll take the berry shake—whatever it's called."

I start to look up to see who it was that ordered Berrylicious Dream, but I get distracted by the chest and arms at eye level when I spin my barstool around. Talk about berrylicious. The muscle t-shirt is definitely doing its job of showing off muscles.

"Hi, Bethany."

My eyes travel upwards, and I know who I'm going to see because I recognize the voice, but I still can't contain the amazement that must be showing on my face. Sure enough—Eric Austin.

"Hi!" I'm overly loud.

"I'm surprised to see you here. I thought you worked at another gym." He doesn't sound surprised—just calm.

Of course he can't be as surprised as I am. "I come here to take my cousin's aerobics class. Are you lifting?"

"I should be." He gives me his adorable smile. "But I usually end up boxing." He points to the corner where the bags and ring are located upstairs.

I squint in the direction he points. Was that Robbie hanging over the balcony? Small world. No wonder my UPS guy is in such good shape. But so is my pastor...the boxer.

"Really?" *Really*? "What about turning the other cheek?" Eric's smile starts to slip so I wave my hand. "I'm teasing. It must help to take out your aggressions. I know ministry can be frustrating. Maybe more pastors should do it."

Eric shrugs. This is a whole different Eric than I counseled with earlier this week. It's kind of cool to know that we can be serious or goofy. I really enjoy goofy.

I motion to his physique. "You're in amazing shape." I poke him in the stomach. Solid. "Flex," I request. His muscles get even harder as I playfully poke a second time. "Flex," I say again as if he hasn't.

45

Eric tilts his head to the side and lets out a "pshah."

I laugh at my own joke. I'm pretty darn...

With no warning, icy water attacks from above. For some reason, the sprinkler system overhead has been activated. An alarm starts to squeal. I look around in bewilderment. Gym members run past us frantically.

I look back at Eric who is ripping his shirt overhead. (Maybe he was serious about getting mistaken for The Hulk.) I have no idea what he's doing, but I yell over the commotion, "I was just kidding about your abs. Now really isn't the best time to show off!"

Eric doesn't look me in the eye. Actually he's deliberately looking away, and when I hear his words I understand why. "Better me than you." He shoves the navy blue shirt my way.

I feel my eyes pop out when I look down at my own top. My *white* top. The sprinklers are pounding on me as hard as hail, the bell blares in my ears, people jostle against me as they try to exit the building, but none of this fazes me. It's not until I realize that I am suddenly a contestant in a wet t-shirt contest that I scream.

I hear another scream as I pull Eric's shirt over my head. I wipe hair out of my face to find Star running my way. Jennica. Oh, no.

Star grabs my upper arms. "There are old women in the pool for water aerobics. Go help them. I've got to get my baby."

I try to dash toward the pool, but my sneakers slip and I end up in a puddle. Eric is right behind me. "Go help the women in the pool!" I yell.

Eric rushes past, and I scramble to catch up. We enter the pool area to total chaos. The water aerobics instructor is trying to instruct a couple of women to go to the locker room, get their stuff, and get out, but they must not have their hearing aids on because they don't understand a word above the noise that surrounds us.

Eric takes one woman by the arm and leads her toward the stairs. I help the other lady. "Is there a fire?" I holler, looking around and sniffing for smoke. I don't want to lead these women into a blazing locker room.

"I don't see anything," Eric looks over his shoulder.

I don't either, and as much as I would like to get out of the building and the rainstorm, I figure that the women we are helping need keys to get home, not to mention clothes and shoes.

The lady leaning on me is shaking. I estimate her to be about my grandmother's age. I bet she never even gets her hair wet when she gets in the pool, but now it is plastered to her head like a wooly shower cap.

"It's going to be alright," I try to comfort her. I pat her arm. Why, oh why, did the locker rooms have to be upstairs?

When we finally reach the locker room Eric holds the door open. He leans toward my ear. "Go check to see who is inside. If it's clear I'm bringing Essie in. I'm afraid to let go of her."

How did he learn the lady's name already? I slide past him, afraid that I'm going to do more harm than good holding onto my elderly buddy. Thank goodness she doesn't have to go far. She collapses onto the first bench and starts pulling wet clothes on over her swimming suit. I keep going and find a few more women gathering their things, but all are dressed. I relay the message to Eric and assume that firemen will probably be in here soon, so what's the big deal if a pastor helps out a little old lady in the women's locker room?

Eric and Essie join us and we all head back down together—half a step at a time. Busting through the front doors into the parking lot was not as great a relief as I expected it to be. The November chill engulfs me as if I'd just fallen into a frozen lake. I shiver uncontrollably expecting my limbs to turn blue any second. My breath fogs the air. Poor Eric doesn't even have a shirt on. He escorts the older women to their cars after a fireman brings them a blanket. Eric wraps it around Essie's shoulders. I dig through the puddle in my purse to find my keys as another fireman wraps a blanket around me.

"Th-thanks."

The man doesn't even hear me before rushing off again.

I see Star struggling toward her monstrous SUV with a bawling Jennica. The toddler is voicing my exact thoughts. My teeth chatter as I catch up and try to ask, "Was there a fire? What happened?"

Star strips Jennica then buries her in her car seat under a winter coat. "No fire. Nobody knows what started the sprinkler system. It's going to cause a lot of damage, though."

"Cr-crazy." I hug my arms to my body.

Eric reappears as Star rushes to climb into the vehicle herself. I try to wave goodbye to my cousin, but I'm frozen so I look like a Tyrannosaurus Rex with a short little appendage. I grab a corner of the blanket and jerk sideways causing it to fall off my shoulders. I flop my wrist over to pass the blanket to Eric. It's only fair since I have his shirt. But boy do I need a hot shower.

Eric doesn't say anything, just takes the blanket. I wonder if he's busy climbing the victim ladder—finding the value in our victimization. I doubt that I'll be able to.

Chapter 7

"I dated a fireman once," is all Dee Dee says after hearing the extended version of the Hurricane Gold's story.

"I've never been so cold in my life," I say, expecting some sympathy. All my clients had asked tons of questions. Brooke even gave me Eric's version of the catastrophe, adding on how brave she thought he was—in so many more words. But Dee Dee's mind is elsewhere.

"Remember A.J.?"

"Uh..." I do remember A.J. And now I remember why she can't focus on my story. I try to play it cool. "The one with the amazing eyelashes?" She'd broken up with him when she started her spa. She said it was because it wouldn't be fair for her boyfriend to have to compete against business for her attention. If only that were the whole story.

"Mmm..." She stares off into space and a car behind us honks since the stoplight turned green and we're not moving.

"Go, Dee Dee," I prod gently. I'd love to talk to her, but this isn't the place.

She turns her little, old Honda Civic into the mall parking lot where, after parking, we are forced to make our way through crowds of high schoolers to an accessories boutique even more crowded with teenagers. Dee Dee zeroes in on the hair accessories and I wait for my turn in the piercing chair.

"Next," calls Cat Woman. She's got an excess of dark make-up around her golden-brown eyes and claw-like fingernails that she could use to pierce my ears if the earring gun breaks.

"Dee Dee!" I wave my cousin over because I don't want to do this alone. I mean, that's why I invited her here in the first place.

Dee Dee wanders over. "Did you want me to hold your hand?" she teases.

That would be comforting, but no. "Help me pick out earrings."

Dee Dee peers in the case. "Why are you doing this again?"

"Remember Babbling Brooke?" They'd met at my studio during one of the lunch walks Dee Dee takes on my treadmill. "She's making me a pair of earrings to match my red dress."

Dee Dee's eyes dart my way. "That's nice of her." She doesn't have to say it—I just know she's pointing out how nice I'm *not* being by calling my client names. But it's such a fitting name.

"She's very nice," I amend.

Cat Woman loads her gun with a cubic zirconium stud. I ball my hands up and squeeze. Closing my eyes, I try to relax as she dabs my lobe with peroxide.

Click. I feel the sting through my entire ear. My eyes water a little. *Click.* A matching pair. I grit my teeth then take a deep breath. I open my eyes.

Dee Dee smiles down. "Beauty from pain." Ah yes, my favorite Superchic song. Also kind of what Eric had been trying to explain to me on Tuesday.

"Let's go watch a movie," I suggest.

Dee Dee is always game for a chick flick. "A romantic comedy."

"Is there any other kind?" I ask as we pay the cashier.

Dee Dee fingers some fake hair at the counter—tiny black braids. I think of Star. "Star had Jennica's hair put in cornrows for the first time," I say.

Dee Dee's expression turns sad. Star was the whole reason Dee Dee became a beautician in the first place. Dee Dee had learned to braid Star's hair in high school. Then when trying to decide what to do after she graduated, Star suggested beauty school.

"It's been a long time since I've done cornrows," she says before looking up at me.

I nod in sympathy. Dee Dee was the one who messed up. She'd made a mistake that couldn't be fixed. But oh how I wish I could fix it.

Her expression changes as she looks at my hair. "I'll give you corn rows," she exclaims with way too much enthusiasm.

I envision myself with braids, arm warmers, and a fedora. "I'm not that cool."

The sales lady is trying to hand my debit card back to me, but Dee Dee tips my head forward holding my cheeks between her hands. I slap the counter randomly to find the little piece of plastic since I can't see.

"I could just do the top half and pull it to one side." She's forgotten the movie. "You could still put it in your standard ponytail."

I have such style.

She lifts my face so I can look at her. "Come on. It will be fun."

"I'll be a whole new Bethany," I say. "Corn rows and earrings."

"That's the spirit!" she says, though I was hoping she would tell me there was nothing wrong with the old Bethany. She grabs my arm and drags me out of the store.

Back at Dee Light's we have the place to ourselves. It's a renovated 1920s bungalow. Dee Dee skips across the taupe and white checked floor to her station. I follow along (not quite skipping) and take a seat.

I'm already imagining what Christian is going to call me. Homie? Fly girl? He called me a punk when Dee Dee convinced me to get a plum-colored weave. The purple wasn't that noticeable in my dark hair, but it did inspire the purchase of my Jeep.

Dee Dee parts my hair and starts rubbing in some kind of thick goo. She picks out a few strands for the first braid and pulls hard. I feel like I'm getting an instant face lift.

"This hurts worse than the ear piercing," I say.

"Don't be a baby."

Her words get me thinking of Jennica again...and another baby. "Can you believe that Jennica is two years old now? I can't imagine having a toddler."

Dee Dee loosens her grip on my locks before yanking harder. "No?" Her voice has an edge to it.

I wait for her to finish the first braid before pressing the issue. She's my captive audience now. Unless of course she leaves my hair half-done. Which I guess is a possibility. But this is the time. It's been eating at me ever since Jennica's birthday and I can't keep quiet anymore. I send up a simple prayer of "help" before diving in.

"Star told me," is all I say. It's all I have to say.

Dee Dee doesn't respond, and I'm afraid I said too much. She finishes a second braid. I'm so on edge that when she finally breaks the silence I jolt at the sound.

"What did Star tell you?" She's not pretending it never happened, she's just being cautious.

I confirm her fears. "She told me about your abortion."

Dee Dee drops my hair. (It's not even half way done, but that's not my biggest concern of the moment.) She sinks into the swivel chair across from me. "Who else knows?" she whispers.

"Nobody," I quickly assure her. "Star didn't even want to tell me, but I overheard her mutter something about how Jennica should be celebrating her second birthday with her cousin. And Jennica doesn't have a cousin."

I'd thought I'd heard wrong. I'd hoped I'd heard wrong. Remember the first rung on Eric's victim ladder—disbelief? That had been me...If Jennica should have had a cousin then Dee Dee should have had a child. And as far as I'd known, Dee Dee had never been pregnant.

"Why didn't you come to me?" I wish I could have helped. I wish it wasn't too late.

Dee Dee looks away as if too ashamed to face what she's done. And as if trying to steel herself for the condemnation she expects to see in my eyes. "I didn't tell anyone but Star."

She tucks her hands under her thighs. "Though I did start coming with you to church, remember?" She bites her lip and my stomach rolls when I realize what she's about to say. "Then your dad confessed his affair. I saw how the church treated him, and he had been such a good man. If your dad couldn't be forgiven, then I don't have a chance."

I want my pillow. The one I cry into at night when life rears its unfair head. My cousin is just one more person hurt by my dad's affair.

I don't want to know anything else, but Dee Dee may not ever talk about this again. "You thought Star would help you?"

The pain on her face is a reminder of the rift between sisters. Her steel supports crumble. The numb mask she wore dissolves and she becomes a heart-broken little girl. She nods and a tear slips down her cheek. "She refused to take me to the abortion clinic. She tried to stop me. She said that if I aborted my baby it was like I thought her birth mother should have aborted her."

Oh no.

Dee Dee wipes impatiently at her tears. "I didn't want to get an abortion, but I didn't see any other way. I'd just signed on the loan and the lease to start my spa."

I leaned forward and whispered. "And the daddy?"

I know who it is before she says. "A.J...He still doesn't know."

I feel my heart twist inside my chest. "Why didn't you tell him? He was a nice guy."

"Because I'm an idiot." Dee Dee closes her eyes, but continues talking quickly. "He wasn't ready to get married. I didn't want to force him into anything, and I didn't want to lose him. I thought if I aborted the baby, we could go on like it had never happened."

Her own child. How can anyone go on with their life normally after making such a choice? I don't have to ask about A.J. anymore. I can now see through Dee Dee's excuse of breaking up with him because of her business. She couldn't continue her relationship on a lie, and she was too ashamed to tell him the truth.

"I'm sorry," is all I can think to say.

Dee Dee wipes her face. "I gave up everything for this spa. I lost my sister, my boyfriend, and my...my baby."

I wish I could bring it all back for her. I wish I had something wise and healing to say. I wonder if she thinks she's risking losing me by telling all this. I consider telling her about Jesus again, but she's heard all that. Maybe just my being here is all she needs for now.

I can't help thinking about Star. "Have you explained this to your sister? Has she seen you cry? Does she know how much you're hurting?"

Dee Dee rubs the arms of her chair. "It's too late now."

"No. It's never too late. That's the beauty of grace."

Dee Dee looks up. The pain is gone from her eyes. It is replaced with a frightening glint of finality. "When Star tried to stop me from going to the abortion clinic..."

I'm afraid she won't finish then afraid that she will.

"I called her a...a name. A racial slur."

I close my eyes. I don't know what to say, and I don't want Dee Dee to see the same hopelessness in my eyes that I saw in hers. I pray. If I were to write down what I prayed, it wouldn't make sense. It's a plea to God. It's desperation for my cousin. It's pain and realization. I don't know how long I sit there, but before I open my eyes Dee Dee is pulling on my hair again.

I'd thought that I'd be able to help somehow—that if I got the sisters together (through a funky sock club or mutual gift for Christian) things would smooth out between them. But it's worse than I thought. I almost wish she hadn't told me. But I still love her. I think I love her more—maybe because I know more of her now.

"Dee Dee," I choke-whisper.

Her fingers pause.

"I love you."

A tear drops onto my hand, and I'm not sure if it's hers or mine.

"Thank you. I love you, too."

Chapter 8

I enter Grace Chapel for the second Sunday in a row. Laurel is sick today and Christian is staying home with her. That's okay. I don't mind sitting by myself. In fact there's only one person I want to talk to.

I see Eric across the sanctuary. He's my safety net. I promised Dee Dee I wouldn't tell anyone about her, but as my counselor I need Eric's advice about what to do. And I have to share this news with somebody. I'm like an overflowing bucket that must be dumped before it starts spilling everywhere.

Brooke surprises me from behind the information counter this time. She pops up with a smile on her face, like a female Jack-in-the-box. A Brooke-in-the-box.

"Bethany! I love your hair!"

She goes on and on, but the compliments roll right off me. My hair is cute, but it's a reminder of my evening with Dee Dee.

"And your ears!" Brooke notices my bling. "I'll have to get to work on making you earrings." She gives me a rundown on her schedule, deciding when she'll be able to start her gift for me. I tell you, the girl does not have an unexpressed thought.

Eric joins us. He points to my hair and gives me a thumbs-up. I guess he doesn't figure he'll be able to get a word in next to his fiancée.

She giggles and grabs his arm. I missed the joke.

Brooke fills me in. "Eric has laryngitis. He lost his voice. I'm sure it's from getting soaked at Gold's. Poor baby. I'm just glad he didn't get hypothermia."

I consider reminding Brooke that I'd been there, too, but she's already moved on to the next subject. Why couldn't *she* have been the one to lose her voice?

"Brooke!" A member of the worship team waves her over.

I nod goodbye as she trots off, feeling guilty that I'd wished laryngitis on her. Then I get a new thought.

"Who's preaching today?" I ask, though I'm not sure how Eric is going to answer me.

He points toward the front row. I feel my eyebrows lift to the middle of my forehead at the size of the man sitting there. Not only is he big enough to use the expression "I'm so hungry I could eat a horse" literally, but he's bald and wearing a black leather vest and biker boots. It should be an interesting sermon.

"Oh." I turn back to Eric and wonder about my next counseling session. "So if you don't get your voice back by Tuesday, I will be able to say anything I want and you'll just have to listen?" I tease though my heart's not in it.

Eric gives me a disapproving look. I know it's in jest. This is like a reverse of The Little Mermaid where Eric was the only one to talk and Ariel used hand gestures and facial expressions to communicate.

"Actually," I look down. "I really need to talk about something. I'm struggling right now."

Eric nods and concern darkens his eyes to the shade of pine needles.

"It's not about me. It's a friend."

I wonder how often counselors hear those words. But he'll understand on Tuesday.

Eric looks like he wants to say something. He opens his mouth and a croak comes out. I can't help giggling like Brooke.

"That was manly."

Eric raises his arms up to boxing guard as if to say, "You wanna fight?"

Piano music interrupts the chatter surrounding us. Eric salutes and heads toward the front row to sit next to the biker/speaker. I make myself comfortable in the back. At the last second Mick jogs in and slides into the seat next to me like he's rounding third base and headed for home. I give him a side wave then try to focus on worship, but I'm kind of out of it today.

The worship leader announces Eric's ailment along with an anecdote about the Gold's Gym's sprinkler system before introducing Mason Lewis. Mason strokes his goatee and squints at us through glasses that are too small for his head. It's then that I notice a whole group of bikers seated in the corner.

Mick leans toward me. "That patch on his jacket says: These are my church clothes."

I like Mason already.

"Hi," the big man greets us. "For those of you who don't know me, I'm the chaplain for the prison. I'm a good size for a prison chaplain, don't you think?"

I chuckle along with those in front of me.

"But I need to say something to Pastor Austin." He has Eric stand up. "Man, I'm worried about your weight. You really need to lay off the Twinkies. What do you weigh? 185? 190? It's just not healthy."

Eric grins then shows off his fine physique to the crowd. He doesn't take his shirt off like he did at the gym, but it's obvious that he doesn't have an ounce of fat on him. We get a good kick out of this, and I think Mason does especially—because Eric can't talk back.

"I'm just kidding, man." Mason waves for Eric to sit down. "But this is a good example of what Jesus was talking about in Matthew 7:3-5."

I nod. I can totally relate to Mason's illustration. I wonder if fitness analogies come naturally when the church service is held in a former gym.

Thinking of Gold's Gym leads me to think of Star. My stomach twists like it's taking a yoga class. I sigh heavily, though I don't realize it until after Mick shoots me a worried look. I curl my lips up for his benefit, but inside I'm trying to think of a way to reunite Star and Dee Dee. It's going to take much more than a sock club and a mutual birthday gift.

I chew on the inside of my cheek as Dee Dee's words of hopelessness play back through my head. If I were Star, would I be able to forgive a sister for not only terminating her pregnancy while I give up my dreams to raise an unplanned child, but to have her call me a derogatory name in the process of refusing my advice? If I truly saw that my sister was sorry—which Dee Dee is—it would be a lot easier. Or I might forgive her for my daughter's sake.

These answers don't satisfy me. I know there is more to forgiveness. I grew up in the church after all. Forgiveness needs to be given whether the other person is repentant or not. And it needs to be given for your own benefit, not for anybody else. An old Sunday school lesson wriggles into my consciousness: Unforgiveness is like taking poison and expecting the other person to die.

I shift in my seat accepting the hard truth. What Dee Dee did is sad—something she'll have to deal with for the rest of her life. But Star needs to step out of the victim role and get on with it. She has to forgive Dee Dee whether Dee Dee deserves it or not. My fingers dig into the leather of my Bible as I resolve to talk to Star. She won't like it. She might even get mad at me. But I want to help her. I want to help her forgive.

Mason clears his throat getting my attention once again. He reads from the Bible. *"Why do you look at the speck of sawdust in your brother's eye and ignore the plank in your own eye? How can you say to your brother, 'let me take the speck out of your eye,' when all the time there is a plank in your own eye? You hypocrite, first take the plank out of your own eye, and then you will see clearly to take the speck out of your brother's eye."*

I jerk back from the spiritual slap in the face. Wow. I'm a hypocrite. It's in front of me written in red letters. When Jesus spoke to the Pharisees, he was speaking to me. I blink a couple times and look down, too overwhelmed by my own realization to hear another word out of Mason's mouth, though I'm sure it's good.

Forgiveness. How easy it is for me to see the speck of un-forgiveness in my cousin's eye though I can't even forgive my dad. What my dad did was devastating. And I don't have to trust him. But I can choose to forgive him. And I'm not doing it for him—he doesn't deserve it. I'm doing it for me.

The decision rushes over me like waves on the ocean, the tide rising higher and higher until I feel washed clean from bitterness and anger. Forgiveness feels like freedom. My stomach untangles from its knot. I'm renewed. I'm ready to run, to feel sunshine warm my skin and wind rush through my hair. It's exhilarating.

I scoot toward the edge of my seat. Nothing can hold me down. I hadn't realized how miser-able I'd been until this very moment because I'd forgotten how amazing life can be. I want to sing and dance. I want to shout. I jump to my feet. The praise band is back on stage and we were all asked to stand up though I think I would have stood up anyway. I laugh, knowing that God's timing is perfect.

Dancing with my father God in fields of grace, we sing and I actually do a bit of dancing. I'm a nutcase and very happy about it.

Sure, I'd invited Dee Dee to come to church with me again today, and I was really disappointed she didn't join me. She missed out, but I was the one God wanted to speak to through Mason. Had she been sitting next to me I would have been focused on her, not on myself. I'm not giving up on her, though. I'll be fighting extra hard now.

Chapter 9

Sean is my client who has worked at a call center for the past sixteen years of his life. Yes, I think this is weird, but God has all given us different gifts, and God can use him when giving technical support to customers on the telephone as much as he can use me to improve my client's health.

Actually, the really weird thing is that when Sean first came in, his head was literally tilted toward his right shoulder from talking on the phone so much. It was painful to look at, not to mention the damage his poor posture was doing to his back. I gave him my business card to keep on his desk. Whenever he sees it during the day, he has to stop what he's doing and stretch his neck the opposite direction. And he's gotten a head-set since. I'm proud to say that besides being much healthier for having come to Lighten Up, he now looks human again.

"Thanks, Bethany," he calls as he heads out the door.

"Bye, Sean."

Out goes one client, in comes another. Business has been this smooth all day, but I'm still anxiously looking at the clock. Dee Dee didn't come over for lunch, and I'm worried that she's going to avoid me now that I know her secret. That's what I did to our whole church when Dad left.

"Hi, Bethany."

I open my mouth to greet Brooke, but I should have known better.

"Get this. I led one of my preschoolers to Jesus today! It was play time, and Allie was just sitting quietly looking at picture books about the Bible. She turned to me and said, 'Miss Brooke?' That's what the kids call me, Miss Brooke. She said, 'Miss Brooke, I can't hear God when he talks.' Isn't that

61

adorable? So I read her the picture book and explained that God can talk to us through the Bible, through worship music, through other people...you know all that. Then I asked if she wanted Jesus to come and live inside her! Oh...I've got to write this date on my calendar. I wish I could go up to heaven and party with the angels right now, I'm so happy."

Brooke does have this radiance about her. It's always there. She's shiny like she got sprinkled with pixie dust. And I'm like Nana barking after her as she tries to fly away with Peter Pan, but I've got to ask... "Did you tell her parents?"

"Of course! Of course! I work at a Christian preschool so I can do that. Though, I'd probably do it anyway. Her mom was thrilled. She asked Allie how they should celebrate. She was thinking Allie would want a cake or something for her spiritual birthday. This is so funny. You're going to laugh." Brooke pauses here to touch my arm and giggle.

Pet Peeve. I hate it when people tell me I'm going to laugh. It never turns out to be that funny.

Brooke takes a breath to control her giggles. "Allie said she wanted to celebrate by going bowling!"

I crack a smile grudgingly. "Bowling?" I repeat as I lead Brooke toward the rowing machine. I usually save it for when clients hit a weight loss plateau, but I'm hoping that it will get Brooke huffing and puffing so hard she won't be able to keep up this constant chatter.

Her story was sweet, and I'm feeling what might be a tiny twinge of jealousy at how on fire she is for God, but I console myself with the knowledge that I'm normal.

"Yes, bowling! Can you imagine? Did I ever tell you what I did to celebrate my conversion to Christianity? I don't think I did. It's only been a few years. I was invited to a Bible study in college, and oh my gosh, well you know how amazing it is."

I'm amazed by how much Brooke can say without really saying anything.

"So I was supposed to go shopping afterwards to buy a dress for this formal dance I was invited to, but as I'm trying on dresses I start thinking about what I was going to wear underneath for when my date took my dress off."

I'm guessing her date wasn't Eric. He said in front of the congregation that he's tempted by porn, but I'd like to think that he's saved himself for his wife. This gets my mind traveling a direction I really don't want to go.

If Brooke had given me a chance to speak I wouldn't have said anything. I busy myself rearranging equipment. I've never had sex, which I'm proud of, but with the whole virgin stigma, I'd much rather avoid the subject all together. Especially with the woman who is going to by my pastor's wife. Seriously.

"So right there in the dressing room, I call my date and say I can't go. It was a hard choice to make, and I was really disappointed because I love to dress up, and dance, and do other things…"

She chuckles, and I feel my face warm as if I were the one on the rowing machine. I'm hoping she'll get breathless from physical exertion and can't continue, but she doesn't.

"I prayed about it. Yeah, I prayed. I talk to God about everything now, from spilled orange juice at snack time to gas money. It reminds me that He's always watching and helps to keep me accountable. And then I also know that anything good that happens is an answer to one of my prayers. Like what happened next."

Whew, she'd moved on. Prayer I could talk about.

"I was feeling sorry for myself over the changes I would have to make, but God reminded me I was a new creature. Then without realizing where I was going, I walked into Build-a-Bear workshop and picked out a doll that looks like me—to represent the new Brooke. Here's the coolest part. When they stuff the dolls you get to put a heart inside. I wrote the name of Jesus on my heart."

I sit down on the edge of my one and only weight bench. I'm surprised by how cool Brooke's story turned out to be. Maybe I could learn something from her if I filtered out all the random thoughts she throws into each conversation.

"That's really neat, Brooke."

"Isn't it?" She throws her hands up and the pulley cable for the rowing machine zips back into place. "Ha! I'm done. I can't row anymore or I won't be able to talk."

She's on to me.

"Now, I wasn't as sore as I thought I would be after last week. Can you work me out harder? I've only got a few months until the big day. I don't know why I planned to get married on Valentines. Sure it's romantic, but that means I have to diet through Thanksgiving and Christmas. It's a good thing I've got you to stay on top of me."

This is a first. My clients usually complain of being too sore. "You don't have to be sore to get results, but we can add more resistance to your workout if you want."

I take the pin out of the weight stack and adjust. Besides added weight I also increase the number of reps she does. I have to admit, she's a hard worker. Her session flies by, and I'm eyeing the clock wondering when she's going to leave. She follows me around as I spray down equipment.

"Eric is spending Thanksgiving with my family, and then I'm going to McCall with him for Christmas. His parents have a cabin up there. Have you ever been to McCall? It's beautiful. I'm not much of a snow skier though, so I'll probably just hang out in the cabin."

McCall is a couple hours north of Boise. It's in the mountains on a lake—kind of like a mini Tahoe—so it's a great place to vacation for water or snow skiing. I do both.

"Nice," I say while rolling up a mat.

The bell over the door jingles and I'm happy enough to kiss whoever just came through it. Hopefully it will jingle again in a moment as Brooke departs. I look over my shoulder and my heartbeat pauses. It's Dee Dee. Brooke greets her before I get a chance.

"Dee Light! I've got to come over to your spa. I bet it's exquisite."

Dee Dee smiles warmly and somehow ushers my client out the door while at the same time listening and encouraging whatever the woman is saying. Such talent. And a little ironic, considering all the jokes Christian tells to Dee Dee about hairstylists being blabber mouths.

"Thank you," I breathe and pretend to wilt into my chair. I'm still not on level ground with my cousin so I tread lightly and hope to ease her nerves with gratitude.

Dee Dee takes the chair across from me, meaning she's here to talk, not to walk. I chew on the inside of my cheek.

"Maybe Brooke talks so much because she's around kids all day and needs adult conversation."

"No," I dismiss her suggestion. "Conversations are a two way thing." Oops, what happened to treading lightly? Uh... "I missed you at lunch. I brought your favorite orange flavored chicken and a broccoli salad."

If you ever ask a personal trainer to give you an example of a nutritious low-fat meal they will say: "Chicken, rice, and broccoli." I've thought about trying to sell a cookbook called *The Trainer's Diet* and offer 365 different recipes for those three menu items. There are so many fabulous ways to cook them. I could collaborate with Jade, except her diet probably consists of raw eggs in a glass.

"Mmm... Do you have any leftovers?"

"Yeah." I'd been tempted to eat it all, but since I tell my clients to have five or six small meals a day I figure I should do the same. On to the not so delicious subject. "How are you doing?"

"I'm fine." Dee Dee shoots me a smile as if she needs to prove it. "I knew you would worry when I didn't come over earlier, but we had some hair dye drama."

I study her face. "That doesn't sound good."

Dee Dee leans back. "My new stylist accidentally used that plum color I put in your hair last year to give a blonde strawberry-colored highlights. I had to fix it and give the woman a gift certificate for a free massage."

"Ooh," I grimace. "Well I'm glad you're here now. I've been praying all weekend for you."

"Thanks," she says heavily.

I think of Brooke's beliefs on prayer, and suddenly feel guilty for not praying enough. "Can I pray with you now?"

Dee Dee shifts her weight as if she's going to stand. "I respect your religion, Bethany, but you've got to stop pushing it on me. I can't accept that Christianity is the only way. Most of the world would go to hell if what you teach is true. That thought would just make me too sad to even get out of bed in the morning."

I'm ready to debate, but her words stop me. That is a sad thought. It's worse than sad. I'm back to my old argument. "Jesus died for *everyone*."

Dee Dee does stand this time. "I appreciate your prayers. But you don't have to worry about me."

When she leaves I worry even more than I had before. Now that I know her problems, I don't know how to reach her.

Chapter 10

Rebecca greets me warmly as I enter Grace Chapel for counseling the following night. She clasps my hand when leading me to Eric's office. Her skin is soft and loose and oh-so-comforting. I thank her with my eyes.

"Hi!" Eric stands and moves with me toward the couches. He sounds a little too loud, like he was tired so he just drank coffee and now the caffeine is kicking in.

"Long day?" I ask as I slump down in my spot. This time I'm more relaxed.

"Oh," he sighs. "Yeah. I'm still recovering from my cold."

His voice is better, but I bet Rebecca acted like a nurse all day anyway, bringing him chicken noodle soup and Vitamin C whenever he sneezed. According to my training on supplements, an excess of Vitamin C doesn't do anything more than the required amount of Vitamin C can do for you when you are sick. But they still sell it.

"Well, I found the value in your laryngitis." I'm a model student. My second session and I'm already using the tools he gave me.

Eric lifts an eyebrow in challenge. "This I gotta hear."

I smile confidently. "Because you couldn't speak on Sunday, God used Mason's sermon to convict me." My smile starts to slip as I remember the lesson.

"Really?" Eric nods in enthusiasm—genuine, not caffeine induced. "I always get a lot out of his preaching. What did it do for you?"

I chew on the inside of my cheek then grab a handful of M & Ms—much tastier. "This is actually a sad story. And I can't tell anyone else." I explain to him my family dynamics. "I want Star to forgive Dee Dee with all my heart. And this is what I was thinking about when Mason spoke about plank-eye syndrome. I realized that just like Dee Dee and Star are missing out on their relationship because of unforgiveness, I'm missing out on having one with my Dad."

Eric leans forward with his chin in his hands. "That's a huge change of position for you, Bethany. How does it feel?"

I press my lips together as I think. I blurt out the first feeling that comes to mind. "Scary."

Eric drops his hands from his face and rests his forearms on his thighs. "You are out of your comfort zone."

"No kidding. I mean, I've decided to start over in the relationship with my dad, but he's hundreds of miles away. I don't know how this is going to work—what it's going to look like."

Eric's eyes lock with mine. "That's something you will get to find out together."

I take this in and try to curl the corners of my lips up. "So it will be exciting at the same time. Scary and exciting."

"Which is better than safe and lonely," Eric comments, and I realize that is exactly how I have been living my life. Safe and lonely. Before I can become distracted by such depressing thoughts, he adds, "I'm proud of you."

I feel bright like the beam of a flashlight. I want to say more things that will make him proud. "I invited Dee Dee to church. She used to come with me before Dad resigned." Resigned is a nice word for what he did.

Eric leans back as if we are through with the serious talk and just having a casual conversation. "Great. Are you bringing her on Sunday?"

My plan to show off didn't work out so well. "No. She actually shared her depressing view on Christianity. I didn't know how to respond." I think through her words one more time trying to come up with an argument. Nothing. "She said that if Christianity is the only way to heaven then most of the people in the world are going to hell. It made me feel self-righteous and smug. Like I think I'm better than everyone else."

Eric cocked his head. "That is tough. Why do we get to spend eternity with God for having faith in our religion and nobody else gets to?"

I lift my hands. When you are raised in the church you don't really think to question its reality. We know that we have the kind of religion where everything a leader speaks should be based on the Bible, that we shouldn't just assume our pastor is always right. We should find out for ourselves, yet we rarely do.

Eric grabs his Bible from his desk. "In Matthew being saved and going to heaven is compared to Noah's ark. There was only one way. One savior, one boat." He passes the Bible for me to read the scripture.

"That's an interesting way to look at it." It starts to make a little more sense but still doesn't seem fair.

Eric's green eyes light up like the go signal on a traffic light. It gives the impression that there is no stopping him. "I was watching the history channel last night about Noah's Ark. I love to see how historians handle the Bible. They usually twist it in a way that they can't see God's glory, but it shines through for me. Anyway, Noah's ark was big enough to hold 569 railroad cars. Figuring in the sizes of young animals around back then that would need to be on board the ark to survive, they would have only taken up 167 of the railroad cars. That leaves 70% of the ark for Noah's family and..."

I catch his drift. "And anybody else who decided to get on board the boat!" It was an amazing thought. "So God made a way for other people, even knowing that they would not take it." This time I lean back because I'm a little blown away.

We sit in silence for a moment. "There's one way to heaven," Eric says finally.

"And we've got to be Noah to the world." I shake my head. "That's good. That's really good. Did you share this with Brooke?" Not that the woman needed more encouragement to witness.

Eric's lips curl into a cocky half smile. "What? She didn't tell you these statistics herself? Shocking."

So he agrees with me about Brooke's motor mouth. I like him even better. "She might have, but sometimes I get lost in our conversations."

Eric chuckles. "Whatever you do, don't go to a movie with her. She never shuts up."

I admire him as a martyr. "How do you handle it?"

He shrugs. "I tease her. You'll see. Someday your fiancée will find the cuteness in your flaws as well."

Flaws? What flaws? I'm an amazing woman. I'm forgiving my dad for running out on us, aren't I? Furthermore..."I'm not getting married."

I expect to hear some joke about how all the ladies in the church will be so disappointed if I don't become Mrs. Mafia Mick. Eric surprises me by getting serious again. "Why not?"

I shrug and try to play it off. "My dad was a strong man of God. If he couldn't make it work, I don't see how I stand a chance."

Eric studies me. "So you haven't always felt this way?"

"No." My voice sounds high. "I thought I was going to marry my college boyfriend, but when I came back from this really awesome mission trip where I got to play soccer with kids in Argentina, he'd started dating my roommate."

Eric blinks. "That would be painful. Was he the reason you decided not to get married?"

I mentally rewind my life. "He was the reason I moved back to Boise, but no, I still had hope for marriage."

"So you still dated?"

Of course. "I still date now."

Eric scratched his head. "What if you fall in love, or if the guy you are dating falls in love with you? You won't consider marriage?"

I shrug. It's kind of a non-issue under my circumstances. "No, because I don't date Christians. I don't want to give nice guys false hope."

Eric guffaws at my statement. "The Bible says not to become unequally yoked."

I lift my hands then let them drop. "I don't get serious. It's just for fun."

Eric gives me a she's-so-hopeless look. "Let's backtrack. Why aren't you going to get married?"

This isn't the reason I came to counseling. I'm perfectly happy with my marriage decision. I repeat my previous words with a sigh. "I don't stand a chance."

Eric watches me for a moment as if I'm supposed to have some kind of epiphany. I don't, so he gives me his. "You haven't really forgiven your father."

I reel as if his right fist had connected with my chin in an upper-cut. "I have!" I cry. "I forgave my father, but I'm not going to get married because I don't want to ever have to go through the pain of divorce again."

"When you use the word 'but' it negates everything you said before it." Eric throws a left hook.

I duck—figuratively speaking. "Then take out the 'but.' I forgive my father, *and* I'm not going to get married."

Eric's eyes flash with humor at my rebuttal. Then he turns sympathetic. "Your feelings are natural for children of divorce. I just don't want to see you settle for less than what God has planned for you."

I hadn't thought of it his way, and I don't want to. I've already justified my decision with scripture. "The apostle Paul encourages staying single."

Eric's face wrinkles at my reasoning. "Anything not done in faith is a sin. You're choice to not marry is based on fear, not on faith. Paul stayed single to spend more time in ministry. You're staying single because it's easier."

I don't see what the big deal is. "I invite my dates to church."

"Ahhh, a dating ministry." He makes it sound like a stupid idea.

"I'm happy being single." There.

"Really?" Eric doesn't fall for it. "Didn't we just agree that it is better to be in a scary but exciting relationship, rather than being safe and lonely?"

I swallow, but say nothing. My spine stiffens. I'm not as messed up as he makes me sound.

Eric senses the change in my attitude. He looks at his watch. "Let's see what Jesus has to say on marriage before you go." He reaches for a different Bible than the one we had used for the scripture on Noah. That seems like hours ago.

"Please." I know I'm right.

Eric flips through *The Message*. It's like Jesus gets agrees with me. He even lists ways in which marriage is hard. Then Eric clears his throat and finishes with, "*If you are capable of growing into the largeness of marriage, do it.*"

I harden my gaze.

"This is the verse I'm claiming as I prepare for marriage. It reminds me that the secret to success is being capable of growing, not in perfection. It's a choice you make—to be capable of growing or not."

I look away as if I'm bored, but really I'm choosing not to grow.

"*If you are capable of growing into the largeness of marriage, do it. Do it.*"

I stand up. "Have a good Thanksgiving."

Chapter 11

Laurel meets me for a late lunch on Wednesday. My client schedule is light because lots of people are already out of town for the holiday, so I agreed to have our accountability group early. She's stressing about cleaning her house and baking for tomorrow's feast—meaning she doesn't want to worry about having me over for dinner tonight.

The Red Letter Bookstore and Café is owned by one of the mega churches that I was attending before Grace Chapel. It's a former Chinese restaurant, but they've done a nice job of remodeling it to look modern. On weekends they often have live music, but today the corner stage is filled with kids attending story time.

Laurel rushes through the door, bringing with her a gusty breeze. I shiver as she joins me.

"Hi," I offer. It would have been easier to skip this week, but Laurel always thinks she can squeeze one more thing in. Actually, she *can* always squeeze in one more thing—because she's perfect.

She smiles sweetly. "I'm not going to be able to stay long. The construction out there ate away some of my time."

See what I mean about her being perfect? I would have been ranting, "That stupid bulldozer made me wait forever!"

She picks up a menu. "What's good?"

I point out my favorite mango salmon salad and the Greek-style sandwiches. Today the special is a teriyaki bowl.

Laurel swirls the lemon in her water. "So how's counseling going?"

I'm tempted to shrug, but the whole point of our meeting is to be real with each other. "Well, Eric gave me some really good suggestions for witnessing to Dee Dee." I hadn't gotten to try them out yet because I'm missing Dee Dee's daily walk to dine with my sister-in-law. I explain the Noah's ark comparison to Laurel. She nods but doesn't get as excited as I did. I guess it's still my turn to talk. "Oh, I've forgiven Dad!"

Laurel's eyes get wider, but she stays quiet as I carefully avoid making the connection with my desire for Star to forgive Dee Dee. I wonder how open I'm supposed to get in accountability, but I figure that my cousin's situation isn't really mine to share. Only Eric knows, and I'm going to keep it that way.

"That's great," she says, though I'm feeling like she's really not here.

We sit silently for a moment. I squirm and give in to the discomfort. I'd be terrible under interrogation. "So that's my spiritual and family life. In my personal life, I've decided that I don't want to get married. Eric is really challenging me on this decision."

Laurel stares past me then jerks like she just woke up. "Marriage is hard," she says.

"My point, exactly!" We sit for another minute. The waitress brings our sandwiches. My mouth waters at the aroma of Mediterranean herbs, so I dig in. Goat cheese never tasted so good. Laurel doesn't move. "Are you thinking about the Thanksgiving menu?" I ask around my mouthful of food.

Laurel's eyes shift to meet mine. "No."

"Scrubbing your toilets?" I try again.

"No."

I'm glad she said no to that one. It's not really a topic I would want to discuss during a meal.

Laurel sighs. "I'm thinking about marriage."

Oh, yeah. She has an issue with my brother being funny. "Did Christian try to pop your toes again?"

Laurel gives a smile as phony as one of those masks used to represent the drama club in high school. "There's more."

I visualize Christian trying to pop her fingers. Or heaven forbid, her back.

She pushes her food aside, and I'm tempted to give her a lesson on nutrition, but only for a moment.

"I wasn't planning to tell you this when I suggested we become accountability partners."

I stop chewing.

"I thought it wasn't really my problem to share."

What? Laurel has problems?

She traces the rim of her glass with her finger as if she's still considering whether to open up or not. "It's about your brother. And you can't talk to him about it."

I feel my eyebrows draw closer together. I have no idea where she's going. "Okay."

Her gaze locks with mine and it's almost like she's apologizing. "Christian is a recovering pornography addict."

I shake my head. I can't believe it. My brother wouldn't do that. Not only does he have a perfect wife, but he's seen the results of infidelity. My sandwich feels like a heavy lump in my stomach. "What?" I must have misunderstood.

Laurel licks her lips. "That's how I felt too, Bethany. I was shocked. If I hadn't walked in on Christian at his computer I wouldn't have believed it."

I'm repulsed. How can I not talk to Christian about this? He'll see the change in my behavior because I won't be able to treat him the same. I feel dirty. Like when Dad admitted his affair. It's happening all over again.

"Bethany," Laurel tries to call me back to reality. "Don't judge him. I did at first, but Eric helped me understand it's not about me. It's about instant gratification. It's a weakness, and it's natural."

I feel my mouth hang open at the way Laurel explains this. How can she so casually justify his behavior?

"Remember when I went on that Girl's-Getaway-Cruise with my mom last year?"

"Yeah." I'd been so jealous, but what does that have to do with my brother?

"That was right after I caught Christian. I'd already had the cruise planned, but if I hadn't, I still would have left your brother. I told him I wasn't coming back until he met with Eric and promised not to look at porn again."

"You've known for a year?" I can't believe all this went on without me knowing. I mean it's natural that Christian wouldn't want to tell his sister, but I should have picked up on some kind of undercurrent or something.

"Yeah, we're better now. I was miserable at first—Chonda Pierce's comedy routine couldn't even make me laugh on the cruise—but I came back to find that Christian had become accountability partners with Eric. And he signed up for Covenant Eyes, which means that everything he looks at online is sent to Eric."

I think of Eric's sermon about David's innocent disaster. It had been planned for my brother, not for me.

"So you've forgiven Christian?" I ask though I already know the answer.

"Of course. And God has rewarded me for my faithfulness. Not only is our sex so much better..."

"Ew." I'm single, people.

"But our marriage is stronger. We made it through this so we know that we can make it through anything."

I tuck my hair behind my ear. "And you can trust Christian again?"

Laurel tilts her head. "That took time. He had to earn it. The internet is such a trap. It makes porn accessible for men not even looking for it." She chuckles. "I actually didn't know if I could trust him or not, until I went to Victoria's Secret online—looking for pajamas—and got Christian in trouble."

I grin at the thought. "Eric busted him?" Eric's probably already done more for my family than I will ever know.

"Yeah."

I take a sobering breath. "So my brother was addicted to porn a year ago. Why did you feel like you had to tell me this?" I'm not sure I want to know.

Laurel sits up straighter. "It's made me who I am, and I still struggle with it. I've forgiven him, but I haven't forgotten it. And I should be able to discuss this with you since you are my accountability partner."

I digest the news. Last week Laurel said that she thinks Dad's sin affected Christian more than he realized. Maybe this is one of the ways. I feel bad for my brother at the same time I'm mad at him. "I'm sorry, Laurel."

Laurel gives me a sad smile. "It's been hard, but you know what? I'm still glad I married him."

I think back to the verse Eric read. *If you are capable of growing into the largeness of marriage, do it.* I still don't think I'm capable, but I see that if I wanted to be, accountability would play a very large role. Again I wonder if it would have prevented Dad from seeking fulfillment elsewhere.

"Laurel, you're so perfect," I say.

She just rolls her eyes, but I mean it. Sure, she's a little more real now that I know she's experienced marital problems, but that was all my brother's fault. And she stuck by him. The strength she must have had to endure the pain only adds to my argument.

"I respect your sincerity," I add.

Laurel looks down embarrassed. Then as if seeing her food for the first time, she waves her hand in the air to get the waitress's attention and asks for a to-go box. "I'm glad we got to talk," she says to me, "but I really have to go. Let's promise to pray for each other."

I take another bite of my almost-forgotten sandwich and nod.

"You're still picking your mom up from the airport tomorrow?"

That's right. "What time again?" I ask.

Laurel flips open her date book to give me the flight I should have written in my date book—if I had a date book. "And you are bringing sweet potatoes?"

"Of course." I hate the traditional sweet potato recipe everyone makes during the holidays. I mean, marshmallows on vegetables? Gross. "I'll just have to go to the grocery store."

Laurel sends me a warning look. I'm sure she never waits till last minute to grocery shop, but that's the fun part. Where's her holiday spirit?

"Don't worry," I console her.

"Alright." She stands up and double checks everything—something else I could learn from her. "Dinner is tomorrow at 2:00."

"I'll be there," I sing-song happily, though it won't be the same without Dad or Trinity. I wish it were the same.

Chapter 12

I trot across the bridge leading from the parking garage to the airport. I'm late because the first grocery store I tried was out of sweet potatoes (in Idaho!), but the Boise airport is pretty small, so I'm not too worried. I rush through the lobby with my eyes on alert then drop into a plastic chair behind a wall of glass next to the metal detectors.

Mom hasn't arrived yet. If she had I would have noticed her. She's the type who stands out in a crowd. Yes, she's beautiful with her dark Filipino coloring and long, lean limbs, but it is her sense of style that draws your eye to her. She dresses like she's still in the 80's.

She has wavy hair to her waist and curls her bangs like I learned to do in middle school (then how not to do in high school), and her eye shadow is either blue or purple thanks to some ancient magazine article telling her she has "cool" coloring. Then there are her long floral skirts—usually black with big pink flowers—and her flowing blouses that belong on the cover of a cheesy romance novel. I don't think anybody has ever attempted to tell her how ridiculous she looks (besides Trinity and me) because she is the sweetest woman you will ever meet. Just her essence is the perfect blend of strength, energy, and tranquility. Nobody wants her to change.

A new wave of people pour through the double doors from their arrival and I catch a peek at a long floral skit. I can't see her face yet, but I know it's Mom. I stand and step around a screaming child. Mom still hasn't spotted me because I can't see her face yet. I skip a couple of steps and start to wave... then the flowing blouse comes into view. I drop my hand. The front of the blouse is tight against the woman's large bosom. That can't be my mom. I mean, I inherited her flat chest. I step back and scan the rest of the crowd, wondering if mom had been on the same plane as her buxom twin.

"Bethany!" I hear Mom's comforting voice from behind me.

How could she have found me first? I'm dressed in my one boring pair of jeans, and my hair is pulled back into a non-descript ponytail. Maybe Mom dressed like a normal person and I didn't recognize her disguise. I spin around and gasp.

Mom is the woman with the boobs! I think it is anyway, I haven't gotten my eyes up above her chest yet. She leans in to hug me and we stick our boom-booms out so our silhouette is the shape of a tent. This is how you hug when you are afraid to touch somebody—or something attached to them.

"Mom!" I keep holding on to her arms, but lean back to look in her eyes. Isn't she a little old to stuff her bra?

"What do you think?" she asks smoothly.

"I can't believe it. I can't believe...you had surgery?"

"Yes." She's all confidence as she swings her jacket over one shoulder and leads me along with her rolling carry-on.

I should probably be happy for her. But I'm not. I'm horrified. I try to keep this out of my voice as I ask, "Why?"

"You, of all people, should know," she quips.

Gee, thanks Mom. "*I'm* not getting breast surgery." That would be too weird. But not as weird as this.

"Well, you are young and perky. My breasts looked like deflated balloons. You kids sucked the life out of them."

I almost gag. "But who is going to see them?" I can't let it go.

She steps onto the escalator. "Me. I did it for me." She seems disgusted that I would think any differently.

I ride down in silence as Mom chirps about the weather... and her new career at a nursing home...and the houseboat she lives on now. I don't hear any of it.

"Would you have done it if Dad hadn't had an affair?"

Mom huffs as we walk to baggage claim. "Of course not. I was a pastor's wife."

I still don't get it. How can she live with herself? "Aren't you still that same person?" Maybe she's not. Maybe my mom changed when I wasn't looking.

"Sugar," she runs her hand against the side up my head, smoothing my ponytail. "I'm still the same person, but I don't have the audience that I had before. I don't have to worry so much what people think of me. I just have to be me."

Really? Her memoir would have to be rewritten and titled "Me as a C." I desperately hope she doesn't run into any people from her past while she's here. I don't need more rumors about my family flying around.

"There…" She waves her hand toward the conveyor belt. "My suitcase is the blue one."

It matches her eye shadow, I think as I run off to fetch it for her. As we head out toward the parking garage, she changes the subject.

"So are you dating anyone, sugar?"

Maybe if I had a chest like hers, I'd have guys lining up, but…"No."

"The right guy will come around when you least expect it."

Sure, I think bitterly. *Then he'll have a nine-year affair and leave me so lonely that I get fake boobs for company.*

"Trinity called the other day. She's getting pretty serious about her boyfriend."

"But he must not be the right guy," I counter, using Mom's reasoning. "Since she obviously went looking for him."

How did my family get so messed up after years of ministry in a Christian church? Dad marrying another woman, Mom having plastic surgery, Christian addicted to porn, and Trinity running off to live with some guy she met online? Oh, and me afraid of marriage—which Eric thinks is messed up.

I push the button on my remote keychain to unlock the Jeep. I load Mom's bags into the back then climb in next to her. I do another double take and wonder how long it will take to get used to the stranger who gave birth to me.

LIGHTEN UP

She's talking about taking a trip to Pennsylvania to meet my sister's new love interest, but I'm still thinking about "the twins." I know some of the ladies at the gym get implants. They disappear from classes for a couple months (because they have to avoid impact) then reappear with their new Barbie bodies. I've gotten used to that, but never thought my mother would be one of them. I mean her idea of exercise is the sign language she did during the worship service at church. And all those lessons about beauty being on the inside...

"How much does it cost?"

She's rummaging through her Marry Poppins-like purse to show me brochures of the Van Trapp lodge that she might visit on her trip to the East Coast, when I blurt out my question.

"I'll be going on an all-inclusive tour so it won't cost as much..."

"No, Mom. The surgery. How much did you pay for the surgery?" It's gonna bug me till I die.

Mom pauses. "It was expensive."

Maybe it won't bug me till I die. Maybe it will just kill me. "You could have bought goats for starving families in third-world countries!" We did this in Sunday School when I was little. "You could have donated toward mission aviation!" Their headquarters are here in Idaho. "You could have..."

Mom interrupts. "I wouldn't have done it except your dad gave me all the money we were saving for our trip to Hawaii. You know I give to missions. You know I pray for missionaries as well. This was my money, and I don't regret what I did with it."

Yeah, I'm on my high horse, but it seems like Mom is in *high school*. She's the teenager and I'm the parent. It's Freaky Thursday—the prequel to *Freaky Friday*.

I turn the steering wheel to my Jeep and we loop de loop toward the lower level of the parking garage. I send up a quick prayer as we wait to pay the garage attendant. I've got to move on, but I can't do it on my own. In fact, I'd rather not move on, but my gawking and squawking won't make a difference now. I comfort myself with the idea of Christian's reaction.

Christian totally lets me down. Laurel greets us at the door and leads us into the basement family room where Christian has set up camp in front of the television. This is the reason I've started to hate Thanksgiving. The guys watch football on T.V. while the women cook. Hardly a celebration—more like everyday life in America.

When we were little, we used to serve at soup kitchens on Thanksgiving. Now that makes you thankful for what you have.

Laurel doesn't even notice Mom's chest, or maybe she does but she's too perfect to show it. I stand behind Mom and watch Christian's face, trying to hide the smile on my own. I expect a repeat performance of his surprise party entrance.

"Hi, Mom!" He stands and gives her a side hug. Now why didn't I think of that?

Okay, he must have noticed them if he's hugging her that way, but he plops back into his recliner and kicks his feet up. How disappointing—like a fire cracker with a faulty fuse. Come on...come on...where's the explosion?

I'm still behind Mom so I cup my hands about a foot away from my chest and pantomime Dolly Parton. Christian shoots me a disgusted look. As if I'm the immature sibling.

I shake my head and run up the stairs after Laurel. Maybe she'll talk in the kitchen. I find her checking the turkey. Turkey always smells better than it tastes—probably because I only eat the white meat. My stomach growls anyway.

"Laurel!" I cry. I need to see a reaction out of somebody else to justify my own feelings. "Did you see them?"

Laurel's eyes slant my way then back to the turkey she's basting. "See what?"

I drop dramatically onto a saddle seat barstool. "Them. The water balloons stuffed down Mom's shirt!"

Laurel covers her mouth and giggles—as if she'd momentarily forgot the punch line to this joke. "You didn't know about them?"

I couldn't be more blown away, even if I'd been walking the giant Garfield balloon in the Macy Thanksgiving Day Parade and everybody else let go of their ropes. "You *knew*?"

The oven rack makes a scraping, clanging sound as she pushes the Turkey back in. "I must have forgotten to tell you. She had them when Christian and I went out to see her in September."

I gasp. "Christian didn't tell me either."

Laurel leans across the counter toward me. "Well, since I found out about his porn addiction, he refuses to acknowledge the female body in any way. We kind of just pretend it didn't happen."

I rub my face with my hands.

"Will you set the table for me, Bethany?" she changes the subject.

I glance at the table. Laurel's already hollowed out the tops of apples to hold tea lights and ironed leaves for decoration. All I have to do is add the dishes.

"So...five place settings?" I ask.

"Just four." Laurel uses her fingers to count. "You, me, Christian, and your mom."

I open the cupboard and dead pan, "You forgot the elephant in the room."

Chapter 13

I glance at the clock on my dashboard. 4:41 a.m. There's only one day of the year that I willingly get up this early. But it still takes me quite a while to get going—a mug of green tea and some kick-boom-boom-day-after-Thanksgiving-sales should do the trick.

Dee Dee's house is as charming as her spa. In the summer her flower garden smells like the perfume section of Dillards. Even now with all the flora frosted over, she's still got the front porch, gingerbread trim, and a dormer window that could get it on the cover of the Better Homes and Garden magazines she orders for me every year. (I think she gets a free subscription for a friend whenever she renews hers, but with the size of my apartment and the one dying plant I stole, she would be better off sending the magazine to…I don't know…Oscar the Grouch? It would be like me sending her issues of Cooking Light.)

I park on the curb of her neighborhood that is so old that nobody has garages then run up to the porch. She's got the light on for me and opens the door before I knock—green tea in hand.

"Thanks." I take the stainless steal mug and stare at her for a moment. I always forget that she wears contacts, so on occasions like this when she breaks out her ten-year-old glasses I'm taken by surprise. The glasses are sadly outdated. She looks like Harry Potter.

She locks the door then we rush through the chill back to my Jeep, which hasn't yet heated up to a temperature warm enough to take mittens off. With a soft top on the vehicle I don't have much insulation, so it takes longer than it should. I'm such a summer girl.

"Where to?" she asks.

"Wal-Mart. They've got a five a.m. sale on twelve-inch bikes. I want to get one for Jennica." That should make Dee Dee happy. She's so thrifty, I don't think she shops anywhere but.

We used to go with both our moms and our sisters every year. This year, Star is going with my aunt, and Dee Dee is going with me. Mom opted to sleep in since that is what Laurel her hostess is doing. (Laurel always takes a weekend trip to Oregon to shop tax free with her sister.)

The two of us are awfully quiet compared to the obnoxious van load of people we used to Christmas shop with. I chew on the inside of my cheek wishing I had prearranged an "accidental" meeting with Star and my aunt at IHOP for brunch. But of course, Dee Dee spent the whole day with them yesterday. I wonder how it went.

"How was your Thanksgiving?" I try to sound peppy.

Dee Dee groans. "I did get to play with Jennica, but Star wouldn't talk to me the whole time. She wouldn't even look at me."

The situation seems so hopeless now that I know the extent of the feud. I should change the subject here.

"My mom got a boob job."

Dee Dee sits and stares at me with her mouth hanging open, the street lights flashing over her face every few seconds. I love it.

"And Laurel and Christian wanted to pretend everything was normal. My Thanksgiving was probably almost as bad as yours." Pour on the sympathy.

"Wow." Dee sips her creamy coffee (so unhealthy) and we cruise in silence. Near Wal-Mart, every other car in the lane merges with us as if we were the Porsche-driving bad guys from that old Disney movie Condor Man. We're women on a mission.

"Man, look at this parking lot," I exclaim. I don't see a single available parking space. "Are we late?" A funny question for 5:00 a.m.

LIGHTEN UP

"No." Dee Dee directs me toward a video store parking lot closer to the street. "The doors open at 4:30, but the sales don't start until five."

I start to feel a little frantic. What if there are no bikes left? "Come on!" I hop out as soon as I've pulled the key out of the ignition. "We've got to run."

Dee Dee waves me ahead. Her caffeine hasn't kicked in yet. "I'm not running that far. I'll radio you inside."

I rush through the parking lot, walkie-talkie in hand, glad that I've worn my Nike Shox. My adrenalin starts to pump. The glass doors whoosh open and a grandpa in a blue vest hands me a map. He moves slowly as if dazed, and I'm guessing he's never experienced this kind of madness before.

The map shows the layout of the entire store and the advertised sales are marked in the aisles. The bikes on sale aren't next to the regular bikes. They're on the other side of the store next to produce. I glance at my watch. 4:58.

If I've taken my health for granted before, I don't at this moment. I make the most of it and sprint across the store.

An announcer blares over the P.A. system. "One minute until 5:00." I dart around a shopping cart loaded with three Easy Bake Ovens and a group of women having trouble reading the map. My shoes squeak against the floor like I'm playing volleyball in a gym.

I slow down as I reach a rack of children's bikes covered with plastic wrap—at least I think they're bikes. It's hard to see through the crowd tightly circling the sale item. I squeeze between a balding man and a short woman in a sweat suit and do a quick scan to calculate the ratio of bikes to people. It's gonna be close.

The P.A. blares again. "10...9...8..."

We all chime in. "7...6...5..."

I elbow my way a little closer. "4...3...2...1!"

Another Wal-Mart employee—one who could use my professional services—rips the plastic away, and I become

87

a Bethany pancake. The crowd presses around me, but I'm no closer to the bikes than I had been pre-countdown. They start to disappear from the rack. I've got to act fast or my early morning workout would have been for nothing.

Moving like a boxer I spread my legs and bend my knees to keep balanced. I bob and weave around the people in front of me, and then as if my middle name is Ali, I shoot my arm out so fast that they don't even see it coming. I'm victorious. The last bike is mine.

Maybe I'm working at the wrong type of gym. Or taking the wrong type of fitness class. I wonder if Eric would give me a lesson or two in sparring. If the adrenalin rush is anything like Thanksgiving morning at Wal-Mart, I would be hooked. Pun intended.

The crowd thins so that I have enough room to hold the walkie-talkie up to my mouth. "Mission accomplished!"

I see Dee Dee jogging toward me before I hear her response. She obviously *didn't* wear her running shoes. She bends over to put her hands on her knees while she huffs and puffs. "I'm glad…" huff, puff "…you got one."

"Barely." I speak modestly, but grin proudly. "I didn't ask you what you want to buy here."

"Oh." Dee Dee stands back up and takes a deep breath. "I'm getting my parents a vacuum cleaner."

We head toward the appliances section. "Good idea."

Dee Dee's parents bought a Kirby vacuum back when we were kids. They still use the dinosaur because it came with a lifetime warranty. Dee Dee's mom refuses to buy a new one even though lifting the vacuum up the stairs is really hard on her back.

I wheel the little bike along. "Did you know that Christian could ride a bike without training wheels when he was two?"

Dee Dee laughs. "Isn't that one of your family jokes?"

We turn down a side aisle. "Yeah. Every time he does something stupid, we're like, 'but he could ride a bike when he was two.'"

"Poor Christian." She actually sounds sorry for him. "Is he going to do the comedy club thing again any time soon?"

"Did I forget to tell you? He's going to be on an improv team at Comedy Sportz. We're getting group tickets. Wanna come?"

We slow down in front of the vacuum cleaners. "Of course. Isn't that where the two teams of comedians compete against each other and get their ideas from the audience?"

"I think so. I've never been." I look at vacuums, too—not that I have much carpet in my apartment. A dust buster is all I really need.

Dee Dee starts digging through boxes under the display. "Your brother is so funny. I'm surprised he didn't say anything about your mom's boob job. That's got to be some great joke material."

I chew on the inside of my cheek. "Well..." How do I explain that? "Dad's decision affected him more than he knows. He's meeting with Eric for help."

"Oh?" Dee Dee looks up from her squatted position. "Like you are?"

"Kind of." I cross my legs and lean against a support beam. I hope Dee Dee is planning to go with me to the mall, as well. Looking at vacuums is even more boring than it sounds. My mind wanders to my sessions with Eric. That reminds me of what I wanted to talk to Dee Dee about. "Eric's got some great things to say." I explain to her the Noah analogy.

Dee Dee stays quiet for a moment. "Interesting."

Ya think? Though I'd probably use the word *profound*. Or maybe *life-changing*.

She pulls a box out and lets it clang into her cart. "This one is light weight. And it's bagless."

And...and...is that it on the subject of heaven and hell? I'd expect her to at least take as much time to look at the options for afterlife as she did on her vacuum cleaner.

LIGHTEN UP

"Come on. I want to get a Christmas tablecloth to go with the snowman tea light holder I ordered from one of my clients."

She takes off toward the holiday section, completely oblivious that she's missed the whole reason for the season.

Chapter 14

Usually I run or ride along with my clients as they warm up, but when I go to put Sean's file away on Monday it won't fit into my file cabinet. Sean's distracted by the jazz music I let him put in the CD player—his choice, not mine—so I use the ten minutes to clean out the drawer.

The front door swings open as I stack another file on top of my desk. I've lost a lot of clients to Gold's, which I'm actually proud of. I haven't just trained them for an hour, but I've given them the education they need to keep themselves fit and the confidence to do it in front of everyone who works out at the giant of a gym.

I spin my chair around and am rewarded by Robbie's gleaming grin. "I need your autograph, ma'am." He's so smooth I get the urge to watch the movie Hitch again.

"What do I get in exchange?" I barter.

He whips a brown package out from behind his back. It must be the new fat caliper I ordered. Jennica broke my old one when using it to dig in the dirt for bugs.

I take the electronic clipboard. "For you," I say as I sign.

We make the trade. I set the caliper down on my desk next to my outdated files and remember the group shower I took at Gold's. "Hey, do you work out at Gold's?"

"Nope." Robbie flexes. "I've got a weight bench at home, and I get my cardio from running around in this uniform all day."

"Huh. I thought I saw you there a couple weeks ago."

"Oh, yeah." Robbie looks around. "I took the tour from a sales guy."

I lift an eyebrow. "And you made it out without signing a contract. That's impressive. The sales department knows their stuff."

"Yeah." Robbie shrugs, but doesn't quite look comfortable. "The sprinkler system saved me, I guess."

A laugh bursts out of me at the memory. "Wasn't that crazy? I still haven't heard what started the alarm."

Robbie studies me for a moment. "I wouldn't have expected *you* to work out there."

"Well, my cousin teaches a class on Tuesdays and Thursdays. It's pretty fun." I think about Star and start to picture her with Robbie. But of course, she's not dating, so there would be no sense in introducing them. I feel a twinge of relief at the idea of having the hunk all to myself—for a couple minutes every week. Boy, I need to get out more.

Robbie looks around the room as if he's looking for an excuse to stay and hang out longer. (I would be too if I had to deliver boxes all day.) But Sean clears his throat to get my attention. I wonder how long I left him on the treadmill.

"Back to work, I guess," Robbie says with a wink, but I don't respond because I don't want Sean to think that I consider my time with him *work*. I basically get to wear sweats and play all day—every child's dream career whether they know it or not.

I give Sean a grueling workout (does anybody ever use the word grueling apart from describing a workout?) and he rises to the challenge. He surprises me every time he comes in. Since I straightened out his posture, he's been able to play tennis again. I swear, it's taken years off him. He now looks young enough to be my grandpa.

He sits down on the weight bench and faces the mirror for his favorite part of the workout—the end. He lifts his hands above his head without me having to prompt him. I lean into his back and pull his elbows wide to stretch his pecs. He groans because he can't let me know how much he enjoys it. I twist both arms behind him so the elbows are bent ninety degrees and pull up.

"Bethany, you're brutal."

I smile at him in the mirror. "I don't know if brutal is the word you're looking for, Sean. I think brilliant would be more appropriate."

"No. In fact I'm pretty sure you have a reputation for being brutal."

"Really?" I puff out my chest in pride. "Then I must be like the Dread Pirate Roberts from *The Princess Bride*. My name strikes terror into exercisers everywhere, but those who know me find me loving and loyal."

Sean snorts. "I do like the pirate idea. You could make your new logo a skull and cross dumbbells."

"Argh," I try to growl seriously, but I can't help laughing.

I hear a tinkle of the bell in the background then I can't hear anything else besides the rush of words coming from Brooke's mouth. "I'm so glad I could make it in today. You did get my e-mail, didn't you?"

I didn't. Maybe that's why I'm not expecting her so early.

"What are you listening to? I love jazz, but I never expected you to like it, Bethany."

I continue stretching Sean, feeling bad that our joke was cut short. I'm hoping Brooke will hop on the rowing machine so I can finish with the client on my schedule.

Brooke steps right in front of us, blocking our reflections in the mirror. "Hi, I'm Brooke Allumbaugh."

Sean wrestles his arm away from my grasp to shake her hand. "I'm Sean Daniels."

Brooke giggles in a totally self-absorbed way. "That's quite a firm grip. Bethany must work you hard."

"Yeah, we were just—" He gets interrupted and I wish I had somehow known to warn him.

"Oh, you're wearing the star of David! It's beautiful. Are you Jewish?"

I've asked Sean questions about his faith before, but never so abruptly.

Sean looks down at his necklace. "I am. I immigrated to America from Europe with my parents in the 40s."

"Ooooh," Brooke nods with understanding though I can't help thinking she doesn't understand much at all. I wonder if I should give her a brief history of WWII after Sean leaves.

I finish with Sean and trot over to my desk to set up his next appointment. You know, demonstrate to Brooke how this whole training session thing works.

"So what do you think of Jesus?" Brooke blurts.

I freeze as if overhead sprinklers had just started to pour water down on us. I'm wishing they would—or at least that I had some kind of alarm to set off when Brooke's mouth starts a fire.

Sean doesn't look offended, though. He just stares at her as if he's not sure he heard her right.

She takes a seat next to him on the bench. "You guys don't believe he's the Messiah, do you?"

Um...couldn't she just read a book? And who talks like that? We believe that Jesus is our brother, our friend... Messiah just seems a little outdated.

"I haven't really researched the prophecies of a Messiah." He says this honestly, openly.

"Oh, you're missing out! It's amazing how the whole Bible fits together so seamlessly. Don't you love that word? Seamlessly." Brooke leans forward as if she's going to let him in on a secret. "If you read the New Testament, you will find that Christianity was started with the Jews and spread to the Gentiles."

Sean is staring at her very intently. "I've never considered it that way."

He actually seems curious. I imagine Nicodemus looking very similar when he met with Jesus and questioned the whole born again thing.

"Oh, you should. You should. Read the Bible and see for yourself." Brooke digs through her handbag (the word purse just doesn't do her satchel justice) and whips out a tiny New Testament—the kind I was given when my parents had me dedicated at church and then I lost either on a camping trip or at swimming lessons. "This book is a top seller, but at the same time it's so underrated." She looks over at me. "How does that work?"

I shrug, not at all sure how Brooke works. She can't be on time for an appointment, but she's a ready witness to a man I've known for months.

Chapter 15

Rebecca waves me into Eric's office. This reminds me of my last visit, causing me to do the Brooke thing and enter babbling.

"I explained your whole Noah theory to Dee Dee and all she said was 'interesting'. Interesting! And then she bought a snowman tablecloth. Of course it was five in the morning, but I still just want to pound her over the head with a Bible." I plop down on the couch and immediately go for the candy dish. I don't even realize I do this until I taste chocolate. I continue my ranting while chewing. Bad manners, I know, but with his fiancée, he should be used to it. "Of course, that's what Brooke would do. She witnessed to my Jewish client today."

One corner of Eric's lips curl up.

"She acted horrified that he doesn't believe in the Messiah then handed him a New Testament."

Eric literally tries to wipe the smile off his face by rubbing a hand across it, but it reappears like fog on a car window. "So she didn't actually pound him over the head with a Bible? Whew. You had me worried."

I laugh and then choke a little on my snack. To hide my embarrassment I toss an M & M at Eric. He catches it (with his quick boxer reflexes) before slipping it in his mouth. Had I known counseling could be this fun I might have signed up years ago.

Eric lips his lips. "Yeah, I joke that when I get frustrated with witnessing to people I can just sic Brooke on 'em."

I picture my newest client on all fours, snarling like a Doberman.

"You've just got to give your cousin time." Eric's voice loses its humor. "So...where were you on Sunday?"

I groan and feel my body grow heavier as I answer the question. "Dying Faith." I explain the name when Eric doesn't get it. "Mom wanted to go to our old church to see some friends."

Eric must have a counseling mask he puts on when he talks to lunatics like me about our crazy lives. All expression just slips right off his face. Of course, he wouldn't want to scare us away with the kind of horrified looks most people give us.

"Is that a bad thing?" he asks.

I lean my head back and roll my eyes to the ceiling. Where do I start? "First of all, I left the church because of the gossip going on about our family. I was 'The-Daughter-of-the-Pastor-Who-Ran-Off-With-His-Secretary.' Have you ever been judged by a person before they even talk to you?"

"Yeah. All the time. Everyone I meet. And I'm sure you even judged me."

He got me. Well, kind of. "I thought you must be a doctor. But—" I raise one finger as if it is an exclamation point. "I was guessing. Those people think they know me because of what they *know* about my family. And lots of them feel sorry for me."

Eric responds as though every sentence he says is a strategic move in the game of chess. "I acknowledge your position."

I don't know if that's a good or bad thing, but I'm going to consider it validation. "Thank you." I start to go on. "Secondly..." I falter.

Eric waits patiently. It's very annoying.

Deep breath. Okay, out with it. "My mom got a boob job."

Eric's jaw doesn't drop. He doesn't reel back. He doesn't even blink. Did he hear me?

"My mom got a boob job!"

He nods that he's heard.

"She used to be the pastor's wife at Dying Faith. She was the perfect model of the Proverbs 31 woman. And now she's...she's...top heavy!"

Eric looks as casual as if he's buying a vacuum, not talking about the female anatomy. "How did the people at church react?"

"Oh, just like Christian and Laurel did. They pretended not to notice. Well, some told her that she looked good, so they pretty much encouraged her. Probably because they were feeling sorry for her. But now they'll talk even more about us behind our backs."

Sometimes it seems like churches are the worst at gossip. *Oh, you need to pray for so and so. I heard they are going through this or that. I'm so worried for them. I can't imagine because I'm perfect.*

Eric challenges me. "How do you know they are talking behind your back?"

My stomach flips a back handspring. "The last time I went to that church, I entered the bathroom where a bunch of women were talking and it got dead silent."

These were women I trusted. Women my mom considered friends. Maybe I can see where Dee Dee is coming from—why she quit going to church.

"I'm sorry about that."

The pain must be showing through my eyes. I look down even though I know he's not feeling sorry for me. He's hurting with me.

Eric pauses. "I'm going to try to explain your mom's decision in terms that you will understand."

I look up and feel a funny wrinkle between my eyebrows. What could Eric know about breast implants that I don't?

"When is an individual most likely to succeed at weight loss?" He asks. "What prompts the largest amount of individuals to enter a gym for the first time?"

I learned this while getting my P.T. Cert (personal training certification). At the big gyms they want trainers to also be salespeople, so we had to study all kinds of bullying techniques. "People are most likely to lose weight when they are going through a big change, like getting married or getting a divorce or something."

"Why is that? Why would someone going through a divorce want to change their appearance?"

Duh. "To feel better about themselves."

Eric watches for this information to sink in.

"No." I refuse to get it. "Surgery is much more drastic than diet and exercise. It's no excuse." But still, I'm thinking of my client Chelsea, whose Dad bought her twelve sessions of training, and she barely went through the motions hoping he would pay for her gastric bypass surgery when I failed to help her meet her goals.

Eric's eyebrows lift. "I'm not giving your mom an excuse. I'm showing you her motive."

"It's stupid. Stupid, stupid, stupid." I know. I sound pretty stupid. "She's supposed to get her confidence from God."

Eric smirks just a little. "Like a spiritual boob job?"

"Exactly!"

"God's the best surgeon. He just doesn't make appointments on our time schedule. You've got to hang out in the waiting room for a while."

I lower my head. "And Mom didn't want to wait."

Neither of us say anything. I don't know what to say. My life is so twisted up. Ever since Dad left..."It's all my dad's fault. Since he left, everything has gone wrong. Trinity took off. Mom...ugh. And Christian! Laurel told me about his addiction."

It's overwhelming. I feel anger toward my dad start to seep back into me, and a tear seeps out. I feel helpless. The sins of the father, and all that. It's like my family is cursed. "I wish he'd never left. It would have been almost better for him to keep hiding his affair. We would still be a happy family."

Eric's hands come to his head and his fingers splay through his thick hair. I've probably given him a headache. All my talk last week about how I've chosen to forgive my dad, and here I am angrier than ever.

"Bethany." The way he says my name demands attention. "I've got to be honest. I should have told you before. And you may not want to keep seeking counsel from me after this."

My body goes on alert. This honesty stuff is tearing my life apart.

"Bethany." The second time he says my name gives me chills. What could make him so intense? "I've met your dad."

I sit up straighter and tilt my head. This is news. But not earth-shattering as he seems to think.

"He stayed at my house during a conference in Spokane. I was a youth pastor up in Washington."

Small world. "You started out as a youth pastor?" My voice gets lower and all-knowing. "Did you keep the teenage boys and girls from holding hands while you prayed? My youth group leader did that. I always thought it was so silly."

Eric's eyes narrow in confusion. Or is it frustration? "I might have. I don't remember. But I'm talking about your dad right now."

Okay, okay. "Okay," I say.

Eric clears his throat. "I really looked up to your dad." Who didn't? He pauses. "The conference was powerful." He takes a deep breath. "On the last night, after three hours of prayer...your dad confessed to me."

Now I'm narrowing my eyes. Confessed? "He confessed... his affair?" My hand flies to my mouth.

Eric closes his eyes for a moment. Then his gaze meets mine and I realize he's scooted closer. "I'm sorry, Bethany."

Sorry for what? For finding out what a creep my dad was before I knew? For not telling me? For the nausea in my stomach?

"He told me that he'd been trying to break it off, but the other woman..."

"Corrine," I fill in her name through clenched teeth.

"Corrine wouldn't leave the church."

I could punch the woman. I see it happen in movies all the time—like Sweet Home Alabama—but I never considered the action to be realistic until now.

100

"Your dad told me that he was weak. He even said, 'Affairs are for the weak.' But he said that he hadn't confessed because he didn't want to hurt his family. And he didn't want to hurt the church."

"Pshah!" I hear the sound of bitterness come from my mouth.

Eric studies my face. "I'm the one who counseled him to confess." He shakes his head as if in self-loathing. "I told him that he was crippling his church by hiding his sin. I told him that your family could make it through this, and that he wasn't putting his trust in God."

I look for a lifeline before I drown in the drama. "But he didn't have to leave us."

"That part shocked me. I was sure by the way he spoke, that his family was the most important thing in his life next to God."

"He had us all fooled." I need to run. I need to get away and clear my head. I can't even think.

"Bethany."

The smoke clears for a moment as Eric continues. "I want you to know that I question my discussion with him every day. I wonder what I could have done differently. When I heard the news of what happened as the result of my words, I chose to take the job down here and pioneer a church. Your dad is the reason I named it Grace Chapel."

I give what might be considered a small smile. "And the reason you speak so much on accountability."

"Yeah."

I rub my face. "Could you do a message on how all things are supposed to work out for good next Sunday? Or on how Christians are supposed to count it all joy? Or maybe you could just plan a church mission trip...to Mongolia...and I won't come back. Where is Mongolia anyway?" My voice cracks.

"You're going to get through this."

I don't see how right now. But maybe I don't have to. Maybe I just have to eat a few more M & Ms and get home to bed. And maybe this will all be a bad dream. I chomp on chocolate and stand up.

"Are we okay?"

"We?" I cannot compute. If I were a laptop, my memory would be full.

"Do you still want to come to me for counseling?" He speaks quicker when saying, "I completely understand if you don't."

I don't know if we're okay. I know *I'm* not okay. But that's why I sought professional help in the first place. "Why didn't you tell me?"

Eric stands in front of me. "I promised your dad that I wouldn't. He wanted to handle everything on his own."

And that's the problem. Dad is on his own. He's left God behind with the rest of us. "Why did you have to tell me now?"

Eric shakes his head as if he had a good reason before, but can't recall what it is. He sighs. "I guess I wanted you to know that your Dad was repentant. And that he was worried about you."

I'm more moved by Eric's concern than by the alleged love of a man who left me. I add on to Eric's answer. "And you care about my family in ways we hadn't realized."

Chapter 16

I'm meeting Laurel for lunch again. I feel bad for leaving Dee Dee behind for a second week in a row, but I do need to be committed to my accountability partner and she's home from work with "female issues." I pick up a couple of to-go boxes from The Red Letter.

She answers the door wearing a pink velour sweat suit and sunglasses. The clothes are great. (I mean, I don't even look that cute on my good days.) The sunglasses make me feel like I'm in a spy movie.

"What's with the shades?" I ask.

She touches a hand to her face like she forgot they were there, and for a brief second I wonder if she has a drinking problem and she's suffering from a hangover, not cramps and bloating. But, no. She's too perfect.

She slides the glasses atop her head. "Oh. I'm doing the dishes. We just put in the stainless steal sink but haven't gotten blinds yet. So when the sun shines in, I get the glare right in my eyes." She leads me upstairs to the dining room table. "Christian calls me Stevie Wonder."

I chuckle as I imagine Christian's impression of the musician. I hope Laurel isn't too prim and proper to laugh at his humor. As I unload our lunch from the bag, I remember the slippers she wore the last time I was over. Her life is so easy. All her problems seem to be solved with cute accessories—ballet slippers, sunglasses.

Okay, maybe not all her problems. My thoughts turn to Christian and Mom. I push them away and try not to focus on myself. "How are you feeling?"

"Mmm." Laurel holds one hand with the palm facing the floor and shakes it side to side. "How are you?"

I try not to let her politeness annoy me. I'll just answer the question she asked. Yeah, as if that were easy. "More counseling last night. And I'll probably need counseling for the rest of my life." I tear into my sandwich.

Laurel squishes her lips to one side and gives me a disapproving look, making me feel immature. Okay, I can do better. "Church with Mom was miserable. So Eric and I talked about that. He said that Mom should have gotten a *spiritual* boob job."

Laurel chokes on her ham on whole wheat with extra pickles. "Explain," is all she can say around her mouthful of food.

She's probably shocked that her pastor is discussing her mother-in-law's chest, but I'm just enjoying her rare display of bad manners. I should try shocking her during meals more often.

"He said that a woman can regain her confidence through reading The Word, and the results are much more beautiful than some silly silicone."

Laurel sips from a glass of ice water that she'd set out before I arrived. "Don't let it bother you so much."

I huff. "Easy for you to say. For starters, this isn't your mom we're talking about, and secondly, you don't have anything to worry about. Your chest isn't flat." I motion to Laurel's bosom for emphasis. I stop mid-motion. I don't remember her being *that* well endowed. "You didn't..."

"No."

Of course not. Laurel is too perfect to need any type of cosmetic surgery. "Are you wearing a padded bra?" That's what I should do.

"No."

Huh. "Well you look bigger for some reason."

Laurel's puts down her food. "I am."

What? Is she holding out on me? "Does that cream in the commercials really work?"

Laurel gives me her amused but condescending look that she does so well. "I'm pregnant."

"Oh…" Comprehension sinks in slowly. "Oh!" It hits me. "I'm going to be an aunt!" I grab her hand and pull her into a weird embrace with the side of the chair poking my ribs. "Congratulations. When did you find out? Who have you told? Why didn't you announce it at Thanksgiving?"

She casually brushes hair out of her face. "We just found out, but we're not telling anyone."

Sure she isn't. "You just told me!"

"You didn't give me much of a choice, dear."

I laugh at my ignorant inquiries. "So I have to keep it a secret?"

Laurel opens her bag of sweet potato chips. "You can't tell *anyone*."

I groan at the burden, though I'm sure "anyone" doesn't include my counselor. "Are you planning some big surprise to let everyone know at the same time?"

Laurel gives me a sad smile. "We haven't thought that far ahead. Being an ultrasound technician, I've seen way too many babies not make it through the first trimester. I don't want to celebrate until we know for sure that our baby is healthy."

"Oh my gosh." I'd never considered this kind of loss before. I hope my brother doesn't ever lose one of his children. He'll be a great dad. Then another sad thought hits me. "Have you had a miscarriage before?"

My heartbeat pauses then beats again as Laurel shakes her head no. "I just want to be cautious," she says.

I'm relieved, but then feel guilty because my relief comes from the fact that I don't have to deal with anymore heartache and not because of how it would have affected my brother and his wife. I try to be more sensitive.

"That sounds wise," I encourage. "Though I'm so excited for you guys that people might guess my secret just by looking at my face."

Laurel gives me a very motherly look. It's one she'll give to her children someday when humoring them.

I stuff another bite of food into my mouth and glance at my watch. I don't have much time, but I have a million questions. Have they picked out names? Do they think it will be a boy or a girl? How are they going to decorate the nursery? Can I be the godmother? I want to dance around and shout, but Laurel doesn't look as exuberant. She must really be worried.

I clasp her hand again—normally this time. "Let's pray."

Laurel squeezes my fingers. "Yes. Let's pray for the baby's body to be healthy and...normal."

I close my eyes and rejoice in my heart, but out of my lips come fervent prayers for nothing bad to happen to my first niece/nephew. And I pray for Laurel's mind. Her worries seem extreme to me, but I really have no experience in this area.

I wonder how my mom reacted when she first found out she was pregnant with Christian. How sad to think that her children are grown and her husband is gone. Is this what Laurel has to look forward to? I'm still excited for my brother's baby, but I'm more certain than ever that this is not something I want to go through.

I'll be the favorite aunt. I'll spoil all Christian's kids so rotten they'll call me Grandma. I'll have all the fun, and none of the worries. Because seriously, I don't think I can take any more pain.

Chapter 17

I forgot my new shoes at Lighten Up and I really want to show them off to Star so I stop by the studio on the way to the gym. It's almost 6:00, meaning I'll have to hurry if I want to make it to her class on time.

The sign on the window reads "open" and I feel a little funny barging in on Jade and her clients. But I guess she's done it to me. I'll be sweet and discreet, not intense and creepy like she was when looking for her BOSU Ball.

I open the outside door and enter the tiled hallway. I share the building with a chiropractor, an insurance agency, and an advertising firm. The crown molding, recessed lighting and cream-colored walls lead to their offices, but I stop at the first door and enter.

I lift my hand to give a little don't-mind-me-wave, but my arm freezes next to my head. Jade and a female version of The Hulk (a relative of Eric's?) take up the whole room. Okay, maybe this isn't that weird, but I'm so used to having wobbly grandmas and chubby spinsters as my clients that I never thought Jade might be training body builders. I would have expected them to want a gym with more equipment—or at least more mirrors—but I guess Jade has a different following.

"Hi?" I pull my hand down quickly after realizing it was still suspended in mid-air.

Jade turns her body to give me her full attention. I have a fleeting thought that she is the exact opposite of Brooke. Her laser-like eyes study me relentlessly. "Did you need something?"

"Uh...just my shoes." I'm stammering in my own studio.

Jade leads me toward my messy corner and ducks behind the screen. "I set them out of the way," she says.

I figure with as big as the two women are, they need as much room as they can get. "Thanks." I grab my new kicks and scoot backwards. I send an apologetic smile to the client/monster. She has a vein sticking out of her neck and I look just a little bit closer for an Adam's apple, but of course none exists. "Have a good work out." I give another awkward wave and retreat.

Too weird. I try to let my misgivings drift away as I speed to Gold's, though I'm thinking I would have been better off wearing my old shoes for one more night. As soon as I pull into the last available parking space I slip them on (cross trainers with bungees instead of laces—how cool is that?) and jog to the massive entry. I scan the barcode on my keychain as I charge past the front desk.

"Bethany!"

I hit the brakes and glance over my shoulder.

"Bethany, right?" The words come from a trainer with a widow's peak and a buzz cut. He's got the look of the Human Torch from the Fantastic Four—when he's not on fire, of course.

I forget about my class. "Yeah." I smile encouragingly.

He leans against the front desk, and I step close enough to see the sides of his eyes crinkle. "If you're headed to Star's class, the schedule has changed. They added a half-hour core class before Jam starts."

"Oh." She hadn't told me. Probably because I haven't been here for a couple weeks. I look around and try to decide the best way to kill time.

The cute guy straightens up. "I'd love to stay and chat, but I've got a client. The apparel is on sale if you're looking for something to do. I think that purple color would be great on you."

Wow. He read my thoughts and he complimented me in the same breath. I scan the clothing displayed behind me next to the entrance and see a plum-colored sports bra that I would never wear in public. But I'm still flattered. "I guess I'll look around." I read the nametag on his lanyard. "Thanks, Paul."

Paul trots away and I glance at my watch. I might as well check out the sales. I find a longer version of the purple top and hold it up in front of me trying to see my reflection in the window.

Tap...tap...tap. The noise on the glass startles me and I jump before refocusing my perspective to make out Eric's face in the darkness beyond my own image. My eyes follow him as he comes in one of the two sets of double doors.

He grins as he makes his way back to me and puts one hand on the top of a rack. "Did I scare you?"

"You...surprised me."

His face sobers. "Are you okay?"

I feel my forehead wrinkle. "I grew up with Christian. I've been surprised before."

Eric gives a little shake. "I meant are you okay after Tuesday?"

"Oh." My dad confessed to Eric. Eric convinced him to confess to the church. My life has changed forever. Am I okay with that? "Probably not. But I've got this really good counselor." I give him an encouraging smile.

"Good." Eric's hand comes up off the rack then settles back down. "Good."

Again I'm touched at his commitment to my family. He may have played a key role in tearing it apart, but he wants to help put it back together. There's nobody else I'd rather spill my guts to. I can tell him anything. Oh yeah, I can tell him..."Christian and Laurel are having a baby!"

Eric's eyebrows shoot straight up. "That's great! I'm surprised Christian didn't tell me when we met yesterday."

I step in closer and lower my voice. "It's a secret. Laurel wasn't planning to tell me, but I kinda noticed." I don't mention *what* I noticed. "They're not telling anyone until the second trimester. Laurel has seen too many miscarriages to get excited yet."

"I'll be praying." He studies me a moment. "Were you supposed to tell me?"

I wave my hand as if it's nothing. "I have counselor/client confidentially and all that."

Eric makes a motion with a finger, drawing an invisible circle around the two of us. "Do I get to charge you for this conversation?"

I click my tongue. "Consider me part of your ministry."

"Ah..."

"Beff!" My lower legs get rammed then hugged by a two-year-old.

I move my left foot as far as Jennica's little arms will allow to regain my balance. "Hey, baby."

Star follows close behind. She's got a fishnet hoodie on and I'm thinking it can't possibly keep her warm in the winter-like weather. "Bethany! I forgot to tell you that my class time changed!"

"That's okay." I arch my back, bend one knee, and lift my foot to my rear in a cute little pose. "I was thinking of getting a top to go with my new shoes."

Star squeals. "I love them."

I grin at Eric. "Eric, this is my cousin, Star, and her daughter Jennica. Star this is...Eric." I leave out the title of pastor because I know how people react sometimes—and Star would be one of those people. Treat him like an alien, or give a lot of reasons why she doesn't go to church.

"Hi," Star greets him and looks to me as if hoping for more of an explanation.

Eric takes over. "So, you teach a class here?"

"Oh, yeah. It's a dance class. Right after the core class."

Eric nods though his eyes don't register understanding.

"The core class is half an hour with a BOSU Ball."

Blank stare.

Star looks at me and laughs. "Why are men so afraid of the aerobics room?"

"You know what a BOSU Ball is." I point out toward the open weight floor. "You were doing squats on it the other night."

Star leans in toward me and nudges me with her shoulder. "Did you know Bethany can do a squat on a balance ball?"

110

She's tying to help me show off.

Eric tilts his head back and squints down. "You mean you can stand on top of a ball?"

Star answers for me. "Like a circus clown."

Thanks, Star.

"I don't believe it."

Star grabs my arm and pulls me toward the railing overlooking the sunken weight room. "Show him, Bethany."

Jennica weaves her tiny body in and out of the railing. "Do it, Beff!"

Eric places his hands on his hips. "Do it, Beff."

I roll my eyes to the skylights. I do kind of want to strut my stuff, but I can't act like it. "Fine." I hop down the two steps and grab a ball.

Eric follows. I hang onto the railing and lift my lower body above the blue plastic ball. Gripping the sides of the ball with the new tread of my shoes I pull my abs in. Bending my knees I let go.

"Oh man." Eric is legitimately impressed.

I feel my thighs shaking as I push my hips backwards. I hold my arms out in front of my body as I straighten back up from my squat.

"You're so awesome, cousin." Star cheers me on. I appreciate this, but then Jennica decides to encourage me, as well. She charges down the stairs toward my legs to give me another hug.

Timber…The ball rolls forward and I fall back. My boom-boom hits the ground so hard I feel my skull reverberate.

"Jennica, no!" Star's warning words are way too late.

Jennica giggles and jumps on me.

Eric stands frozen only a foot behind me. My hero. I climb slowly to my feet. "You could have helped me out a little there," I shoot at him, but he's too busy laughing.

He's got a great laugh. I don't hear it too often, but now is not the time. Star is cackling away also. I don't know if my boom-boom will be bruised, but my ego sure is.

Star looks at her watch and speaks through gasps as she tries to catch her breath. "I've got to get Jennica to childcare. Nice meeting you, Eric."

"You, too." Eric tries to wave, but his body is still convulsing in mirth.

I act confident in the face of my humiliation. "As much as I love being laughed at, Eric, I think I'll go with Star."

Eric sits down on the ball I just rolled off of. He's wiping his eyes, so I figure he can't see me leave. I'll just try to forget I was ever there.

Star slows her pace so I can catch up to her outside the kiddie playland. "So...who was he?" she half-whispers.

I guess I can tell her now. "My pastor."

"Girl," her head bobs side to side as she talks, "*I'm* gonna have to start coming to church."

I lean against the counter as she signs Jennica in. "He's engaged to one of my clients."

Star looks up. "Huh," is all she says.

She kisses Jennica goodbye and we head upstairs. Her bright striped socks peek out from underneath cargo dance pants.

"Nice socks."

"From the sock club," Star replies. "My class loves to see what socks I'm wearing when we lay down on the floor and stretch."

"Do you have trouble finding matching socks?" I usually buy all plain white socks so I can mix and match. When each pair is different I seem to end up losing one. This morning, for example, I couldn't find the other puppy dog sock, so I've got one puppy dog and one palm tree sock on. I was in a hurry. Maybe I'll skip out on the stretching section of the class so nobody will notice.

"You won't lose socks if you wash them together," she replies.

So only the dryers at the Laundromat eat socks? I wonder if Dee Dee has my problem. Dee Dee. Here goes..."Dee Dee like her socks, too. Her favorites are the Care Bears."

Star's eyes shift my way. Why won't she say anything?

"I talked to Dee Dee about what happened between you two." I just blurt it out. It's bad timing. It's not thought out. But now it's too late.

"Stop it, Bethany." The bitterness in her voice makes me cringe. "You're the only one who knows. But that's not going to change anything. You sign us up for the same sock club. You got us to go in together on a birthday gift for Christian without talking to us about it first. Just stop it."

How can I? "Star..."

"Stop it. I've got to teach a class. I don't want to think about it, and I don't ever want to talk about it. It makes me sick."

"Of course it does! Unforgiveness will..."

We're at the top of the stairs and Star pauses to refill her water bottle in the drinking fountain and to interrupt me. "How would you know?"

I can answer that question. "My dad..."

"Ha!" She snaps back up from the drinking fountain to face me. "You haven't forgiven your dad."

I stare speechless. She doesn't know what I've been dealing with. We haven't talked for ages. "You don't understand..."

"Exactly." She spins on her heel and talks over her shoulder. "And you don't understand what I've been through."

I tail after her like I'm the puppy dog on my sock. "You're right. But I do know that Dee Dee is so sorry. She regrets everything. She's miserable."

Star gives me one last look as she grabs the handle for the door leading into the aerobics studio. She's telling me to shut up with her eyes. But she also wants to get the last word in. "She should be."

Chapter 18

"You are horrible!" My client's words don't surprise me. This is actually a tame statement coming from her mouth. But I know she doesn't mean it.

"Come on, Abby. Only two more."

She grunts and gives me a dirty look. "I hate you."

"You'll love me when you reach your goal weight." Abby has these great legs, but they're attached to a torso that resembles Humpty Dumpty's—which is fitting since her attitude usually stinks like a rotten egg. "Last one."

She lowers the weight down into the cradle from the leg press she is doing and collapses back against the seat. "Are you trying to kill me?"

"I've thought about it," I reply sweetly.

"Ohhh." Abby stands up. She's one of those people who needs a trainer like me to force her to work out. "You know after our last session I couldn't even lift my hands to drive home. I had to do this." She shifts her weight side to side and her arms flop about. She jerks one shoulder higher and pretends that her left arm has swung atop a steering wheel.

I laugh at her reenactment. "Wow, I must be better than I thought."

Abby rolls onto a mat and lifts one leg in the air for me to stretch her. "If you ever get tired of training, I'm sure the CIA would hire you for your torture techniques."

"Hmm." I consider her suggestion as I bend down on one knee behind her lifted leg and press it toward her chest. "What doesn't kill you, makes you stronger, right?"

"Whatever helps you sleep at night."

I bend her knee and place her foot in the "pocket" between my thigh and hip. I hold down her straight leg and press the bent knee up and out.

114

"Ahhh!" she screams. Even during stretches she makes my personal training studio sound like the Pit of Despair.

"Ahhh!" The second scream comes from behind me as the door swings open.

I glance over my shoulder in alarm. Brooke comes charging in as if her hair is on fire. I want to tell her to stop, drop, and roll, but naturally she doesn't give me a chance to speak.

"It's party time!" She announces and starts doing a bad version of the Macarana.

I smile down at Abby—whose eyes have tripled in size—and give a small shake of my head so she knows that she has no need to worry about her safety. And I thought *she* was the drama queen.

"Is it your birthday?" I guess.

"No!" Brooke looks as if she might explode with excitement.

"Did you lose a pound?" I guess again. Usually my clients are delighted to see changes, but never this happy.

"Better!" She bounces up and down. She holds her hands up. "I just got a manicure at your cousin's spa!"

I motion for Abby to sit up and turn around so I can stretch her arms. I feel bad that I can't give her my full attention right now because I have to focus on Brooke's nails. "Yippee."

She giggles and slides down on the floor next to me. "*That's* not what I ran over here to tell you."

What a relief. Though the way she says this makes me think she wonders about my sanity.

She holds a hand (with new French tips) to her heart and suddenly turns serious. "Dee Dee accepted Christ as her savior."

I've finished stretching Abby and I'm giving her a nice little shoulder massage to finish her hour, but Brooke's words cause me to pinch instead of squeeze.

"Ouch!" Abby reaches for her neck, and if I wasn't so shocked, I might have wondered if I was about to experience the battle of the over-actors. I barely notice when Abby leaves with a pout.

"What? My Dee Dee? My cousin?" That would be so wonderful, but there had to be a mistake. I've been witnessing to her for twenty-seven years. If she had become a Christian, I would be the first person she would have told.

"Yes! I was talking about my relationship with Jesus and she started asking questions."

I can't even imagine the scene Brooke is describing. My hard-hearted cousin would have said something like, 'You actually believe in immaculate conception?' Well I guess that would be a question. Maybe that's what she asked Brooke.

Brooke stands then pulls me up with her. "Then I led her in the sinner's prayer."

I don't believe it. I have to go find out the truth from Dee Dee. Not that I don't trust Brooke, I just don't think she communicates with reality sometimes.

She hops up and down holding my hands. "Aren't you thrilled? I know the angels in heaven are breaking out balloons and streamers...and maybe some noisemakers, too. Woo-hoo!"

Brooke is noisemaker enough for me. "That's incredible," is all I say. I'm trying to act ecstatic until she leaves and I can rush over to Dee Light's Day Spa and hear it for myself.

Brooke giggles and spins away. "You're speechless. That's so funny. I guess I would be, too."

I doubt it.

"Well, I have to get back to work. I just came over for the manicure on my lunch break. And then I had to tell you the news. But don't worry. I'm eating lunch, too. The kids had tuna fish and carrot sticks. They didn't like it much, so I ate the leftovers. See, I'm being healthy. I want to weigh myself later!"

I nod (which is all anyone can do when Brooke talks), but my mind is across the street. I don't walk out with Brooke because I don't want her to think I'm walking her out. She has enough trouble saying goodbye as it is. I watch her from my window, and as soon as she hops in her Mazda and zips away I lock the door to Lighten Up and zip away myself.

I bust through Dee Dee's front door as if I were Brooke. The desk girl and the manicurist look up from the customers they are assisting. I don't see my cousin anywhere.

"She's in the back room." The desk girl points toward an arched doorway as she looks me up and down. Oh yeah, that's why I don't come to the spa very often. I always get the feeling that the technicians are sizing me up: "Sure, she's got muscle, but a body wrap wouldn't hurt. Did you see that stray eyebrow? I would totally schedule a brow wax if I were her."

"Thanks."

I dart down the hallway past the hanging water fountain. Dee Dee is sitting on the stairs that lead to her office. This is kind of strange, but not as strange as what she is doing on the stairs. She's reading the Bible.

She looks up at the squeaking sound of my running shoes on the laminate floor. "Hi."

Her face is relaxed and energetic at the same time. If I took a picture of her right now it could be used on a billboard for her spa.

"You're reading the Bible." I state the obvious because I don't know where else to start.

"I am." Her voice is soft and awe filled. "Brooke told me to read the book of John. It's amazing. I was headed upstairs, but I couldn't read and climb at the same time." She scoots over so I can join her on the step. "You know, I always thought of Jesus as this peaceful but naïve character. Like if he walked a mile in high heels or made it to middle-age, he would have stopped yapping about loving your neighbor and being humble and meek and that kind of thing."

I sink down into the carpet as thick as teddy bear fur. Whenever I witness to Dee Dee I get a whole new perspective on Jesus. I know him. I know what he went through for me. I know what he taught. So I have no clue how misguided unbelievers are. Where do they get this stuff?

"What do you think now?" I twirl my ponytail around my finger. I have the feeling she's going to tell me everything I've been trying so hard to tell her.

"Jesus could talk smack! He made the Pharisees look like idiots." She's enthralled.

I rest my arms on my knees and lean forward. I'm happy for her. I'm sooo happy for her. But I'm sad for me at the same time. "You...you asked him into your heart?"

"I did!" Her dancing eyes shine with tears.

The last time I saw her cry, her face had been filled with pain. I can't help being jealous of the experience she had with Brooke. What could I have said? What could I have done differently to get her to this moment sooner? I tried everything I could think of.

"What did Brooke say that got through to you?"

Dee Dee sighs. "She..." her voice breaks. "She told me about her abortion."

I feel my mouth open. No words come out. Brooke had an abortion? I blink.

"All this time I didn't want to know about Christianity because I didn't think I was good enough. But if God can restore Brooke from her brokenness to the position as a pastor's wife, then maybe I have a chance, too."

My mind is still reeling. Eric is engaged to a woman who has been with other men? Did he know that she'd killed her child? Pastors are called to a higher standard. Shouldn't the pastor's wife be, too? Was Brooke fit to be in ministry?

I shake the questions away. Of course, she is. My dad's best friend who was a pastor had been a drug addict before he got saved. We all get a second chance. That is the whole reason Jesus came to earth. But...but...is she fit to be Eric's wife? He deserves better.

"Bethany?"

I have to talk to Eric. I look at my watch. I've got another client in ten minutes. Can I wait until tomorrow night at counseling?

"Bethany?"

I turn my head to face my cousin. Was she talking?

"What do you think?"

"Congratulations!" That was a stupid thing to say. I envelope her in a hug to make up for it. It's a pretty weak reaction compared to Brooke's dance. "The Bible says that angels celebrate whenever there is a new believer."

"Really?" Her face shines as if she'd just been in the presence of God. "I have so much to learn."

"We all do." I'm thinking of myself again...and Eric and Brooke. I try to snap out of it. "If I ask you to church again, will you accept this time?"

"Tonight? Is there church tonight?"

She'd be ready to go right now if I said the word. I look down and smile. "Let's start on Sunday. Then maybe we can get you into a Bible study or an accountability group. Eric is really big on accountability."

Dee Dee rolls her eyes to the ceiling. "That would have kept me out of a lot of trouble."

I nod at the irony. How often do we wait until it's too late to see the need for accountability?

Chapter 19

Tuesday evening I burst through the door of Eric's office. I'm getting pretty good at these Brooke-like entrances—sans the screaming and dancing. Maybe I can add those on later.

Eric raises his head from his desk and his lips quirk up. "Did you miss me?"

"I'm just in desperate need of therapy." I wish I could close the door to make the session more private, but it's not like Rebecca is eavesdropping out there. I'll just speak in hushed tones...after the good news.

"My cousin accepted Christ." I say this matter-of-factly—as if I hadn't been praying for since we were kids.

"Brooke told me. That's great."

I take a deep breath. I wonder if I should have called him last night instead of using my appointment to talk about his life. (He's not the one who needs therapy.)

I didn't get a chance however because Dee Dee showed up at my apartment with the Bible Brooke gave her. I guess that was good—no, it was great—but I've been dreading this moment for over twenty-four hours now.

"Um...did Brooke tell you what she said that got through to Dee Dee?" Maybe he already knows. Maybe it's no big deal. Or maybe they had it out last night and now they're not engaged anymore. I mentally slap myself on the hand for having such a thought.

"Brooke talked about it all night, but I couldn't really put the pieces together."

Hmmm. I can relate. But I'm still not sure if he knows his fiancée's past. I look down, unsure of how to proceed. "Dee Dee couldn't stop talking about it either. She has so many questions."

Eric nods. "Meeting Jesus for the first time is pretty powerful."

I'm sure it would have been. I lift my hand helplessly. "I wasn't there. I've witnessed to Dee Dee for years, but I wasn't there when she asked Jesus into her heart."

Eric studies my face. "You still played a huge part. Do you feel like you missed out?"

"Well, yeah." Here goes. "I hit her with the gospel from every angle I could think of. But what made the difference was Brooke's...um, testimony, which is something I could have never given."

Eric's eyes get soft...dare I say dreamy? Not a look I would expect from a man thinking about his fiancée's past relationships. "Brooke usually breaks out her testimony the moment she meets somebody new. This isn't the first time it has impacted a life."

"Huh." I pause, trying not to sound too cynical. "I hadn't heard it. So I was kind of surprised to find out that she had an, uh...abortion."

Eric's eyes look down. "Terrible, I know. But somehow God uses our worst sins for good. Now Brooke can speak from experience when counseling unwed mothers. And she can relate to those who feel unworthy of God's love."

I'm amazed by Eric's objectivity. Especially with the speech he gave my dad about sin. And then he just accepts an impure woman to become his wife? I feel my eyebrows lift.

"How did it affect you when you found out about her fornication? And murder?" Okay, I'm definitely not being politically correct—in fact I'm being a little judgmental. But I'm stating my beliefs.

Eric crosses his arms and leans his head back, reminding me of how I sat my first time in the room. The tables have turned. "Let's see. The first time I found out about Brooke's past was in a bar."

I blink and cock my head to one side. Does *Eric* have a past that I don't know about?

His teeth flash at me—grinning at my discomfort—as he reads my mind. "My brother called me to pick him up because he was drunk, and Brooke had taken his keys away from him even though they'd never even met."

This scene isn't too hard to imagine. Brooke has no inhibitions.

Eric continues. "She had just gotten saved. So when her friends invited her to go drinking she would go with them and order Coke. Then when they asked why she was drinking Coke she would say, 'Let me tell you...' and just start preaching the Good News."

A surprised little laugh escaped from my lips. Now I'm not only jealous that Brooke got to lead my cousin to Christ, but I'm envious of her boldness. Rather than become a pious, boring Christian, she excitedly hung out with drunks. The phrase "What Would Jesus Do" runs through my mind.

"That's really cool," I admit.

"Yeah, so I found out everything that first night. I thanked her for watching out for my brother and gave her my business card. Then when she started coming to church here and signed up for the worship team we got to know each other better. I was concerned about her past so I tried to ignore my attraction to her." He frowns at the memory. "But the whole congregation loves and respects her so I figured I could too."

Everybody loves Brooke. Everybody except me. And I don't have an excuse. I'm just bad at forgiveness, I guess. I try to think of something encouraging to say. Complete blank. "Did she tell you that she did the Macarena at Lighten Up in front of another one of my clients yesterday?"

Eric chuckles. "She didn't."

I give a cute little shrug. "It's true."

"Did you join in?"

I laugh at myself. "No. I thought she was just excited about her manicure."

Eric runs his hands through his hair. "Her excitement can be a little overwhelming at times. I remember on our first date I almost drove off the road when she gasped. I thought something terrible had happened, like a dear leaping into the road or her appendix bursting. But no, she had just forgotten to call her mother on her birthday."

I feel the laughter throughout my whole core. Who needs a BOSU Ball? And my cheeks hurt from smiling. It's not one of those smiles you give to make the other person feel good. It's one of those smiles you can't stop because you feel so good. Eric makes me feel good. He's an amazing counselor. "So she's always that dramatic?"

"She's got the joy of the Lord. And she's on fire for God. It humbles me." Eric's expression sobers. "She wasn't always this way."

I try to imagine a poised, serious, quiet Brooke. I can't do it. "No?"

"No. Before I met her...And I'm only telling you this because I know she would tell you if she was here."

I feel my eyes get wide as I nod.

"Brooke battled with depression for a long time. She had low self-esteem. After her abortion she started hating herself."

I feel my heart go out to her. My crazy client used to be sad and self-conscious?

"She tried to kill herself on Mother's Day."

My hand flies to my mouth and my chest squeezes tight as if I've been holding my breath under water for too long.

Eric waves a hand. "This is all before I met her and she got saved."

"She tried to kill herself?" I squeak. I've only heard of suicide on T.V. shows and in the news. Well, and Judas in the Bible.

"Yeah, she overdosed. Her neighbor found her and called an ambulance. She had her stomach pumped and spent a week at Intermountain."

Intermountain is a mental hospital. I get the heebie-jeebies just thinking about it...that and the shower scene from *Psycho*.

"So." Eric slaps both legs with his hands. "How are you doing?"

I sit speechless. I think my mouth is even hanging open a little bit. I blink.

Eric grins. "That story should give you a little hope for your future and the future of your family, right?"

Chapter 20

Star completely ignored me through the entire dance class. She must be angrier than I thought. Or maybe she's sulking, feeling sorry for herself, justifying her anger. I've been there. Oh, who am I kidding? I'm there now.

"Good class, Star," I call on my way out of the studio. I'm being the bigger cousin.

She gives a little wave as if shooing a fly. It makes me feel like a pest. Maybe that's how she sees me—buzzing around, landing where I'm not wanted. Fine. I'll fly away.

Downstairs I spot Eric doing bicep curls and instantly get a craving for chocolate. It must be like how Pavlov's dog started drooling at the sound of the dinner bell. With a sigh I head to the front desk to buy an Apex bar. It's not real chocolate, but it will satisfy my sweet tooth...and my depression.

Paul, the cute trainer, pops behind the desk to help me since the desk girl is on the phone. He's got a contagious smile, and I'm feeling better already.

"What can I do for you?"

My mind starts to wander. He can take me out Friday night. He can bring me flowers and real chocolate. Then we can go for a run together on the green belt the next day to work off the calories. "Um..." I'm still lost in his brilliant blue eyes. "Can I have a chocolate peanut butter bar?"

His gaze doesn't leave mine as he reaches inside the storage container. "That's my favorite."

"So I have good taste?"

He hands me the protein bar and leans forward with his elbows on the counter. "I see you bought the purple top I recommended, so I'd have to say you've got great taste."

Correction: I *really* like his attention. I step away from the counter so he can see my whole torso. "I actually bought the long version of the top you recommended."

Paul clicks his tongue. "My loss."

I should be embarrassed and blushing, but I'm flattered. It's been way too long since I've been on a date. And as unwanted as Star made me feel, I could use a few more compliments. I climb up on a stool and make myself comfortable. "How much do I owe you for the bar?"

Paul waves his hand in the air. He's got strong hands I notice. And clean—as if he gets *ma*nicures. "It's on me. I'm having a productive day, so I'll pass on my good fortune."

I rip into the bar. Our conversation has cheered me up, but that doesn't stop my hunger pains. "Did you sign a new client?"

"Two." I absolutely love how he focuses on me as if I'm the most interesting person in the room.

"Nice." I chew and nod. "I saw that you were number one trainer of the year."

Star got number one instructor. And that's out of six award-winning locations. It's a big deal.

"Oh, yeah." He looks down humbly. It's adorable.

Star did a dance across the room when she told me of her award. But Star is always dancing across the room.

"Maybe you could train me." I say this then can't believe I said it. I know what's coming, and I'm amazed at my own brashness. But sometimes fitness professionals do hire their own personal trainer—it's the accountability thing...and justification for my actions.

Paul looks back up. "Aren't you a trainer? I've seen your ads for Lighten Up in the newspaper."

I tilt my head and smile. "Yes, I'm a trainer, too."

His eyes slip away from mine and roam over what he can see of my body. "And you're in top shape. What do you want me to train you for?"

I'm a shameless flirt...but then, so is he. We're a good match. "So I can get to know you better."

Paul's eyes narrow, but his lips curl up. "So do you really want me to train you? Or should I just ask you out?"

Yes. That was way too easy. It must be meant to be. I lean forward and rest my elbows on the counter. "You can ask me out if you want to," I offer coyly.

"Alright..." He says slowly, his face only inches from mine.

My heart pounds as if I'm experiencing an adrenalin rush. Or maybe it's just a combination of endorphins, chocolate, and romance. Now that's a good mix. I wait in anticipation for Paul's next words.

"Paul, your client is here." Desk Girl isn't on the phone anymore. She's interrupting my interlude.

Paul glances away. I groan inside. But if it's meant to be, we *will* meet again. Gee, I'm starting to sound like Scarlet O'Hara. This must be a side effect to this heady concoction I've created.

Paul straightens up and winks at me before leaping out from behind the counter to greet a client. The woman glows as if she's already worked out. Maybe it wasn't the endorphins or the chocolate at all. Maybe Paul makes every woman feel this way.

I sigh a dreamy little sigh and take my chocolate back upstairs. I feel like relaxing in the hot tub so I head to the locker room to put on my swimming suit. Normally, I would head home and order a Pay-Per-View romantic comedy, but I've got my own little movie to relive in my head for at least one night.

I'm rounding the corner to the hallway overlooking the pool and leading to the women's locker room when I hear my name called from behind. It's Paul. My breath gets stuck in my lungs.

"Bethany," he says again as he jogs toward me.

He's got great form and he's not even out of breath. To me, that's sexy. He stops with a mischievous grin when he reaches me. I know I'm grinning back like a fool.

"Is there a reason you're chasing me?" I can't wait to hear his answer.

"Oh, yeah."

He acts like he's forgotten. Like just seeing me is enough. My toes curl in my cross trainers.

"I had something else I wanted to say."

Goody. This is it. I lift an eyebrow. "What's that?"

"I…" He leans closer, and before any more words come out of his lips they are touching mine.

We're kissing! Well, actually, as my eyes close, my mouth opens into a huge smile and I think he kisses my teeth. Quickly I resume pucker position. It's unbelievable. It's got to be fate.

His hand comes to rest on the wall next to my neck and he leans in closer so that I can feel his warmth. His lips taste salty from sweat. Or maybe that's my lips. But I'm a fan of sweat so it doesn't bother me. And it obviously doesn't bother him either. His other hand circles around to the small of my back. I melt in his arms.

"Bethany!"

Paul jerks away from me at the sound of someone calling my name. His passion disappears and he's suddenly as cool as the weather. I'm so out of it, it takes me a moment to realize who is talking. I look past him to see another male. It's my pastor, but I'm not repentant in the least.

"I always run into you here, Bethany."

Baloney. There is nothing in this hallway except the women's locker room. Eric isn't running into me accidentally.

He turns to Paul. "And you are…"

"I'm Paul Alexander. I'm a trainer here." He's all about business. I wish I could be as smooth.

"Ahhh." Eric nods wisely and I'm getting more annoyed by the second. "So how long have you known Bethany?"

Paul shoots me a cocky smile. "We're just getting to know each other."

"I see." Eric shoots me a look, too, but it's not a smile. "So maybe she'll bring you to church. I'm her pastor. Oh, and I'm her counselor, too."

I want to scream and pull my hair out. Aughhhh!

Paul holds out his hand, acting respectful. "Nice to meet you." They shake. "I've got to get back to my client. See you around Bethany." He doesn't look my way. He hasn't looked my way since Eric told him I was loony, that I needed therapy.

I'm too humiliated to respond. I wait for him to disappear then turn on Reverend Austin. "What was *that*? What *was* that!?"

Eric looks amused and concerned at the same time. "I'm a guy, Bethany. I saw how he was watching you when you walked away. Then when he ran after you I figured I better follow."

"My hero." I stomp past him back toward the gym. I won't be relaxing in the hot tub now. I need to race a couple miles on the treadmill.

Eric follows. "Can I ask you the same question? What was that you were doing?"

I stop and whirl to face him. "It's called kissing." I talk to him as if he were stupid. "It was a mutual attraction. Absolutely no reason for you to *save* me from him."

"Maybe I was saving you from yourself."

This time I really pull at my hair and give a little scream. "It was a kiss. No sin there."

Eric places a hand on his hip. "Your actions aren't any different than your sister's."

I feel every muscle in my body tense. "Excuse me? I must not have heard you right because it sounded like you compared me to my sister. Trinity sleeps around. She gives guys whatever they want. She has no boundaries. I..." I point to myself. "*I* am a virgin."

"Not for long if you keep acting the way you're acting."

I jerk back. I blink. "It was a kiss. I've got self-control. I made it this far. I'm *not* like my sister. Give me a little respect."

Now both of Eric's hands are on his hips. "First of all, most Christian virgins don't think they are going to have sex until they've had it. Second, I'm treating you with more respect than you're treating yourself."

I lean my head back and look to the aluminum rafters for support. He just ruined my night, and now he's talking in riddles.

"Bethany, the definition of flirting is making the other person feel good about himself. You give them what they want so they like you. Then you like yourself more. You are not being true to you. And that is why I compared you to Trinity."

I throw my hands up. "This isn't one of our counseling sessions." I don't want to hear what he has to say. "And you had no right to tell Paul that you're my counselor."

The thought makes me angrier. One amazing kiss is probably all I'll get from Paul. Now he knows that I'm a Christian and a psycho. I was hoping to reel him into my world gently.

"You're right. I crossed the line. But you'll thank me later."

I give a spastic little shake of my head. "What are you? My dad?"

I shouldn't go there. But he deserved it. He compared me to my sister.

"Whoa..." He sounds offended—and like he could lecture me for hours.

I can't do this. I hold up one hand and strut away with all the attitude of Star. Eric trots past me and turns around so we are facing each other as we walk. I avoid his eyes. I can ignore him until he goes away. I try to get around him to a treadmill.

"Move, Eric. I've got to work off some steam." It is a very small percentage of Americans who exercise when stressed. I'm proud to be one of them. Maybe that's why I'm so skinny.

Eric's arm shoots in front of the treadmill so I can't climb on. Gold's has about 900 treadmills, so normally I would be able to climb onto one next to me, but they are all filled. Usually I love the energy in the building at this time of night. Tonight I just want to be alone.

"Come with me. I'll teach you how to really work off some steam. And you might get to punch me in the process."

The treadmills overlook the weight room below, and I spy Paul rubbing his client's shoulders after she sits up from the bench press. My stomach knots up. "I'd like to punch you now."

Again the amused/concerned glint flashes in Eric's eyes. He removes his arm from my path and leads me in a different direction. I should have known—the boxing ring.

"Here." Eric grabs gloves from a box in the corner and tosses them my way before climbing between the ropes and onto a huge square mat.

I scrunch my eyes closed before preparing for battle. Am I really doing this? Going rounds with a pastor?

I've taken kickboxing before. I even have a punching bag at my studio I use for training. I climb in the ring across from Eric and lift my hands to guard my face. I wonder how he'll explain it if he gives me a black eye.

"Light on your feet." He demonstrates a boxer's shuffle, and I mimic him. This is so ridiculous.

He demonstrates a few punches in slow motion, and I repeat at full speed—shadow boxing.

"Alright!" He's enjoying this way too much. "Now you try to hit me."

"Really?" I'm like Jennica in front of a bowl of macaroni.

He nods so I swing. He knocks my arm away before I even knew what happened. My shoulder stings a little so I punch with the other arm. *Wham.* He defends himself again.

I roll my shoulders. "This is supposed to calm me down? Because I'm getting angrier."

Eric's teeth flash. "Good."

I go for his head with a hook. You know, like Rocky Balboa when the blood and sweat fly sideways from his face. I'm a little relieved that he ducks. I decide to target his abs, though remembering what he looked like I'm afraid my hand is all that is going to hurt afterwards. I give my hardest jab. His block knocks me backwards.

131

Two jabs in a row. My movements aren't as fast as I remember them to be in Body Combat. It's like one of those dreams where you can only move in slow motion.

I remember the fake. I bring my shoulder forward as if I'm going to punch then pull back for a fraction of a second before actually jabbing. He saw it coming before I even remembered how to do it. Maybe I can't do this. I go for an uppercut. Block.

"Not bad." Yeah, right.

Eric brought me over here to toy with me. To show me that he can read my mind. To humble me. I'm so frustrated I could kick something! That's it. I'll use a combination from kick boxing. Jab. Cross. Jab. Knee.

Eric ducks, blocks, ducks, and I expect him to block again, but he's watching my hands and doesn't see my knee coming. *Crunch.* He's down.

"Oh!" I gasp. I thought it would feel good to make contact, but as I watch him curl into a ball and slap the mat, I'm starting to feel guilty.

"Ohhhh," he moans rolling on the floor. "I didn't know you were *that* mad at me." His voice is high and squeaky.

My arms are still in guard because I don't know what else to do with the big gloves on. And it's not as if I could tend to his wound anyway. "I thought you were going to defend yourself."

"That was below the belt." So that's where the saying came from.

"I learned it in kickboxing class." Now I'm defending *myself.*

"This isn't *kick*boxing."

Oops. "Are you...are you..."

"Going to be able to have children? Probably not."

My mouth falls open. I don't know what to say. Yeah, I was mad, but I didn't mean to ruin his life.

He sees my face through his tears and gives a gurgled laugh. "I'll be fine...in a few months."

I take a tentative step forward. "Let me help you up."

He waves me away, dismissing me the same way Star did. "You've done enough."

I feel the same pinch of pain. "You asked for it," I remind him.

"I know, I know," he says through gritted teeth.

I climb down from the ring and remove my gloves. If life is like a boxing ring, do we all ask for the pain we receive? Did my dad ask for it when he was unfaithful to Mom? Did Christian ask for it when he stopped monitoring himself on the internet? Was I asking for it by making out with a stranger in a public place? Do I regret making out? Nope. I just regret not making out longer. And Eric's paying for that one.

Chapter 21

It's Saturday and I'm sulking...in my bathrobe in the afternoon. I did go for a jog this morning after watching the holiday parade from my window. But then I came home, showered, and messed up my kitchen in an attempt to make Christmas cookies. The dough is in the fridge "chilling," and I'm pretty sure that's all it will ever do.

I should have gone skiing with the youth group. Christian invited me, but I was afraid Eric would be there. I don't want to see him for two reasons. First, I'm still mad at him for crashing my kiss. Second, I'm still embarrassed about introducing my knee to his nah-nahs. (Nah-nahs: An anatomical term I made up for Star to use if she ever has a son—it kind of goes with boom-boom.)

Oh, Star. That's another relationship that makes me queasy. I slouch onto my couch. I don't know what to do about my cousin. We used to be so close. My stomach spins like the carousel set up across the street for the month of December.

Was it better just to be her good-time buddy and not call her on her blind spots, or did I do the right thing trying to reunite family? I know I'd be just as troubled with this question had I not confronted her.

I grab the remote control out of a pile of clothes I should have taken to the laundromat already and flip through the channels. What I need is a good Christmas movie—something that will lighten my mood.

Like the time Dee Dee and I saw *Premonitions* in the movie theatre. The message was powerful, but the end was so heavy that after driving out of the parking lot quietly, I flipped a U-turn and we went back to see a midnight showing of *Wild Hogs*. We both fell in love with John Travolta's squinting scene, not to mention William H. Macy's geekiness, and our second exit was much more enjoyable.

Bummer. *White Christmas* isn't playing for another hour. I settle for *Home Alone*. Its lack of romance is made up for with physical comedy and "The Carol of the Bells."

Thud-thud. There's a knock on my door. Who the deck? What the halls?

I jump up, suddenly full of energy. I imagine Paul on the other side of the door—crazy, I know—but I pull my one pair of jeans and an Adidas sweatshirt out of the pile on the floor and stuff everything else in a basket under my coffee table just in case.

"Coming," I call as I whip my hair into a ponytail and grab some chap stick and chewing satisfaction from my gym bag. Chomp...chomp...the juices start to flow. Deep breath. I swing the door open. "Hi!"

Of course it's not Paul. He doesn't know where I live. And even if he did, I'm sure he wouldn't come near my apartment knowing that I'm a lunatic and undergoing professional counseling. I don't let my disappointment show—probably because I'm not disappointed. "Star!"

"Hey." She looks a little sheepish.

"Beff!"

The child may be tiny but she's got the force of a top tackler. I hang onto my doorframe as she embraces my legs.

Star shrugs. "Kids are so funny. I took her on the merry-go-round and she remembered that you lived nearby. She wanted to stop and say hi."

I don't doubt Star's motivation. Though I hope it's also an apology...or at least a truce. She doesn't need more family members to avoid. I bend over and sweep Jennica into my arms. She smells like peppermint.

"Did you see Santa Clause?" I ask.

Her big eyes get bigger as she nods. "I want a bike."

Gotta love her honesty. And the fact that I've already bought the perfect gift for her.

"You're not old enough to ride a bike are you?" I act shocked.

I put her down and she props hands on her hips in a position I'm sure she's learned from her mom. "Yesh."

"Oh, well then Santa better get you a bike." I grin at Star. We've already discussed my gift purchase.

"Come. Come Beff." Jennica pulls on my hand with sticky fingers, trying to get me out my front door.

"Are we interrupting anything important?" Star asks politely, looking over my shoulder. She lifts her expressive eyebrow at me as McCulley Culkin slaps his cheeks and screams.

"Not really. I was just *home alone*." I joke before grabbing my keys and locking up.

I'm not wearing any shoes, but that's okay. I know where Jennica wants to go. We take the elevator to the first floor where a play area is set up in a corner room. It's like a backyard for kids with no backyard—or guests of residents with no backyard. I wonder if I'll ever have a backyard as I unlock the door to reveal a structure of rainbow colored slides and tunnels.

Star makes herself comfortable on a side bench and I follow suit. I'll give her the first chance to talk, too.

She smiles sweetly. "I actually wanted to come over to ask you something."

My heart skips a beat. She's going to ask about Dee Dee. I just know it.

She turns her upper body to face me and rests her arm on the back of the bench. "Who were you kissing in the hallway leading to the women's locker room the other night?"

My spine snaps into perfect alignment. How did she know? Who else knew? If she didn't know it was Paul who kissed me then who was telling the story? Not Eric. "How did you know?"

Star doesn't do quiet giggles. Gales of laughter pour over me. "The water aerobics instructor saw you from the pool."

Oh no. I must have put on a real show.

"Who was it? And why do I have to hear this through the grapevine?" She nudges me.

I go into defense mode. "You weren't even talking to me on Thursday."

She waves her hand in a similar fashion to her dismissal of me from her Jam class. "I've got my own junk to deal with. So? Who was he?"

I narrow my eyes. "By junk, do you mean your sister?" Now, I'm just stalling. I talk about my problems a couple nights a week with Eric and Laurel. It would be nice to talk about somebody else's problems.

Star leans in towards me. "Was it your pastor? Did you kiss your client's fiancée?"

"Ahh!" I gasp. "Of course not. Why would you think that?" No, no, no. This is how rumors get started. And what a horrible rumor. It would be like my Dad's affair all over again. Me and Eric? Not with Brooke in the picture.

"Okay, okay." Star speaks in a calming tone. "You were avoiding my question, so I thought that might be why."

"No." I give a shake/shudder. "No. Though Eric did show up."

Star sits up straighter in triumph. "Tell me everything."

I relive the nightmare, leaving out the boxing ring. She was already way too interested in my relationship with Eric. It was better to focus on what could have been with my dream lover. "It was so romantic. But now he'll never kiss me again."

"It was Paul?" Star's face scrunches up. "I thought he had a girlfriend."

I sigh. "I could have been his girlfriend."

Star rolls her eyes. "Cousin, from what I've heard about Paul, you aren't missing out."

"But you haven't kissed him." I sink back into my seat.

"Get over Paul. Aren't there any other guys in your life? With your body, you should be able to get anybody."

"Thanks," I mutter. I know she's trying to help, but it makes me think of the blind dates in movies where "She's got a great personality" really means, "She's not much to look at." I must be the reverse. Star says, "You've got a great body," but really means, "You are about as interesting as the soy milk you always try to feed my daughter."

Star gets up to help Jennica whose pant leg somehow got stuck between the steps. "No guys at work?"

I think of Sean and giggle.

"I heard that." Star calls back over her shoulder as she gives Jennica a little push down the slide. "What made you laugh?"

"I was picturing myself on the arm of an old Jewish guy with a kink in his neck."

Star cha-chas back toward our bench. "That's a start." She spins, does a body wave and lands next to me.

"No. Really it's not. The only half-decent man at work would be the UPS guy." I pause. Star is going to run with this information, but I kind of like the idea. "Robbie."

A name is all she needs—she starts planning my wedding. I forget to mention the fact that I'm not getting married. Anyway, it's probably a non-issue to a woman who refuses to date at all.

"Sure, Jennica can be my flower girl."

"Woo-hoo." She's out of her seat and dancing again. Jennica comes running and joins right in.

"...hot like me." The little girl chants as she moves.

I tilt my head. "Is she singing Pussycat Dolls?"

Star gives me an evil grin. "It's on the latest Body Jam CD."

I bite my tongue. A two-year-old should not know the lyrics to such seductive songs. I don't even listen to that kind of music. Star better be careful or her little girl was going to find out what nah-nahs were a lot sooner than she should. I'll broach the subject later. Right now, I still need to discuss Dee Dee.

Yep. I've decided. Being Star's good-time buddy is fun, but I'm not a true friend unless I'm honest and caring.

"With all this talk of kissing and weddings I think I need to watch *White Christmas*. Do you want to come back to my apartment? I've got some cookie dough and cookie cutters for Jennica to play with."

Hopefully she won't eat too much. And hopefully I'll get a chance to talk to Star more about her sister. I'll get her good and cozy then ask concerned questions before sharing my own ideas. Then we'll hug and cry and a soft snow will start falling outside my window as "Silent Night" starts to play in the background. Jennica will have fallen asleep and the sweet smell of baking cookies will surround us. If only life were that easy…

"*White Christmas*? That's an old movie." She's not interested.

But wait…"You haven't seen *White Christmas*? There's dancing involved."

"Dance!" Jennica shakes her boom-boom in a way that would make Ricky Martin proud.

Star's lips curl up at the sight of her adorable daughter. "We do like dancing. And we like cookies, too. Don't we Jennica?"

"Cookie?"

So I resorted to bribery. It works. I just hope the talk I have planned will be as successful.

Chapter 22

It's 4:00 on Monday and I'm hoping Brooke doesn't show up for her appointment. Not that she's ever not shown up, but if anybody was going to miss an appointment it would be Brooke. And I wouldn't even charge her for the time as my 24-hour-cancellation-policy sign says I will. I just want to go home and fall asleep.

The day started off with the discovery of a broken mirror in my studio. I called Jade and she apologized, promising to pay for it. I still don't understand how it happened, but I'm over it. I'm just still out of it, too.

It's partly the gloomy weather, partly the shorter days, partly the fact that I haven't been sleeping well because I'm analyzing all the deep conversations I've been having, and partly the huge lunch I ate with Dee Dee today. Or maybe it's the soft Christmas music I've got playing over the radio. *Silent night, holy night, all is calm, all is bright...*

I lay my head on the desk. This is why they always play heavy rock music at the gym—it pumps you up. I could change the station. I've got the remote right in front of my nose. Or I could just close my eyes.

Ding-Ding. The bell over the door causes me to jolt as if it were an alarm clock. I widen my eyes to keep them open and sit up straight.

"Bethany, I need you!" Brooke blasts in. "Oh my gosh. I don't know what to do. If you don't help me out, I won't be able to get married. I'll have to cancel the wedding. And my parents have already rented the church—which is really hard to do on Valentine's Day. And I've hired the caterer and the D.J. and the photographer. Photographs are the most important part of the wedding, you know. I won't get any of the deposits back. I'll lose..."

I hold out a hand and blink very slowly. Am I dreaming? Did Brooke say she's not getting married to Eric? "Hold on. What's the problem?" What could be so wrong? Did the happy couple get into a lover's spat? And how am I supposed to help?

"Oh!" She sinks into the chair on the other side of my desk and buries her head in her hands. "How could she do this to me?" As are all Brooke's questions, this is rhetorical. "I've had my wedding planned since we took Home Ec. together."

Am I still half asleep or is Brooke talking nonsense? I feel like Alice in Wonderland. "Who did what?"

"My best friend from high school refuses to be in my wedding unless I make her Maid-of-Honor." She stomps her foot. "This is unbelievable. Just because I was Maid-of-Honor in her wedding, she thinks that she should be mine. But she doesn't have a sister. I've got to make my sister Maid-of-Honor. Eric's brother is his Best Man. It wouldn't be right. And she got married right out of high school so we were closer then. I hardly ever see her anymore. I don't..."

"Brooke." I reach across the desk to wrap my fingers around her arm. "Calm down. Breathe. We'll figure it out." I say this though I'm not sure why I'm even involved at all. This is what you hire wedding planners for, not personal trainers.

"Okay. Okay." She fans herself with her hands and makes little gasping noises. "That's better. I'm peaceful. I'm in control. I'm relaxed..." Her voice gets squeaky again. "I need help!"

She does need help, and I'm thinking she should be sitting across from Eric's desk, not mine. She's loony. "How can I help you?" She'll figure out in a minute that I can't— unless she wants to talk about diet and exercise.

"I need you to take Rochelle's place." Her eyes shine with unshed tears and she's unusually quiet.

Rochelle. Who's Rochelle? I mentally rewind our conversation. Now my voice sounds squeaky. "Your best friend from high school? You want me to be in your wedding?" In Eric's wedding? That would be too weird.

"Please, oh please. I'm begging you. You're my friend now—I see you much more than I see Rochelle. You wouldn't have to do anything except wear a beautiful dress." She leans in closer and her voice gets lower. "They are red, of course, for Valentine's Day, and I know you look gorgeous in red. You could even wear the earrings I made you. Hey, maybe I could make earrings for all the bridesmaids. Matching jewelry!" She comes back from her tangent. "Please. I need one more bridesmaid. Eric's got five groomsmen. He can't take back his invitation to be in the wedding from any of them, and I can't have one walk down the aisle by himself. How strange would that be?"

I wonder who I would be walking down the aisle with. Maybe Christian is in the wedding. Then she should ask Laurel to be her bridesmaid. I'll suggest this when she takes a breath.

"I'd ask Laurel, but Christian said that she's been really sick lately and doesn't have much energy."

There goes my brilliant idea.

"And I know you have energy, since you can beat up Eric in a boxing ring!" Her laugh grates like fingernails on a chalkboard.

"I didn't beat him up." Somehow the story had leaked out at church on Sunday. I'm guessing Brooke was the source. Anyway, I made a hasty retreat after the service. I've gotten way too much attention at church in the past, and I'd rather not be the topic for discussion again.

"Oh, sorry. You didn't beat him up, you just took him down. See. You owe us. Make it up to Eric by being in our wedding, and he'll promise not to file a restraining order." She's cracking up at her own joke.

I look to heaven for a guidance...and patience. "Um. This really isn't that big a deal. You wouldn't have to cancel the wedding if I wasn't a part of it. Don't you want the ceremony to be more personal?" Curiously, my stomach twists at the idea of walking down the aisle past Eric. Can't I just cry from the pews like I do at every other wedding—then eat some cake?

"I want a big wedding! The bigger the better. It's gotta be perfect. Please say you'll do it."

I want some time to think about it. I want to consider my options—or more appropriately, Brooke's options. I stand from my chair to lead Brooke to the treadmill, but as I walk around the corner of the desk she leaps up and wraps her arms around me. She thought I was coming over to give her a hug.

"Thank you. Oh, thank you." She squeezes the breath out of me. "Hey, you can walk down the aisle with Mick. You two would make a great couple. I saw you sitting together at church a couple weeks ago."

She's off and running, or at least she should be. I untangle myself as she talks and set her up at a 2.0 incline and 3.5 miles per hour. Now she's running more than just her mouth.

"Mick thinks you're precious…"

I sigh and slink back to my desk. With my other clients, I like to walk and talk with them, but since Brooke can carry on a one-sided conversation, she really doesn't need me.

The bell over the door jingles again. I turn my head to see what else I have to deal with. I really don't feel like smiling.

Robbie bounds in. My lips curl up of their own accord. Robbie glances at my client, and I realize what he is hearing.

"You and Mick would make a great couple. You both have dark hair and are athletic. Your kids would be absolutely adorable."

Nothing is going my way.

"So," Robbie holds out the electronic device for me to initial. "Mick is your boyfriend?"

"No," my smile feels a bit pathetic. "I accidentally agreed to be in Brooke's wedding, so now she thinks she needs to hook me up with a groomsman."

I say this loud enough for Brooke to hear, but I know she's not listening.

She walks and talks. "Mick restores vintage cars. He's going to let us use a classic Corvette for after the reception. Isn't life grand?"

She doesn't wait for an answer before continuing on. Robbie and I stare at her for a moment.

He turns back to me. "So maybe if you don't start dating Mr. Corvette, I can take you out sometime."

My cheeks start to hurt from the width of my smile. "What took you so long to ask?" I tease. This is what I need—a getaway, a mini-vacation, an escape from reality. And no Eric looking over my shoulder.

"Alright. How's this weekend?"

I groan. Just when I think life starts to play fair. "I'm going shopping with my sister-in-law."

"Wow." Robbie tries to read my expression. "Either you're blowing me off or you take your shopping way too seriously."

I laugh at myself. "We're shopping in Oregon, so yeah I guess I do take my shopping too seriously."

Robbie shrugs. "I understand."

I don't think he does. "Their outlet malls are ten times the size of ours, plus they have no sales tax. My sister-in-law goes every year. This is the first time she's invited me."

"Hmm." He stuffs one hand in his pocket. "Well the following weekend I'll be gone for Christmas. How about we get together in January? I'll make it my New Year's resolution to take you out."

I sit up taller. I've never been a part of a New Year's resolution before. "What do you have in mind?" I'm thinking dinner train or the Philharmonic. A Broadway in Boise production wouldn't be bad.

His grin is pure mischief. "We could go bowling or play laser tag with my buddies."

Earth to Bethany. He's a UPS delivery guy. At least he's being creative. And he's super cute. "Bowling it is."

144

"Great," he says.

"Great," I echo.

He turns his back on me and we stare at Brooke for another minute.

"I met Mick when I had to take my car into his auto body shop. I'd been rear-ended, and he thought it was weird that I prayed for the person who hit me. So I told him all about my prayer life and he agreed to come to church." She's like the Energizer Bunny. She keeps going and going and going.

Robbie nods at me. "I'll see ya soon."

I stand up and walk to the door with him. "If not," I say, "I'll just have to order something UPS."

Robbie's eyes twinkle. "Or maybe I can send you a package."

I imagine a brown paper wrapped bowling ball. "Tis the season."

Chapter 23

I sprinkle some chili powder into the tomato mixture for my huevos rancheros. My brother would be pretending to barf into my skillet if he were here. He hates tomatoes—claims they were the forbidden fruit in the Garden of Eden.

I bump my head on the range hood as I stand up. I rub the spot and look out the window at the streetlights twinkling. Of the two apartment styles, I picked the one with the window in the kitchen instead of the bedroom since I spend a lot of time cooking. When I do move into a new place it will be for a bigger kitchen.

I crack an egg into a Pyrex measuring cup and slide it gently into the pan. My stomach rumbles as I get a whiff of the tangy scent. I've just started to grate the cheese when the phone rings.

My phone doesn't actually ring. It barks. *Ruff...ruff.* It's annoying, and I've even had neighbors report me to the apartment supervisor for hiding pets. It's all Christian's fault. He programmed the phone when I bought it, and I don't know how to change it.

"Hello?" Maybe it's Eric calling to cancel my counseling session because he's afraid I'm going to inflict another injury. Or maybe now that I'm in his wedding, he doesn't think it is appropriate for me to be a client.

"Hi, Bethany." The deep voice is one I've known all my life.

"Hi, Dad." I may be mad at him still, but it makes me feel good to know he's thinking of me.

"How are you doing?"

Everything inside me smiles. "I'm hanging in. My life has gotten kind of crazy lately. I'm going to be in my pastor's wedding. You've met Eric Austin haven't you?" I quickly remember how Dad knows Eric, so I don't give him a chance to respond. "And Mom got a boob job. And Laurel..."

Dad clears his throat just in time to stop me from spilling the news of Laurel's pregnancy. Whew, that was close. "Your mother had breast augmentation?"

Ew. Icky. I don't want to be in the middle of this. "Yeah, she used the money you were saving for a vacation to Hawaii." New subject. I ramble on about the first thing that comes to mind. "I could use a vacation. I'm looking forward to seeing you. It will just be you and me Christmas Day because Christian and Laurel are going to her folk's house. We'll celebrate Christmas Eve with them and you can stay there of course, but I'll make Christmas dinner here in my apartment. It's kind of small, so we can walk along the greenbelt or go out for a movie."

Dad used to take me to movies when I got grounded. He would feel sorry for me being stuck inside, so he'd take advantage of our time together. He also used movies in his sermons a lot. I know he'll love this idea. I just won't be able to see the new chick-flick.

"Honey, that sounds wonderful."

I expect him to tell me about the last movie he watched or suggest the latest sports film.

"But I'm not going to be able to make it."

Dead silence. I'm not sure I heard him right. I don't want to acknowledge what I think he just said because I don't want him to confirm it. If it was Christian I would know he was pulling my leg, but why would Dad tease me this way? And if he's not teasing, what reason could he possibly have for not keeping his word? For leaving me all alone on Christmas day?

"Sweetie?"

Finally I stammer. "You're...you're not coming?" I slide down a cabinet to the floor. "Why? You planned to spend Christmas with your kids. I haven't seen you since last year at Thanksgiving." I sound helpless. But I can't help it. I guess that's where the term comes from.

"I know. I even bought my plane ticket. But before I promised to spend Christmas with you, I told Corrine that

I would fly to Florida with her when her first grandchild is born. I just found out that they are scheduled to induce on the 26th of December." He's way too calm and logical about this. Just the idea of breaking my heart should break his heart.

Well, I can be calm and logical, too. I try to swallow through my constricted throat and refuse to believe that we can't work this out. "That will work, Dad. You fly to Boise on the 23rd. Then go straight to Florida from here."

Dad's quiet, and I pray he's considering my idea. "I really want to, Bethany. I do. But I have to go with Corrine because she's afraid to fly."

"So what? Tell her to get over it. Send her to counseling or have her take a drug. There's other ways to get her to Florida. I'll buy her a bus ticket." Desperation makes my voice squeaky. "Or a train. Or she can drive."

Dad pauses as if waiting to see if I'm done with my rant. "From Montana? On Christmas?"

"It's been done." In fact I'd really like to ruin Corrine's Christmas right about now.

"Bethany, I'm going with my wife to meet her first grandchild."

Irony screams at me. *His* first grandchild has been conceived and he has no idea. Now, I hurt for Christian because he's not going to get to tell Dad the news in person. I've got to make this work.

"Why can't they change the date? Why does Corrine's daughter have to induce on the 26th? Did she plan it this way to get an extra tax exemption?" Yeah, I'm bitter. Dad is choosing his stepdaughter over his own daughter.

Dad's sigh is loud. "I'm not in charge here. If the baby is induced on the 26th, then that's when I have to be there. It's a once in a lifetime thing. I can see you anytime."

I feel like a door was just slammed in my face. "That's a good point, Dad. You could see me anytime." I close my eyes and knock my head back against the cabinet a couple of times.

"But you haven't."

This isn't happening. My own father isn't really abandoning me on Christmas. My mind reels back through all the dates this year when he could have seen me. Father's Day he refused to come out here and leave his step kids. He did invite me to be with his family. The idea made me sick. Then in September I went to Missoula for a fitness conference, but the drive was too far for him with his back condition. And what about Christian's birthday? That would have been the best surprise.

"I'm sorry." He sounds more angry than apologetic. "I wish I could make it work."

"You could if you really wanted to." I jab the disconnect button.

The stovetop timer buzzes, but I don't move. It would be so much easier not to care. So what if my dad leaves our family and moves to another state? It's his loss if he doesn't want to see me, right? I shouldn't have to compete with children that are of no blood relation to him whatsoever.

But I do care. All I want for Christmas are my two parents back...my two parents back...my two parents back. I would give up everything to go back in time to a place where I was a priority—where I was taken care of and cherished. Now I have to figure life out on my own, and I'm pretty sure that I'm making a big mess of it.

I click my phone back on and dial Christian. His answering machine greets me coldly. I wonder if they've heard the news yet. But it won't affect him as much. He's got his wife and a child on the way. He's got in-laws who will bake pumpkin pie and laugh at him while playing charades. He's not going to spend any time alone.

What am I going to do? Bake myself a ham? Go to the theatre alone amidst groups of families and friends? Walk along the river listening to Christmas carols on my headphones? That's festive.

Maybe I could walk right off a bridge. Of course, I wouldn't really do that, but now I understand the spike in suicides during the Christmas season. I'm George Bailey before the angel rescued him. And my dad is that mean, old man in the wheelchair.

A burning smell starts to accompany the buzz of the timer. My neighbors will really love me now. Maybe I'll get kicked out of my apartment and then I can be homeless for the holidays. I drop the phone with a thud and rub my temples.

I'm not hungry anymore, but I know I have to eat. I click the stove knob above my head to the off position and swing the cupboard next to me open. Power Bars. Yum. That'll be all I need for my Christmas dinner, as well. Nice and simple.

Who am I kidding? I throw the bar across the linoleum room. My kitchen is tiny, so it only sails three feet before crashing into the wall and dropping to the linoleum floor.

I need to run. If only I could take my dad inside a boxing ring right now. Then I could show him how I feel. Eric's crumpled position on the mat was a great comparison to the blow I just received from my dad.

Eric. Oh, yeah. I look at my watch. Counseling. I'm so lonely I would pay people to talk to me.

I'm not feeling any better when I reach the church. Eric's secretary is in the sanctuary wrapping empty boxes to put under a fake tree—my Christmas is going to be just as hollow. I'm glad she doesn't look up so I don't have to wave. Her smile might have made me feel better, and I just want to feel sorry for myself.

Eric is reading the Bible as I enter his office. It makes me feel guilty for how often I've been putting off my devotional time. I slink over to the couch and sprawl on my stomach. My head rests on a pillow that smells a little like wet dog—confirming my suspicions that this living room set was a garage sale find.

Eric looks up and evaluates my position. "What's going on?"

I decide to start off with small talk. I'm not ready to admit my patheticness. "I'm going to be in your wedding." I wonder if he knows.

"Ahhh." He stands and moves to his place on the loveseat. "So this must be the always-a-bridesmaid-never-a-bride-depression."

He almost gets a small smile from me. "Is that a clinical disorder?"

"Nah. Just an observation."

"Well then, Freud, you are way off. Remember, I don't want to get married?"

"Hmmm." He's full of deep-thinking sounds today. "You do look lonely, but what's the problem? You don't like the dresses Brooke picked out?"

He was correct the first time. I might as well explain. It's not as if keeping it to myself will keep it from happening. "My dad isn't coming for Christmas." My chin trembles as I say this, and I lose the battle against the urge to cry.

Eric leans forward, resting his forearms on his thighs. "Why not?"

His voice is so warm with concern that I can't keep the emotion from showing. I curl into a ball on my side and let the tears dampen my face. All that has happened lately... and I'm crying because I miss my daddy. I feel like a lost little girl. I can't answer his question because I can't even talk.

"I remember you had plans for him to come." He hands me a box of tissue.

I roll onto my back and sop up my tears. I stare at the ceiling, trying to separate myself from the emptiness and pain. "Yes." My voice is low and hard to understand. I try again. "Yes. But his new wife's daughter..." Another rush of tears forces me to pause. "She's having a baby in Florida." I hate Florida. I'm never visiting Florida—even though I would love to drive along from island to island in the Keys. Maybe if I boycott Florida I will somehow boycott this memory.

"Did you explain to your father how this makes you feel?"

I roll my wet eyes. This is when it would be nice to have a sympathetic female counselor rather than an objective male trying to dissect my life. "Of course. I can't remember what exactly I said, but I made it pretty apparent that I wanted him to visit."

"What did he say?"

I give a laying down version of a shrug. "Just that he was sorry it wouldn't work."

Eric does this wise/understanding nod thing. "He's probably pretty torn up about it."

I want to throw the stinky pillow at him. "No. If he wanted it to work, he could have made it work. I told him so and he got mad."

Eric sighs—sounding a little too much like Dad. "I'm really sorry, Bethany." Now he sounds a lot like Dad. "You're a victim here."

"You bet I am."

Eric lifts his eyebrows at my response. "Have you tried to find the value, yet?"

I stare back up at the ceiling. I'm still wanting to feel sorry for myself. "Yeah." Sarcasm at its finest. "I'm really looking forward to wrapping presents—to me from me."

Eric's lip quirks up on the right side. "That would make shopping easy."

I really do throw my pillow at him this time, but I'm thinking about the Adidas outlet at the outlet mall in Oregon. I roll to a seated position and take a scoopful of M & Ms. I knew I should have eaten dinner.

"Let's climb the victim ladder," he suggests, reminding me of an old Bob Newhart sketch comedy routine. Bob played a therapist and whenever a patient came to him with a problem he gave two simple words of advice: "Stop it."

If only it were that easy. But then we wouldn't need God.

"Alright," I roll my head back to the couch cushions. "What is the first rung on the accountability side?"

"Acknowledgement."

Fine. That was easy enough. Or I thought it was. "My dad is not coming for Christmas." As I say the words, my voice fades in and out.

"Good." Eric waits for me to wipe my nose again. "Now own it."

I shake my head. "What do you mean? I thought I just did."

Eric's nose scrunches up as if he just caught a whiff of the pillow. "Own your part. What choices do you face?"

This isn't fair. Dad messed up my life. He should have to fix it. Deep breath. "I can choose to be miserable...or not." The miserable part of my situation seems like a given. What am I going to do? Bake cookies and take them to a nursing home?

"Great." Eric encourages me. "Now take the next step. Make a plan. What can you do since your father's plans have changed?" I wonder if Eric still respects my dad. I don't know how he could.

I mutter my answer as if I'd been called to the principal's office and wouldn't be let go without saying the right words. "Bake cookies for old people."

Eric's eyes sparkle like he's not sure if I'm trying to be funny or not, and he doesn't want to laugh if I'm serious. "That's a nice idea. It would make you thankful for your youth and health. Do you know many old people?"

"No. Just one dancing granny from the gym, but she doesn't eat cookies." Nancy would douse me with mineral water if I tried to feed her sugar.

"Okay...any other ideas? What about your brother? Or your cousins? Or your mom?"

Eric's way too good at this. Though I've got a rebuttal for his every suggestion. "Christian is going to his in-laws. My cousins aren't even talking to each other so their Christmas will not be merry. And Mom is going to the East Coast to see my sister." There. See, I deserve a good sulk.

Eric rubs his hands together and purses his lips. He at last looks at me. "I'm thinking of a family that would love to take you in. It's a couple about your parents' ages who used to be missionaries and are very warm and welcoming."

"Ha! I'm not homeless." I remember doing this as a child. A homeless lady stayed with us for Christmas.

When she brushed her teeth the toothpaste foam ran all down her hand.

"It's my family, Bethany."

I have my mouth open to argue, but his words are like dry ice the way they cause me to freeze. "What?"

"Would you like to join us? My parents live in Spokane, but they have a cabin in McCall. We go skiing every Christmas."

His eyes are dark and serious. I'm mesmerized by their depth. I don't know what to say. I know what I want to say, but... "I can't possibly accept."

"Sure you can. My parents love to meet new people. My brother will be there, too. And Brooke is coming up. You can share a room with her."

It sounds too easy. It's unexpected. I'm overwhelmed. "You need to talk to all of them about it first. Especially Brooke. I mean it's your first Christmas with her, isn't it?"

Eric tilts his head. "Yeah, but it's not like we'll be alone. It's a family thing."

I blink a couple times and look down. I feel like crying again. It's an emotional day. "Thank you, Eric. If your parents are okay with the invitation then I will consider it."

Eric's gaze pulls my eyes back up. "What's to consider? You've got my mom's amazing cooking, Brooke's lively conversations, and three handsome gentlemen."

"And skiing," I add.

Eric shakes his head at me as if he should have known. "And skiing."

"And a partridge in a pear tree." I'm feeling much better now. If it doesn't work out, at least I'll know I was invited. And maybe I'll just go skiing by myself. With Eric's help I've climbed the accountability ladder once again. I'm still hurt, but I'm moving on.

Chapter 24

Comedy Sportz is located on Entertainment Drive, be-tween the biggest movie theatre in town (twenty-two screens), an arcade, pool hall, ceramics studio, and a me-nagerie of restaurants. This will be Christian's first time on stage. All participants have to go through a comedy class, which was Laurel's Birthday gift to Christian—a fact that I find humorous in itself since Laurel is so often annoyed by his jokes.

Dee Dee parks behind Legend's Sports Pub, and we jog through a light sprinkling of snow toward the entrance. I blend right in with my surroundings since Dee Dee dressed me up like a snowflake. I'm wearing a white sweater, cream-colored gouchos, and matching knee high boots with heels. (The heels are the scariest part.) Besides that, Dee Dee pulled my hair back and pinned ringlets all over my head. My yellow parka kind of clashes with the look, so she has me shed it the moment we get inside.

The building is small, so after we pay at a corner conces-sion booth, we take seats facing the other corner. The place is packed with Christian's friends, though Laurel is the only one I know.

A whistle blows and I see my brother step out on stage dressed like a referee. "Welcome to Comedy Sportz. We'll get started in a few minutes, but I just want to have you all move forward. The seats are funniest in the front."

If comedy is all about timing, Christian's got it made. He connects, he knows how to work a crowd, and he doesn't seem nervous in the least.

We all grumble good naturedly, but stand up to move for-ward one row. I'm just getting situated in the last seat when Eric rushes in.

He looks over my head to talk to Laurel. "Hey, sorry I'm late."

"I think you made it just in time." Laurel smiles.

I smile, too. "I didn't know you were coming."

Eric glances at me in surprise. "Whoa. I didn't even recognize you, Bethany. You look…fancy."

I'd forgotten I was so dressed up. Dee Dee even put makeup on me. Now I'm self-conscious, but flattered. "Oh. Well, my cousin is always giving me makeovers."

"She does good work."

The lights start to dim so Eric slips behind me to the seat I just vacated. He's all alone.

"Is Brooke coming?" I whisper since the show is about to start.

Eric leans forward to whisper back. "She was planning on it, but she couldn't get out of bed this morning. She was too sore from personal training yesterday."

I gasp then giggle. "I warned her! But she kept saying she wanted me to push her harder. I wish she would have called me. I could have recommended a hot bath and pain killer."

Eric chuckled along. "I already suggested that to her. She'll be fine."

An old 2 Unlimited song blasts over the loudspeaker. "Welcome to the big game!" Cheers ring out from all around me.

Laurel has her arms in the air clapping for her husband who is jogging around on stage. I pull her arm down and yell in her ear so she can hear me. "Brooke couldn't make it, so I'm going to sit with Eric."

I'm not sure if she heard me, but she nods anyway. Her entire focus is on Christian. I grab my purse and do a squat walk back to Eric so that I don't block anyone's view.

Eric gives me a quick smile as I join him. Then we watch as the two opposing teams of players take the stage to the Rocky theme song. The blue team and the red team face off. Christian calls the captains to the field—meaning they meet at center stage.

They start off with a game of freeze tag, but this version has two players acting out a scene. The other players have the option to call "freeze" any time, causing the first actors to become like statues in whatever positions they are in. The third player has to pick a player to replace, then start a whole new scene that fits the position the actors froze in.

Christian explains the game then asks for audience participation. We're supposed to yell out suggestions for a scene.

"Body building!" I call out, but Laurel's answer is louder... or maybe just more meaningful to my brother.

"Having a baby!" she hollers.

Christian claps his hands. "Having a baby it is." His eyes are on his wife and I feel warm all over at their secret connection. Nobody else knows they are expecting. Nobody but Eric.

I look over at my pastor and we share our own private moment. It's a thrill to be a part of something so meaningful.

The actors become a doctor and a patient. The funny thing is it's the guy who lays down on the stage with his knees spread, huffing and puffing like he's doing Lamaze. It's unexpected and gets the audience in the mood for more.

The blue team wins the game by calling freeze the most times, so they get to challenge the red team. They send the three players outside into the snow, while the audience thinks up phrases. The slips of paper containing our ideas are scattered along the floor for the performers to pick up and read in the middle of their scene.

The red team comes back in and takes their places.

Christian directs them then calls to the audience again. "I need an action. What should they be doing in this scene?"

"Getting married!" Dee Dee yells first. I raise my eyebrows because she's usually not very loud.

Christian looks a little surprised at first, too. "Getting married," he continues as if he hasn't missed a beat. "Now I need a location. Where are they getting married?"

A guy on the other side of the aisle responds. "On a fire engine." He's looking our direction instead of at my brother.

"Why not?" Christian hoots. "Alright. We're all attending a wedding ceremony on a fire engine."

One of the actors makes a screeching sound as if to imitate a siren, but I'm looking between Dee Dee and the mystery man. I lean over to Eric as the scene starts. "Does that guy look like he has really long eyelashes to you?" I ask.

Eric gives me a look to tell me that my question is more bizarre than a wedding on a fire engine. "Sure."

I lean back in my chair though I'm figuratively on the edge of my seat. Maybe I'm crazy, but I can't help thinking that the guy with the long eyelashes is the father to Dee Dee's aborted baby. And if you could see Dee Dee's face, you would think so, too.

The game's over, but the laughter sounds distant to me. I can't take my eyes off the fire engine guy.

Eric mumbles something to me about staring, and I hear Christian on stage requesting a volunteer, but I'm not really paying attention until I feel a sharp jab in my ribs. "Oh!" I yell, pulling my arm up to protect myself from any more pain.

"I love to see such excitement!" Christian jokes. "Miss, come on up."

I see faces turn my direction, and when I look to the stage in surprise I see my brother motioning toward me.

"Yes, you. The lady dressed all in white."

I give Eric the big-eyed-help-me-plea, but he can't do anything, and even if he could, I doubt by the way he's laughing that he would. After all, he's the one who made me "volunteer" in the first place.

I stand to my feet, wobbling just a little. Christian sets a chair next to him and has me take a seat facing everybody.

"This next game is called 'Hey waiter.'"

I have this sudden vision of myself ending up on the floor in the birthing position the way the first game had started. I shoot Eric a death glare, but my job's not so bad. I just have to call, 'Hey, waiter, there's a (fill in the blank) in my soup," and wait for the actors to respond with punny answers. We start out with a mint.

"I'm Certs-ainly sorry."

"Take a hint, lady."

Then there's a shoe, a lamp, and a jack hammer in my soup. We end with this cute, chubby girl doing the running man and singing, "It's Hammer time." A guy from the back runs up to take a snapshot of me with the cast before Christian tallies the score and announces half time.

Unfortunately I'm still on stage when I see Dee Dee slip out the door. I have the feeling she won't be coming back. I run to catch up with her but by the time I make it outside, she's gone. I pretend I'm headed back to my seat, but really I'm looking for the guy with the eyelashes.

Eric turns to face me as I wander up the aisle. "No hard feelings, right?"

I'm not even sure what he's talking about. "What?" I mumble. Then I see the guy with the eyelashes. It's A.J.—and he's got his arm around a redhead. No wonder Dee Dee left. I'm a little hurt myself, even though it doesn't involve me—and even though A.J. has every right to be dating somebody else. I mean, he could even be married to the woman. It's been a couple years now since Dee Dee broke up with him.

"Do I need to elbow you again for staring?" Eric asks.

Oh, yeah. I should be mad at him for getting me called on stage. "That guy over there..." I look at Eric and tilt my head A.J.'s direction. "That's Dee Dee's ex-boyfriend."

Understanding washes over Eric's face. "The father," he says quietly.

This is something else only Eric and I know. We look at each other for a moment. I don't know what else to do. Dee Dee's gone and if I were her I probably would have left, too.

Eric faces forward once again and leans back in his chair. "It's hard letting go."

The way he says this causes my brows to draw together in suspicion.

He sees my look and gives me a half-smile. "I was engaged before."

Before? "As in before Brooke?" He must have dumped *her*, because there is no way any woman would give up a guy as great as Eric.

Eric shrugs. "It was my college girlfriend. I had just accepted the youth pastor position up in Spokane, and I had this preconceived idea that all pastors should be married."

Not a bad idea, but kind of funny coming from Eric, since his youth pastor looks like a skater who just experienced electric shock, and the prison chaplain is an obese biker. Eric seemed to have higher standards for himself. I could mention this, but I just want to know about the girl. "What happened?"

Eric's eyes wander away. "It would have been a big mistake. But I was still devastated when she cancelled the engagement to pursue her modeling career."

My lips part. I smack them back together as soon as I realize my mouth is hanging open. "You dated a model?" I choke out once I find my voice. "No wonder Brooke is so obsessed with losing weight for your wedding."

Eric waves my words away. "My ex just looked like the girl next door. She was photogenic though, so she started posing for a photographer to make a little extra money. It took off from there."

"Where is she now?" I ask. What I really want to ask is how Eric could make such a big mistake. And how can he be so sure that Brooke is the one? What is he doing differently the second time around?

"She was in Milan, last I heard."

"Wow." He should elbow me again—this time for staring at him. "You were engaged before."

Eric rolls his eyes. "It was the thing to do at my college. We used to joke that girls attended to get their M-R-S Degree."

I shake my head. Marriage is serious stuff. "How close were you to the altar? Was it like the movie *The Wedding Singer*, where the bride simply doesn't show up?" Poor Eric.

He gives me a knowing smile. "Nothing like that. We didn't even get around to setting a date because we couldn't work it around her schedule."

I want to know more. I want him to share everything with me. How did he meet her? What was she like? How long did it take for him to get over her? I open my mouth, but I'm interrupted by the announcer—"Mr. Voice" as Christian calls him.

The players take the stage and do a Beastie Boys type rap. The audience comes up with a name and the actors have to make up lyrics that rhyme with the name. If the audience fills in the rhyming word, the team gets a point. The names get longer and longer and pretty soon the players are making up words. It's entertaining, but my thoughts are still on Eric. How could he come so close to committing his life to the wrong woman? Was he not listening to God? Or did God allow it to happen for a certain purpose?

Luckily, I'm still thinking of Eric when Christian calls for another volunteer. I hold my hand over Eric's head and point. Christian obliges.

"Ha!" is all I say when Eric squeezes past me with eyes narrowed.

He has to play a spelling game where the audience thinks up words and the players take turns spelling the word and giving a definition one person at a time. They stand straight and tall with their hands clasped in front of their chests as if they were the Von Trapp Family Singers. Eric looks ridiculous...and he's a terrible speller, too.

"Serendipity," suggests A.J.'s redhead.

They take turns. S-E-R-E-N-

It's Eric's turn. "Dipity," he finishes.

He's not much better at definitions.

"Madrigal," calls a balding guy from in front of me.

The players answer on cue. Pronoun: Describing-the-act-of-Eric fills in the blank. "Madrig."

He gets his picture taken at the end like I did. But this time Christian announces that Eric is his pastor and he's going to make sure the photograph gets posted on the church's power point presentation on Sunday.

"You're horrible," I tease Eric when he returns.

Eric plops down. "It's your fault," he retorts.

"Oh," I coo. "Are you a victim?"

Eric just shakes his head at me. We're having so much fun giving each other a bad time that we stay to hang out with Christian afterwards. He introduces us to the owner before we head over to Legends—Laurel is craving onion rings.

The owner of Comedy Sportz is actually one of the performers. She's young and gangly, with tight blonde curls.

"This is such a great idea," Eric tells her.

"Thanks." She beams. "We're trying to bring clean comedy to Boise."

It is clean. Even kids can attend. If anything foul is said, a *foul* is called—that's part of Christian's job.

"Is she a Christian?" Eric asks my brother when we leave.

"No." Christian puts his arm around Laurel. "She's actually Mormon."

The LDS have high values, and do the family thing right... when they're not practicing polygamy.

I think of the Christian comedy DVD I gave my brother last Christmas. "Hey, *you* should start a comedy club," I suggest.

Laurel snorts—the most unladylike noise I've ever heard her make. "He'd have to get fired before I'd let him do that," she tries to joke, but I don't think she's joking.

"Why?" I challenge. "It's a great idea."

Eric tries to lighten the mood. "Small businesses do run in the family."

"That's right!" He's brilliant. "You could even use the name Light, like Dee Dee, Star, and I do!"

Christian glances at Laurel and the gleam in his eye is put out. "You've already taken the name Lighten Up. What else is there?"

"What about Light Heart?" I turn to Eric, the expert. "Isn't that Biblical?"

Eric opens the door to Legends for us to enter. "There might be something in Proverbs. I know 'happy heart' is mentioned."

"There we go. How about Light Hearted Comedy?" I love the idea. It's perfect. "And instead of saying 'A Christian Comedy Club' we could call it 'Christian's Comedy Club'." We follow a waitress to a booth.

Christian smiles at me encouragingly. "I take it you enjoyed my performance?"

He's just looking for compliments. I slide into the seat next to Eric. "It was okay. What do you think Eric? Is it worth going to again?"

"I'd go." Eric hands me a menu. "Which reminds me, are you coming with me to McCall for Christmas?"

I feel both Christian and Laurel's eyes on me, so I explain. "Since Dad's not coming for Christmas, Eric invited me to join his family."

Laurel eyes turn serious. "Did I not invite you to my parent's house?"

She hadn't. But that's okay. "Do your parents go skiing in McCall?" I ask in return.

"No." She looked over toward my brother as if communicating non-verbally. I wonder what she said.

"Then I'll go to McCall with Eric." Now it's my turn to speak non-verbally. I look over and thank Eric with my eyes.

Chapter 25

Laurel shops like she does everything else—efficiently. I'm surprised she can spend a whole day at an outlet mall, but I guess if she has a list and gets everything done at once, that's pretty efficient.

Of course she gets to visit with her sister, as well. I would have thought this to be an enjoyable occasion, until I hung out with Laurel's sister.

Chloe pulls her Audi into the humongous parking lot off I-5, south of Portland. "I'm never going to find a parking place." Her tone is low and full of disdain.

I'm squished in the backseat, but I don't say a word. It's way too easy to be sucked in by her attitude. Often when I'm with people like her I start looking down my nose on the world without even realizing it. "Can you believe so and so said such and such?" or "What was he/she thinking to wear whatever?" I become an expert on everyone's life but my own.

The sad thing is that Chloe has so much to be thankful for. She's beautiful, for starters. She's more petite than Laurel, with stunningly silky hair and features like Michelle Pfeiffer. I once read that the more evenly balanced facial features are, the more pleasing they are to the eye. Michelle Pfeiffer was used as the example of perfect balance, and I'm guessing that Chloe could be, too. On top of that she has a brilliant career at an advertising firm and is engaged to the heir of a major athletic shoe industry. Believe me, we heard all about it.

Laurel and I drove into town last night and stayed at Chloe's house in the West Hills. Unfortunately, the eight-hour ride was more fun than the two hours spent with Miss Precocious. The best part of the evening was giggling at

Conan O'Brien. Well, Laurel and I giggled. Chloe lectured about how Conan is in desperate need of a haircut.

Chloe honks as a rude driver cuts in front of us to get the last parking place in the row. She then circles the parking lot and cuts in front of a silver Suburban. Classic Chloe.

So I don't know why I'm surprised when she deserts us later to run to the bridal store with a friend. I lift an eyebrow at Laurel. If I were her I would be ticked. "Wow," I say.

Laurel turns on her heel and takes off for the back corner of the shopping center. (I knew it--she's got a plan mapped out.) She speaks to me over her shoulder. "Chloe can't stop thinking about her wedding. And I haven't even told her yet that I can't be in it because my baby will be due about the same time. I feel guilty every moment I'm with her."

Yet another negative emotion the baby has caused. I lengthen my strides to catch up with her. "Don't you think Chloe will be excited for you?" I want to cheer Laurel up, but maybe these are not the right words to say.

"Sure." She doesn't sound sure.

We round the corner and I catch a glimpse of Carter's and Osh Kosh. "I know! Let's go buy your baby an outfit." There's nothing cuter than pink dresses and tiny shoes.

Laurel pauses and looks in a window. "I don't know if I'm having a boy or a girl." She doesn't sound dreamy the way an expectant mom should.

"We could buy one of each," I suggest.

Laurel looks away. "I should do that with Christian."

Yeah. As if my brother would ever willingly go shopping. "Okay," I say. I'm not going to fight her.

We move on and I wonder which store she's planning to attack first. My eyes wander from window to window. I freeze and grab Laurel's arm. Now I'll fight her if I have to. It's Motherhood Maternity.

"No." Laurel tries to back away. "Huh-uh."

"Why not?" She's a strange one. I remember Star ordering maternity clothes on-line before she was even showing.

Laurel looks at me blankly before answering. "I'm not shopping for me today."

"Alright." I swing the door open. "I'm shopping for you. Let's pick out your Christmas present."

She hesitates.

"Come on. You don't want to wear Christian's sweatshirts for nine months do you?"

She looks down at her shirt. I'm surprised Chloe didn't make any rude comments about her weight.

"I'll try stuff on, too," I tease.

The right side of Laurel's lips starts to curl up. "Is that a deal?"

I laugh, picturing myself in a pair of pants that comes up to my bra line. "Deal."

The clothing store actually has pillow-like "stomachs" you can attach with Velcro to make yourself look pregnant. It's not very natural, but kind of fun. I pull a velvet dress over my head and turn sideways to get a good look in the mirror. I look like I'm wearing a curtain.

"Laurel, you've got to see this." I step out from my dressing room and scan the store. I don't see Laurel, but my eyes lock with those of a cute male. He's very cute. In fact he's Paul from the gym. I gasp and step away.

"Hi." He looks me up and down like he's always done, but there's amusement in his expression this time. What is *he* doing here?

"I...I'm not pregnant," I blurt out. Great. Now his suspicions of me being a nutcase are confirmed.

Paul gives a slow nod. "Why would I think you're pregnant? It's not as if you're trying on maternity clothes."

Ha. Very funny. "I'm here with my sister-in-law. She's pregnant and I'm just...um...keeping her company." How did I ever get this beautiful man to kiss me? I'm a total loser.

"Right. Your sister-in-law." He looks around to emphasize that we're all alone.

I stick a thumb over my shoulder pointing to the dressing rooms. "She must be in there."

166

Paul's eyes sparkle. "You should let her try on that little number." He gestures toward my tent/dress. "It's breathtaking."

"I do have good taste." I try to joke and remind him of better days at the gym. My words fall flat. We look at each other in silence. "So why are *you* here?" I blurt out.

Paul points toward the dressing rooms now. "I'm with my girlfriend."

I try to take this in. I blink a few times. Did I hear him right? "Your girlfriend?" I ask to be sure.

"Yeah. Meagan is finishing up the semester at college here in Oregon. She'll be moving in with me after Christmas."

I stare.

Paul's eyes get narrow. "Don't tell me you didn't know."

My hand goes to my heart. So he thinks I was flirting with him while aware that he's dating somebody else? And she's expecting his baby? "She's pregnant?" I whisper. All of a sudden our past "relationship" has to be a secret.

Paul gives an annoyed nod. "Most people are when they try on clothes here."

"How..." A million questions race through my mind. "How far along is she?"

"She's due in February—Valentine's Day, actually."

I poke him in the chest. "You were cheating on her." It's an angry whisper now. "With me!"

Paul holds up one of those strong hands to stop me. They aren't so sexy now. "Hey. You came on to me." He's eyeing the dressing room and starting to sweat.

"Well, I didn't chase *you* up the stairs. I didn't initiate the kiss." I'm innocent. I'm just as used as the girlfriend.

"Calm down, will you?"

Calm? How can I be calm when my blood is racing through my veins?

"Nothing happened," he grunts.

Nothing? The most romantic kiss of my life is considered nothing by the guy who kissed me? Well what if something had happened? What if this pillow under my dress was actually a baby? My stomach beneath the "stomach" starts to churn.

One of the dressing room doors swings open and Paul immediately walks away. "Hey, babe. Are you getting the black top? It made your boobs look good."

Her boobs do look good. They're almost as big as my mom's though she looks younger than Trinity, with wispy blonde hair and a nose ring. I feel sorry for her because her boyfriend is a creep, but at least she's not the other woman. She's not Corrine. I am.

Chapter 26

"So you really don't mind that I'm coming to McCall?"

Eric convinced me that his parents wouldn't mind if I came. And then he left the weekend before Christmas. Brooke and I had to work until the 23rd, so now the two of us are driving through the snow on Christmas Eve.

"Of course I don't mind," she chirps.

I think I would mind if my fiancée asked another woman to join us when I met his parents. But I don't tell Brooke this.

She raves on like usual. "I'm just thankful you can give me a ride. I'm a terrible driver in the snow."

The drive usually takes two hours, but traffic is especially slow because of the weather. It's pretty dangerous where the road winds along the river with no guardrail. My uncle once helped an older couple from their car after it slid over the edge and into the water. My aunt still hits him out of fear for his life whenever he tells the story— as if that will keep him from doing good deeds in the future.

Brooke hums along with the music for a minute—Amy Grant. Amy Grant and Christmas have become synonymous in my mind since her Christmas album is the only one of her CDs I listen to anymore.

"How often does a girl get to take a friend with her when meeting her in-laws?" She's talking again. "I think Eric really invited you up for me. I mean, you're more my friend than his, ya know?"

I *didn't* know that.

The sign for McCall greets us along the highway as the log cabins become more frequent. Brooke digs into her purse for directions.

"Turn right at My Father's House. I wonder if that's a church. Cool name. It kind of goes along with the many mansions in this area." She giggles.

I turn right. My Father's House is a burger joint.

"Left at the golf sign. I heard they have snowshoe golf up here during the winter festival. How fun would that be?"

They also have ice sculpting. It's very fun.

"Just think. The next time I'm up here I'll be Mrs. Brooke Austin." She squeals. "Eric and I will be able to share the same room. The same bed."

I get a strange tickle in my belly. I change the subject. "There's the golf sign. What next?"

I slow down as Brooke and I peer down a side street. I spot Eric's truck first, but you wouldn't know it by the noise Brooke makes.

"There it is! Eric's truck is parked out front. Oh, the cabin is adorable."

The cabin is an A-frame with a big porch and smoke sifting through the chimney. I smell the welcome scent of burning wood as soon as I stop the car and open my door.

Brooke jumps out as well. "The 4-Runner must be Trent's. Have you met Trent? He's Eric's brother."

Oh, yeah. The drunk guy Brooke stole the keys from the night she met Eric.

"He's separated from his wife right now because of his alcoholism." She's like a gossip encyclopedia. "But I think he brought his daughter with him."

The front door swings open. Eric looks good in jeans and a hooded sweatshirt. He leaps down the stairs and envelopes Brooke in a hug. "Hi, Bethany," he says to me over her head.

"Hi, yourself. Thanks again for the invite."

He turns toward the house with one arm still slung around Brooke's shoulder. "No problem. My family will love you. But that doesn't mean you can kiss them before you get to know them."

He winks at me and I roll my eyes. We'd had a short counseling session over the phone before he left. I'd made the mistake of telling him about Paul.

"Hey, you want to have this conversation in a boxing ring?" I not-so-subtly remind him of the damage I inflicted the last time he upset me.

"Ooh," Brooke taunts while Eric flinches.

An older woman comes through the front door with open arms. "Girls! I prayed you would have a safe trip. The roads are nasty today."

Brooke steps forward first. "Oh, I prayed too. But I had nothing to worry about. Bethany has four-wheel-drive. I'm so glad to be here and finally meet you."

The women hug between Eric and me. He stands tall and proud. I feel like an intruder for the moment, but his mom doesn't let me stay that way.

"Bethany," she turns to give me a hug and I find myself wrapped in her softness and the scent of lavender.

"Mrs. Austin." She's wonderful.

"It's Sharon. We're not formal up here."

I kiss her on the cheek after glancing up to make sure Eric was watching. Then as his mom turns her back to lead us inside I give a sassy little air kiss. Smack talk from my smackers.

Neither Sharon nor Brooke witnessed my attitude. They're already inside, and Brooke is listing off all of the attributes she loves about the place. No, it's Eric's dad who saw my show. He steps out from behind the house carrying a load of firewood.

"So this is Brooke." He shifts the logs to one arm so he can shake my hand.

I'm mentally more unbalanced than the firewood until I realize that Mr. Austin thinks he saw me blow a kiss to his son. Oops.

"No, Dad. This is *Brooke's* friend, Bethany."

Interesting how all of a sudden, I'm Brooke's friend. But I guess I am one of her bridesmaids now.

"Oh?" The man looks from me to Eric.

"Yes. Bethany, meet my dad, Gabe."

I grasp his huge hand. "Nice to meet you, sir. Thank you for inviting me into your home." I think I sound a little too Orphan Annie.

"You're not *in* my home yet. Come on, kids. Let's get out of this cold."

We follow Eric's dad. And even though this is the last place I would have expected to be for Christmas, I certainly feel welcome. And I'll get to ski, too.

The men plop down in two large chairs in front of the fire. Gabe asks about the wedding so I politely leave them alone. What do *I* have to say about the big day?

Sharon and Brooke sidestep each other in the tiny kitchen at the back of the house putting together a pie. It's clearly not Brooke's gifting. Or maybe she's really gifted at pie making, but she won't close her pie hole long enough to find out.

"I'm having a bridal shower in January if you want to come down. Actually I'm having two. My mom is throwing me one for housewife crack, as Eric calls it, but then my friends from work are giving me a lingerie party."

Sharon becomes busier as Brooke brings up the subject of underwear. Her fingers fly around the edges of the piecrust to create a scalloped look.

"I just love the little see-through baby-dolls with the g-string underwear."

I fake a cough to cover my surprise...and my smile. Does Brooke realize who she is talking to?

"I'm so excited for my wedding night. I feel like we've been waiting forever. There've been times when I've begged Eric to elope with me just so we could..."

Sharon's pinched face jerks up and her eyes meet mine. I give an apologetic smile and retreat so I don't have to hear the end of the sentence. Brooke is just too embarrassing to listen to.

I join the guys again and perch on the edge of the ottoman. When Gabe leans over to toss another log on the fire I
whisper a warning to Eric.

"Your fiancée is talking about sex with your mother."

My pastor sits up straighter than I've ever seen him before. He should have warned his mom about Brooke. Or he
should have brought a muzzle along for such situations. But
now it's too late, and he obviously doesn't know what to do.

The front door swings open, releasing a rush of wind so
cold it should be colored blue.

"We're back!" yells a big man standing at the entrance. He
reminds me of a grizzly bear. Next to him is his little cub
hidden underneath a red scarf.

Another round of introductions and hugs for Eric's brother and niece. Emma Austin is ushered to the kitchen by her
grandmother to drink hot chocolate and talk about her ad-
ventures in ice skating. I join them since Brooke is talking
to Trent. The kitchen is now safe.

Emma climbs up on the counter. "I'm good, Grandma!"
The little girl's cheeks are almost as red as the scarf I un-
wind. "I can go half-way around the rink without falling.
Can I get an ice skating dress?"

Sharon smiles at me. "It's always about the clothes with
Emma."

Emma gulps her cocoa and grins at me from underneath
a chocolate mustache. Her eyes are a beautiful green like
Eric's. "Do you ice skate?" She asks me.

"Sometimes." I used to play roller hockey with Christian, but
I don't think she cares about that. "I took my cousin's daughter
to the rink last summer. They have Monday Madness with free
lessons and zambonie rides. You would love it."

I'm in the middle of explaining how the zambonie is the
machine that cleans the ice when Eric calls Emma out to
play a game of Candy Land with him and Brooke.

Emma drops to the floor. "I always win Candy Land," she
tells me before running off.

I can't help smiling. "She's got positive self-esteem."

Sharon's smile fades away. "If only her dad did, too."

I shift my weight uncomfortably at her comment then sit down on a bar stool to watch her roll out dough for biscuits. I'm not sure what to say. "Eric's self-esteem seems pretty strong. Are Eric and Trent a lot different from each other?"

"Goodness." She pauses, probably figuring out how best to answer my question. "We were missionaries in Africa when Eric was little. He was the only white kid around. The other kids would rub his skin to see if the whiteness would rub off. Then they would follow him around the village. He's been a dynamic leader ever since."

This I did not know.

"When pregnant with Trent I was so sick we moved back to the states for health care. We lived in this big old castle in Pennsylvania that was actually a missionary compound. He cried a lot, and I didn't want it to disturb the other missionaries so I held him all the time. I believe that's why he's never really been able to do anything for himself. I've always wondered how his life might be different had we stayed in Africa."

She's looking down at the flour on her hands—they've gone still. I reach across the counter to touch her. "You can't blame yourself. We are who we choose to be. Trent can still turn his life around and start making good choices."

"I know." She shakes her head and picks up the biscuit cutter. "I just wish I could do it for him."

I climb off the stool to grab a cookie sheet and arrange the perfect circles of dough. "I'd say you're doing a lot for him right now. You love him unconditionally. You are being an example of Jesus to him."

"Thanks, sweetheart. That's nice of you to say." She wipes at a rogue tear and leaves a trail of flower on her face. "Trent is my mission field now."

I wonder if she knows about my family and what a mess has been made out of my parents' ministry. I hope she doesn't because I don't want to talk about it. "You know, I'd heard you guys used to be missionaries, but I wasn't aware that Eric lived in Africa with you."

Sharon's face lights up like sunshine on a cloudy day. "I should show you his baby book. My favorite story is of when he was learning to talk, and I was trying to teach him about Jesus. I would point up to heaven, but in Africa we had lizards on our ceiling. So he thought..."

I finish the sentence with her. "The lizards were Jesus!" That's hysterical.

Eric hears our laughter from the other room. "Are you talking about me in there, Mom?"

Sharon and I grin at each other conspiratorially. "I'm just getting started!" she calls back. Then she tilts her head toward the great room. "You go play, sweetheart. I'll finish up in here."

"Are you sure?" I slide the baking sheet into the oven. "I was hoping to hear more stories."

"Ahh. I'm going to get myself in trouble. Though I do enjoy talking to you." She rinses her hands off in the sink.

"Well, let me know if you need anything."

My mom was never this fun in the kitchen. She was graceful, but distracted. She was all about giving the gift of service and forgot about the gift of quality time. Quality time is my love language. And I'm loving my time at Eric's cabin for this reason. My family can't make time for me, but I've found a family who will.

I sink onto the floor in front of the coffee table, filled with contentment. Eric's not so relaxed.

"If I land on 'miss a turn' one more time, I'm tossing my gingerbread man across the room," he growls.

Brooke laughs as she stands up. "I went out first," she tells me before engaging Gabe in one of her one-sided conversations. I guess that wouldn't be considered 'engaging', would it?

"I'm going to beat you too, Uncle Eric," Emma sings.

"We'll see about that." Eric picks up the last card in the pile. It's the ice cream. "Ha!" He's ahead of her.

"No!" Emma covers her face dramatically.

"Here, I'll help." I pick up the cards to be shuffled. "Don't worry, Emma, you'll win," I say confidently as I place the candy cane in a position for Eric to pull.

Emma moves her guy. Eric flips over the next card.

"Hmm. The candy cane. I wonder how it got there." He narrows his eyes at me while moving back toward the bottom of the board.

"Yes!"

Emma celebrates as the game continues, but Eric lands on the secret passage. I pick up the deck and rig it again.

"Another candy cane?" Eric acts shocked.

Emma is almost to the finish line now. I shuffle the deck one last time for good measure.

"I don't believe it." Eric deadpans. "Another candy cane."

I smile innocently. "There are always more candy canes this time of year."

"I won! I won!" Emma jumps up and down. I expect her to shout, 'I'm going to Disneyland.'

"I won," Brooke corrects from across the room. "You got second."

This doesn't inhibit Emma's pleasure one bit. "I beat Uncle Eric. I beat Uncle Eric."

Eric shakes his head at me then turns when his fiancée calls.

"Eric...Oh, Eric..." Brooke is curled up on the window seat. "I'm under the mistletoe," she sings.

I can't keep my eyebrows from drawing together. Do guys really enjoy being pursued so hard? Could Brooke be any more obvious? I look at Eric, who has only got eyes for his fiancée. He smiles before crossing the room for a quick peck. Pathetic.

I look away to find Sharon's eyes on me. She doesn't seem too thrilled about her future daughter-in-law. I give her a little shrug. I'd feel the same way if I were her.

Chapter 27

As good as the ham was on Christmas Eve, breakfast is even better. The coffeecake is practically a cheesecake so I balance out the fat-gram-to-calories ratio with Sharon's amazing fruit salad—as if dieting worked that way.

"So," Trent teases from across the table the next morning. (Emma got us all up early to check out stockings.) "Brooke brought her personal trainer with her to keep her accountable for all the food she eats on Christmas."

Brooke laughs. "Oh my gosh. Bethany is a slave driver. I could eat everything on this table and still not consume more calories than I've burned this month."

"What about the rest of us?" Trent asks around a mouthful of food. "I feel guilty eating like a pig in front of her."

Eric takes a sip of sparkling cider. "I don't. I've seen her inhale a bowl of M & Ms in one sitting."

Brooke's jaw drops down toward this gorgeous cross necklace she's wearing. "You eat chocolate? And you look like that?"

"Hey." I nudge Eric with my elbow. "What happened to counselor/client privilege?"

Eric snorts. "I should charge you extra for eating all my candy."

"Candy?" Emma licks the cream cheese off her fork. She's wearing a princess tiara that she found in her stocking.

"No candy." Eric's dad can be a little gruff.

"How about presents?" Sharon smoothes out his rough edges.

"Yippee!" Emma runs across the wood floor then slides in her socks, colliding with the piles of presents under the Christmas tree.

I think of the gifts I bought for my family and wonder if they like them. I wish I could have given Jennica the bike in person.

"Let's get dressed first Emma," Sharon calls to her grand-daughter then stops behind my chair. "Dear, you didn't see your stocking."

I look up to see if she's talking to me. She is—which totally confuses me. "I don't have a stocking."

"Why?" Eric glances over. "Were you on Santa's naughty list?"

I make a face. "Of course not. I just figured he would leave my gifts at my house. I wouldn't want him to get mixed up with me traveling for the holidays."

Sharon places a hand on my left shoulder. "Well Santa found you. And he must have known about your M & M cravings." She hands me a felt stocking with an M & M candy cane sticking out the top.

It's not much, but it's more than I expected. I feel the grin pull my skin tight as I accept the gift. "You?" I ask Eric.

"Nope."

"I didn't want you to be left out," his mom says to me. "Though I didn't realize we share the same taste in candy."

I place the stocking next to my plate. "Well, I didn't used to eat any candy at all before I started seeing Eric."

"For counseling," Eric adds, making me realize what I just said.

I can't think of a good retort, and I'm too uncomfortable to meet anyone's eyes. Of course I meant for counseling. I focus my attention on Brooke who has moved over to the fireplace with Gabe. She has started a monologue about the first time she found out Santa Claus wasn't real. I hope Emma has already discovered the truth for herself and Brooke doesn't shatter the child's illusions. The woman doesn't know how to think before she speaks. Not even when she's asleep. I should know, we shared a bed last night.

"Oh. Eric," I choose to forget my embarrassment and move on. "I hate to tell you, but Brooke talks in her sleep."

Eric smiles in surprise and his eyes start to twinkle. "What did she say?"

I rack my brain. It had been the middle of the night and I told myself I wouldn't forget as I fell back to sleep, but... "It didn't make enough sense for me to remember."

"Darn it." Eric looks toward his fiancée. "Honey, did you know you talk in your sleep?"

Brooke prances over. "What? I talk in my sleep? Why do you think that?"

"You said something last night," I explain.

"Really? Oh no. I did have a weird dream, but I can't remember it now."

Eric rubs his hands together. "This is going to be fun."

Brooke giggles and falls into his lap. I hadn't expected Eric's reaction. I would think that when the person you spend the most time with talks all day, you wouldn't want to listen to her at night, too. I bet Brooke falls asleep talking.

I get up to help with the dishes while the happy couple teases and tickles each other. It's annoying. I think about taking a quick shower—I don't actually do it because when you are used to showering after sweating for hours at the gym all other showers seem pointless. So I just put on my one pair of jeans. They're tighter than I remember. I must be bloated from breakfast.

Opening gifts is fun. Eric wears a Santa cap and passes out the packages one at a time. I brought the presents from my family so I have something to open, too, but watching Emma is the highlight of the morning. By the time we finish, she is dressed in an ice skating costume (grandmas read minds, you know) and a bike helmet (from Brooke—to go along with the bike Eric bought her.)

Gabe whips out his new board game for entertainment. I'm kicking everybody's butt in the charades portion, so when Eric and I are supposed to act for our teams at the same time he concedes and goes into the kitchen to help his mom. I'm thinking Sharon never leaves the kitchen. I offer to bring back a round of hot chocolate as my team moves into the winner's circle.

"She's not bad for a personal trainer," Trent says to Brooke, as I get up.

I'm still laughing at my impersonation of Jennifer Lopez as I climb down from the loft. No wonder Eric bowed out. Or maybe he's just thinking of the way I came onto him when we first met, and I had J. Lo's name taped on my back. I'm glad we can be friends now.

"So what do you think of Brooke?" Eric's voice travels from the kitchen and I tune in to listen on my way to join him.

"She's something else." Sharon would make a good politician.

Eric knows his mom too well. "Did she make you uncomfortable with her...candor?"

Sharon pauses. "There are some things I would rather not know."

Eric sighs. "She's honest."

"She's immature."

I freeze in the silence that ensues. Sharon's response was so quick that I'm betting she's regretting it.

"I'm sorry," she says softly. "I guess I just expected you to fall for someone as um...deep as you."

"I find Brooke refreshing and real. Those are respectable qualities." His voice has a bite to it.

I take a couple of quiet steps backwards. Maybe I can escape to the bathroom.

"Will you try to get to know her?" Now he sounds challenging.

"Naturally." I hear movement, and I guess that she's trying to make light of the situation. "I really like getting to know Brooke's friend, Bethany. She's very thoughtful and easy to talk to."

I take two steps forward. I like Sharon, too. I can interrupt the discussion now.

"Mom, she connects with everybody." Eric's words are nice, but his tone is judgmental.

My eyebrows draw together as I stop again.

"She's manipulative. She knows how to make people feel good about themselves so they like to be around her. But there are no real roots to her relationships. She'll kiss a stranger just for fun."

Now that blow was below the belt. What the heck? I'm so real with Eric that it's painful. I thought he was one of the few people who could know my garbage and still like me. I mean, he's my pastor, so he's supposed to love me. But here he is telling my secrets behind my back.

I see Sharon's elbow stick out beyond the corner, and I picture her putting her hand on her hip. I feel like I've just let her down, but she stands up for me. "Perhaps she's not manipulative, but skilled at conversation. And didn't you see that her motivational gift is encouragement. She makes other people feel good about themselves because God has given her that gift. So what if she knows how to have fun? You need a little more of that in your life."

Hearing Sharon's words makes me mad. I'm not mad at her. I'm mad at Eric. Before she reasoned with him I felt sorry for myself. I felt like scum. But she makes me sound like an amazing person. Who is Eric to put a negative twist on it?

"Mom," he grunts. "We're not talking about Bethany. We're talking about Brooke. She's the one I'm getting married to on Valentine's Day."

"I know." Sharon's voice is quiet. "You're in my prayers."

My emotions are reeling. They've just been yanked all over the map. I don't know what to think, and apparently I'm not thinking because I'm still standing in the middle of the family room when Eric steps out of the kitchen.

He sees me and the anger on his face drains away into what looks like guilt. I blink quickly as our eyes meet and my own anger melts away to devastation. I give a little shake of my head. I wish I was anywhere but here at the moment. If I hadn't just heard him rip me apart then I would still think he cared about me and my family, I wouldn't feel like running away from him forever, and I'd be able to breathe.

He reaches out helplessly. "Bethany..."

I have to get away. Until I do I'll have to pretend I'm fine—pretend his words don't sting like the icy winds outside. "I'm getting hot chocolate," I choke.

I walk past him on autopilot and watch as my hands dig through the pantry for the blue canister. I don't look at Sharon because I don't want to see the empathy on her face.

Eric follows me in. "Bethany," he says again.

My eyes start to burn and my throat constricts. With all I've been through, how can this even affect me? My own dad didn't want to spend Christmas with me, why should I expect more from another man?

I remove four mugs from the mug tree and fill them with tap water. I'm going to focus on my task. Nothing else matters.

I turn to stick the water in the microwave but Eric is in my way. I don't look up from his chest. I can't if I'm going to keep from crying. I hold out two mugs. "Will you heat these up?" My voice is overly loud, but he takes them quietly.

I hear soft footsteps as Sharon leaves us alone. I need to get out of the kitchen, too. I move to pass Eric, but his arm shoots in front of me sloshing water on his sleeve.

I'm careful not to touch him. "Please move."

"Look at me first."

I am. I'm looking at his arm. But I don't think that answer will appease him. I lift my eyes without moving my head.

His green eyes plead with me. "I'm sorry. I was out of line."

"Yeah." My laugh sounds hollow—bitter.

He sets the mugs down on the counter and runs one hand over his face. As soon as he lets down his guard, I'm outta there. He whirls after me. I can't focus on him, though. Brooke is climbing down the ladder from the loft. Where am I supposed to go? I hang a left and retreat to the room we shared—it's the room Brooke will share with Eric next year. I'm only in the way. What am I doing here? Sharon needs to get to know Brooke. I think "connect with" was the term Eric used.

He's right behind me, though he can't really close the door with the two of us in here. That would be inappropriate for one, but also attract excessive attention. I grab my suitcase.

"What are you doing?" he demands.

I'm not going to lose it. Deep breath—more like a shaky breath. "Thanks for inviting me Eric, but I don't belong."

"Come on. I didn't really mean what I said."

I must trust way too easily if he thinks I'm going to buy that line. "Then why did you say it?" I stop him with my hand. "Wait. I don't want to know."

"Please. Forgive me. I was just...I don't know, upset that Mom was comparing Brooke to you, I guess."

I stare him down. My tears have dried up. I'm going numb, which with all I've been through would probably be a preferable state. "I didn't experience your mom that way. I think she was done talking about Brooke. She was only remarking on the really good conversations we'd had." And they were good. "I like your mom. I'm not just putting on a show so she'll like me. And by the way she stood up for me, I think she likes me more than I like myself right now."

"Okay. Okay. You're acting on emotions. You don't have to leave."

What am I supposed to do? Hang out for dinner with such an awkward undercurrent?

He continues. "Please. You're right. I'm wrong."

Now I'm starting to feel sorry for him. Starting to, I said—I'm not there yet. "It's not about being right or wrong. It's about working or not working. And this isn't working. Didn't you teach me that little tool?"

Eric's eyes wander the ceiling. "What can I do to make it up to you?"

I'd been looking forward to skiing with him the next day. That's what I really want. "You can carry my bag to my car while I thank your parents for their hospitality."

"I'm an idiot."

I leave him to his accurate conclusion. Sharon's eyes study me with concern as I thank her for making me feel welcome. I don't mention the way she stood up for me because Brooke is with us, and all I've told Brooke is that I want to get home to my family.

Sharon squeezes my hand. "I've enjoyed getting to know you Bethany. You are a very special woman. Don't let anyone tell you differently."

Brooke totally misses the meaning of the message, but what should I expect? "With you gone I can eat all the pie I want," she laughs. "But I'll be good. And I'll miss you."

"Merry Christmas," I call to all as I follow Eric out the door.

He swings my suitcase into the rear of the Jeep. "I shouldn't have said what I did," he apologizes again.

"But you believe it." And he should know me best, right?

He closes the rear door. "My mom was probably closer to the truth. You've got a gift. But God has given us all different gifts to balance each other out. Each gift has drawbacks. Like my gift of perception. I'm often overly negative."

"Noooo," I say in mock shock.

He gives me a sad smile. I open my car door to get in and see the gift bag that I hadn't been sure whether to put under the tree or not. Well, it's too late to worry about what Eric thinks of me now. He's made his professional opinion clear.

"Here you go." I hand him the sparkly red bag.

"Oh, man. You saved this just to make me feel even worse right now, didn't you?"

"Is it working?"

"Yeah. I shouldn't accept it. I don't deserve it. I..."

I interrupt him. "Too true. But I gave it to you anyway. So open it."

Eric's eyes tell me again that he is sorry as he flips the bag over. I know what the gift is so I keep looking at his face. I should still be ticked at him, but for some reason I feel closer to him than ever. As if he's a brother I can despise at one moment then be crazy about the next.

184

"Thanks Bethany." His voice is soft and low. I love the sound of it.

I gave him a couple of documentaries on Bible times. An archeologist found remnants of chariot wheels from the time of Moses at the bottom of a sea. "Have you seen it yet? I know you like the history channel, and this is kind of a Christian version."

"I've heard of it, but I haven't seen it." He turns the DVDs over in his hands. "When I was little I wanted to be either a pastor or Indiana Jones. This is perfect."

I chuckle warmly. "When I was little I wanted to be either a professional volleyball player or a unicorn."

His eyes crinkle at the sides. "I got you something too, but..." He looks down. "Brooke saw me wrapping it and thought it was for her. She put it on and I couldn't take it away from her. I'm totally whipped, aren't I?"

Unfortunately. I wonder what he bought me. Oh... "Was it the necklace she had on this morning?" It was antique-looking bronze cross on a ribbon.

"Yeah," he mutters and runs a hand down his face.

"It was lovely." And now I'm even more disappointed.

Eric shrugs. "I thought it might encourage you with your witnessing."

"Because I suck at it compared to your fiancée?"

Eric's eyes meet mine. "That's not what I meant."

The front door of the cabin swings open. Brooke pops her head out. "Eric! Are you coming to eat? Oh, Bethany, I thought you'd left. Have a safe trip."

I climb in my car then pause. "One more thing."

I've got his full attention even though Brooke is still talking.

"Just because I connect with you, doesn't mean I connect with everybody. Merry Christmas."

Chapter 28

I climb from the backseat of Christian's Acura. "This is our pastor's house?" I ask in awe. My dad was a pastor and we never lived in a house half this size or nearly this new.

Christian shrugs as if it's nothing—as if he's responsible for the splendor before me. "I pay my tithe."

Laurel walks up the pathway with me and gives me a serious answer. "Eric's brother is in construction. Every two years they build themselves new homes for a fraction of what they're worth. Eric makes more from real estate than he does from Grace Chapel."

Huh. I guess this way Eric doesn't have to have a second job like many pastors of small churches do. And the perks are amazing.

I climb the steps to a beautiful wooden door that could easily be ten feet tall. It's a monster house.

The door is yanked open by Brooke. "Happy New Year!" She's wearing glasses with the year printed on them. Somehow she pulls it off without looking ridiculous.

"Happy New Year," we chorus back to her.

Brooke pulls me in, rips my parka off my shoulders, and tosses it on a nearby table. She leads me past the office behind French doors on my right and the formal dining room framed by Roman columns on my left.

"I'm going to live here soon," she squeals. She waves her free arm around while she gives me the tour. "I want to paint the kitchen red. Not a cherry red, but more like spaghetti sauce. The coffee shop around the corner from the preschool uses that color. They also have warm sunshine yellow walls, which I want to do in the living room."

We stop in front of a stone fireplace and I step closer to the warmth. "If I ever buy a home it's got to have a fireplace," I say.

Brooke does a little cheerleader clap. "This house has a fireplace in the master bedroom, too. Isn't that romantic?"

I sigh. If I ever get a house with a fireplace in the bedroom it would not be romantic because I don't plan to share it with anybody. The thought kind of makes me sad.

"Come on," she takes off down a hallway. "You've only seen a third of the house."

I follow, wondering what more there could be. The hallway Ts with another hallway. I see two bedrooms and two staircases—one going up, one going down.

Brooke pushes a bedroom doorway open. "These bedrooms have a connecting bathroom, so I'm going to have to have twin girls."

Uh, right.

"Then our son will sleep downstairs. Come on."

Nobody is in the basement and it feels cold, but it would be the perfect environment for working out. Eric even has a weight bench and treadmill set up in the main room.

"This will be the play room. Eric will have to move his icky exercise equipment when I get pregnant. Or we can sell it since he works out at the gym anyway."

I wonder where Eric is. I didn't see him in any of the rooms we'd been through so far.

"Here is our son's room." She says it as if the poor boy is already born. "Eric's a big Boise State Broncos fan so we'll paint it orange and blue. And this is the guest bedroom. I'm thinking of going with a lavender theme. Maybe get one of those canopy beds from the Pottery Barn catalogue."

I look around the barren rooms. This house is too huge for a bachelor. Currently he doesn't have enough stuff to fill the place.

Brooke runs out of words for a rare moment—maybe she's waiting for me to tell her how lucky she is.

"You're so lucky."

"I know. It's like a fairy tale. Just wait until you see the bonus room. I've saved the best for last."

Brooke races up the two sets of stairs like she's spent a lot of time on a stair stepper—which she has, thanks to me. I take the stairs two at a time to catch up. I collide into her back when we reach the top. Oh, joy. She's in Eric's embrace. It was his solid chest that stopped her.

I look around the room full of church members so I can ignore the happy couple. On my left is a media area where an overhead projector displays oversized video games on a screen. On my right are a pool table and a pinball machine. I'll bet the rest of the house is just for show. This is where Eric lives.

"Nice place," I say casually.

Brooke bounces away. I don't know where she's going and I don't look to see.

"It's huge, huh? The basement and bonus room are a cheap way to add square footage. And we did it right before construction costs skyrocketed. My next house isn't going to be this big." Eric explains as if he's embarrassed by the luxury. "Did you get the full tour?"

"From tour guide Barbie."

"She's just a little excited."

"A little? She has your children's rooms picked out and decorated."

Eric chuckles and leans back against a marble wet bar. "I've tried telling her that won't happen. We have to move in a year. Not only will we not be having children here, but we won't be painting the walls anything but white."

I feel a little bad for Brooke. Maybe I can show her the article in Better Homes and Gardens where the entire decor is white with wood accents. It has a very calming feel to it. "Why do you have to move?"

"That's the whole reason I built the house. It's income, which we'll need if she's going to have twins." Eric's lips turn up, making fun of his fiancée.

I smile too and secretly wonder if he's marrying Brooke just for the blonde jokes. She's pretty easy to make fun of.

"Plus," he tilts his head, "it would offend some members of my congregation if I owned such a large house."

His comment makes me frown. "Really? That seems kind of petty."

"Yeah, well Rick Warren set the bar."

Rick Warren, the pastor who wrote *Purpose Driven Life*, gave a lot of his earnings back to his church, and never moved from the parsonage. He's the type who tithes ninety percent and only keeps ten percent for himself. Amazing, I know, but Eric built this house. He should be able to enjoy it and thank God for the blessing. It's not like he's a televangelist begging for money.

"Well, maybe if you'd buy new couches for your office, they wouldn't make such a big deal about it." I suggest the absurd.

He gives a mock thoughtful nod. "I'll think about it."

I'm giggling as Mick joins us.

"Hi, Bethany."

"Hi, Mick." The New Year's glasses aren't so attractive on his sinister looking face.

Eric slips away leaving the two of us standing awkwardly.

"Did you have a good Christmas?" Mick tries to start a conversation.

I try not to grimace thinking about how I spent the holiday. "It was okay, but I'm ready for a new year."

"Yeah," he sips his soda. "Me too."

"Well, I'm going to go find my brother. I'll talk to you later."

"Okay. Later."

Christian and Laurel aren't upstairs. I head back down to the first floor and find them in front of the fireplace with the lights off. They're all alone and sharing an intimate moment.

"Hi guys," I flop down on the couch set at a right angle from them. "Am I interrupting anything?"

Laurel leans her head on Christian's shoulder. "We're just practicing for our New Year's kiss."

I sink lower in my seat. "I don't have anybody to kiss," I pout. Then I think of Mick. I wonder. Maybe if he took off his party glasses...

There's a flat screen television over the fireplace. Enough of this romantic garbage. "Do you guys want to watch the ball drop in Times Square?"

Christian shifts his gaze from his wife to me. "I think you've mistaken me for a fourteen-year-old girl."

I thin my lips and narrow my eyes. I'm trying not to laugh at my brother's obnoxiousness. It would only encourage him.

Eric appears from the hallway and grabs a case of soda from the kitchen behind us. "You guys are missing the party."

"Christian and Laurel have to practice their kissing for the midnight hour," I explain to get even with man across from me.

Unfortunately he's still a boy—he always has to have the upper hand. "And Bethany is pouting because she has no one to kiss."

I cross my arms defensively. "Mick might kiss me."

Eric sets the soda down and plops onto the sofa beside me. "Don't you think you've kissed enough guys recently?"

Will he ever let it drop? "I made a mistake...once."

Christian chuckles and looks at Eric. "I seem to recall you kissing somebody by mistake, too, my man."

My eyebrows shoot up. I scoot to the edge of my seat. This is juicy news. "Who was it?" Who had Eric kissed? Huh-ha! And after all the grief he's given me.

"It was me." Laurel's face is tinged pink.

"What?" I swivel from my sister-in-law back to Eric. Laurel's married. It must have been ages ago. They dated and I didn't know it? I'm surprised there's no bad blood.

"It wasn't a mistake," Eric corrects. "It was an accident... just the other day."

My jaw drops into my lap. Even Laurel's accidents get her kissed by handsome men. So unfair. She's not even looking at us now, but hiding her face in Christian's shirt.

"How?" I'm holding my breath.

Christian chuckles mercilessly. "He was congratulating us on conceiving a child after you told him the news. He went to kiss Laurel on the cheek just as she turned her head. Got her right on the mouth."

"Ahhh," I squeal. Unbelievable. I wonder what an accidental kiss would feel like. Probably not so good with your husband watching, but it my case...

The doorbell rings. Eric hops up to answer, giving Laurel time to come back out of her shell. "I've never been so embarrassed," she whispers to me.

We hear Eric greet whoever is at the door. It's a male and a female. The woman's voice sounds familiar. It sounds like my sister. I look at Christian to see if he is having the same reaction. He's staring at the ceiling.

I watch in anticipation to see who Eric leads into the house— who it is that sounds like Trinity. I wonder if she'll be like Trinity. Maybe she's the exact opposite and moved from the East Coast out to Boise to be with some Idahoan she met online.

Eric's eyes meet mine as he comes around the corner. I can't read his expression. He's just watching me. Strange. I look past him at a girl with chin-length dark hair flipped up on the edges. It's hard to see in the firelight, but she's got the same dark eyeliner that Trinity likes to wear.

"Bethany! Christian! Laurel!"

It's a Trinity impersonator.

"It's so good to see you guys. We've been driving for, like, six days. Are you surprised?"

I think of Chevy Chase's line in the movie Christmas Vacation. *I wouldn't be more surprised if I woke up with my head sewn to the carpet.*

Laurel gasps. "How did you find us here?"

Trinity hops over the back of the couch to land in the seat Eric had vacated. "Christian."

Laurel and I turn accusing eyes on my brother. He lifts up his hands innocently. "I told her on the phone that we were going to a party at my pastor's house. I had no idea they were in town."

"We looked him up," Trinity exclaims. She turns toward me and pulls me into a hug. I don't remember her being this happy when she left.

Christian stands up to shake hands with the loser Trinity brought home with her. He looks like a stray dog. Maybe it's because he's wearing a dog collar.

"Guys, meet Donovan." She introduces the rest of us.

Donovan seems shy. I wonder if he writes poetry and plays the guitar when he's not seducing women over the Internet.

"Well," Eric speaks up as we quiet down. "Why don't you all come upstairs? The countdown is going to start in a few minutes."

He's so polite. He wants to be at the party, but he doesn't want to leave us behind. At the moment I wouldn't mind leaving everyone else behind. I mean, I'm thrilled that my sister's home, but has she thought past today? Is she planning to stay here? And where? Is her new pet going to stay? Are they going to get jobs? This is crazy.

We go upstairs. Eric has a bowl of M & Ms on the bar. I wonder if he bought them just for me. I stuff a few in my mouth so I don't have to talk.

The countdown begins. "10...9...8...7...6..."

Laurel snuggles up to Christian again. Brooke bounces over to Eric. Even Trinity has someone. My eyes scan the room for Mick. The guy is holding a pool cue. I'm sure he would find a warm body preferable to a piece of wood. I take a step forward, but then my eyes meet Eric's.

"5...4...3..."

Eric's eyes narrow and he gives just a little shake of his head. He's like a brother and a father combined. He's a bother. I narrow my eyes right back, but stay in place.

"2...1...Happy New Year!"

Cheers rise all around me. This has got to be the only time when married couples in the church make out in public.

And I'm right in the middle of it.

Mick crushes a soda can on his forehead. Okay, maybe I'm glad I wasn't there for that.

A noisemaker pierces the air. I look the direction it's coming from. Trinity stands up on a chair. "I've got an announcement to make."

What in the world? Trinity doesn't even know these people. Did she get drunk before she came over?

"You may not know me," she starts. Where can she go from there? "I'm Trinity Light. I'm Christian and Bethany's sister." Oh good, she's pulled me into this. "I left here a few months ago to find a guy I had met online. Donovan, come here."

Donovan takes a baby step and gives a little wave.

"The reason we drove out to Boise, is because on Christmas Day, Donovan proposed to me."

I gasp and the M & Ms in my stomach turn to lead.

Trinity's bright smile beams down on me. "So, I just wanted to announce that...I'm getting married!"

A couple catcalls come from Mick's direction. Clapping from all sides of me. The noise fades away as I focus on my sister. She's impulsive. I always knew that. But this is insane.

First of all, why would she want to get married after what happened to Dad and Mom? And second, how well does she know this guy? People can make up all kinds of lies over the internet. Has she checked to see if anything he said was true? Third, I don't know the guy. If she expects her family's support, we need to know what we are supporting.

She's been gone for almost a year then just swoops in out of nowhere and drops a bomb. Do Mom and Dad even know? How soon do they want to get married? I mean, she doesn't even know that Laurel is pregnant. I gasp. Is Trinity pregnant?

Whoa. I've got to talk to her. I spin on my heel to find her in the midst of well-wishers. She always did know how to draw a crowd, but I'm going to have to pull her out of that crowd. I've got to talk some sense into her.

I storm past the bar. An arm shoots out in front of me, blocking my path. It's Eric.

I don't have time for him right now. My sister's life is in jeopardy.

Eric bullies me down a couple of stairs. "Don't do it, Bethany."

"Don't do what?" I ask innocently. I just need to get past him.

"Don't steal her moment."

He knows me too well. "She's making a mistake," I hiss through my teeth. "Did you see that guy? He can't even take care of himself. How is he supposed to take care of her?"

"This is not the time to talk sense into her. She's happy. So be happy for her."

I want to kick something. Or shake something. Star's dance class would do me some good right about now. "How can I? I don't even know her. She left me, Eric. And I'm supposed to be happy for her?"

His calmness is so irritating. "Bethany, you're being like the prodigal son's brother in the Bible."

That stung. "How would you feel in this situation?" I challenge him.

Eric takes his arm off the wall. This would be my chance to dart past, but I wait for his response.

"I would feel the same way," he admits.

Ha. Victory is mine.

"But," he adds, negating everything he just said. "I wouldn't let my feelings get in the way of supporting the ones I love."

The fight drains out of me. I need a white flag to wave.

"Unconditional love," he says. "That's what Trinity needs right now."

And he's right. It's just so much easier to receive than to give.

Eric steps out of my way. "It's a party. Go celebrate."

My voice is devoid of joy. I speak in a defeated monotone. "Happy New Years."

Chapter 29

Trinity is staying with me. Donovan is at Christian's house. They've been living together for the past year so I think it's a little too late to separate them. It's not like we can restore Trinity's virginity or anything. Besides, she's driving me crazy. Or maybe it's the fact that I haven't spoken my true feelings yet that is driving me crazy. They're ready to boil over the surface any minute, but I decided I need to meet with Eric before I talk to her so that I'll be ready (and perhaps rational) during the confrontation.

"How are you holding up?" he asks as I arrive on Tuesday night.

"She's a slob." I collapse on his couch just glad that I don't have to move a pile of my sister's laundry to sit down. "And she barrows my clothes without asking. I looked everywhere for my bungee shoes this morning only to find out that she was wearing them."

Eric nods, but I don't see the sympathy I deserve. "What are you going to do about it?" he asks.

Yes, I'm being a victim, but it's not my fault…Hey, that would make a great bumper sticker or keychain or something.

"Honestly, I want her to find her own place. The only problem is that she would be looking for an apartment to share with Donovan."

Eric keeps asking annoying questions. "So you still don't like the guy?"

What's to like? "You saw him at church on Sunday. He didn't sing. He didn't even stand up. And he drew pictures all through your sermon. Even if I did like him, he's not a Christian and should not be getting married to Trinity."

Eric plays such a great devil's advocate—an interesting role for a pastor. "He agreed to marriage counseling with me. And he's not living with Trinity right now. He obviously cares for her and wants to make this work. The whole church thing could be brand new to him."

I frown because I don't want to agree.

"Have you talked with Trinity yet?"

"No." I look down. "She asked me to be her Maid-of-Honor."

"Does that surprise you?"

I sigh. "No. But she'll probably change her mind once I tell her that I think she's ruining her life."

Eric looks slightly amused. "Maybe you should phrase it differently."

He makes life sound so easy. "Like tell her that I'm worried about her?"

"Sure. Tell her how you experience her without being judgmental. State how you see her decision and why it worries you."

I think over Eric's suggestion. What could I say that she doesn't know? Does she have a blind spot? "I see her as impulsive, and it keeps her from seeking God first in her decisions."

Eric nods emphatically. "There's no guarantee on how she's going to receive it. But when your words are spoken out of love, not out of fear, you're, in a way, giving her medicine."

I think about that. If she chooses to listen, to take the medicine, she'll grow stronger and healthier. That could be said for each one of us. I wonder what kind of medicine I need to take. My thoughts return to Christmas day.

"So I should accept what you said about me at your parent's cabin as medicine? I can learn about myself from the way you "experienced" me?" It hurts to ask the questions, and I hope that Eric just apologizes again and simply tells me how amazing I am.

Eric looks down at his interlaced fingers. "What I said was not out of love, Bethany. It was out of fear of what my parents thought of Brooke. But yes, at that moment, I did experience you as manipulative and shallow."

I feel an emptiness inside me start to grow. I'm a giving person. I care about people like Star and Dee Dee and Eric. It hurts to think that maybe deep down I'm self-centered.

"The thing is," Eric pauses to meet my eyes, "you don't have to own feedback. Just because I saw you as manipulative, it doesn't mean you are manipulative. You simply acknowledge my position and weigh it carefully. What might you be doing to make others think you are manipulative? Some feedback is good, some is not, but it's your choice to grow."

I quote a line from Eric's last sermon titled: MORE. "If we think we've arrived, we're dead." I lean back and rest my head. It's overwhelming to question whether my motives had been in the right place through attempts to reunite family.

The sock club. Christian's birthday gift. I was manipulating my cousins.

Guilting my dad. Yelling over the phone. I was trying to manipulate him into coming for Christmas.

The talk I'm planning for Trinity. I want to stop her wedding. I'm manipulative.

"All this time I've been trying to fix everyone else when the problem is me." Oh, I'm a mess.

"Bethany."

"You're right. I'm just feeling sorry for myself, and I think it's everyone else's fault. So if I fix them, I'll be okay."

"Bethany."

"When I was little Christian once said, 'Bethany helps people so everyone will adore her.'"

"Stop, Bethany." Eric's raised voice gets my attention. "You're owning all of it. I'm not entirely right. I only see a part of you. My mom saw another part. Balance it out. What are your strengths? What are your weaknesses? Now learn from them."

I don't want to be here. I want to disappear until I've licked my wounds. What's the saying? *When I point one fin-*

ger, I've got the rest pointing back at me. I take a deep breath, rolling my head back then angling it so I could see Eric. "Should I not talk to Trinity at all?"

Eric studies me for a moment. "You've made some valid points that it sounds like she needs to hear. Ask her first if you can give her some feedback. And remember that after you state your beliefs, you need to let her choose what to do with them. It's her life."

He's right. And I don't want him to be. "She met him on-line," I groan.

Eric's eyes crinkle at the corners. "Brooke and I went to a marriage conference a few months ago and a good portion of the engaged couples met through the Internet. It's not that uncommon anymore."

I shift in my seat thinking about how I'm going to be in Eric's wedding, too. I groan. "Everybody is changing so much. Dad's got a new life. Mom got a boob job. Christian and Laurel are having a baby. Trinity's getting married. You're getting married."

"Those aren't bad things." Eric pauses.

My arms flop on the couch in an attempt to shrug. All the energy has drained out of me. "I wasn't ready for them."

Eric does look sympathetic this time. Okay, he's not so bad. "It sounds like you were in a comfort zone. And now you're being pushed out."

"No kidding."

"Maybe you need a change, too." Eric suggests.

That's an interesting thought. But I don't know what I would change. I reevaluate my life. "My business is great. I'm not planning to get married or to have kids. My church is okay except for the pastor who thinks he's Dr. Phil."

"Hey."

I send him a small smile to let him know I'm just giving him a bad time.

Eric's eyes turn serious as if he's got more psychoanalysis to share. "What about your apartment?"

I love my apartment. "Getting Trinity out of there will be a good change."

Eric leans forward and supports his chin with his clasped hands. "Have you thought about getting out of there yourself?"

I'm surprised by the idea, then surprised that I'm surprised. It's an intriguing thought. "It would be nice to have more room."

Eric's enthusiasm builds. "Have you thought about buying a house?"

"Well, yeah. Eventually."

"My brother is building in a subdivision of smaller houses. The mortgage wouldn't be any more than rent. Now is a really good time to buy, and Trent could get you a deal."

Visions of a large kitchen and a fireplace float through my mind. It wouldn't be Eric's monster house, but I don't need that much space. A tiny house would be a mansion compared to my apartment. I'm suddenly full of energy. "Would I be able to pick my own floor plan? My own colors?"

"Yeah, if you get on it right away." Eric pauses. "Do you have enough money saved for a down payment?"

I hope so. I should. "I need to check with Jade. She does all the finances from the studio. I have quite a bit saved for a Reformer—that's Pilates equipment—but I could always buy one later."

Eric's thrilled. He grabs the phone to call his brother right away.

I fill like a huge weight has lifted off my shoulders. I'm actually doing something. For the first time in a long time, I'll be too distracted by my own plans to meddle in other people's.

I go through my checklist of changes once again: Dad remarried. Mom top heavy. Christian parenting. Trinity and Eric married—not to each other of course. Me a homeowner. Maybe it's not so bad.

Chapter 30

I haven't seen Star for weeks. Christmas and New Year's were both on Thursdays so she didn't have class. I'm kind of glad though. When she left my apartment last time I wasn't at the top of her favorite people list. I hope she's cooled off by now because I'm feeling pretty guilty.

Trinity sits on the bench with me outside the aerobics room waiting for the core class to finish. Star doesn't even know my sister's big news. And though Trinity hates any kind of organized exercise, she came with me to surprise Star.

I did get my chance to talk with Trinity. She listened with a hard heart then stated matter-of-factly, "Well, if you're worried about Donovan not being a Christian, then pray for him. I am."

I didn't say anything after that. For one, I hadn't prayed at all for Donovan. I'd been trying to fix stuff on my own again. Secondly, to hear that Trinity prays was a big relief for me. For all I knew, she could have joined Wicca and started listening to Marilyn Manson. But no, she has a better relationship with God than I do.

Half the core class starts to stream out the door to go take a spinning class, lift weights or go home. The other half stays put for Jam. Trinity and I join them.

"How bad is it going to be?" Trinity asks nervously. She's worried about dancing, not about seeing Star—the exact opposite from me.

"Just have fun with it," I encourage. It's gonna be impossible for her to remember all the moves, let alone move to the beat, but I don't want to scare her.

An African-American woman with short-short (but cute) hair moves to the front of the room. She puts the headset microphone over her head.

LIGHTEN UP

"It looks like Star's not here today." I try to keep the relief out of my voice.

Trinity points toward the woman's back. "That's not Star?"

Trinity has been gone so long she must have forgotten what our cousin looks like. "No. Star has lots of long braids. She'd never cut them..."

I stop as the instructor turns around. She's got Star's sultry eyes and bright smile.

"That *is* Star," Trinity announces triumphantly. "Star!" She jogs toward our cousin.

Star looks up, and it takes her a minute to recognize Trinity. "Hey, girlfriend. You're back in the B.O.I." She makes Boise sound ghetto.

"And I'm engaged!" I follow Trinity so I'm close enough to hear the announcement.

Star hugs her. "Congratulations!" Her voice reverberates over the loudspeaker. She switches off her mike—which is a first. (She's a total microphone hog. I once made the mistake of going to a karaoke club with her and found out the hard way.) "You wanna celebrate after class?" she asks. "This calls for some serious ice cream. And you've got to see Jennica. She was only one when you left, I think. Now, she's almost a preschooler!"

I'm still getting used to the chic cut. "Your hair!" I blurt.

Star fingers what is left of her locks. "Drastic, I know. I'll tell you about it later. We can go pick up some bridal magazines and take them to Maggie Moos. How's that sound?"

"Great!" Trinity gushes. She'll be in heaven.

"Great," I echo, but I'm not thinking about weddings or ice cream. I'm just glad Star wants to talk to me again.

Trinity is worse at Body Jam than I expected. I should have given her a private coaching session beforehand. But she's in too good a mood to mind her three left feet—notice I said three and not two. She has a good time laughing at herself, so she got an abdominal workout even if she didn't burn many calories.

We meet Star and Jennica at Maggie Moos. Jennica giggles at the cartoon paintings of a female cow all over the walls. Trinity orders buttery popcorn flavored ice cream mixed with nuts and caramel. She claims it tastes like caramel corn—and I thought popcorn flavored jellybeans were bad. Star orders a banana split with the award winning vanilla and chocolate flavors and an ice cream cupcake for her daughter. I try not to let my concern show, but Star reads my face as if she grew up with me or something. I order a mango smoothie.

"Lighten up," Star says, which I find a little ironic.

We crowd around a tiny table and Trinity starts flipping through fragrant magazines that are more about the ads than anything else. I wonder if Mom and Dad will be able to pay for the wedding or if they'll even want to. Trinity hasn't talked to either of them as far as I know.

"When are you planning to get married?" I ask.

"As soon as possible," Trinity giggles, reminding me of Brooke.

I consider pointing out that there is a reason for an engagement period. You know, like if somebody has a change of heart. Instead I say, "I thought you always wanted an outside wedding." This wouldn't be possible for a good four months.

"Now I'm thinking a Valentine's wedding would be romantic."

My heart stops. "I'm already in a Valentine's wedding," I say. Star's eyebrow shoots up.

"Eric's," I explain.

Now her mouth drops open. "The hot pastor?"

Trinity nods. "He *is* ridiculously attractive. And he's got the strong and silent thing going for him."

I'm not surprised that the other women think Eric is good looking, but... "Eric? Silent?" I wish he would be more silent. He's always saying stuff I don't want to hear.

Trinity corrects herself. "More like deep-thinking—perceptive. Like you can't keep a secret from him, and every word he says has a purpose."

"Wise," Star paraphrases.

Huh. I thought it was only me that Eric understood so easily. I guess..."He is a counselor."

Star's attention swings my way again. "You're in his wedding? Are you a groomsmaid? I've heard of some people doing that."

"No." I shake my head. "I'm a bridesmaid. His fiancée asked me."

"Really?" Trinity sounds apprehensive. But she doesn't know I've been training Brooke for over a month. Not that a month is all that long in the way of meeting a bridesmaid. "I guess I'll have to pick a different date for the wedding. Especially if the hot pastor is doing my ceremony."

Dad did Christian's wedding. Though I don't think Trinity will want him to do hers. She'll want him to walk her down the aisle. That's one way to get Dad to visit, anyway.

"Now this is an amazing dress." Star points to a bridal gown in the magazine that I would more likely term 'outrageous' than 'amazing.'

"Elegant but fun," Trinity agrees. "I like this one with the black sash."

Black at a wedding? Wasn't that a color reserved for funerals? It fits in with "'till death do us part" but I'm guessing that Trinity is going to do the trendy thing and change her vows to "'till love leaves us." My parents might as well have done that.

"I adore it," Star gushes.

Is my fashion sense really that conservative? "It's like the dress on display over at David's Bridal," I offer lamely. The wedding boutique is a part of this ritzy shopping plaza along with Maggie Moos, a golf/tennis shop, a kiddie salon, and my favorite Thai restaurant.

Trinity looks thoughtful. "Donovan and I are paying for the wedding ourselves. I wonder how much I can spend on a dress."

Respectable—and practical, since Mom and Dad aren't likely to approve this union. But I'm guessing the happy couple blew all their money on the cross-country road trip. Maybe it *will* be a while before they get married.

"Oh, girl. Didn't you see the sale advertised in David's window?" Star wipes ice cream off Jennica's face while she talks. She's momentarily distracted. "I'm so glad I didn't buy her an ice cream cone. I'd have to lick all the drips for her."

Gross.

"What sale?" Trinity sits up straighter.

Star looks up from her Maggie Moos mustachioed child. "The $100 sale. Maybe the dress Bethany saw in the window was part of the sale."

Trinity jumps up. "I'll be right back."

Wow, is she going to be sore tomorrow. Not only did she take Star's dance class, but she's actually jogging of her own accord.

I shiver as a blast of cold wind rushes in at her exit. Why again, are we eating ice cream in January?

Star leans toward me as soon as Trinity leaves. She probably wants the gossip on Trinity's fiancée.

"He's shy and has a soul patch and wears all black." I try to sound non-judgmental. I'll let her form her own opinions.

Star's mouth is open. She stares at me for a moment. "What?"

As if she wasn't about to ask for all the dirt. "Donovan Cross. Trinity's new last name will be Cross, by the way. Maybe she can carry on the crazy name tradition your mom started and name her kid Chris Cross or something."

Star's eyebrow goes into active mode. "I think that's already been done."

Oh, yeah. The old school rapper. I'm so hip...or funky...or whatever them young whippersnappers are saying nowadays.

"I wanted to talk to you about something else." All of Star's diva-ish drama act is gone. Her tone is low and serious. I'm in trouble.

"Okay." I try not to sound too nervous.

"I had my hair cut at Dee Light's."

I suck on my straw so hard that I finish the smoothie and start to slurp air. Ouch. Brain freeze. I rub my temple and try to register the significance of Star's confession. "Did Dee Dee cut your hair?" I haven't spoken to Dee Dee since our lunch of tuna salad—which really stunk up my studio by the way. This is huge.

"Yes."

My first thought is that Star did something horrible and so Dee Dee hacked her hair off for revenge. I'm already preparing to calm the storm. "It looks amazing. She did a great job. I love it. Don't you love your mommy's hair, Jennica?"

Jennica's round eyes are as serious as her mom's. "No."

I laugh nervously. "She's two. She probably says no to everything."

"She does," Star allows, "but she truly hates my hair. She wouldn't look at me when I picked her up from my parents' house. She turned around and backed up to me so I could hold her and talk to her without her having to look at my hair."

"She's looking at you now."

Jennica glares. "Mommy's a boy."

Star bursts out laughing. "I guess now that I look like a man, I don't have to worry about her father being out of the picture."

That really isn't funny. And if Dee Dee chopped her hair to make her mad, she's taking it quite well. "It looks beautiful, Star. It's a fabulous style." Though only someone with Star's personality could ever pull it off.

Star leans in close again and stops laughing. "I need to thank you for talking to me about Dee Dee. I didn't want to hear her side, but because of what you said, I started to feel guilty about ignoring her during the family Christmas dinner."

I hear myself gasp. Star waits for me to say something, but I'm frozen—not just because of the smoothie, but in anticipation of her next words.

"So today, I decided to work it out. I went to her spa but didn't know where to start so I just stood staring at her.

She asked me what I wanted. I said I needed a change. She thought I was talking about what I wanted for my hair."

My hand flies to my mouth. I wish I could have been there. I can't wait to get home and call Dee Dee. I don't have a doubt in my mind that Star's actions are a result of Dee Dee's recent prayer life and not my bumbling interference. There is so much I can learn from my baby Christian cousin. I burst out in laughter and tears at the same time. I grab for Star's hands. "You didn't correct her assumption?"

Star is laughing, too. It's the laughter of relief and freedom from bitterness. She squeezes my fingers. "Nope. I already felt like an idiot. So I picked the first hairstyle in the book she handed me and then we made small talk as if I was a regular client."

"Star...Star!" I'm overflowing with everything except words. "Oh, Star!"

Star reels me back down to Earth. "It was a tiny stitch in the mending of our relationship needs."

I'm still flying like Rudolph. "But it's the hardest stitch to sew."

Star's eyes shine. "Thanks, Bethany," she says again.

Chapter 31

I've been waiting all year for my date with Robbie. Granted, that's only nine days, but with all the brides-and-babies-to-be in my life right now, it's not a day too soon.

He's picking me up at Lighten Up. It's Saturday so I didn't work, but I lifted weights this morning then hung out at Dee Dee's spa to talk about Star and the Bible and Trinity's wedding and the possibility of me building a house. I could have stayed and talked all night—especially since she gave me a manicure and massage for free when a couple of clients didn't show up.

But now I'm ready for my hot date...even though my jeans are feeling a little snug. If I'd dressed at home I probably would have changed into some loose cargo pants. Man, my jeans are so tight that if I were trying them on in the store I would think there was some manufacturing defect. I can't get them up all the way. Hopefully my belt will keep them from slipping down over my hips.

Seriously, I must look like my brother Christian did when he was seven and painted the lower half of his body blue. My mom thought he was wearing tight pants at first until she discovered that his legs matched the neighbor's new exterior. He had to be dipped into a bathtub full of turpentine.

Gasp. I can barely breathe. I know that the average American gains ten pounds during the holidays, but I avoided all the sweet stuff. Maybe I should put my sweats back on. I mean, Robbie is taking me bowling so it's not like I need to dress to impress. I dig through my bag looking for something comfortable to...

The chime over my door rings. What's the opposite of being saved by the bell?

"Hey, Gorgeous."

"Hi!" I sound overly cheerful. But I will have a good time. Robbie's relaxed posture and intuitive smile reassure me.

"So you never take a day off, huh?"

I shrug. "I lifted this morning. Then I helped out my cousin with her business."

Robbie looks around the room, not missing a thing. I'm glad I dusted for cobwebs yesterday. "What kind of business?"

"Vanity, basically. It's amazing how much money people will pay to look and feel better about themselves—even if it isn't healthy." I think of Dee Dee's tanning beds. I've convinced her not to use them, but then she got a spray-on tanning booth that always leaves her with orange splotches on her hands. I know darker skin gives the appearance of muscle tone, but natural is so much healthier. Dee Dee says I don't understand because I was born with an olive complexion.

Robbie's curious gaze clues me in to the fact that I've spaced out. He smoothly changes the subject. "You look good. Like you've been building muscle."

Sure. I'll let him think my thighs are larger because of extra squats. "Thanks."

We stare at each other for a moment. All of a sudden the dynamics of our friendly UPS man/recipient of packages relationship has changed.

Robbie claps his hands. "Are you ready to go?"

"Oh yeah." I trot toward the door. "Let's get out of here."

Blaring techno music greets us at the entrance to the bowling alley. The place is completely dark except for the black lights turning all things white into a shimmery purple color. Robbie grins and his teeth become illuminated against his shadowed face.

"Do you do this a lot?" I ask. The atmosphere is new and exciting to me, but it could be routine to my date.

"Not me. But my buddies come often." He leads me to the shoe counter. "I'll introduce you."

Oh? His buddies are here? There goes all chance for romance, but maybe Robbie is just supposed to be a friend.

It goes with my dating for fun philosophy. Eric might even approve.

I give the Ben Franklin look alike behind the counter one of my chunky-heeled boots in exchange for a pair of shoes that don't even have matching shoelaces, then hobble after Robbie to lane fourteen.

"Hey everybody, this is Bethany. Bethany this is…"

"Everybody," they chorus before breaking out into laughter and back slaps.

The group seems tight. As if they know each other on more than one level.

"Bethany," a tall woman greets me. Even though she's wearing jeans, she has a professional air to her. Maybe because of the pleat she's ironed into the denim. "How did Robbie convince you to go out with him?"

So this is what I have to deal with. It can't be any worse than hanging out with my family. They can dish it. Let's see if they can take it. "Oh, he bribed me with a promise of bowling and of being interrogated by strangers."

"Oooh," tease a couple guys behind her.

One guy stands up. "I like her," he announces, as if I'd passed some kind of test. He holds out his hand to me. "The name's Beau. Welcome to our club."

I shake, but my grip isn't nearly as strong as his. His face looks rough and I wonder if in normal light it's considered ruddy. This combination makes me think of David from the Bible, and I picture Beau ripping apart lions with his bare hands.

The female Goliath introduces herself as Therese. Then there's Preston and Hallie.

Robbie becomes the perfect gentleman—showing off for his friends more so than for me, I think—and helps with my shoes, finds me a ball, and buys me a Sprite. Everyone else sets up on their own.

"Are you a good bowler?" asks Beau.

"I played a pretty mean game of bumper bowling with my niece recently," I reply.

Beau laughs, but Robbie laughs louder. He's got a great laugh. I could listen to it all night. I smile over at him.

Therese picks up her ball, but stops to talk to me before taking her turn. "You've got a heavy ball. You must be pretty strong."

Wow. All this attention. It's like I'm a star...or maybe just Star. "I *am* a personal trainer." What else am I supposed to say?

"She's buff." Robbie adds.

"Maybe I should train with you," Therese says before charging the lane and rocketing her ball like a ninja...if ninjas bowled.

"I have a trainer," Hallie chimes in from her spot in front of the monitor.

"A yoga trainer," Preston informs me with mock condescension in his voice.

This makes sense. Hallie is so little I could huff and puff and blow her down. But she's really cute in a nerdy kind of way—glasses and a polo shirt.

"My trainer just got arrested for selling steroids," Preston tells us.

He's a muscle head so I just ignore him. I've met too many muscle heads in my line of work. They are arrogant problem-causers.

I stand up to bowl. My jeans restrict my form, so I kind of hop on one foot to maintain my balance after swinging the ball into the lane. It almost rolls into the gutter, but ends up knocking over the last pin on the left. I try again. The ball takes the exact same course as if it were magnetized. I start off with a score of one after my first frame.

"So what do you think about that?" Preston asks when I return to my seat.

"I think I'll need to bowl with you guys more often if I'm going to get any better."

Robbie apparently likes my answer because his arm comes around my shoulder and his eyes twinkle down at me approvingly. I like the fact that Robbie likes my answer. Maybe we'll become more than friends after all.

"No, I meant what do you think about trainers selling steroids?" Preston interrupts my moment.

"I've heard of it happening," I reply quickly and look back at Robbie, but the moment is gone.

He's up and making the first strike of the night. He does a little air guitar in victory.

Therese calls above the blaring music, "We didn't tell Bethany our rule."

"What rule?" I'm imagining that the losers have to buy a pitcher of beer—which means I'll be forced to explain why I don't drink.

Robbie plops back down next to me. "If you get a strike or a spare you have to dance."

I giggle. No worries. "Is that what you call your little performance?"

Robbie's eyes narrow in challenge. "You think you can do better?"

Beau whoops. I'm guessing he likes competition.

"If I get a strike, you'll know I can do better." Thanks to Star's Jam class. I mentally steal some of my cousin's moves.

"This I gotta see." Robbie leans forward in his seat and gives me a bowling lesson before it's my turn again.

It doesn't help. My ball knocks over the exact same pin. My score has now doubled to two points.

"Maybe she's afraid to get a strike and have to dance," Preston taunts.

Hallie swats him away. "She's just warming up."

I wish. I don't get any better.

"You've really got it out for that one pin." Robbie observes.

"What has that pin ever done to deserve your wrath?" Therese plays off him.

Christian would fit right in with this group. But I'm feeling a little suffocated. It's my last turn. I want to get a strike, do my dance, and then spend some time alone with Robbie. Get to know him without the wild lighting and pulsing beat.

"You're up, King Pin," Robbie winks at me.

As I take my spot, I hear Therese start an argument about how there should be a Queen Pin. I block it out and focus on the lane in front of me...on the pins...on the arrows leading to the pins. I take my first step, swing the ball back, assume my position, then swish...let it go. It's rolling, rolling, rolling straight toward the middle. Pow! Down they all go.

Woo-hoo! I did it. Time to bust a move. I break into a hip swivel then a spin. I go for a big Star-like-finish with a kick-cha-cha and a pose.

Rrrrrip. That didn't sound good. Fear grips me as I look down. The front seem of my pants just above my thigh has come apart. And to make it worse, my white underwear is ultraviolet. It shines like a spotlight.

I get a standing ovation. All of Robbie's friends are on their feet cheering and laughing. I laugh too, but out of utter embarrassment, out of stupidity for wearing my tight jeans, out of disgust for the fact that I must have gained weight, and out of disbelief that I could let that happen.

Robbie is out of his seat, too, but he comes toward me, rips off his sweatshirt and ties it around my waist. My hero. Not that I'll ever see him again. In fact, I'll be hiding under my desk the next time he delivers a package to Lighten Up.

"She showed *you*, Robbie!" Therese calls.

"She said she was a dancer," yells Beau, "but I didn't know she was going to give a strip tease."

I'm thankful for the dark lighting keeping Robbie from seeing me turn bright red. I hide my head in his chest anyway.

"Do you want to get out of here?"

No, I want to humiliate myself some more. Maybe I can get the back of my pants to split, as well. "Yes."

"I'll get your boot."

Robbie takes my shoes off and leaves me for what seems like eternity.

"You're still up," Hallie announces.

Figures. I finally get a strike and I can't bowl my bonus turn. "Somebody else can go for me."

Therese tries to make me feel better now that she's done laughing. "It's just a little rip."

The rip heard 'round the world. The family in the next lane over is pointing at me.

Preston takes Robbie's seat. "So, you're really bulking up, huh? Are you going to be in a body building competition or something?"

I'm too mortified to tell him that my weight gain is not lean body mass. I would think it's obvious, but if not, I won't voluntarily make myself look any worse at the moment by pointing it out. "I'm more into Miss Fitness," I reply vaguely.

"Really?" Preston's interest is starting to annoy. "I know a guy in one of those competitions. He took anabolic steroids and his heart actually grew so that it's no longer safe for him to do cardiovascular training."

When you work a muscle it normally grows larger, but with the heart, the walls get thinner so that the space inside is larger. That way it becomes more efficient by pumping a greater volume of blood with each beat. "You've got to be careful." Where is Robbie?

"Do you think it's worth it to use drugs to win competitions?"

There's Robbie. Heading this way, thank goodness. I look down at my lap to make sure my underwear is covered by Robbie's sweatshirt sleeve. I look back up to find Preston's intense gaze still on me. What did he ask, again?

"Ready?" Robbie reaches down to take my hand.

It's about time. "Yes." I stand and wave at the rest of the group. "Bye, guys. Glad you enjoyed my show. I'm taking the act on the road now."

Robbie tucks my hand into the crook of his arm. "You're planning to tour?"

I wrinkle my nose. "If that's what my fans demand."

Therese gives me a quick hug. "I'm a fan."

Preston shakes my free hand and his grip is just as strong as Beau's—and a little menacing. "I'll catch you later."

Chapter 32

I trudge into Eric's office on Tuesday night. I know I'm going to get a lecture for skipping church—if nothing else.

"I have an excuse," I say before he even has a chance to ask.

"Really? Because I would think that if your sister who is staying with you can make it to church, you would at least come with her."

Good point. But I've got one as well. "It's not as if she came to hear the Bible. She just wanted to see Donovan."

"Donovan—the guy you don't think is good enough for Trinity. He was asking a lot of questions after the sermon. He seems more open to God's word than you are." I can count on Eric to tell it like it is...or how he sees it anyway. He's probably thinks he's giving me "medicine" of some kind.

Ugh. I miss one service and this is what I get. "I spent time with God Sunday morning. He was my hiding place. I had a late night Saturday."

Eric's eyebrows lift. "Dee Dee said you had a date. It must have gone well."

Now even Dee Dee is coming to church when I'm not here. No wonder I'm starting to look bad. "Hardly." I instinctively reach for the M & Ms. I pop the candy into my mouth then freeze mid-chew. I jump out of my seat to spit into the garbage can. Strings of saliva hang from my lips. I grab a tissue to wipe it all off.

"Are you okay, Bethany?" Eric's voice rings with concern and a dash of bewilderment. "Is there something wrong with my candy?"

"It's the M & M's." I declare. "Of course. No wonder I've gained five pounds."

Eric's expression deepens the creases in his face. "What's the matter? Are you anorexic?"

Pu-tooey. I spit again. "You can't let me eat any more chocolate!"

"There are other counselors that can help you with that. I'm not trained..."

I collapse onto the couch—on the opposite side from the end table. "I'm not anorexic Eric."

Eric's face relaxes.

"I just had a horrible date Saturday night because my pants split while I was bowling."

Eric's face contorts again. It's twitching as if he's trying to control his mirth. He looks like he has to sneeze.

If it hadn't been for the candy there is no way I would have told him, but now I might as well explain everything. "Robbie brought me straight home after that happened, and I'm sure he'll never ask me out again. That thought kept me up until the wee hours of the morning trying to figure out what I've been doing differently that would cause me to gain weight. I can't believe I forgot about your M & Ms."

Eric can't get past the first part of my story. "You seriously split your pants? And I thought splitting the bowling pins was bad." His joke is so lame I would have expected it to come out of Christian's mouth.

"Welcome to my life. My pants—my only pair of jeans—split in the front, and the black lights lit up my underwear like a neon sign."

Eric leans forward to rest his face on his hands as if he's deep in thought, but I know he's really hiding a smile. What kills me is that his fiancée has lost over ten pounds because of me, and here, thanks to him, I've gained weight.

"Shut up." I know he's dying to make another dumb joke. I think I just bring dumb jokes out of people. I gave Christian his start in comedy.

"Can I remind you of one thing?"

"No."

"Well, then you're wasting your money on counseling."

Why does he have to be so right all the time? "Okay, one thing."

"No accidents."

He's taking his beliefs a little too literally. "Splitting my pants *was* an accident."

"Then it's your job to make it a no accident."

"Really?" Why can't I just call it an accident and move on? "What? You want me to climb the accountability ladder? Don't be ridiculous."

Eric grabs his Bible from his desk and hops into his chair with wheels to roll closer to me. Now that I've scooted to the other side of the couch he can't share scripture verses with me from where he was sitting.

"I won't make you climb the accountability ladder, but I do want to talk about Romans 8:28."

Now *that's* where my favorite verse is found. I remember now. "All things work together for good to those who love God and are called according to his purpose."

Eric's eyes remind me of the lake in the morning (when I get up early to water ski before any of the other boats go out). They are still and deep. "Do you believe the verse?"

I'm lost in his eyes for a moment. Finally his words penetrate my thoughts and I respond. "Yes."

"Do you believe that before anything happens to you it has to be allowed by God?"

This is tough to comprehend in a world of evil, but I believe the key word is *allow*. God doesn't cause these things to happen, but he will allow them and use them for good just like his scripture says. "Yes."

"And the only reason God will allow something to happen is for the sole purpose of blessing your heart?"

Whoa, now. There have been a lot of things that have happened lately that have not blessed my heart. I might say that God has allowed them to punish me or to get me moving when I've become stagnant. Like a good kick in the pants... or a knee to the groin. I'm not sure I agree with Eric. "Was your heart blessed by my knee in the boxing ring? Was that a move God allowed?"

Eric flips to Romans 11:33. "How unsearchable are His judgments and His ways past finding out."

Extreme faith. Offensive faith. "So you went home that night and thanked God for the pain I put you through?"

Eric's chuckle sounds sarcastic. "Actually, I was pretty angry at first. I was mad at you. Victimized. But then I thought, 'What can God be trying to teach me?' Because of that night, I really started to evaluate the time I spent boxing. I've decided to give it up."

I feel as if *I* just received a physical blow. "You gave up boxing?" I'm shocked. He'd been so defensive when I first questioned his sport. "Isn't it like your therapy of choice?"

Eric shrugs. "It was a problem for some of the people in the church. I was being selfish to keep doing it."

I sit back in my seat. So that's why I hadn't seen him at the gym on Thursday. And I'd been part of his decision. It's a decision I don't support, though. For as wise as Eric is, he seems to make a lot of stupid choices—like marrying Brooke. But it's not my place to call him on it. I shake my head. "So has God blessed your heart, through this?"

Eric's shoulders lift a fraction of an inch. "It's been pretty hard, actually. But like King David said, 'I'm not going to offer God sacrifices that are no sacrifice.'"

What a heart for God. And I don't know if Eric's heart has been blessed by God yet, but I'm guessing God has been blessed by him. Like his hero, Eric is a man after God's own heart. I can learn from him. "So what do you think I'm supposed to learn from splitting my pants?"

Eric is smiling again. I'm sure the image of me with a big hole in my pants is enough to lighten his mood for weeks to come. I start to smile, too. What's the point in becoming a laughingstock if I can't laugh at myself?

"That's your job to figure out." He says this and stops, but he obviously has more to say. He struggles for a moment (his mouth opening and closing a couple times) before giving me his own opinion—or medicine as he calls it. "You might want to relate your date disaster with your kiss catastrophe. It doesn't seem like your relationship strategy is working. Maybe God is trying to get your attention—get you to consider the possibility that He has something better planned for you."

I narrow my eyes. "I know you think that. So of course you are going to read the situation that way."

Eric imitates my expression. He's still sitting in his desk chair directly in front of me, so it's like a staring contest. "And you don't agree, so of course you're going to dismiss the idea immediately."

I look away first. "This is what's called an impasse."

Eric beams, triumphant for some reason. "Now see…I just gave you feedback. What you're supposed to do is acknowledge my position and promise to weigh it carefully before taking further action."

That sounds so ridiculous. But it makes sense. I wonder if he learned this tool at his marriage conference. "Do you communicate this way with Brooke?"

Eric's chair squeaks as he leans back. "That's what she says to me when I give her feedback. What I've learned to say when she gives me feedback is, 'You're right and I'm a jerk.'"

Eric's statement is funny, but I'm smiling dreamily. What would it be like to have a man care for me that much? I'm staring up into space, so Eric wraps up my challenge for the day.

"Pray about it," he says. But I've forgotten what it is we were talking about. I'm too busy imagining what it would be like to be loved by a guy like Eric.

Chapter 33

Laurel and I aren't doing so well with our accountability meetings. She's pregnant. There were the holidays. Then today I'm looking at houses with Eric's brother Trent. And I'm babysitting Jennica...something about Star using too many of the daycare hours at the gym.

Laurel didn't want to skip another week, so she's coming with us to the new subdivision. And Dee Dee heard me mention the idea of buying a house...I couldn't keep her away. Though I think she's going to be pretty disappointed when she finds out I want something that's been built in the last century. She'll give me her "cookie-cutter-houses" speech.

Dee Dee runs across the parking lot toward my Jeep as I get ready to leave. I roll down the passenger window to see what she needs.

"Can I ride with you? My car has been making funny screeching sounds lately when I slow down."

I let her in and give her advice on getting her brakes checked. Her poor car. She can grow an amazing garden and keep her house smelling like an apple pie when she's not baking, but all she knows how to do to a car is pump gas, and even then people probably think she's from Oregon where every gas station is full service.

"Hey Jennica," she grins at her niece as she climbs in.

I spin the steering wheel to turn onto the main road. The action (or maybe it's the metallic mess on my fingers) gets Dee Dee's attention.

"I see you had a manicure," she makes the overstatement with a straight face.

What a great time to run out of nail polish remover. "Jennica wanted to paint my nails."

219

Dee Dee gasps as if each nail is a masterpiece. "Great job, Jennica. I should hire you to work at my spa."

Jennica giggles. "Paint your nails?"

"Oh." I see Dee Dee's pouty face out of the corner of my eye as I glance down at my GPS. "I wish you could. But I just had my nails painted yesterday." She waves one hand in the air as evidence.

"Pwetty," Jennica coos.

I turn left into Pepper Hills. That's what the sign on the large rock at the entrance to the street says anyway. I don't see any hills to prove it. But I guess if you can call Boise the City of Trees, you can make up any ridiculous name for a subdivision.

Dee Dee groans. "You aren't building a *new* home are you? The lots are so tiny."

"Oh," I mock her. "I hadn't thought of that. Where will I put my tennis court? Oh wait. I don't have one. My entire apartment is smaller than the swimming pool at Gold's. This place is a paradise."

I'm actually feeling rather giddy. I'm going to get to buy a lawnmower. And I can even put up Christmas lights. I can invite guests over and have more than just one couch for them to sit on. I'll have a guest bedroom for when Mom visits or an exercise room like Eric's basement. I feel so mature.

Dee Dee covers her eyes. "Pinch me. I need to wake up from this nightmare."

Jennica laughs. "Peek-a-boo," she calls.

"It's not that bad." I park in front of a spec home. "This one has a front porch. And look, the garage is on the side so that when you look at it that's not all you see. It's charming."

"Charming?" Dee Dee moves her hands from her eyes, but I wish she hadn't because she's looking at me like I'm crazy.

I turn toward Jennica. "We need to teach Aunt Dee Dee some manners." I face my passenger again. "Watch it, Missy, or you won't be getting a ride home." Gee, is it too much to ask my family to be happy for me?

Laurel climbs out from the car in front of us. She's not looking any bigger belly wise, but she's holding her back. We get out to join her though I have to be careful what I say since Dee Dee doesn't know about the baby yet. I think I really need to throw Laurel a shower to get her more excited for her baby. Speaking of showers…

"Hey, girls. We need to plan a wedding shower for Trinity."

"Is Trin-ty stinky?" Jennica hugs her stuffed dog close.

We laugh and Dee Dee explains the difference between a bathroom shower and what we were talking about.

"We can have the shower at my house." Laurel starts the planning process as we head into the office. She'll take over from here. I won't have to do any of the work, but I'll get to take credit for the idea.

Trent greets us with a file of paperwork. Dee Dee rolls her eyes in disgust and takes Jennica to the toy corner while I look at floor plans and lot availability. I hold my breath as he brings the prices out, but it's better than I expect. And having checked with Jade, I know that I could put ten percent down today if I wanted to.

My stomach starts to do flip-flops. This is exciting stuff. I'm so glad Eric suggested I buy a house.

Dee Dee returns for the color selection. She runs her hand along the tile samples. She doesn't say anything so I know she grudgingly approves.

"See?" I say in my I-told-you-so voice. "I'm even having a fireplace put in."

Dee Dee smirks. "Is it a real wood-burning fireplace or just one of those fake flip-the-switch kind?"

"It's the *awesome* flip-the-switch kind." I resort to the retorts a grade-schooler might use.

Trent overhears and offers to give us a tour of the floor plan I like the best. "Our contractors worked with *Extreme Makeover: Home Edition* when they came to Idaho," he says causing Dee Dee to follow him as if he were the Pied Piper.

221

I round up Jennica and follow the little group back outside into the chilly air. I hug her close for body heat.

We enter into the living room of the house across the street. It's not a grand entrance, but the ceilings are 10' high, giving it a spacious feel that I'm not used to. I would love the chance to get used to it.

The kitchen is the best part. It's old fashioned with room for a table and the *awesome* stone fireplace. Dee Dee even looks impressed.

The tour doesn't take very long because all that is left is the three bedrooms...but that's two more bedrooms than I have now. I want it. I want it. I want it.

Dee Dee looks as if she's thinking hard about what advice to give. "Get Berber carpets. They last forever."

I'll take her word for it. All I know about carpet I learned from the ads in the magazine subscription she bought me.

"You are getting real wood floors, right?"

I don't know. I look at Trent.

"I can run back across the street and get the pricing sheets for you to look at again," he offers.

He seems like a nice guy. "Thanks."

Dee Dee starts listing the merits of hard wood. She slips one foot out of her clog and rubs a toe across the floor. Jennica must think it looks like fun. Her bungee shoes (we have the same taste) go flying off and then she's slipping around as if on ice skates.

I smile. "I think I would like hard wood." This will be a huge change from the linoleum where I live now. I slip off my shoes as well and slide next to Jennica. One small slide in the new living room, one giant slide into a new lifestyle.

"Come on, guys," I invite Laurel and Dee to join us. I told you I was giddy.

Laurel gives me her not-gonna-happen look. She and Dee Dee move down the hallway into the bedrooms. Well, at least Jennica is here for me.

"Try this," I say to my playmate, before running and sliding in my socks. Just as I reach full speed and begin to sail, the front door opens.

I should have expected Trent to come right back. Only it isn't Trent, it's his brother. Eric watches as I glide past him into a wall.

"I hope I didn't miss your triple axel," he deadpans.

I push off the wall to turn around. It's got great texture to it—kind of Italian and creamy looking. Funny, I've never noticed wall texture before.

"Jennica and I were just warming up," I say.

Eric looks around the room. Jennica isn't here anymore. She must have sock skated down the hallway. "Right," he says. Moving on he hands me a stack of papers. "I stopped by to see what you thought, and Trent asked me to bring this over. He got a phone call."

I take the papers. "Thanks." I run my finger down the flooring options. "Ouch. I don't know if I can afford hardwood."

Eric taps the papers. "I told you Trent will get you a good deal, didn't I? I'll have him throw in a free flooring upgrade."

"Ooh, I've got connections." I do a pirouette.

"So, you're interested?" Eric turns into a salesman before my eyes.

I grin. "What do you think?"

Eric winks. "I think I'm the answer to your prayers."

Hmm...I probably should have prayed about this decision a little more, but if my pastor thinks it's an answer to prayer, then I'm in. And I've got that jittery feeling in my stomach. That's a good sign, right?

I'm so excited I call all the Light girls back into the room so I can go put down the earnest money. Eric says they'll be breaking ground in March.

Dee Dee doesn't say another negative word on the way home. "You like the house I picked out, don't you?" I want to hear her admit it. She just smiles, so I try again. "Tell me you like my house, or I'll increase the incline on the tread-mill for your walk tomorrow." My house. *My house.* It feels so good to say it.

"I like your house." She acknowledges. "Though, about your treadmill, I don't think I'm going to be using it much anymore."

I start to frown at her, but the Jeep swerves causing Jennica to scream. I look straight ahead again. "Why not?" I can't think of any reason why she wouldn't want to come walk with me. If it were nicer out I would think she was going to walk outside, but not in this nasty weather.

Dee Dee sighs. "Oh...I'm trying to read the Bible all I can, but I just don't have enough time in my day. Brooke recommended a Bible study to me that has lots of homework, and Laurel gave me a couple books tonight about creation that I want to read. I just don't have time to do everything."

I blink. "You still need to exercise!" What kind of cousin would I be if I didn't care for Dee Dee's health?

Dee Dee slides her hands under her legs. It's a move I've seen her do many times when she's feeling defensive or shy. "I know...but I read a verse last night. Have you heard I Timothy 4:7?"

"I've read I Timothy," I reply quickly, though it's been too long since I opened my Bible and I have no idea where she is going with this.

"Oh. I just thought you might know it because it talks about physical training."

Now there's an idea...memorize scripture verses about health and strength and the body—my career. But still I have no clue what verse she's talking about. The Bible is a pretty long book, you know. "Quote it for me. I'm sure I'll recognize it." I hope I do.

"Okay." Dee Dee clears her throat. "Rather, train yourself to be godly. For physical training is of some value, but godliness has value for all things, holding promise for both the present life and the life to come."

That's in the Bible? Why had I never noticed it before? Of course, I know it to be true, but... I can't think of any buts. "That's good," I say quietly.

"I should focus on God right now."

I'm a little taken aback by Dee Dee's spiritual desire. I mean, it's great that she is pursuing a relationship with God, but it was me who witnessed to her in the first place—and it was while she walked on the treadmill.

We've arrived at the parking lot of the spa where her car is parked. She doesn't get out though, and I can't think of anything to say, so she continues. "I fasted the other day for the first time." She fasted? Who fasts anymore? "I stopped at The Red Letter Café and Bookstore to get a smoothie, but I started looking at all the books there, and I had this thought: I'm hungry. The funny thing is that I wasn't hungry for food."

I'm still trying to get over the fact that Dee Dee fasts. I've never fasted. It slows down your metabolism causing your body to think it is starving and store fat. I've always thought of fasting as, like, holy anorexia. But maybe lots of people fast—they just don't talk about it since the Bible says not to brag. And Dee Dee hasn't read the whole Bible yet so she doesn't know she's not supposed to talk about it. But then, where did she learn about fasting?

"And I *am* really hungry, Bethany. I have so much to learn. Now that I'm looking for the truth, I'm finding it everywhere. One of my clients even left me a little tract yesterday about angels and demons. I don't know anything about the subjects."

"I've never studied angels and demons either," I say quietly.

"Really?" Dee Dee sounds shocked. As if I'm the authority on all things Christian. And maybe I give out that vibe.

I have an idea. I've never considered it before. But it would be pretty awesome if it worked. "What if we do a Bible study together while we walk on the treadmill every day? I could probably answer some of your questions, and you would inspire me to think deeper. It would be training for our bodies and souls."

Dee Dee's eyes double in size. "I never thought of that. It would be a whole new side to my relationship with Christ. I could worship God through my exercise."

And as simple as Dee Dee's statement sounded, it was something I had never tried. I prayed to God to grow my business. I believed that I was improving the quality of life for those I trained. But I'd never really worshiped God with my whole body. I'd kept them separate like church and state. I'd been missing out.

Chapter 34

"You're skinnier than Rochelle so the seamstress will have to take in a little material around your waist."

Brooke's words makes me feel a lot better after my bust-a-move/seam performance at the bowling ally.

"And take in a lot around your chest."

Okay, not so good anymore.

Brooke's bridesmaids giggle and chat at David's Bridal while I get poked with pins and needles. The dresses are stunning. I even feel glamorous. But I really don't belong here.

I change back into my warm-up pants while Brooke puts on her wedding gown for us to see. She looks amazing. Yeah, the sweetheart neckline and yards of tulle are elegant, but it's her body that takes my breath away. She's got the hourglass figure I've always dreamed of.

I knew she was dropping pounds, but her baggy gym t-shirts hid the transformation. She's like a shrinky-dink version of the woman I started training over two months ago. It's time for an after picture for my before-and-after wall.

The other bridesmaids are just as amazed as I am. They gasp at the change. I sit back with pride and wait for Brooke to refer all her friends to me. Instead, she starts to blabber about some movie actress she saw wearing a gown like hers, so I zone her out to hear what the bridesmaids have to say about the groom.

"Oooh. Eric is gonna go gaga when he sees her." *Gaga?*

"They should put a Ken and Barbie on top of their cake because they are going to look that good together." *How cliché.*

"I'm so jealous. Brooke is having a dream wedding with a dream lover." *Dream lover?*

A chubby bridesmaid (who could look like the new Brooke if she hired me and had a mole removed) sinks down on the velvet ottoman next to me. "Have you met Eric?" she asks.

"Yeah." I don't say anything else because I don't know if she's met him yet. And if she has, I bet she doesn't know him as well as I do.

"I wish he had a twin brother. The world needs more men like him."

I doubt she's thinking about the world.

Brooke's sister overhears and joins us as Brooke goes back into the changing room. She sighs. "I think Eric is one of a kind. He's handsome. Funny. Smart. Respectful. Good--"

"Looking," Chubby adds, as if being good-looking is valued over just being good. I guess in our society it is.

Brooke's sister carries on. "But it's more than that. He's genuine. When you talk, you know he's listening. He really cares about people. Can you imagine having those qualities in a husband?"

Chubby grunts. "I bet Brooke will never have to ask him to mow the lawn or help with the dishes."

"Have you seen his house?" Brooke's sister interjects.

I'm feeling a little sick of the whole conversation. Okay. I get it. Eric is a superhero. Everybody loves him. It's not just me...I mean Brooke.

I leave the conversation behind and walk to the window to wait for Trinity. I get to try on two bridesmaids dresses in one day. Lucky me. It's a good thing that I haven't let Eric's comments get to me, and I still plan to stay single. Because, you know, if I were wanting to be the bride, today would be a pretty depressing day.

I watch as Trinity slams the door to Christian's truck. It's an extra vehicle they just use for towing their boat—talk about an easy life. Trinity walks quickly toward the boutique. Her head is down and she wipes at her face. Is she crying? She is. She grabs a tissue from her pocket and blows her nose. Maybe her wedding is called off. The thought doesn't upset me except for the fact that I have to console my sister.

"Trinity." I rush over and wrap her in my arms. *It's for the best*, I think. *No accidents.* "What's wrong?" Donovan better get his butt back across the country quickly before Christian finds out that he broke our sister's heart. See? This is why I'm not getting married.

Trinity opens her mouth to answer but only sobs come out. She uses her tissue again. "I'm fine. I'm fine." She stands up straight and lifts her head but doesn't look me in the eye.

"No you're not. What happened?"

Trinity shudders as she tries to maintain her composure. Then she breaks down again. "Dad's not coming to my wedding. He's not going to walk me down the aisle."

Indignation rises within me, and empathy pours from me. How could Dad do this again? Isn't skipping Christmas enough? He had to go see his wife's daughter give birth, but he can't even give away his own daughter? Wow. If I were getting married, I wouldn't even invite the man—see how he likes the taste of rejection.

"Oh, honey," I soothe. Her head is on my shoulder again. I stroke her hair. "Leave and cleave. You're going to have a new man in your life." If Donovan can be called that. "And I'm sure Christian will walk you down the aisle. This is a time to celebrate. Don't worry about Dad."

I say this, but I'm mentally preparing to call my father. What reason could he possibly have for missing his daughter's wedding? Well, besides the fact that Trinity ran off and chose to marry someone Dad had never even met or given his blessing to. But all the more reason for him to come down here and see for himself who his new son-in-law is going to be.

"I'll try." She looks at me with eyes begging for hope and guidance. It's a different side of Trinity. I've always thought of her as hard-hearted and rebellious. But maybe she is the prodigal daughter. Unfortunately, my dad is no example of Christ in this parable.

"Have you talked to Mom, yet?" I'm pretty sure Mom's response will be softer and more supportive than Dad's. I hope so for my sister's sake.

"Oh, she was there when Donovan proposed."

That's right. I hadn't made the connection. "And she likes Donovan?" I try not to sound too surprised.

"Of course. She'll be here for the wedding."

I picture my flowery mom relating to an antisocial punk. The Lord works in mysterious ways.

"Maybe it's too hard for Dad to see Mom again," I suggest. Corrine definitely wouldn't be invited.

Trinity sinks onto a corner bench. "Dad said he would come, except the wedding is the same weekend as the cruise he's going on with his new wife."

I blink a couple of times. I hate to be the bearer of bad news, but Dad's lying to get out of the wedding. "Um…That can't be right. Dad's cruise is in a few weeks."

"No, it's right. We're getting married the week before Valentine's Day."

My eyes feel like they're going to pop out of my head. "What?"

Trinity's voice isn't whiny anymore. It's rushed…to go along with her animated motions. "There was a cancellation at the old train depot. I've always wanted to get married there. The next opening isn't until the fall."

First of all, are they insane? You can't plan a wedding or be emotionally prepared for it in a matter of weeks. Secondly, the depot is expensive. How can they afford it? And third, "Eric is counseling you guys. I don't think he'll agree to do your wedding until you've completed his course."

Trinity rolls her eyes. "This isn't *License to Wed*. Eric does want us to finish a book and do the exercises, so we're meeting with him twice a week." She stands up and starts riffling through racks of dresses. "The funny thing is that Donovan is really into it. If I mention the wedding, he turns talk back to a chapter in the book."

I never would have expected that from a slacker. "Is his family coming out for the ceremony?"

Trinity holds a black dress in front of me. Morbid. "He doesn't have much family, but his mom is coming for sure."

I'm trying to picture what the wedding will be like. The train depot is beautiful—on a hill overlooking the city. The outside is stucco, and the inside is simply hardwood and windows. Why would she make the occasion so elaborate when not many people will be attending. How can she afford to?

"Is…um…is Donovan's mom helping pay for the ceremony?" I have the right to ask. It's because I care about my little sister.

"I didn't tell you?" She places a hat on my head. Very 80s. "Donovan still lives with his mom so I didn't think he made very much money, but I guess being a computer consultant brings in six figures a year."

What?

"Most of it he's put in savings or invested. I get to spend whatever I want on the wedding and for the honeymoon we are going to Europe."

Double what? My little sister can't even hold down a job of her own. She didn't finish college. She had her car repossessed. And now she's going to have the life of a princess? I don't know what to think besides NO FAIR. "Wow!"

Her grin lights up her face. "Donovan can work from anywhere, so I think we're going to move to Boise. He's been looking at real estate. He wants to get a place where his mom can live with us."

I feel the skin between my eyebrows crease. "What are *you* going to do?" I can't picture her with children yet. Or in any kind of domestic setting.

Trinity has moved on from black to brown dresses. Boring. "Dee Dee offered me a position managing the front desk of Dee Light's."

It fits. Though I don't know about the word "managing." It's more like an answer-phones-and-set-appointments position.

"What do you think?" she asks when I don't respond.

I don't know what to think. The run-away rebel is turning into a Stepford Wife. "I think…you are growing up." I've *got* to buy my own house now.

She holds up a cheetah-print gown. "The black spots will go with the sash on my wedding dress."

Maybe she hasn't grown up after all. "I also think that if you want me to wear that dress, you should hold your ceremony in the jungle so I'm camouflaged and nobody will see me."

Chapter 35

I've gotten it all written out. I know exactly what I'm going to say to Dad. I rip the paper out of my notebook with aggression.

The Bible is confusing to me on this issue. It says not to let the sun go down on your anger, but it also says to sleep on it. I figure I'm doing a little of both by calling Dad the next day. And I'm using Eric's confrontation tool, as well.

Dad tried to call me on Christmas, but I was up in McCall so we haven't spoken since I hung up on him. He answers on the third ring. I wonder if he's expecting my call, knowing that I would have heard the news from Trinity by now.

"Hello?" He answers as if he can't read caller ID and doesn't know it's me.

"Hi, Dad." My words are familiar, yet my voice is businesslike.

"Hi, Bethany. How was your Christmas?"

Too bad his question is more like small talk than caring conversation. "I spent it with some friends. How was yours?"

"I'm a grandpa," Dad says. He has no idea how true the statement really is.

"Congratulations." Corrine's daughter Felicia used to sing in our worship band. I really am happy for her. But I think Dad is going a little far to consider her child his first grandchild. I sigh because that's not what I called to talk about.

"Thank you." Dad's voice is hesitant. "I heard about Trinity's wedding."

This is another tricky subject for me. I don't agree with Trinity's choice of spouse, but I agree even less with Dad's choice to not attend the ceremony.

"Don't you think you should meet the guy?" I momentarily revert to being a hurt little girl. I want my Daddy to care enough about his daughters to give his blessing...or not give his blessing.

He used to be my protector. Like when Mom let me ride my tricycle down a hill and it rolled out of control. He came running. After lifting me out of the rosebush, he carried me and my tricycle home. I used to think he was so strong. Now I know better.

"I would like to, Bethany, but Trinity didn't give me much of a heads up. It's actually my anniversary and I've promised to take Corrine on a cruise."

"Who cares?" I want to scream. But I don't. I grip my sheet of notebook paper like a weapon. I could let him have it right now, but he would become defensive and shut down. I have medicine to give him, and I want him to be receptive. "May I give you some feedback?" I ask calmly...I mean *icily*. It's the best I can do.

Dad doesn't respond at first. He'd probably prepared for me to yell and hang up on him. He doesn't know how to handle the mature, reasonable side of Bethany. "Okay."

I'm leaning over my kitchen counter, too pent up to sit down. I smooth the edges of my notes where I'd clutched them in my fist. I'll focus on the words. (The emotions are only going to get in the way.)

"Dad." I take a deep breath before reading what I have to say. "I experience you as selfish and it keeps you from having a close relationship with your children." Trinity is his child. Not Felicia.

I'm his child. I'm his firstborn daughter. Mom said that he used to pray over my cradle every morning. He used to grab my littlest finger and tell me that I had him wrapped around my pinkie. He taught me my alphabet and bought me my first bike and came to all my swim meets.

"Honey..." He says this in a way that tells me he's not mad. In fact his voice kind of breaks as if he's hurting like I am. "I'm not doing this out of selfishness. I'm..." he doesn't finish.

"You're going on a cruise," I fill in for him. Oops. Even I can hear the bitterness in my words. But I'm not going to let myself be a victim. I've acknowledged his choice, I've owned my decision to call him, I made a plan to give feedback, and now I'm moving on.

"Yes," Dad admits. "I'm going to miss the wedding, but I'll be in Boise in March and I would really like to see you then. I do want a relationship."

So he says. "What's in March?" You wanna bet he's not just coming to see his kids?

"I'm speaking at Living Faith."

He's got to be kidding me. First of all, why would they have him back? Second, why would he want to go back? "Why?" I blurt out.

Dad clicks his tongue. "You know that Corrine inherited land here in Montana and that's why we moved away, right?"

Another excuse to leave his first family behind. "Sure." Where's he going with this?

"Well, Corrine and I have prayed about it, and we decided to use the property to start a retreat center for fallen pastors."

I feel the gasp rise from deep inside my chest. "You're what?"

"There's a huge need. The church I go to now has four fallen pastors attending. And Felicia's church down in Florida has a pastor who just got caught for using the church phone to call phone sex lines."

I'm horrified. Would being around other broken ministers make my dad feel better about himself?

"What are you going to call it?" I ask sarcastically. "Adulterers Anonymous won't work because AA is already taken." I'm instantly hit with guilt. Adultery is in the Ten Commandments, but so is honoring your father and mother. "Sorry," I mutter.

Dad must have figured out the whole anger issue because he responds slowly. "I've sinned, Bethany, but I've been redeemed. And now I'm in the perfect position to offer hope to families who are going through similar circumstances."

What he says makes sense, even though it reminds me of the charity to help out retired NFL football players. I'm thinking there are others in more need. And I'm also thinking that there is another person better suited to lead it. You know, like a pastor who sinned, but stayed with his family and got his priorities back in order.

"So you're talking to Dying...I mean Living Faith about your retreat center?" I'm still trying to figure all this out.

"Yes."

"And they support you?" I've got reasons to ask this in disbelief.

"Yes."

"Wow." A million questions run through my mind, but they are so jumbled that I can't disconnect them. I want to know what Mom has to say about this. And Christian. And Eric. "Does anybody else know?" I choke out at last.

"I've been networking quite a bit, and I'm getting a great response."

So maybe that's why he hasn't had any time for me. Before it was the church and now it's the retreat center. I'm never going to be the first ministry in my father's life.

"I hope you'll come out and visit sometime. We're putting in a pool the shape of a dove. And we'll have horseback riding—sleigh rides in the winter."

It sounds more like a resort than a retreat. "Will you have counseling and worship and speakers and prayer and—"

"Of course."

I don't want to like it. But I do. I just don't like my dad being in charge of it. It's like hiring an obese personal trainer. This can't possibly be God's will.

"I don't know, Dad. The land you are using came from the other woman. What kind of message does that give?"

He doesn't miss a best. "It shows that God gives second chances."

"Second Chance Ranch." The name comes out of nowhere. It's good, and I'm afraid that it will encourage Dad.

The name Adulterers Anonymous fit better.

Dad repeats the name. "I like it, honey. But I'd like it even better if my daughter gave me a second chance."

I tried. He took it and ran. "Dad, I think you're working on seventy times seven." I state the number that Jesus said we are to forgive. I'm sure Jesus meant we are to forgive an infinite amount of times, but I wonder if I would be let off the hook if Dad used up all 490 I-forgive-yous, and I told him I didn't have any left.

"Well," Dad pauses. "Once again, I'm sorry I can't make it to Trinity's wedding."

The words are empty. I bite my cheek. Why do I even let it matter anymore? "I guess I'll see you in March."

I hear my clock tick in the silence. Finally Dad asks, "Will you come hear me at Living Faith?"

Dying Faith? I don't think so. "Been there. Done that. It ended badly." Yes, I'm being cruel, but it's the truth.

I hear Dad's enormous intake of breath, and prepare for an explosion like that of an over-inflated balloon. I flinched for no reason. Dad lets the air out slowly. "Alright then, Bethany. I'll call you when I get there."

I want to say, "Don't strain yourself," but I refrain. If Dad is serous about coming to visit then I'll just let him prove it. But so far, all he's done is let me down.

Chapter 36

I'm early to counseling, but I can't wait to talk to Eric. Not only did I climb the accountability ladder after my dad victimized me (yet again) by refusing to come to Trinity's wedding, but I calmly gave him feedback. He wasn't happy to hear it, but I do think I earned his respect. This is a huge change of position.

Eric's secretary isn't behind her desk so I walk past it to announce myself. I peek into Eric's office before knocking. I do plan to knock, really I do, but my fist pauses in mid air when I see Eric and Brooke in an embrace. Wow, Eric really is a passionate pastor.

I cover my mouth with my hands to keep a giggle from escaping. I feel like I'm back in third grade when my best friend and I stole Christian's love letters written to his girlfriend.

Eric's hands cup Brooke's face and I hear her moan. He kisses down her cheek to her jawbone then back to her ear.

I should step back and give them their privacy. But their door is wide open. And I do have an appointment. Besides, this is the closest I've been to romance in a long time. (Movies don't count.)

A stapler falls onto the floor as Eric turns Brooke's back toward the desk and leans in over her. Ooh. I fan myself. No wonder she's so excited for her wedding night. I feel a twinge in my gut. It can't be jealousy. It's probably more like guilt. I'll step back now and let them finish their interlude. I'm obviously not invited.

"Bethany!" The voice comes from behind me. The secretary is back. She doesn't know that I'm spying, just that I'm waiting for Eric.

But now Eric knows I saw everything. He lets go of Brooke and wipes his mouth as his eyes meet mine.

The secretary keeps talking. "Sorry I didn't see you come in. You're a little early. Eric should be here soon."

I look over my shoulder at the older woman as Eric walks toward the door to show himself. "I'm here, Rebecca," he says.

She looks startled. "Oh. I didn't see you come in either, Pastor."

Brooke chooses this moment to exit. She stops right between Eric and me. "Oh my gosh. I didn't know you were here, Bethany. Sorry for that little scene. Eric can't keep his hands off me." She doesn't sound sorry. And she doesn't act sorry when kissing Eric goodbye. And my guess is that *she* is the one who can't keep her hands off her fiancée.

Rebecca busies herself with paperwork so I follow Eric back into his office. He's acting embarrassed. He doesn't even sit in the loveseat next to me. He moves behind his desk. The longer he looks down at his computer keyboard the bigger my smile grows.

He clears his throat and looks up. "How are you today?" He fidgets with his pen and his face is tinged pink. He's adorable.

I shrug as if I don't have a care in the world. "At the moment I'm feeling pretty good. I can't remember what I came here to talk about, but I won't ever forget what I just saw."

Eric purses his lips. "I don't...we don't usually..."

"So that's why Brooke can't stop talking about you—not that she ever stops talking."

Eric shakes his head at my teasing. Now he gets a little gleam in his eyes. "A pastor *should* be passionate."

"I agree." I laugh. "Though most don't give a demonstration."

Eric chuckles, too. I love that he can laugh at himself. "A couple more weeks and it won't be such a big deal."

I give him my best innocent look. "Who's making a big deal out of it?"

"Not you," he plays along.

"Not me." I say, though my wicked grin is back.

"Good." He comes around the desk and joins me on the

couch—trying to bully me into moving on. "So, how are you really?"

I'm still high on the fact that I caught my pastor making out with his girlfriend. "Um..." I sit sideways facing him and rest one arm along the top of the sofa. I play with a string from the seam of the cushion. "I'm great."

Eric doesn't know how to respond to my answer. How many clients go to counseling to tell their counselor that they feel great? "Great," he echoes. A safe response.

Maybe I don't need counseling anymore. Eric got me out of the victim role. He showed me how to become accountable. He taught me how to give and accept feedback. I was tested this weekend with my dad, and I passed.

"Wanna go out for coffee?" I sound like Star suggesting we celebrate with food, but I do deserve a celebration.

Eric's gaze meets mine. He hesitates. "I shouldn't."

Because I'm a client? "Come on. I'll pay." There.

"Bethany, you should know better than anyone why I can't go out for coffee with you." His voice is low and almost admonishing.

I'm confused. Doesn't he drink coffee? I don't usually, but it would be nice to get away from the stuffy office. We had so much fun at Comedy Sportz, just the two of us goofing off...

"Oh." He doesn't want it to be just the two of us. But I hadn't even thought of it that way. It's not like I'm Corrine. "It's just coffee," I offer one more time, willing him to reconsider.

"I know." He runs one hand through his hair. "And I would like to go out for coffee with you. But if I don't draw the line now then I won't know where to draw it. Brooke and I agreed not to ever be one-on-one in a social setting with members of the opposite sex."

I drop my hand into my lap and sink deeper into the cushions. I hadn't seen this coming. And even if I had, I wouldn't have expected to feel this great loss. "Brooke wouldn't mind. We're just friends." Eric is one of my best friends.

Eric now turns sideways and raises an arm to the back of the couch. "You're right. Brooke wouldn't mind. But I'm sure your mom didn't mind your dad helping out his secretary at first either."

"That's not fair." I've never once thought of stealing Eric. I've never tried to cozy up to him or seduce him. I'm not like that.

Eric holds up a hand. "I'm not trying to be mean. I'm just saying that I can't make any exceptions. I'm keeping myself accountable in this way."

It's not about me. He's planning to make his wife a priority in his life. That's great. But for some reason I thought I would be on his list of priorities, as well. I mean, I feel like family. I spent Christmas with him. We fight like siblings. We love to tease each other.

I don't feel so great anymore. I'm left out. I'm lonely. If *I'm* not planning to get married, but all my male friends do, that will leave me with only girls to hang out with. I'm going to be the third wheel everywhere I go. Even Trinity is getting married.

My thoughts eventually lead to my dad. I guess I should have brought him up to begin with. I sink even lower in my seat. If we're not going out I might as well get comfortable. "Dad isn't coming for Trinity's wedding."

Eric pauses, as if to change gears and catch up with my train of thought. "I hadn't heard. How's Trinity?"

I shrug. He should have asked how I'm doing. I'm the one in his office. "She's stressed. If she changes the date of her wedding he can come, but I'm pretty sure she won't do it just for him."

"Hmmm." Eric looks like he's still thinking about my sister.

"I called him," I announce, even though he didn't ask. "I gave him feedback."

Now I've got Eric's attention. He's looking pretty concerned.

"I didn't yell or cry." I'm feeling kind of numb, actually. Like, who needs a dad, anyway? "Though I did get a little upset when he told me he's planning to start a retreat center for fallen pastors."

Eric kind of does a double take, though he was already looking at me. "What an amazing idea."

I chew on my cheek. "It would be amazing if somebody else were to run it. Dad should be a visitor."

"I don't know," Eric tries to reason with me. "Think about how Brooke was able to lead Dee Dee to the Lord because she'd had an abortion. Because of your dad's mistakes he's going to be able to relate and minister to the visitors."

I press my lips together because I don't want to agree. I've taken steps to forgive my dad, but that doesn't mean I have to trust him.

Eric encourages me to pray about it. He then commends me for the changes I've made. He affirms the way I gave feedback. But somehow that numb feeling doesn't leave me.

Yes, I've moved forward, but it's like I've climbed to the top of a hill where I can clearly see how much farther I have to go. It's the same in the world of exercise and movement science: the more I learn, the more I realize I don't know.

Eric's words seem hollow, too. I know he does care, but he doesn't care enough. I thought he was hurting with me, but maybe all along he was just trying to fix a problem he felt like he created.

I want him to take up my offenses. Sure, I handled the conflict well, but the bigger point should be that Dad's choice to go on a cruise instead of walk Trinity down the aisle is wrong. Eric should get angry. He should want to protect me. But I guess he can only fill that role in Brooke's life now.

I head home feeling worse than I did when I arrived. I stick a potato in the microwave and pull some leftover homemade chili out of the refrigerator. Curling into a fetal position on my bed I close my eyes. Is this what the rest of my life will be like? Dinner for one and a cold bed? Nobody here to ask how my day was. Nobody here to wipe away my tears. Nobody to take my side...or challenge me when I'm on the wrong side.

I think about the road ahead of me. It's not only long, it's lonely. Christian has Laurel. Trinity has Donovan. Eric has Brooke. All I have is humiliating dates and stolen kisses. Maybe Eric is right. Maybe my journey isn't supposed to be made alone, no matter the risk.

Dad messed up his relationship with Mom. I'd always thought their marriage was perfect, and when I discovered it was a lie, my hope was shaken so badly that I lost it for a while. I want to hope again.

I stretch and roll over. I rub my eyes. I'm groggy, but I should call Eric and tell him my decision before I fall asleep. It seems so unreal, that if I wait until morning, I might think it all a dream.

But it's real. I want somebody to look past my faults the way Eric looks past Brooke's. I want somebody to stand up for me the way Eric stands up for Brooke. I want somebody to kiss me the way Eric kisses Brooke.

I fumble through my purse on the nightstand to find my little address book with Eric's phone number. I've never called him at home before. I could just call Laurel and tell her my new desire and the faith God has given me, but Eric is the one that inspired this change. He interrupted my kiss with Paul. He suggested that the rip in my pants was not an "accident." And most importantly, he read me the verse about growing into the largeness of marriage and believed that I could do it.

I smile softly into the receiver and get comfortable under my covers as I wait for Eric to answer the ring. Maybe he's not home yet.

First there is a crash, then Eric's voice answers. "Hello?" He sounds like he needs to clear his throat.

"It's me. Bethany."

"Are you okay?" His voice goes up an octave.

How cute is that? He does care. My bed is so warm. I

couldn't feel any more peaceful. "Yeah. I'm just calling to ask you to marry me."

The phone is silent. I snuggle deeper into my pillow waiting for his response. He must be shocked that I've become open to the idea of a wedding.

"What?" His voice sounds deep now.

"I've decided that if God wants to bring a man into my life I will consider marriage." He's still silent, so I continue on. "When that time comes, will you do my ceremony like you're doing Trinity's?" Maybe my dad will give me away. Maybe Christian will. But if Eric gives his blessing, I'll know that I'm going to be fine.

"Uh…" Eric is out of it tonight. "I thought you meant…Sure."

"I know it's a huge step for me, but you are the one I have to thank for it. That's why I called you instead of Laurel."

He's quiet again for a second. "At midnight?"

Now it's my turn to say, "What?" I jerk up on my elbow and squint at the neon green numbers on my alarm clock. My potato has been done for hours. "I must have fallen asleep." I'm so embarrassed. If Eric isn't allowed to go out for coffee with me, then having late night conversations is probably taboo, too.

Eric chuckles. "As long as you are awake right now, it's okay. What made you decide to want to get married?"

I sink back down and stare at my ceiling light that is still on. If I'd picked the floor plan with the window in the bedroom I would have seen how dark it was outside and this wouldn't have happened. I sigh. "Seeing you kiss Brooke… among other things."

"Huh." That's all he says and I start to wonder if I'm giving the wrong impression. But then he says, "You have my permission to kiss Mick, now."

"Mick?" The guy who probably has Al Capone in his genealogy? I guess I did want to kiss him for New Year's.

"He's had a crush on you since you came to Grace Chapel. But I didn't want him to start anything if you weren't willing to commit."

"A crush?" Gangsters get crushes? It's been a while since anyone has had a crush on me. Since, like, sixth grade.

"Yeah. He was burned pretty badly by one woman, so now he's kind of shy...intimidated, you could say."

A shy gangster. "What happened?" I'm more nosy than interested.

"Bethany," he sounds weary. "He'll have to tell you himself. And I'm going to go back to bed."

"Okay." I guess it's late...and none of my business. "I just wanted to..."

"Ask me to marry you." Eric finished.

I let out a loud he-haw. "Is that what I said?" No wonder he hadn't answered right away.

"That's what you said." I'm visualizing his smile. "And the answer is yes. I will marry you."

Chapter 37

I'm fasting today. I'm not excited about it, but I have this feeling that if I don't do it I will be missing out. Kind of like when actor Stephen Baldwin's wife became a Christian. She would lie down on the floor and talk to God every morning and every night for an hour until Stephen started to think she knew something that he didn't. Now he's got a huge ministry.

Like I said, fasting goes against everything I teach my clients...but like Eric (and King David) said, you can't give God a sacrifice that is no sacrifice. After feeling led to research fasting I found some convicting scriptures. Jesus fasted—which I knew, but I didn't know about Daniel, David, the whole city of Ninevah and all the Jews in Esther's time. Esther's story was the most intriguing to me. Not only had I dressed up as Queen Esther for a harvest party one year, but the story of Esther was listed under a reason to fast that I could relate to. *Reason #7: We fast in times of crisis.* I should have been doing this a long time ago.

Here's my plan. I'm going to fast the last Saturday of every month. (I picked Saturday because I don't usually have any clients.) I will drink liquids and probably have a smoothie like Dee Dee does. I'm going to spend extra time in the Bible and prayer. And last, I'm not going to tell anybody what I'm doing. It's going to be private, between me and God.

Okay, I can get excited about this. Eric gave a sermon on Sunday about how we so often use the phrase, "I'm waiting on God," when maybe God is just waiting for us. So I'm taking a step forward in faith. If only I'd realized that Laurel had planned Trinity's bridal shower for the last Saturday of this month.

"Are you done with the balloons yet, Bethany?" Laurel calls from the kitchen where she is mixing the punch.

I tie the bouquet to the top of the banister. "Finished," I yell back at Laurel. I'm trying to avoid the kitchen where she's got fruit-kabobs and sub sandwiches and cream cheese mints overflowing the serving trays.

"Great. Will you put the sherbet in the punch for me? I've got to run and change before anybody else shows up."

Laurel is wearing sweats and one of Christian's t-shirts. Apparently her clothes are becoming too tight for comfort, but she doesn't want to buy maternity yet.

I'm not going to tell her I'm fasting. I'm not going to tell her I'm fasting. "Okay."

My stomach rumbles and my head starts to pound. I have no idea how Jesus fasted for forty days. This one day is killing me.

I try not to inhale the scent of fresh baked rolls stuffed with roast beef and cheddar. Mmm. I am so going to Arby's for breakfast in the morning.

"Hey Lord," I pray. "No accidents, right? You are teaching me a lesson here. And You want me to talk to you now instead of stuffing my face with delicious..." I can almost taste it... "delicious..." What was I praying about again?

My tongue feels dry and swollen from neglect. I pour the last of the 7-Up over the sherbet and scoop a cup for myself. The sweetness almost makes my eyes water. I down the rest as the doorbell rings.

I trot down the half-flight of stairs to the front door. Everybody arrives at once. Star and Dee Dee came together which makes my heart glad. Their mom arrives right behind them, followed by Brooke and a couple of Trinity's old high school friends. Brook is talking as if she was the one who grew up with them.

Finally, Trinity arrives. She claps her hands and gives hugs all around. She looks good. Happy. I'm happy for her. So happy, in fact, that I'm wearing a Cheetah print dress in her wedding next week. I have no idea what I will do with the thing when the wedding is over. Her wedding pictures are so going to get made fun of by her children.

She steps to the middle of the room and holds her arms overhead as if she'd just jogged up the stairs with Rocky Balboa. "I have an announcement!" she exclaims.

My pulse flutters, and I wonder if Dad has rescheduled his cruise and will be coming to the wedding after all.

"Donovan and I had our last counseling session this morning." She's more excited than I've ever been after counseling. "Donavan asked Jesus into his heart. He prayed the sinner's prayer with Pastor Austin."

My mouth drops open. What a year. First Dee Dee and now Donovan. "That's amazing." I rush to hug her, but Brooke steps right in front of me.

"My prayers have paid off." Brooke shouts.

I can't believe what a loud mouth she is. First of all, Trinity is *my* sister. I should be the one hugging her. And second, it's like Brooke just took credit for Donovan's conversion. It's not as if she was the only one praying.

But even as I think this, deep inside I feel a twinge of guilt because I know Donovan's newfound Christianity is not a result of my nonexistent prayers. Still, she doesn't have to be the center of attention. I step around her to hug Trinity second.

I pour myself another glass of punch and wonder if anyone has ever become a punchoholic before. Though I doubt it will take the edge off the way alcohol is supposed to.

Laurel leads us in a couple of her creative games, which everybody plays while stuffing their faces—everybody except me. Then she cuts the cake. It's not just any cake, of course. Laurel special ordered a cake that looks like an actual computer because that is how my sister met her fiancée. It's covered in fondant so it's smooth. The letters on the "keyboard" spell out Donovan and Trinity's names.

I back away as everybody digs in. I bet it's delicious. *I love you, Lord. I love you, Lord. I must really love you, Lord.*

"Hey, Bethany," Star calls. "Aren't you hungry?"

Umm, yeah. Even if I were talking about my fast, Star is the last one who would understand. She smiled politely, of course, when Trinity made her announcement about Donovan, but she's not "into religion." I pick up a third cup of punch. "I'm just going to drink some punch for now, Star. Thanks."

Star gives me a disgusted look and pops a cashew in her mouth. She probably thinks I'm anorexic.

We all gather around Trinity as Laurel pushes the coffee table laden with presents her way. I'm having trouble focusing, though. I really wish people would throw away their cake plates when they finish eating because I'm imagining myself licking off the crumbs. I start to feel a little shaky.

A loud giggle draws my attention back toward my sister.

"That's from me," Brooke sings as Trinity holds up a long nightgown. "I bought myself a matching one for my honeymoon."

I wonder where Eric is taking his bride. I imagine him running through the surf of an exotic location in his swimming trunks. I bet he would enjoy surfing. My head starts to spin.

Trinity grabs another gift bag. She pulls out something black and lacy.

Brooke gives a wolf whistle. I hold my throbbing head. I can't take it. "Brooke!" I blurt in exasperation. My voice sounds overly-loud even to me.

I remove my fingers from my temple and look up to find all eyes on me. I'm about to explain that I have a headache, but Brooke explodes in laughter. I'd meant to quiet her down, but she turns up the volume.

"I guess I'm a little excited." She begins a monologue on her wedding, and I want to ask if she's forgotten who we are celebrating today, but I keep my mouth shut...until Trinity gets to my gift.

"I love it." Trinity giggles as she pulls out a Minnie Mouse pajama set. "It's so..."

"Sexy," we say together and laugh. As little girls we used to think Minnie Mouse was beautiful.

"Thank you." Trinity leans over and gives me a hug. This last month of sharing an apartment started out rough. And while she's still a slob, she's also a really good listener and has my same sense of humor. It's been nice getting to know her on an adult level. I lean back in my chair, feeling short of breath for some reason.

"Minnie Mouse?" Brooke questions my taste. "Bethany, I'm not so sure I want you to come to *my* bridal shower anymore. I get enough of cartoon characters at work."

I can't bite my tongue any longer. She's being rude. Even if she is only voicing what everyone else is thinking, she still needs to use a little discernment. "Really, Brooke? Because sometimes you seem like an adolescent to me." Everybody has stopped talking, and I should too. Instead, I rashly decide to finish what I've started. "You're going to be a pastor's wife in a couple of weeks, so you might try to act like it." As soon as it's out, I realize it sounded more harsh than I meant it. But I did mean it.

Laurel's face is white. She stands up and starts gathering empty cake plates—about time. Trinity folds her new pajamas gingerly, her eyes watching for my next move.

Brooke's mouth opens and closes. I wonder if I should remind her how she is supposed to accept feedback: I acknowledge your position, blah, blah, blah... Of course, I probably should have asked her if she wanted feedback first, then phrased it in a loving way—even though I'm not feeling loving at the moment. I feel...weird.

Brooke is as quiet as I've ever heard her. She starts to stammer. "I...I was having fun. I didn't mean..."

"Bethany," Laurel calls from the kitchen. "Will you help me pour coffee?"

I don't know what to say to Brooke. I don't want to say anything else in front of an audience. So I get up and respond to Laurel's call. She's not going to be happy with me.

"Can you believe her?" I half-whisper when I get to the kitchen.

"She's my guest," Laurel says shortly, pointing out that my behavior reflects poorly on her hostessing. She hands me four thick mugs made out of pottery. I bet she made them herself. "Do you want coffee?" she asks.

Coffee makes me shaky and hyper-sensitive, even when I eat food with it. If I were to drink it today I would be out of control. Oh! It hits me. All that sugar from the punch has gone straight to my head.

It reminds me of the time I went to Jade's body building competition. She'd gotten first place, but when I congratulated her afterwards she didn't even remember receiving the award. She'd cut down so low on carbs that her brain wasn't functioning properly. The opposite must have happened to me.

"Laurel." I set the mugs down. I can't tell her that I'm a fasting fool. "I'm not feeling very well. I need to lie down." Even as I say it, I'm holding onto the counter to stay steady.

Laurel looks at me and nods. She's probably thinking that if I'm sick, she'll have an excuse for my cranky behavior. "Go ahead. I'll explain your absence."

She wants to be rid of me. I oblige her unexpressed request, and make a hasty exit. I doubt Eric will let me off as easily.

Chapter 38

My stomach gets me up early the next day to eat breakfast. Eggs, hash browns, toast, and orange juice. My strength is back. Since I'm up, I decide to go to church early and apologize to Brooke. I wonder if she'll still want me in her wedding, let alone keep me as her personal trainer.

I leave Trinity sleeping on my couch and am one of the first to arrive at Grace Chapel. The worship team is running through a couple songs on stage. I stand at the back and wait.

"Bethany." My name is called from the office area. Chills run down my spine as I turn to see Eric waving me over.

I remember how he didn't take offense at my dad's behavior—didn't fight for me. But Brooke is his fiancée. I'm guessing that he's got a few choice words to say in *her* defense.

Guilt causes my heart to pound in my chest as I make my way over. I know I said I wouldn't tell anyone that I fasted, but Eric is my counselor. He's going to want an explanation, and I need to be honest. I hold up my hand to stop him from attacking so I can get my defense in first.

"I'm going to apologize to her. That's why I'm here early," I say. "I wasn't myself yesterday. See, I was fasting for the first time. Without thinking I drank a lot of punch and the sugar in it..."

Eric tilts his head. "What happened yesterday?"

I pause. He doesn't know? "Um...nothing?"

Eric's eyebrows draw together. "What did you do?"

I squeeze my lips tight for as long as I can, but then the story bursts out anyway. "I called Brooke adolescent and told her to start acting like a preacher's wife."

"Really?" He sounds contemplative, though I have no idea what he's thinking. "What did *she* do?"

I can't believe Brooke didn't tell him. I would think she would want to tell her side first and get him to back her up. "She..." I don't want to say it too rudely. "She kept talking about *her* wedding and *her* honeymoon while my sister was opening shower gifts—nothing major. I just had a headache. I'm really sorry."

Eric looks down, and I might be wrong, but I think I spy a small smile on his lips. "She's embarrassed," he says. "I've given her feedback on this kind of thing before. Don't worry. She'll forgive you."

Relief rushes over me. "I don't normally..."

"I know." He nods. "Fasting is always a humbling experience."

We look at each other for a moment. I'm expecting him to say something else. He doesn't. "So if you didn't call me over to talk about Brooke, what did you want to talk about?"

"Oh." Eric pauses and rubs his chin. "Your check bounced."

I don't follow. I paid my tithe at the beginning of the month and the statement showed that it cleared already. "No..."

"Your earnest money."

I stand up straighter. "Are you sure? I verified the total of my bank account with Jade. She told me I had plenty more in the bank than what I paid your brother."

Eric studies me with concern in his eyes. "You should double check with your bank. And call Trent tomorrow. He'll be expecting it."

Confusion clouds my mind. It didn't make any sense. "Okay." My voice is high and hesitant. Thoughts tumble through my mind and out my mouth. "I wouldn't have written a bad check. I hope I'm not a victim of debit card theft. It must be some accounting mistake."

"Okay. Don't worry about it. I just wanted you to know." Eric looks past me. "I've got to go fill in for the greeter today."

"Sure." I'm not really listening. What could have happened to my money?

I take a seat on the right of the sanctuary where Christian and Laurel usually sit. Dee Dee, Trinity, and Donovan sit

with us now, too. We take up a whole row. And if I was paying attention, I would have saved them the seats, but I'm
calculating numbers in my head.

Mick plops down next to me. I glance up and immediately
wonder if Eric passed on the news that I'm looking for a
husband now.

"Hi." He smiles. He does have a nice smile—not cocky
or fake.

I might as well give him real back. I could flirt with him
and make him feel good about himself the way I did with
Paul and Robbie. I could act like I've got it all together
and wait until we've been dating a while to show my true
colors. But I won't get his hopes up. Eric said he's already
had his heart broken. And honestly, he could do better
than me.

"I lost $15,000," I say.

Mick takes this in slowly. "Are you a gambler?"

"No." I shake my head. "No. I'm just an idiot." He doesn't
look like he believes me so I have to convince him. "I kissed
a guy who already has a pregnant girlfriend. I split my pants
open while bowling. And yesterday I called the pastor's fiancée names."

"Interesting," he surmises.

"Scary," I correct.

"Wait 'till you hear what I've done."

Uh-oh. Is this where he confesses that he's a contract killer?

"I hit a mentally-challenged woman with a golf ball when
golfing last summer. I accidentally painted a client's car
black instead of white. And before I got Lasik surgery, I wore
glasses with one lens that always popped out."

I can't keep from giggling. I think I've encouraged him.

"As for the romance department, my fiancée left me for
my brother."

"Oh no." So that's what Eric had been talking about. I
momentarily forget about my money, but the sick feeling in
the pit of my stomach doesn't go away. In fact it gets quea-

sier thinking about what it would be like to lose the person you love to your own sibling. "When did that happen?"

"It's been a couple years now. But I have to see them together at holidays and reunions."

And I thought *I* had a messed up family. I don't know how to respond. Mick must be the nicest guy ever to attend family functions when it obviously rips his heart out. But nice guys finish last, don't they?

I'm saved from saying something stupid when Trinity and Donovan slide into the seat next to me. Donovan is holding a brand new Bible with his name engraved on the cover. And he's wearing a tie instead of his dog collar—it's an interesting look for him. The rest of my family slides in behind us as the music starts.

I totally lip synch my way through worship. It's pretty hard to concentrate when you don't know if somebody has assumed your identity and wiped out your whole bank account—kind of a distracting thought.

Finally Eric steps up to the microphone. "It's been a great week," he announces. I beg to differ. "I had the privilege of leading someone to the Lord." He looks everywhere but at Donovan. "I don't want to speak for him, but if the individual wants to name himself, now would be a great time."

The congregation applauds and looks around. I look at Donovan and clap along. He's staring down at his Bible and might as well be asleep for all the moving he's doing.

I nudge Trinity who nudges Donovan. He doesn't react.

"Come on, Donny," she whispers.

The applause dies down. Eric leans forward to the microphone to continue, obviously realizing that he's embarrassed my future brother-in-law. "Well..."

Donovan leaps out of his seat, arms flung wide. "It was *me!*"

If the term thunderous applause hadn't already been a common phrase, I still would have used it to describe the moment. The roar comes from clapping, stomping, and woo-hooing. Emotion fills the room and tears spring into my eyes. This must be how the angels celebrate each new birth into the kingdom. It's divine.

The clapping continues and we all lean in to embrace Donovan. This has to be the best moment in all my church-going experiences. Donovan changed his position and publicly became accountable for his decision. And by the way he shouted, there's no way he's ashamed anymore. I can't wait to see how God uses him.

The joy that surges through me dispels the anxiety that had been attacking. I'll worry about my money later. For the rest of the service I make up for my previously unholy behavior.

Chapter 39

The train depot is all wooden floors and soaring ceilings, but the rows of windows that earlier let in the bright winter sunshine now outline a view of the lights from downtown Boise. Twinkling white Christmas lights continue the pattern around the room, giving the place a warm glow. The soft scent of roses is unmistakable. It's going to be a simple, yet elegant wedding. Not what I would have expected after seeing the bridesmaid dresses Trinity picked out.

I'm wearing it now. And I just wore it to The Red Letter Café. Us girls have been primping all day and now that the guests are about to arrive, we realized we were hungry. Being Maid-of-Honor meant I had the honor of running errands in my feline frock. With the looks I got, I might as well have been wearing a headband with cat ears and eyeliner whiskers.

I plop the bag of sandwiches and container of drinks down on the table in the back room and stare at my little sister. Since I'd left, Dee Dee had twisted her hair up and pinned her veil in place. I feel my heart skip a beat. Is that really the little girl I used to lock out of the bathroom when getting ready for school? Is she the same teenager who got arrested for putting shaving cream all over her ex-boyfriend's truck? It can't be the slob who only last week ate the Thai food that had been left out on the counter all night.

My hand raises to my chest as if I'm about to say the Pledge of Allegiance. "Trinity. You're a woman."

I hear a sniffle from Mom before she wraps us both in a hug. "My baby is getting married," she whispers.

This had not been what we expected when Trinity ran off to meet a guy from the Internet. We wanted her to stay home where she was safe, to meet a guy from church, and

257

keep a job or at least go to school. But now Donovan is a Christian. And he's going to take good care of Trinity.

Our lives must be like one side of a Rubiks cube in God's hands. We try our hardest to get our own colors to line up, but God often twists us out of alignment to get the colors of other people's lives to come together first. Like how Brooke was able to witness to Dee Dee because they both had abortions. Or how Dad is going to help teach fallen pastors at his retreat center by being an example of what not to do. Or even how Eric only came into my life because he was there when my dad confessed.

As if thinking of Eric causes him to appear, he peeks into the room at the same time he knocks. Seeing that we are all dressed, he joins us inside. He's wearing a suit—something I have never seen him in before since everyone wears jeans to Grace Chapel.

"You clean up well," I say over a bite of turkey on wheat.

Eric's smile is humble, yet sure of himself. How does he do it? "You look—" he looks me over "—like a wildcat."

"This dress is a cat-astrophe," I make the pun quiet enough to keep Trinity from hearing.

Eric squints at me with the you-know-better eyes. Then his gaze softens. "How are you doing? Besides the dress, I mean."

Deep breath. Wow, he even smells good. And I probably smell like a deli. Um…what did he ask me? Oh yeah. "I'm fine. The money magically appeared back in my bank account. As for the wedding, I wanted to be mad at Trinity, you know, but now I'm hopeful."

Eric nods. "I've done some weddings that I regretted. But I don't think this is going to be one of them." He clears his throat. "Ladies, the wedding will be starting in a few minutes. I came back to pray with you before I pray with the guys."

Trinity twirls around to face us, almost tripping Jennica on her train. "I'm so nervous. Look at me, I'm shaking. Why am I shaking?"

Eric consoles her while everyone gathers around for prayer. "There's no such thing as the perfect marriage, Trinity. But you can have a successful marriage. One of my favorite verses in the Bible says, *If you are capable of growing into the largeness of marriage...*"

I recognize the words and join in as Eric looks at me. "*Do it,*" we say together. Good stuff.

Then Eric's hand brushes mine. I shift to make more room for him, but his touch continues. In fact his hand slides into mine. I almost gasp and look down in alarm. I know we just shared a moment there, but he can't hold my hand. He's getting married next weekend. What's he doing?

Oh. My pulse slows down. My face warms as my mom takes my other hand. We're holding hands to pray.

I mentally laugh at myself. Hadn't I given Eric a bad time about being one of those youth group leaders who didn't let boys and girls hold hands during prayer? And here I am acting as if it's a big deal. So what if we're holding hands? I can still focus on the prayer. I close my eyes.

"Thank you Lord for bringing Donovan and Trinity together..."

Eric's hand is warm and rough. I want to smooth it with my thumb, but that would be inappropriate.

"We ask for your covering of protection over their marriage..."

But why would it be inappropriate? Eric and I are close. He's one of my best friends. I tell him everything. And I want to support him. It would be just like a pat on the back. A hug.

The thought stops me. We've never hugged. He's never even touched me—not even when I fell off the stability ball and he should have caught me. I did touch him in the boxing ring that one time, but I'd like to forget about that.

I wonder if he's thinking about how *my* hand feels. It's not too sweaty. And I'm sure it's soft—Dee Dee gave us all manicures for the big day.

I peek down to see our hands joined together. And now I'm thinking about Romeo and Juliet. *Let lips do what hands do.* My breath catches. Oh no.

The Bible says if you think lustfully about someone, you have already committed adultery in your mind. But I'm not being lustful. I care about Eric. We have a connection. Yeah, I flirted with him when we first met, but now our relationship is so much more. And it wouldn't be adultery anyway, because he's not married yet.

Now I'm trembling like Trinity. This is ridiculous. It's all in my head. Why am I doing this to myself?

My mind reels to answer. Because he defended my honor from Paul at the gym. Because we had so much fun together at Comedy Sportz. Because he really listens when I talk. Because he took me to meet his parents. Because he's the entire reason that I've decided that I want to get married. Because he's holding my hand…and it makes me feel alive.

"Amen."

What am I going to do? I will be walking down the aisle toward him in just a few minutes. And then I'll be doing it again next weekend when he marries Brooke.

Eric's grip loosens from around my palm. My fingers tighten in response.

"Bethany."

My head jerks up. All the other bridesmaids are starting to disperse. I can't look at Eric. I'm sure he'll read the feelings in my eyes.

Eric squeezes my hand then gently slides it away. I'd still been holding on. I need to escape into the bathroom.

"Are you sure you're okay?" His gaze is hot on my face.

"Yes." I'm anything but. I look down. I give what I hope will pass as a smile to Jennica. I glance out the window at the skyline. But Eric is still looking at me. Never before have I cared so much what he thinks, but never before have I made such an idiot out of myself either.

I want him to feel the same thing I do. How could he not have sensed the electricity that he zapped me with when we held hands? But what if he did feel it? What then?

I need an excuse to escape. I rub my lips together. That's it. "My lip gloss is coming off."

I rush away, but my imagination travels with him. He's going to pray with Donovan. He'll probably say something funny then offer words of wisdom. He's a man of God, with a sense of humor, and the gift of perception. He's everything I need, so why did it take me so long to figure out he's everything I *want*?

Music blares from the speakers at the reception. Y...M... C...A... I watch as Brooke bounces around and does the arm motions to form letters. She doesn't look as good as Star on the dance floor, but she does have a killer bod now, thanks to me.

The D.J.'s smooth voice cuts in at the end of the song. "It looks like it's ladies night out here. This next one goes out to all the bridesmaids. Come on girls, grab your man. Get some guys on the dance floor."

The slow melody to "Lady in Red" replaces the enthusiastic beat of the Village People. I look down at my dress as the lyrics entrance me. Instead of a sweet ballad, I hear empty words and feel my lonely heart throb. I look across the room to see Brooke swaying towards Eric. Now it's my whole chest that aches.

It's too late now. Like Sylvester Stallone in *Cliffhanger* watching his wife slip from his grasp and fall to her death, my chance at a relationship with Eric is out of reach. (Okay, not a chick-flick, but, hey, I have a brother who I used to watch movies with.)

To my surprise, I see Eric shake his head and step away from Brooke. A ridiculous glimmer of hope starts to brighten within me. As Brooke takes Jennica's hand and heads back out to the dance floor, Eric makes his way across the room. I feel my throat constrict as he heads my direction. The room is full of people so it's not likely he's coming to talk to *me*, but our eyes meet and he continues my way. This would have not been big news a couple hours ago, but now my every skin cell goes on alert and I panic about whether to look away, smile...what do I do? I think I smile, but then I look away, too. I've forgotten what it's like to act nonchalant. I look back up at him as he reclines into the chair across from me and loosens his tie.

"Hey," he says.

I should say hey back. Act *casual*, I tell myself. *As if you didn't just figure out that you're in love with the guy.* My little pep talk doesn't work. "Why aren't you dancing with Brooke?" This comes out sounding like an accusation because I'm so desperate for a reason to believe he would rather be with me than her.

"Some people would leave the church if they saw me dancing," he answers simply.

This ticks me off. Not because he's not dancing with Brooke, but because if I were the one he was going to marry, I would want to know that he considered me a higher priority than his job—even if it is a ministry. "Do *you* think it's wrong to dance?"

Eric gives a mischievous smile. "You saw me kiss her. You should know that I'm dying to dance with her."

That hurt. A moment ago I was terrified he would be able to tell how I was feeling. Now I want to smack him because he has no clue. "Oh my goodness!" I can't hold my frustration in any longer. "You can't please everyone. First you give up boxing. Then you refuse to keep your house. And now you won't dance with Brooke—the woman who is supposed to be second in your life only to God!"

I sense Eric stiffen. He slants his eyes to look at me, but doesn't turn his head. It's as if I'm a bear, and he's afraid to move because I'll attack. "You're *mad* at me?" I hear a note of disbelief.

"Remember King David?" I think back to the first sermon I heard Eric preach, and wonder if I'm headed toward an innocent disaster. "He danced in an undignified way. It didn't matter what people thought of him. His wife even ridiculed him. But he lived what he believed. I don't see you doing that."

I've got Eric's full attention now. "I'm avoiding the appearance of sin." He says this sharply, and I know I've offended him.

"Premarital dancing is a sin?" A mocking laugh slips out. "And even if it was, my dad *appeared* sinless until he confessed his nine-year affair."

Eric's arms fly into the air as if playing defense in a game of one-on-one. I don't let him speak. "Which is more important? Purity before God, or keeping every one of man's laws?"

Eric leans forward and growls quietly. "You know I'm not legalistic."

I lean forward, too, so that we both have our elbows on our knees and our faces are only inches apart. In a romantic comedy, this would mean we're going to kiss, and believe me I'm giving that a lot of thought, but my mouth has switched into argumentative mode and it can't be shut down. "Remember the boyfriend who broke my heart?"

"Yeah." He says this grudgingly.

I probably sound like a lunatic bringing up my ex now, but I've got a point. "He didn't become a Christian until high school. His parents bribed him to go to a church campout. He'd always thought religion was stuffy and fake until he accidentally ended up golfing with the pastor and his wife. The pastor hit the ball. My boyfriend hit his ball. Then the pastor's wife hit her golf ball. Her ball flew a lot farther than either of theirs and the pastor cursed."

Eric narrows his eyes and I get the feeling he wants to curse at *me*.

"My ex-boyfriend became a believer on that campout, because he realized that he could relate to the pastor."

Eric is rolling his eyes. "I don't think..."

I don't want to hear his side. Not yet. "I'm not saying that the pastor was right or wrong. I'm just saying that he didn't try to be somebody he wasn't. It worked." I want this for Eric. I really do. "Eric, think about the witness you could have been to your boxing buddies."

Eric blinks and looks down. I'm getting to him. "I gave up that hobby to serve God."

"I know. Your heart was in the right place." I truly respect him for this, but I think he's missing out on an opportunity that God put before him. "I'm sure it was a sacrifice. Just like your house. But think about that one, too. The Bible says to enjoy the work of your labor. Where's the enjoyment? And what do all the guys in your construction group think? What does your brother think? All they know is that you won't keep a nice house because you're a Christian. Why would they want to get saved when you make religion seem like a chore?"

Eric's eyes bore into mine. He's really thinking, but he doesn't like it.

"Jesus died to set us free. Where's your freedom? And what about Brooke? Is the church more important than her?" I can't say anything else. Not only do I feel my chin start to quiver at the mental image of Eric and Brooke as husband and wife, but I'm picturing my own parent's disastrous marriage.

Eric reads my expression and interprets half of it. He takes a deep breath. "Are you thinking of your parents?"

I nod and try to swallow my thickening saliva.

"Now I see where you're coming from."

Oh, he still doesn't get it. He thinks this is only about my parent's divorce.

He touches my hand. His warm fingers brush my wrist. We have spent the past three months together, yet he hasn't touched me once until today. I can't believe that he doesn't feel the same electric current I do. My eyes frantically scan his face trying to read more into his expression.

"I'm not your dad."

I'm sure he meant that to be reassuring, but it only confirms that he's missed my entire point. I snatch my hand away. "Okay. Okay." *Get it together girl. Or at least act like you have it together.* "Haven't you read Galatians? What I'm telling you does come from the past, but not my past. It's in the past of the apostle Paul."

Eric leans away from me. "I've read Galatians. Are you talking about circumcision?"

"Exactly!" I fling my head and arms back in exasperation.

Eric's mouth hangs open slightly. He's trying to connect the dots I've made. "Galatians 5:4. *You who are trying to be justified by law have been alienated from Christ; you have fallen away from grace.*"

Ooh, good verse.

Eric rubs his face and kind of shakes his head at me. "I'm not so sure you can compare what I've been doing with circumcision."

He continues, but I zone out. He's talking about circumcision. I don't want to go there.

I jump to my feet. My chair crashes to the floor behind me. Eric's eyes widen is bewilderment.

"I can't do this," is all I say. I've already said enough. He can choose to read Galatians again, or not. He can think about my input, or not. But I have to get out of here for me.

Chapter 40

I pull Eric's shirt on over my head. It's the one he gave me when the sprinklers attacked us in the gym. I'm sure he didn't mean for me to keep it. And I never thought I'd be wearing it again. But here I am, huddled in my bed, skipping church on Sunday morning.

I can't face him yet. I can't see him with Brooke. I can't act as if I'm fine.

I have a choice. Either I tell Eric how I'm feeling with the hopes that the feelings are mutual and he calls off his wedding (as if he's the romantic lead in my favorite movie), or I keep my feelings to myself and change churches.

The first choice is risky, and half the time I think that if he's attracted to me then he should call off the wedding and profess his feelings without me saying a word. But the fact is, when most people are on their deathbed, their biggest regret is that they didn't take more risk. (It's true; I read it in a magazine.)

If I don't tell Eric how I feel, then I will never know how he would respond. Is it arrogant of me to think that he might love me more than his fiancée? He didn't meet me until after they were engaged. And we are truly a better match than Eric and Brooke. I think I've already mentioned that she doesn't always act like a pastor's wife, haven't I?

There. I made my decision to talk to him. I just have to wait until our counseling appointment on Tuesday. And that's the problem. If he were here right now I would tell him. But he's not, so I have time to think, and I start thinking that I'm not being fair to Brooke. I'm being selfish. I'm being Corrine. The thought makes my stomach churn.

My phone barks causing my heart to pound. I scramble out of bed. Eric could be calling to check up on me. He's been awfully attentive lately.

The caller ID shows my brother's cell number. I consider not answering, but push the button anyway. "Hello." My voice is as flat as my chest.

"It's Laurel. Are you sick?"

"Kinda." No lie.

"Well, we missed you in service, but everyone is going out to eat. I was calling to see if you want to come."

I feel my muscles tense up. "Who all is going?" Now that's a rude question. As if Laurel isn't enough.

"Uh...your mom, your brother, and me."

That isn't enough. My heart plummets in disappointment—not that I'd go if Eric was going to be there. Because he'd probably bring Brooke. "Oh."

"Well, do you want to join us?"

I don't want to do anything. But how do I say that nicely? "Thanks for inviting me, but I'm not even dressed." I doubt it would go over well for me to show up in Eric's old muscle tee.

"Maybe I'll bring you some soup on my way home."

Who does that anymore? "Don't worry about me. I'm just going to take it easy today." I'm going to stay at home and alternate between daydreams and day nightmares. "How was the service?" I try to ask about Eric in a discreet way.

"Amazing. I'm really sorry you missed it." Laurel's voice fills with energy. "After Donovan's announcement at church, Pastor Austin had the idea to do a service of all testimonies. I don't think anybody left without crying."

"Sounds powerful." Normally that would have been my favorite kind of service, but today I'm so focused on my feelings that I might have stood and professed my love in front of the entire congregation—a la *The Graduate*.

"Yes. Powerful." Laurel is quiet as if lost in thought.

"Okay, well, have a nice dinner."

"Thanks," Laurel chirps. "I hope you feel better soon."

I sigh as I hang up. I wish it was Eric who called. I just want to hear his voice again. Listen to him tease me, or even lecture me. I'm okay with that. What am I going to do?

I glance at my Bible guiltily. *Father God,* I pray, *let your will be done.* I can't leave it there. *I'm ready to get married now. Eric showed me that. And if he's the one for me, don't let him marry Brooke. Please. Amen.*

I plop down on the couch, but can't stay still. There's no use in trying to watch a movie, and I'm not likely to fall asleep—I stayed in bed till 11:00 this morning. I need a distraction, but at the same time I don't want to be around any people.

I walk to the kitchen and grab a container of yogurt. My fridge is a disaster. I still have turkey leftovers that Laurel packed me on Thanksgiving. Pulling them out, I toss the Ziploc bag in the garbage then spy some alfalfa sprouts I used to make a veggie bagel the day I got my Christmas tree. There is an oozing puddle under the slimy plastic container. Grossness.

I clean out the fridge, sweep and mop, scrub down appliances, and am attacking light switches when I hear a knock on my door. Too bad I didn't take care of my appearance as much as I did the appearance of my apartment.

I rip Eric's shirt over my head and stuff it under the couch before answering the door in my pajamas. Just as I swing the door open, I have this thought: What if it's Eric at the door, coming to ask for his shirt back? Will I pull it out from under the couch in front of him or lie and say that I lost it at the laundromat?

But it's not Eric. It's Laurel. With soup.

"Hi," I greet in disappointment. Even having to explain an embarrassing situation to Eric would be preferable to a pleasant conversation with anyone else.

"Hi." Laurel looks down at the sanitary wipe in my hand. "Are you *cleaning*?" She acts shocked.

I find myself offended—even though I normally practice the cleaning method of mess transfer. "Yes."

"That's...good." I'm thinking she wanted to use the word miraculous.

"Do you want to come in?" Usually she doesn't.

"Okay." She makes herself at home in my kitchen. "So, you're feeling better?"

No. "I'm okay."

Laurel pours the soup into a bowl and sets it on the tray she gave me for Christmas—a tray I've never used. Next she gets out a pitcher to make orange juice. "We haven't met for accountability for a while. Is there anything you want to talk about?"

I tuck a strand of hair behind my ear. What should I tell my accountability partner? Something nudges me internally. Maybe the hardest things to tell are the most important. "I'm...I'm struggling." I'd like to leave it at that. Everybody struggles. Laurel's prayers should be sufficient, right?

Laurel's eyes flick my direction before she searches for my salt and pepper shakers. She doesn't look at me as she asks, "Is it your dad? Or your cousins? Or your pastor?"

I can feel every nerve in my body come to life. "Why would you think I'm struggling with Eric?" Whoa, I sound defensive.

Laurel sets the tray on the coffee table and studies me like I'm her ultrasound monitor at work. "Oh, I don't. But your mom does."

Mom. A bolt of fear zaps through me. "What...what makes you say that?"

Laurel bites her lip before responding. "At lunch today she told Christian that if she were Brooke, she would keep her eyes on you."

My breathing starts to hurt. I sink onto the couch.

Laurel joins me calmly, but her stiff motions give away her tension. "I told your mom she's being paranoid. You're in their wedding, for goodness sake."

I stare at the wall. Mom is worried that I'm going to be to Brooke what Corrine was to her. But there is a huge difference. Eric isn't married to Brooke. I'm not stealing a husband; I'm rescuing a fiancée.

Laurel stood up to Mom for me. Suddenly I need her on my side. I have to tell her the truth. I turn my head to look her in the eye. "I'm in love with him."

Laurel blinks then frowns. "How do you know?"

Her curiosity encourages me. Her question emboldens me. "How did I *not* know? That is the question!"

Laurel twists her fingers together in her lap. "When did you come to this...realization?"

"Yesterday." I feel a rush of relief and adrenaline. Putting words to my feelings confirms them. My thoughts are finally free to bounce around the room like a racket ball. "It was so unexpected. I mean, I was attracted to him when we first met. But then it became so much more than that. I connected with him as if we were siblings. I learned from him as if he were my mentor. I laughed with him as if he were my best friend." I pause, my voice becoming softer. "Then when he held my hand for prayer yesterday it hit me. I don't want to ever let go."

I'm holding Laurel's hand now. My eyes beg for understanding. My spirit pleads for confirmation. Mom's perception of my confession would be colored by her pain, but surely Laurel can see that this is real.

Laurel's mouth hangs slightly open. "What are you going to do?"

I collapse backward and cover my face with my arms. "I don't know." I sit up straight. "I have to tell him. I have to know how he feels."

Laurel bites her lip. "You already know how he feels. He's getting married to Brooke."

My mind flashes back to my late night phone conversation. "He said he would marry me. We were just joking around, but maybe he was part serious. He's perfect for me in every way. Even his dad thought I was his fiancée when we first met. And he's been wrong about a fiancée before." I'm desperate now. But the more memories I recall, the more sure I become.

270

"What about Brooke?" Laurel plays the devil on my shoulder. Or maybe she's the angel. "Bethany, you're not in a bubble. Your actions aren't only going to affect you. It could very well affect the entire church—like your dad's affair."

"Ohhhh," I groan. "I didn't mean for this to happen. I don't want to hurt anybody. But it feels so right in my heart. Eric is perfect for me. We make sense."

Laurel looks down. How can she argue? Weddings are called off all the time. It's better to have a little bit of drama than a life full of regret. I tell myself this, but still I'm torn. I need her encouragement. "Laurel?"

"I wish I could help you, Bethany. All I can think of is a scripture verse that says, *Only a fool trusts his heart.*"

My passion dampens. "You don't think I should say anything?"

"I wouldn't," she says simply, and it sounds like an apology.

Hope seeps out of me. "So, I'm supposed to pretend I don't feel anything? I'm supposed to hide the truth? Keep it a secret?" The alternative is even worse.

Laurel looks almost as confused as I feel. "If your right eye sins, pluck it out. Flee from evil. Maybe you should go to another church."

I'm reignited—this time with indignation. "How is this evil? How am I sinning? I haven't done anything wrong."

Laurel is slow to answer. "You're innocent now, Bethany. But you could be headed for disaster."

"No." I refuse to believe it. "I'm not going to do anything wrong. I'm just going to tell my counselor how I'm feeling. I do this every Tuesday."

Laurel's eyebrows lift like a red flag being raised. "Pray about it first."

"I did," I respond quickly.

Laurel nods thoughtfully. "Did you just talk to God, or did you listen, as well?"

I look down. "Sometimes I have trouble hearing."

"Me, too," Laurel sighs. "Especially when I don't like what he has to say."

Chapter 41

I toss Mom's bags into the back of my Jeep the next morning. I'd offered to take her to the airport.

"All set?" I ask.

"You bet." This is the question and response format she led us in as children.

I give her a small smile and climb behind the wheel. "Too bad you can't stay for Valentine's Day," I comment, since I can't get my mind off the upcoming wedding.

Mom settles into her seat and angles her body to face me. "You won't miss me. You're going to be busy as a bridesmaid."

The way she says this makes me feel like she has a lot more to say. I glance at her as I pull into traffic. "That's right."

Mom imitates the expression of Cinderella's wicked stepmother perfectly—you know, when the woman found out that Cinderella was the one who wore the glass slipper and so she locks the girl in her room. "You've decided not to tell Eric you love him?"

"What?" The car swerves dangerously as I merge onto the interstate. "Laurel told you?" I feel so violated.

"She didn't have to, sugar. I knew before she confirmed it."

I focus on slowing down my breathing—and on easing my foot off the gas pedal. "You probably knew before I did."

Mom doesn't look concerned. Well, not for me anyway. "Don't tell him," she commands.

"Mom," I half-whine, "If I don't tell him now, then I can never tell him."

"Then never tell him."

If only it were that easy. "Everything in me longs to be with Eric. And I can't help believing that the feeling might be mutual."

He does care for me. I know that for a fact. He invited me to his family cabin for Christmas. He came to sit next to me when Brooke was dancing. And when he looks at me, it's not like he's seeing what everybody else sees, but he sees through me to my emotional DNA. He reads my thoughts and predicts my actions, like when he stopped me from confronting Trinity on New Years.

My mom's eyes blaze with a controlled anger. "If you have to tell somebody, it needs to be Brooke." I knew she would put herself in Brooke's shoes.

"You don't know Brooke. She's not like you, Mom." I can't even imagine telling Brooke that I'm in love with her fiancée. What good would it do? She'd hate me forever and tell everybody why. I'd never get a chance to see Eric again.

Mom clicks her tongue. "So you're going to sneak around behind her back and try to steal her husband?"

"No!" I would never do that and..."She's not *married* to Eric!"

"Yet."

I'm exasperated. "Mom, I am not Corrine. Can't you see my side at all?"

"There's only one side." Mom studies me up and down. "Eric is not yours. That's a fact."

She's right. But it hurts to hear. Why couldn't I have discovered my feelings weeks ago? Better yet, why couldn't he have discovered his feelings for me? If he'd only touched me sooner...I should have shared a blanket with him after the sprinklers went off at Gold's Gym, or we could have skied together after Christmas and gotten cozy on a chairlift, or had I collided with him when I was sock skating in the spec home he might have caught me in his arms and kissed me unexpectedly. My toes curl at the thought.

I missed each one of those chances, but I'm not going to miss another one. "I have to tell Eric, Mom. If he doesn't have feelings for me then there's no harm done. If he does have feelings, then it would be wrong for him to marry Brooke."

"Step away, Bethany."

She's not even listening. She's reliving her own experience. I take a deep breath. "Mom, me giving up Eric is not going to bring Dad back for you."

Mom's face gets hard. I knew she was strong, but I'd never seen her so fierce. "I don't want your father back. He didn't leave me, I left him. There was no way I could trust him after years of betrayal."

I gasp and almost miss the exit for the airport—even with the neon airplane wings designed to look like they're flying up the curving ramp of the parking structure. "Dad wanted to work things out?" Too bad I'm avoiding my counselor because I could definitely use his advice on this turn in events. Just when I think I've got my life headed in the right direction it spirals out of control again.

"Of course. He still loved us. But I never wanted to see him again." Mom looks out the window now. "It would have been easier had he just died."

I blindly change lanes and get honked at by a taxi. The sound is as jolting as reality. "Mom!" What a horrible thing to hear your mother say.

Mom shrugs. "It's true. If he'd died then you wouldn't have been hurt when he cancelled your Christmas plans, and he couldn't have turned down the chance to walk Trinity down the aisle."

Who was this woman? "But if you'd stayed with him he wouldn't have done those things either," I reason. What? I'm on my dad's side?

Mom gives me a thin smile as I pull to a stop in front of the terminal. "I'm not to blame. It was Corrine who made a pass at your father and stole him away from all of us. Remember *that* when deciding what to do about the attraction for your pastor."

She makes it sound so dirty. I'm almost ashamed. Almost.

I pop the hatch and help her with her bags. "Call me when you get home so I know you're safe. And I'll call you after I talk to Eric."

Mom takes her suitcase, and stares me in the eye. "The sins of the father…" she quotes ominously. This is her good-bye.

"Laurel!" I crash through her front door. I've never entered without knocking before, but I've had the whole day to stew over the fact that she betrayed my confidence. Just as Mom couldn't trust Dad after he cheated on her, I can't trust Laurel to be my accountability partner anymore.

"Laurel!" I yell again as I charge up the stairs. Mom might have guessed that I had feelings for Eric, but she wouldn't have known for sure or said anything to me if Laurel hadn't blabbed.

We wouldn't have had this discussion until after the fact—after I open up to Eric and after he leaves Brooke for me. Then I could just announce my new relationship. But now, I'm questioning my every thought, feeling like a home-wrecker.

There she is—slouched in a sofa chair facing away from me. "How could you tell my mom what I told you in private? She lectured me all the way to the airport. She made me sound like…"

Laurel turns her head sideways so that I can see her profile…and tears dripping down from her pink eyes. What in the world does she have to cry about? She's got her beautiful home, her successful career, her perfect hair, and what I envy most…an adoring husband. "What's wrong with you?" I ask grudgingly.

Laurel wipes at her eyes and takes a shaky breath. "I'm sorry I told your mom. I was just worried about you." She does sound sorry, but also distracted.

I stand in front of her and cross my arms, too revved up to sit down. "If you were worried about me you should talk to *me*…or God. Mom is biased and judgmental."

Laurel tilts her head as if she is too tired to hold it up. "Maybe you should listen to her. She's biased because she's been through a similar experience."

"Similar? How can an affair be similar to me telling an *unmarried* man that I'm in love with him?"

276

Laurel sighs. "I don't know."

Way to get out of an argument. "What's with you?"

Laurel's chin puckers and her bottom lip quivers. "I might as well tell you," she blows her wet and slimy nose. Gross.

"Tell me what?" I'm gonna have to drag it out of her.

"Christian," she wails. I wait. She tries again. "Christian got fired today."

A heavy weight pulls me down next to her. "Why?" Christian is the number one salesman in the region for his company.

Laurel wipes at her eyes. "For viewing pornography on the office computer."

I hear myself gasp.

"I'm so mad at him I could..."

I've never seen Laurel mad before. I wonder what she is capable of.

"I could sell his golf clubs."

Ooooh. But seriously... "What are you going to do?"

Laurel's shiny face looks at me helplessly. "I want to kick him out. And go to counseling. And fast forward life until this is all over."

I awkwardly caress her forearm. "I'm sorry." I'm sorry it was my dumb brother who hurt her so badly. Why couldn't he learn the first time?

"Me too," Laurel squeaks as she looks down. "I won't be able to quit my job to stay home with the baby now. And we might have to sell the house..."

"He'll get another job," I assure her. He's got to.

"I'm going to have to work extra hours," she continues her list. "I'm just so tired."

Sleep is a sign of depression, and I don't want Laurel to get depressed. I try to think of something encouraging to say. Laurel knows that all things work for good to those who love God, so I don't want to reiterate a Sunday School lesson making her situation seem trite. But maybe Eric's version will bring her hope. "Laurel, you're hurting and angry right now. I know I would be."

Laurel's eyes glance at me warily, expecting the but.

Here it is. "*But* God has allowed this to happen for a reason. As crazy as it sounds, He's going to use this situation to bless your heart."

If I were Laurel I would give me a dirty look right now. She doesn't. She nods reluctantly. Wow. She's amazing.

"Can I pray for you?" I ask, feeling ashamed that I haven't been doing it consistently.

She nods, so we take it to God. She's still sitting there crying silently when I finish. I'm wondering if I should say something else, but the front door swings open. Laurel frantically wipes at her tears.

Christian pounds up the stairs and his gaze goes directly to his wife as soon as his eyes clear the railing. "I'm just here to pick up a couple more things," he mumbles before heading back toward their bedroom.

"Where's he going?" I ask in alarm. I thought Laurel said that she wanted to kick him out, not that she already had.

Laurel swirls her hands through her hair looking defeated. "He's staying at Eric's until the wedding."

My heartbeat doubles. I try to nonchalantly glance out the window to see if Eric had driven Christian over and is waiting in his car. Only Christian's Acura rests next to my Jeep, and I feel disappointment zoom through me. Then shame at my selfishness. My brother got kicked out of his house and I'm thinking of flirting.

"I should go talk to him," I say.

Laurel doesn't respond so I make my way down the hall and knock on the last door. "Christian?"

He opens the door for me then resumes piling his bed with clothes from his closet.

"Why would you *do* that at work?" I can't help it. The question just pops out of me.

Christian jerks the top drawer of his dresser open. "Because I'm an idiot, okay? Because since Laurel got pregnant her sex drive has been non-existent. Because I've got Covenant Eyes on my computer here at home and Pastor Austin sees everything I look at online. Because I based my actions on my feelings and not on facts."

I take a seat next to Christian's pile of clothes. He's going to be a mess without Laurel ironing for him. I run my hand along a teal shirt sleeve. "What did Eric have to say?" I'm sure it was wiser than anything that's ever come out of my mouth.

"He said that I need to fill myself with good fuel right now." Christian picks up a Bible from the nightstand giving me a clue as to what he's talking about. "Living my life is like engineering a train. The engine is the fact."

Fact: God loves Christian. Fact: Christian and Laurel promised to love each other for the rest of their lives. Fact: Christian is hard-working and lovable. "Okay." I want to hear the rest.

"To keep the train moving forward, I have to feed the engine with good fuel."

I expand on the analogy. "Good fuel would be the Bible, church, prayer, counseling…"

"And bad fuel would be Internet porn." Christian gives a defeated shrug. "Without enough good fuel my train can't make it up the mountains in life. I start rolling backwards. Then the caboose is leading. The caboose would be my feelings"

Eric told him all this? I'm a little jealous. This was good stuff that I could have used. I can still use…like when I'm acting on *feelings* of attraction to my client's fiancée. I shake the thought away.

Christian throws everything in a duffel bag. "If you live your life based on feelings, you will crash."

I look down at the floor even though he wasn't talking to me. He was speaking metaphorically of his own life. I try to lighten the mood. "Well, now you can start your comedy club."

"Because my life is such a joke?"

He's still witty, but understandably lacking in humor. I don't know what else to say.

"Do you want me to walk you out?" I offer.

Christian pulls me into a hug. "I'm sorry, sis. Man, I feel like I let everyone down."

My big brother suddenly seems so small. I bite the inside of my cheek to keep from crying.

He leans away. "If you want to help me, why don't you stay with Laurel tonight? I don't want her to be alone."

I have the feeling that Laurel would like to be alone, but I agree because I'm not going to base my actions on *feelings*. Maybe I can even be good fuel to help her.

One more client, then I'll be heading to my counseling session. This is it. I've got to let Eric know how I feel. It can't be contained inside of me anymore. Even if he doesn't feel the same way, I owe it to him to be honest. He is my counselor and my pastor after all.

I fidget in my chair, feeling an overwhelming urge to eat some chocolate; M & M's to be specific. But I don't have any, of course.

I look at my clock again. The countdown has begun.

Mom was wrong. I'm not trying to steal. I'm going to be real. And even though Christian's talk of feelings leading the train made me think of my desire to be with Eric, I've since realized that Eric is my good fuel. I need him to help me keep moving forward.

I know it's not going to be easy. But I'm capable of growing. And I want to grow with Eric. There's nobody else who has ever challenged me or blessed me in the ways that he can. Now that's something to hold on to.

The bell over the door chimes. I should have cancelled the training session. I really don't have the patience to deal with Amber today.

I swivel in my chair to find an unexpected face. It takes me a minute to recognize Robbie out of UPS uniform. When I do, I want to crawl under my desk.

"Hi." Yes, God allowed me to have a disastrous date with the guy so I would reevaluate my marriage plans, but that doesn't mean I'm happy to see him again.

Robbie's face is grim. He doesn't look happy to see me either, and he's not carrying a UPS package. So why is he here?

"What's up?" I ask, even more confused when his bowling friend Preston follows him in.

Robbie flips open a wallet-looking thing. There is some kind of badge inside. "Robert Browning, D.E.A."

I blink between stares.

"We have a warrant to search your premises."

My mouth is hanging open so wide, I'm sure I'm drooling. "For what?" is all I can think to ask. None of this makes sense.

Two uniformed officers enter with dogs.

"Anabolic steroids." Robbie responds. "We've had you under surveillance. Your partner Jade Dixon has been arrested for drug trafficking."

I must be dreaming. How could this have happened without me knowing it? Sure, she was as big as a man, but that doesn't mean...my memory unfolds past events like a map. Jade had been very protective of her BOSU Ball shipments. Maybe they weren't BOSU balls at all. Robbie and Jade had both been at Gold's the night the sprinkler system went off. Perhaps she had triggered the alarm to keep Robbie from catching her. Could my broken mirror have been a result of 'roid rage? And the bowling night must have been other federal agents...they had even asked me questions about steroids. How stupid am I?

Robbie looks official standing in front of my desk while everybody else tears the place apart. "You're not a suspect."

"Thank God." I truly am praying here. With the way I was acting on our date, this has to be a miracle.

Robbie continues. "But because funds from your business checking account have been used to purchase narcotics, we have to search the premises."

My hand goes to my heart—to keep it from bursting through my chest. "My money."

"Your money is safe." Robbie drops a card with his name and phone number on my desk. "Ms. Dixon used your account to purchase the substance then would reimburse you with a fraction of what she got paid."

That's why my check bounced. I should have asked more questions. "I can't believe it."

Robbie whips out a notebook and takes my statement, though there's nothing I could tell him that he doesn't already know. He requests Jade's client roster, and I get a sinking feeling that the name of Lighten Up is going to get dragged through the mud.

My 4:00 client shows up and faints. I'm not kidding. It's like she's Lois Lane, and she might as well be a reporter with how fast she's going to spread the news.

The crew leaves a mess in its wake. I'm feeling just as emotionally destroyed. Robbie is the last to leave.

"You're good at your job," I compliment, but make it sound like a put down.

Robbie pauses and turns around. "Do you mean the investigating or the undercover part?"

"Undercover." I sound like a bitter ex, when really I hadn't wanted to see him again after my embarrassing display. "I never would have guessed you were investigating me."

Robbie's shrug looks elegant in his suit. "That's because you're attractive and expect men to ask you out."

I shake my head. "Well, then I'm a horrible judge of men, aren't I?" My words ring through my head.

I'm a horrible judge of men. First Paul, then Robbie, now Eric. *No,* I argue with myself. *Just Paul and Robbie.*

I look at my watch. I'm late for meeting with Eric. I grab my purse and usher Robbie out the door.

Driving to the church is like a race against my thought process. I know what the conclusion is going to be, but I want to make it to counseling and talk with Eric before my conscience informs my conscious. No such luck. The moment I tear into the parking lot is the moment I know I can't go inside.

There's a huge invisible wall between me and the entrance. It's filled with facts...the fact that my dad cheated on my mom because it felt good at the time, the fact that Christian lost his job because he chose instant gratification over sacred vows, the fact that I've completely humiliated myself over a couple of men in the last few months. It was the Robbie thing that really threw me. I had no idea what I was getting myself into when I accepted his invitation to hang out. I could have faced legal trouble by acting on my feelings.

My conversation with Christian plays through my mind. I have to act on the facts to keep my train moving forward.

I cut the engine and run my hand over the smooth steering wheel. I can see inside the foyer of the church—the corner of the reception desk. My pulse picks up speed as a tall, male silhouette steps in front of the desks holding something flat like folders. It's Eric.

Without any premeditation whatsoever, my cell phone is in my hand, and I'm instant dialing. My heart drums in my chest as I listen to the rings. Words bounce around my head and I wonder which ones I will speak in panic.

"Thank you for calling Grace Chapel, this is Rebecca. May I help you?" The worn, but warm voice greets me.

"Rebecca." I blurt out. What next? "I need to talk to Eric." I talk fast and loud, feeling disconnected as if I'm reading a bubble over my head in a comic strip.

"He's right here, darling. Hold on."

I wonder for a moment if she recognized my voice. Then I don't care because I should be more worried that Eric will recognize the anxiety in my voice. I watch through the glass doors as he sets his folders down and reaches for the receiver. He's the epitome of casual strength.

"Hello?" So smooth, it's almost sensual.

"Eric..." I stammer. "I can't come in." What would he think if he knew I was in the parking lot spying on him?

"Are you alright? We missed you at church on Sunday."

Did he miss me? The idea almost crushes my resolve. "I've...got a lot going on."

"I know you do." If his comforting voice can turn me to jelly this easily, it's a good thing I'm not fully in his presence. "Christian told me that you are staying with Laurel for him."

Oh, I mentally groan. I need to be in his office right now. I need to pour out my frustration with my brother and evaluate the hateful statements from my mother. I grab the door handle to do just that, but Mom's parting words haunt me. *The sins of the father...*

I collapse back into my seat. What were we talking about? Laurel. "I'm not sure how much help I am, but Christian told me your train analogy, and I'm trying to put it into practice." He should be able to hear the *chugga-chugga choo-choo* from inside the building.

"Oh, the train analogy has been a huge tool in my life," Eric muses. "It is so hard not to act on feelings, isn't it?"

I run my thumb along the mouthpiece of my phone. I can see his lips almost touching the receiver on his end. "You have no idea."

"Hmmm," Eric murmurs in a way that sounds like he can see me, even though he doesn't know that I'm parked out in the dark. "I'm disappointed you can't make it tonight. I won't be able to meet again with you for a few weeks."

He's thinking that we'll continue counseling after his honeymoon, but I know better. Our last session is long since over. "Thank you, Eric."

I watch the man on the phone turn and prop his hips on the desk as if he's settling in for a comfortable conversation. "For what?" Now his voice is teasing.

I smile sadly. Before I would have risen to the challenge and accused him of fishing for compliments or just coyly given a vague response. But now I prepare to say goodbye. I take in the details of our last conversation—his long, built body in it's relaxed position—a position that makes others feel relaxed as well, the sound of his voice that wraps me in warmth and can bring me to tears or inspire giddiness, and the words that are always caring even if they aren't what you want to hear.

"I've learned a lot from you," I say simply. I need to end this conversation and get away before he coaxes anymore out of me. The problem is that I want to linger and stretch out this moment into the length of a lifetime.

Eric tilts his head back. "You mean God taught you a lot in spite of me."

I don't know what to say. I need something memorable for when he realizes that I've left the church and won't be coming back to counseling, but I can't clue him into the fact that this is the end. He'd ask too many questions. And the whole reason that I'm having this conversation from my Jeep is so that I can stay firm to my decision of not revealing my desire.

I take a deep breath. "God used you. I'll never forget all you've done for me."

Eric pshaws my statement. "I'll see you Saturday."

Saturday. Valentine's Day. The wedding. I'd made the decision to avoid Eric, without considering his lesser half—Brooke.

I can either dress up as a bridesmaid and plug my ears while singing la-la-la when the pastor asks us all to "speak now or forever hold your peace" (can you imagine?), or I can become accountable to the bride. Mom told me to talk to Brooke. Everything in me resists the idea, but it also resists the thought of walking down the aisle toward Eric when I'm the one who wants to be saying "I do."

I sigh and close my eyes. I can't confirm that I'll see him this weekend. But he'll find out why soon enough from Brooke, I'm sure. "Goodbye," is all I manage to choke out.

Chapter 42

The day rolls by like the ocean on the Washington coast when you've stood in the icy water too long and your feet have become numb. I train my clients. I respond to their questions. I make small talk. But I'm not aware of any of it.

Brooke is my last client of the day. I remember how she burst in here on her lunch break for the first time three months ago. I'd had no idea that helping her prepare for her wedding would mean the end of my own future.

I can't sit still. I pace to the window then grab another drink of water. I think about picking up the phone to call Dee Dee since she didn't make it over for our Bible study today, but then I decide to pick up my Bible instead. I flip through a few pages, praying for guidance. God should have some scripture tucked away just for me.

"Yay! You're reading the Bible." Brooke's cheerleading voice is as startling as the ring of the bell over the door. How was she able to speak a whole sentence before I even heard the warning jingle? "Eric was just telling me that even though reading the Bible should be as essential as breathing air, it's not easy to stay committed. I think it's because the Devil knows that if he can just keep us too busy or too bored then we'll lose our connection with God. That's how a pastor falls. Oops. I wasn't thinking about your dad."

She never thinks—that's the problem. But she's got me thinking. I know Dad read the Bible to plan his sermons, but how often did he do it for himself? And what about me? I haven't been reading the Bible as much as I should, but I had the one day of fasting where I really focused on scripture. I wonder where I would be right now if I hadn't.

Brooke hops on the scale. I guess we're done talking about commitment to God, though I still have some important things to say on the subject of commitment. I don't get a chance.

"Today you are taking my body fat again, right? Hey, look! I lost nineteen pounds!"

I'm happy for her. She reached her goal. But she's not going to be happy when I tell her what I have to say. I've practiced it over and over in my head. The problem is that I've only practiced my part. I have no idea how her part is going to go.

I snap a picture of my star client in front of my corner screen and turn off the camera without even looking to make sure I didn't cut off her head. I blindly set it on my desk, hoping for an opportunity to speak. She's not going to make it easy.

Brooke grabs her purse and starts digging through it. "Oh, I finished your earrings! They turned out so cute. Are you able to take out your studs yet?" She hands me a couple of hoops covered in dangly beads.

I take the gift in one hand wondering if she'll want them back in a moment. I touch my ear with the other hand. "I think so. I…"

"Well, try them on!" She's grabbing at my ear now. "I want to see how you look. For the wedding we should put your hair in a French twist and then spiral curl the ends. Then you could really show off the earrings. You would look fabulous."

I step back away from Brooke's helping hands and finish taking out the CZs by myself. "About the wedding…" This isn't how I planned it at all.

"Oh, don't worry. I made earrings for everybody else, too." She claps. "Natalie and Marissa get here tomorrow. I haven't seen them in forever."

I have no idea who she is talking about. If I could just get her to listen. "Brooke…"

"Hey! I heard that the cops searched the studio yesterday. That's so CSI. What happened?"

I've got the dangly earrings in now. They feel heavy and I can hear the beads clicking a little bit. If only they were louder then I wouldn't have to listen to Brooke.

"The trainer who worked evenings was selling steroids. But I'm not in any trouble." I think of Robbie and how the event sent me flying to Eric's office. In truth, I'm in big trouble. I give a little shake of my head, sending the earrings clattering. "Brooke, I need to talk to you."

"Okay." She sits down on a weight bench and leans forward, pressing her palms together between her slender thighs. And that's it. She waits silently.

I'm momentarily stunned. This was the opening I've been waiting for, but now I don't know what to say. "I don't think I should be in your wedding."

Brooke waves her hand in the air to push away my worries. "Of course you should. I know I made you mad at your sister's shower. I'm sorry. I just get so excited…I'm excited to have you in my wedding party."

She's not helping. I stuff my hands into my pockets to hide my shakiness. "I'm not…I'm not mad at you," I stumble over the words I had prepared. I have to get this out before I mess it up any more. "It's my feelings toward Eric that are the problem."

"What?" Brooke leaps out of her seat and I imagine her smashing a chair over my head WWF style, but I relax from my flinch when I hear her next words. "You're mad at Eric? What did he do? Sometimes he sees things a little too black and white, but I'm sure we can work it out."

I pull my arms across my chest, feeling cold. "No. I'm not mad at Eric. I'm in love with him."

Brooke must feel the chill as well, because she freezes. She's never been so quiet. Maybe I've shocked her into a catatonic state. Like when people hold their emotions inside and then they explode—Brooke is the opposite. She's kept nothing in and now she's imploding. If I don't say something quickly I might be sucked inside, as well.

"I know you wanted five bridesmaids, but..."

She starts fanning herself with her hands. "Oh my gosh, oh my gosh." Her breathing becomes squeaky.

Oh, no. Not another fainter. I expected her to hate me, or at least yell at me. I look around for a paper bag for her to breathe into. The closest thing I can find is an Adidas knapsack.

I try to ease her back down into a sitting position. "I'm sorry, Brooke. I didn't mean to hurt you." Even as I say this, I'm not sure why she would be hurting. I'm the one who doesn't get the guy. And now I'm wondering why I should even say sorry. It's not like I planned this.

She jerks away. "You're in love with him? Does he know?"

I hold my hands up defensively. "I didn't tell him. And I'm not going to. I'm not even going to come to Grace Chapel anymore."

"Well *that* doesn't matter." Brooke turns from me and moves toward the door, her fingers in her hair. She spins around. "I'll have to tell him that you're not going to be in our wedding. Then I'll have to tell him why. And if he knows you're in love with him he's not going to marry me," she wails.

A ridiculous rush of hope surges through me. She just spoke my dream. She thinks he would choose me over her. And she knows him best.

My pulse pounds like hoof beats so I mentally rein it in. "Why would you think that?" I try to make my question sound like I think she's absurd, but really I want to hear the answer.

"Look at you." Brooke wildly motions to my reflection in the wall mirror. "You're everything a pastor's wife should be. I'm just...I'm just a dumb blonde with a horrible past."

Now I might have once thought the same thing about Brooke, but I remember Eric's story of how she tried to kill herself on Mother's Day. The visual of Brooke committing suicide on her wedding day overpowers my selfish desires.

"Brooke." I have to repeat her name because she's roaming my studio like she's in physical pain. "Brooke, Eric loves you. *You*. He knows your past. And your past does not define you."

I don't think Brooke even heard me. "I knew it was too good to be true. I don't deserve him." She wipes mascara tears angrily down her cheeks.

"Are you kidding me?" I grab a roll of paper towels from next to my disinfectant spray. "You may be a new Christian, but your faith is so strong that I feel guilty just being around you." I listen to my words and am surprised to realize they're true. I'm not only jealous of her relationship with Eric, I'm envious of her relationship with God—as if God should love me more just because I've known Him longer.

Brooke's laugh is harsh. "Eric's mom even liked you better. I pretended I didn't notice, though she made it pretty obvious."

I let myself have the tiny triumph. Eric's mom is awesome. "It doesn't matter. This isn't an arranged marriage. It's a commitment between you and Eric, and I'm not going to get in the way. I'm not going to call him. I'm not going to him for counseling. I didn't even go last night. There is no way I will ever be alone with him again." My chest squeezes tight as I make this promise. Because all I want is to be alone with him forever—I don't want to let go of the tiny chance that it could still happen.

Brooke shakes her head and won't look at me. "Why couldn't you tell me sooner? Why did you have to wait for the week of my wedding? Why did you have to tell me at all?"

"I don't know." I seriously don't know anything anymore. I'm just trying to do the right thing, but everyone has a different opinion of what right is.

Brooke tosses the wadded up paper towels in the garbage. She stands tall and speaks with bitterness. "I should have seen this coming. You two are perfect for each other. Well at least now I'm skinny so I'll be able to attract somebody new." Her voice breaks. "But I don't want anybody else."

I'm a little afraid. I'd feel better if she'd just yell at me and call me names and tell me that I don't have a chance with her man. Why would she give up so easily? I mean, I've already waved the white flag.

"Brooke, this doesn't have to be a big thing for you. Nothing has changed..."

"Not a big thing? Eric adores you. Oh, I'm so stupid."

I've never seen this side of her. She's out of control. I think of Eric's train analogy and what happens when feelings lead. "Brooke, you need to live your life based on facts. The fact is that you are getting married on Saturday. You have heard Eric explain the train, haven't you? You may feel insecure, but you can't base your actions on your feelings, or your caboose will be leading."

Brooke's eyes narrow up at me. She turns and slaps her boom-boom as she walks out the door. "You can kiss my caboose."

Chapter 43

The silence that marks Brooke's exit consumes me. It fills me with anxiety. I did what I had to do. Now I have nothing to do. It feels terrible.

I can't stop thinking of Eric. How long until he hears the news? Is Brooke talking to him this moment? My stomach twists at the thought. Will I ever see him again?

I'm edgy. I can't concentrate on my paperwork, not that I can ever concentrate on paperwork, but now my nerves have me itching. Every inch of my body is uncomfortable.

I power on the treadmill before I've even decided to run. It's like my mind and body are disconnected. I rip off my tear-away pants from over my running shorts and climb onto the conveyor belt without really focusing on what I'm doing.

My feet start to move. It's not fast enough. I instantly relate to cutters—those who cut themselves so that the physical pain overcomes the emotional pain. I speed up until I'm panting. I crank up the incline.

My new earrings jingle in my ears. Normally I would take them off, but now I feel like they are part of my punishment. They are my scarlet letter.

Outside the sun is setting. My day is over and normally Jade would be coming in. I haven't heard from her, but I'm pretty sure our partnership is through. I could stay here and run all night if I wanted to.

Directly in front of me between the windows is a framed scripture verse. It actually used to read, "You are who you choose to be," which is one of my favorite quotes, but after Dee Dee's conversion, I've been inspired to change a few things. The words in front of me now cite Hebrews 12:1. *Let us throw off everything that hinders and the sin that so easily*

LIGHTEN UP

entangles, and let us run with perseverance the race marked out for us.

I've got a race to run, but I'm not sure of the direction. I've made an effort to get rid of the entanglements with Eric and Brooke, but now I feel purposeless. It will take perseverance to make it up this hill in my life.

Perseverance/endurance is something I know about. I've got slow twitch muscle fibers, meaning that I'm great at endurance sports. It takes longer to fatigue my muscles.

Fatigue is a good thing in weight training. You want to work to fatigue—till you couldn't possibly do another rep. This is what makes you stronger.

Sweat trickles down my spine. I don't have a towel with me so I tear off my shirt and mop at my skin. I should turn on a fan, but I don't want to slow my pace.

One step at a time. This is all you can do in life. The next right thing. If only it didn't hurt so much.

I jab some more at the *up* arrow for the incline. My high school track coach would be proud.

I think of Eric again...or I should say I think of Eric *still.* Because I haven't stopped.

I'm not going to be in his wedding anymore. I shouldn't even go. We've spent the last two major holidays together, yet I won't be part of his Valentine's.

The thought of Valentine's Day makes my heart ache—and not just from exertion. There's a spot for Eric in my heart that will never be filled.

He's only a memory now. His dry wit and slow smile. His strong muscles and stronger beliefs. His sweet concern and tender touch.

I close my eyes for just a fraction of a moment, imagining Eric touching my hand the way he had at Trinity's wedding. That's all it takes. I don't see where I'm stepping. I lose my sense of balance. One foot touches down beyond the treadmill belt, and before I can pick up the other foot, it's pulled backward. For a fraction of a second I'm practically doing the splits then I'm thrown across the room. My legs twist awkwardly before I hit the ground. *Crunch.*

Pain rips through me so ferociously that I'm not even sure of the source. *Why me? Why now?* I'm afraid to move. As my mind begins to clear from the snowstorm that fuzzed my consciousness, I realize the sting is from my ankle. From the way it feels, I would expect it to be absolutely mangled—unrecognizable, but as I inspect the injury it looks normal. I try to slide my neon green sock down to inspect further, but even the softest contact causes me to grit my teeth to keep from crying.

Well, if I wanted physical pain to distract me from my emotions, I got it. Not that I need more trauma in my life.

Gently, I shift my weight to roll onto my hands and knees. I don't make it. The moment the toes on my right foot graze the ground, another wave of pain grips me. I collapse onto my back.

My skin is slick from sweat, but now that I'm not moving, my body temperature has cooled, causing my limbs to tremble. I curl up, wrapping my arms around my knees hoping to generate some body heat. I lay there, staring at the ceiling, wondering what to do.

Dee Dee. Maybe she's still at work. I could do a one-legged crab walk/boom-boom scoot toward the desk and grab my phone. Dee Dee would take me to the hospital.

I wonder how long I'm going to have to use crutches. Hey, at least now people might think that I'm not in Eric's wedding because I broke my ankle, not because I fell in love with the groom.

The bell over the door jingles. I give a huge sigh of relief at the thought of Dee Dee here to rescue me. Who else would it be? My business is closed.

I turn my head and gasp for breath. It's Eric.

My heart is in my throat. What is he doing here? Brooke must have told him everything and now he's here to torture me—I mean counsel me. Can't he just leave me to lick my wounds? I'm never going to heal with him hovering around.

At the same time I'm thinking this, I'm longing for his presence. As much as I don't want him here, I don't want him to leave.

"Bethany." His eyes pop open wider at the sight of me on the floor.

I can't speak. I hadn't prepared for this. And even if I had something to say, I wouldn't be able to verbalize it without an emotional breakdown. Methinks I'm already a big enough mess.

He shuts down the whirring treadmill before kneeling beside me. "You fell off while you were running?"

He must be a detective. My lips curl up at the thought. Before I would have been able to tease him about his sleuthing skills, but now I have to keep thoughts to myself so I'm not in danger of flirting. It's a bittersweet revelation. Bitter because it's over, sweet because we had once been so close.

I nod and look down. Oh no. I'd taken my shirt off. I'm only wearing my sports bra—not a pretty sight. I let out a garbled cry and tilt my head crazily from my supine position trying to find my t-shirt. It's still hanging from the treadmill, but in the chair next to Eric is my sweatshirt. I point and motion past him like a mad woman.

Eric picks up the hoodie from the seat and hands it to me. Being on my back, I don't know how to put it on, but I'm desperate to cover myself. I promised Brooke that I would stay away from Eric, but here we are alone together, and I'm topless. Turning the sweatshirt backwards, I stuff my arms through the sleeves so that the hood hangs under my chin.

Eric watches me with concern. "Where's it hurt?"

It takes me a moment to remember, with my heart throbbing and all. Then the stabbing pulses up my leg take over, forcing the first tear to slip out. The pain alone would be unbearable, but I have to deal with saying goodbye to Eric, as well. It's a loss that will be mourned like a death. "My ankle," I say through gritted teeth.

"We better get you to a hospital. Here, let me help you up."
As he says this, he slides an arm under my neck and around
my shoulders.

"No!" I shout, as his skin touches mine.

Eric shifts back to his squatted position. "Did I hurt you?"

Of course he hurt me. He chose another woman over me.
I poured my broken heart out to him. I let him put it back
together. And now I'm never going to see him again. I would
hope that it hurt him, as well.

"Eric." I try to sound reasonable, but my voice breaks. I
feel my chin pucker, but I continue anyway. "Eric, you can't
touch me."

Eric's brows knit together. "We have to get you to my truck."

My chest constricts at the thought of riding with Eric. I've
never been in his truck before. And I can't get to his truck
without his help. Since I've admitted my feelings and tried
to step away, we've become more intimate than ever. "Call
Dee Dee. Call an ambulance. Call a taxi." Tears slip into
my ears. "Now that you know I'm in love with you, you
shouldn't even be around me." My voice is high pitched and
hard to understand, but I want him to know that I'm doing
this because I care for him. "I know you need to avoid the
appearance of evil." I even make a sad attempt at an apology for my attack at Trinity's wedding.

I chance a look up at him. His eyes roam my face, and his
lips part but no words come out. He gives a little shake of
his head.

Then I have a horrible thought. "Brooke didn't tell you?"
How did I get myself into such a situation? I'm crippled and
crying my eyes out to a man who has no clue what kind of
pain I'm in.

"Did you say," Eric pauses as if in disbelief, "that you're
in love with me?"

My nod is so small that I don't know if he's seen it. "I'm
sorry. I didn't mean for it to happen." I close my eyes, wondering if my feelings could have been waylaid. "And I know

you even took preventative measures, like not going out for coffee when I wanted to. I didn't even know how I felt until Trinity's wedding. That's why I didn't come to church on Sunday. Or counseling yesterday."

Eric blinks. "You told Brooke?"

"I was trying to be accountable." I wipe at my cheeks with my sleeves and consider pulling the hood up over my face. "Though I would have rather been like my dad."

There. I confessed. The thing that I'd been unable to forgive my father for has now happened to me. I want what I can't have. *The sins of the father*, my mom had said.

Eric gives a bewildered sigh. Like it's his fault for being so wonderful I couldn't resist.

The song Brooke sang at the first Grace Chapel service I attended rings through my mind. *We are all guilty of the same things. We think the thoughts whether or not we see them through.*

Eric looks down. I'm sure he'd love to leave, but he's too responsible for that. "Bethany, Dee Dee isn't across the street, and we need to get you to the hospital."

I want to scream, but instead I nod my head meekly. I don't have much choice.

Eric tucks his arm around me once again. "We'll roll you to your good foot on the count of three." He says this into my ear, sending chills up my neck and emptiness into my core. I try to numb the pain—pretend it's not happening. But every part of me wants to curl into his embrace.

My right arm is wrapped around his neck now. He's my crutch as I hobble to the door. He's so close. I want to lean my head on his shoulder and nuzzle. But I'm reminded of promises I made. I choke them out so Eric knows—because apparently he hasn't been told anything. "I promised Brooke I wouldn't be alone with you. You need to call her right now. Tell her that you're just taking me to the hospital."

Eric leads me outside into the freezing temperatures. I hardly notice the goose bumps because I'm so focused on him...and the throbbing of my ankle.

"I'll talk to Brooke when I get a chance. Right now we need to take care of your injury. Maybe Laurel can help you when we get to the hospital if she's not too busy."

Laurel. She's kicked her husband out and still she's going to be my rescuer. How messed up am I?

Eric lets go of me at the door to his truck. I miss his warmth already. "Let's turn your sweatshirt around," he offers, taking hold of the material to help me out.

"No!" Knee-jerk reaction. But I'm already longing for a relationship I can never be in. Having him undress me is not going to help. "Just zip it up. Please."

Eric connects the zipper behind my back. I'm dressed worse than I was for "Wacky Wear Day" during high school homecoming. Not only am I wearing my sweatshirt backwards, but I've got huge hoop earrings on with running shorts and mismatched socks—my left sock has little frogs printed on it and I didn't think anyone would notice under the track pants I had on earlier.

Eric then opens the passenger door. I look at the seat and wonder how I'm ever going to get up there. Normally I would step on the running board, but my right ankle won't allow me to put any weight on it.

"Turn around," Eric directs.

I turn to face him with the truck behind me. Eric steps closer and puts his hands to my waist making my imagination run wild. I've heard that just as men are attracted to appearance, women are attracted by touch. I've never known it to be true 'till now. But it's not just a physical desire that draws me to him. It's an emotional longing that can't be described in words, but could have been lifelong had it the chance to grow. And that's what hurts the most—knowing how great it could have been.

"Put your hands on my shoulders."

I'm afraid to oblige, knowing what I'm going to feel. My palms tingle and ache to explore. I meet his gaze, knowing that my expression has got to be as open as his is closed.

The moment is over before I can experience the full impact of it. I swivel in my seat so that my feet are out of the way for Eric to close the door. I buckle automatically while watching Eric walk around to the passenger side.

The ride to St. Luke's is quiet and uncomfortable. This is the only time we've never had something to say to each other. I wonder what he's thinking.

"I'm sorry," I say again to fill the silence.

Eric doesn't say anything and my tears start to stream. It's like he said goodbye to me before he even left.

The cab heats up and the pain in my ankle intensifies. It's like my whole leg has been lit on fire. I notice the distant lights shining from atop the ski hill at Bogus Basin, making the clouds glow. That's something else I'll be missing out on this winter. I can't ski in a cast.

Eric pulls around to the back of the hospital for emergency care. Rather than help me hobble to the door this time, he scoots me off the seat into his arms. I'm sure he just wants to get it over with as quick as possible, but I'm finding misery and ecstasy in every second. One last chance to study his profile, memorize his movements, smell his cologne.

If only he would suddenly realize that he doesn't want to let me go and skim his lips across mine. I'm so close. I have this feeling that if our eyes meet it will happen. It would be inevitable. But he continues to look straight ahead.

Has it only been four days since he held my hand in prayer? Why couldn't he have prayed that way with me the day we met? I want to go back in time and start over, like a patient on their deathbed realizing how much life was wasted. But I'm not dying. The rest of my lonely life expands before me.

"Eric," I say.

He sets me down in a wingback chair before meeting my eyes. "What?" His voice is concerned but wary.

"Eric, I...I don't know what to say"

Eric looks down for a second. "I don't know what to think."

I hold my breath. "What *are* you thinking?"

Eric is calm and controlled as he studies my face. "I'm actually…"

"Bethany?" Laurel sounds dazed as she moves from a hallway into the lobby. Where did she come from? And why now?

I glance back up at Eric wondering if he can finish his sentence before she joins us. But he's studying the leaf print on the carpet now. We've lost our connection.

Chapter 44

Laurel sits next to me and gazes off into space as if she's already forgotten I'm here. I know she's going through a lot with Christian, but I'm the one who needs hospital care. Turning slowly to look at me she asks, "Are you okay?"

I could tell her the truth about how I doubt I'll ever be okay again. She doesn't know that I've talked to Brooke or that I was even planning to talk to Brooke. But she does know that I'm in love with Eric, and here she sits lost in her own world oblivious to the fact that Eric and I were having a private conversation before she wandered over.

"I flew off the treadmill and hurt my ankle," I explain though my every thought is still on the man in front of me.

Eric turns but he speaks to me over his shoulder before walking away. "I'll get your paperwork."

"Thanks." I want to hop after him, but I'm afraid that might appear too desperate.

As soon as he's out of hearing range I lean over and whisper to my sister-in-law. I know she failed at being my accountability partner, but I'm in serious need of moral support. "I told Brooke that I was in love with Eric today."

Laurel digests this slowly. Her forehead wrinkles. "Then why is Eric with *you*?"

My hope flutters back to life for an instant, but that is all the power I will give it. "He came in to Lighten Up and found me lying on the floor after my accident, so he brought me here."

"Hmm..." Laurel watches fish float around in the tank across from us. "So he went to your studio for closure?"

I shrug then really start to think about it. "No...Brooke didn't tell him what I said. I don't know why he came by. He's never done that before."

301

Why did he stop by if it wasn't to talk to me about Brooke? I watch him at the lobby desk talking to a Hispanic woman. What had he been about to tell me when Laurel interrupted?

I look over at Laurel to find her blue eyes filling with tears. Is she crying for me or is she overwhelmed from the situation with my brother? Either way, she's not being the support I expected.

"Bethany," she squeaks then pauses to control herself. "I'm…" she dabs at her eyes with a tissue. "I just gave myself an ultrasound."

I glance over at Eric. I need to make sure I know when he's coming back so I can catch my breath before it gets stuck in my chest again. He's on the phone now. Jealousy grows inside me at the thought of him talking to Brooke. "Are you supposed to do that?" I ask vaguely.

"Nooooo," she wails.

I jump in my seat from the startling sound. "Well, I'm sure it will be okay," I try to comfort her. So what if she gave herself an ultrasound? She's still married to the man she loves and about to have a child with him. I can't even dream of such a day.

Laurel sits very still with her hands covering her mouth, as if she's afraid another frightening sound will escape her lips. She moves her hands and whispers to me. "I'm having twins."

My hand flies to my heart. She gets two babies? Twins are so adorable. She can dress them alike and give them rhyming names. That's great news. So why is she acting as if it's the end of the world? I wish I had her problems. "Congratulations," I say. Now can we get back to my life?

Laurel slouches in her seat. I've never seen her slouch before. "I don't know how we are going to afford raising two babies. And I don't know if I want to bring twice as many kids into the middle of my messed up marriage."

I try to position myself so that the pressure is taken off the ache in my leg. It doesn't work. I cringe, then encourage. "Remember what Eric said when he prayed for Trinity at her wedding?" It's a moment I'll never forget. "He said that you have to be capable of growing into the largeness of marriage. You can do that, Laurel. You're so perfect, it should be easy for you."

Laurel's laugh is bitter. "You think I'm perfect?"

Isn't she?

"Do you know why I gave myself an ultrasound? Why I haven't been excited about being pregnant?" Her harsh voice makes me question everything I know. "Because I'm afraid my baby is going to have six fingers on each hand and six toes on each foot."

Say what? Images from *The Princess Bride* and the six-fingered man sweep through my mind. *My name is Inigo Montoya. You killed my father. Prepare to die.*

My laugh is loud and abrupt. "Why would your baby have six fingers?"

Laurel waves an arm wildly to show off her own hand. "Because I had twelve fingers and twelve toes when I was born and so did my dad."

I feel my jaw drop and my eyes bug. "Are you kidding me?" This Martha Stewart impersonator must have escaped from a circus.

"No. I'm not kidding. But you're the first person I've told. Christian doesn't even know. Can you imagine the jokes that he's going to make at my expense?"

I imagine.

It's a good thing you're not deaf too, because your sign language would be really hard to understand with extra fingers.

Oh babe, you shouldn't have chopped off your extra finger because you would have made an awesome court reporter with how fast you could type.

So how do you give the peace sign when you have six fingers?

It is kind of funny. Though Laurel is not the type to laugh at herself. "You had surgery?" I ask.

"Yeah. But my older sister Chelsea never let me forget it. I was a freak all through school."

Suddenly I see Laurel in a different light. No wonder she always tries to appear perfect. It was to make up for past imperfections. "You're not a freak."

"Maybe not now, but my baby...my *babies* are going to be. Think about it. There are twenty-four fingers and twenty-four toes in my womb right now. And there's no way we have enough money to pay for the surgery to have the extras removed." Her speech is fast and frenzied. "Maybe if there was only one child...or if Christian still had a job!"

I take Laurel's hand to comfort her and can't help looking down at it. It looks the same as my hand except for the taupe fingernail polish and humongous rock on her ring finger.

What am I supposed to say? "I think you should talk to Christian about this. He's not going to make fun of you." The truth is that he might have before, but not now that he got fired. He's humble and willing to do anything to keep his wife and child...children.

Laurel sighs and looks away. "I didn't want anybody to know."

I give a shaky smile. "That's the beauty of having an accountability partner. Once you share your secrets, they don't have power over you anymore."

Laurel grimaced. "That doesn't make this any easier."

I look across the room to find Eric headed back toward me. "No, it doesn't."

Laurel follows my gaze. "You did the right thing, Bethany."

I chew on the inside of my cheek. "I wish I felt the same way. Right now all I feel is regret."

My heart starts to thump in my ears again as Eric gets closer.

He hands me the clipboard, careful not to touch me. "As soon as you get the paperwork completed they can take you back to an exam room."

With the throbbing in my ankle, this news should fill me with relief. But instead I'm clinging to every second with Eric. "Okay."

Laurel rises to her feet. "I've got a job to do. I kinda left my station without telling anybody."

I understand what she's saying, but Eric has no clue why she wandered away from work. "Have a good night, Laurel," I say quietly. "I'll be praying for you."

I plan to be putting in some serious prayer time. In fact, I should pray right now. *Lord, be with Laurel and Christian as they plan their future together. Give them peace and direction and two healthy babies. And be with Eric and me right now. Be the center of our last conversation together. Help me to find the value. And heal my ankle. It's killing me.*

Eric lowers himself into the seat Laurel vacated. "How are you doing?"

I press my lips together before answering. "Do you really want to know?"

Eric ignores the real problem and focuses on my injury. "I bet I could get you some pain killer."

I give a small shrug to show that I'm not thinking about meds at a time like this. "Did you call Brooke? Is she coming out to join us?" That's what I would do if I knew my fiancée was hanging out with a love-sick psycho.

"No, that wasn't Brooke on the phone." He looks at me intently—eyes boring into mine.

I don't really care who he was talking to on the phone. I just want to know what he's going to do about Brooke. "Well, you need to call her. Or you need to leave. I made her the promise not to..." my voice breaks. I swallow, hoping to choke down my rising emotions. "I said I wouldn't try to steal you away from her."

I look down at my hands clasping the clipboard. If I looked at Eric he would see how shallow I am—how if it were up to me I would have gotten him alone and flattered and teased him until there was enough chemistry to light a fire. I could say that it just happened and it wasn't my fault. I would have gladly become Corrine if it meant that I got my way.

I feel, more than see, Eric shift away from me. I'm ashamed to know that his wisdom is what separates us.

He clears his throat. "We're not going to be alone long."

I lift my eyes to see him without looking up. I feel like a naughty kid in the principal's office, waiting for my punishment. What surprises me is that Eric actually responds as if he were the principal.

"Your dad is coming."

My whole head snaps to attention now. "What?" I couldn't have heard right.

"I came to Lighten Up to tell you that your dad is in town. He wanted Christian to talk to you first and prepare you, but Christian thought you were more likely to listen to me."

I lean back in my chair. Of all the times I'd begged my dad to visit, he chooses the night I break my ankle and profess my love to my pastor. I cover my face with my hands and pray aloud. "Oh God."

"That's a move in the right direction."

I need Eric more than ever. How can I do this without him? I look to him for help. "I'm not ready. What do I say?"

I've planned speeches out in the past. There's the one where I nail Dad for not coming to Trinity's wedding. And now that I know Christian is expecting twins that will be good ammo for attacking him on the issue of abandoning me at Christmas to meet his wife's first grandchild. Or my favorite...I call his wife every dirty name I can think of.

My heartbeat skips. I can't call Corrine a single name that I don't deserve myself. I've never understood before how she could come on to Dad. It was just wrong. You didn't do that.

I look at Eric. His charming half-smile. His challenging green eyes. His strong, inviting arms. She must have felt what I feel. She must have mixed up right and wrong in her head. *The spirit is willing but the flesh is weak.*

I'm still not even sure that it would be wrong for Eric to break up with Brooke. In my mind, we make so much more sense as a couple. And it feels right. But as Christian learned the hard way, you can't base your actions on your feelings.

LIGHTEN UP

Eric tilts his head. "You're ready to talk to your dad. You don't need me to answer questions for you anymore, Bethany."

I'm like a baby bird he just pushed out of the nest. Except the mommy bird sticks around to catch the baby if it can't fly. I'm on my own. Eric can't be my wings anymore. I have to let him soar away.

My throat constricts. "I'm going to miss you."

He looks away and nods to no one. What could he say? Great knowing you? Take care?

I wish there was something I could say that could fix all this. Something I could do that would make it okay for us to be friends—more than friends.

He stares across the lobby in silence as I fill out my paperwork. I'm acutely aware of his every action. We're side by side, but we couldn't be farther apart.

I run a list of possible conversation topics through my head. I want to hear his voice again. I want to make him laugh. "You know the guy I went bowling with when I split my pants?" Oh, great start. But at least I'm trying.

Eric doesn't try as hard. "Is that really what you want to talk about right now?" He leans forward, propping his elbows on his thighs.

I *do* sound like an idiot, but I'm going somewhere with this. "Well, I was just going to tell you...the guy is actually a DEA agent. He's been investigating Lighten Up because Jade was selling steroids."

Eric's head turns to look at me. His eyebrows shoot up. "Are you in any trouble?"

He cares. And I love him for it. "No. But that is why my check to your brother bounced. Jade used my account to pay for her shipment of drugs then replaced the money as she sold it."

"Crazy." His one word hangs in the air.

I won't let our conversation die. I wish we were back in his office. I might as well be as real with him here as I was during the counseling sessions. "Tuesday I was planning to keep our appointment and tell you how I feel about you."

Eric shifts in his seat, but he can't be any more uncomfortable than I am. I'm the one being rejected here. I continue with a courage I don't feel.

"But then when Robbie brought me the search warrant, it made me think about my choice in men. I don't know how to pick 'em. First a player with a pregnant girlfriend. Then a DEA agent who only wanted to pump me for information. And now my pastor who is engaged to one of my clients."

I pause to gauge his reaction.

He blinks then finishes my explanation. "So you cancelled your appointment with me in order to keep your feelings from running your train."

"Yes." I couldn't have explained it better…except for the feelings part. "But the other guys don't compare. It's always been you whether I knew it or not."

Eric's gaze caresses my face, but I can't read the look in his eyes. He's guarded, which is a good thing at the moment. Any encouragement on his part and I would be in his lap—not even a broken ankle could slow me down.

"Bethany," he says slowly. I love how he says my name. I want to wrap it around me like a warm blanket. "There are no accidents. I…"

I hold my breath, but Eric's words are interrupted again. This time by the only other man who knows me better.

"Bethany." My father emerges from the revolving door. He comes to me with outstretched arms as if he's been longing to see me—not avoiding me.

The past two years don't matter at the moment. "Daddy!" I start to stand, forgetting that my right leg is not whole. He swoops in and crushes me to his chest to keep me from stumbling.

I never expected a reunion like this. And I never expected to feel so little and so needy. I hang on for dear life. Tears spring to my eyes, and I look at Eric through my blurred vision.

Eric gives me a sad smile. He may not love me, but I am loved. My dad is here. He still wants me. I'm safe in his arms.

Eric stands and shakes my father's hand behind my back. I can't see him now.

"Thanks for taking care of her for me," my dad says over my head.

I hold my breath and listen for Eric's response with the ear that is not pressed to my father's chest.

"She's an amazing woman, sir. I may have been her counselor, but I've learned just as much from our relationship."

I close my eyes. Eric's words are kind, but it is his mention of relationship that tears at me. Our relationship is over. And I can't help thinking that if it wasn't over, we could continue to learn so much more from each other.

"Bethany Light?" A nurse calls my name. I'm ready to escape.

"We better go." Dad twists around to support me the way Eric did on the way to his truck. I feel much less vulnerable this time. "Bye Eric," Dad says.

"Goodbye," Eric says to both of us, but the word has a whole different meaning for me.

Dad has me turned toward the exam rooms so I look over my shoulder for one last glimpse of the man I would have loved to have called my husband. Eric stands still with his eyes on me. His face is expressionless, but just the fact that he is still looking at me, touches me deeply.

"Goodbye," I say softly before hobbling away.

Chapter 45

Dad makes a better nurse than the lady in the pink scrubs. He helps me lie gently on the table then wipes my tears away.

"Does it hurt that much?" He asks then gives orders to the nurse before I can respond. "She needs some pain killer."

The nurse reads my temperature and blood pressure, gives me an ice pack, and promises a doctor will be with us soon. As much as my ankle aches (I want to throw up), I'd rather have my dad all to myself than have our conversation chopped up by x-rays and analysis.

Dad lays his jacket across my bare legs. "Remember when you were little and I put your shoes on the wrong feet? It wasn't until you tripped for the upteenth time that your mother realized what I'd done."

I'd forgotten that story. "Oh, yeah."

Dad motions toward my feet. "At least I always dressed you in matching socks." His eyes travel to my backwards sweatshirt, but he doesn't say anything else.

I rest on my side and smile at the idea of how I must look. I don't explain, though. I'm just enjoying the attention. I didn't realize how much I missed being taken care of.

"What brought you to Boise?" I ask, avoiding his previous question about my pain—and the twisting in my gut that thinking about Eric brings.

Dad scoots a chair close to me. "I missed my little girl," he says simply. This would have been an appropriate response had he used it during a visit sooner. At the moment, I find it lacking.

"Well you completely missed your baby. She's married and on her honeymoon in Europe right now." I'm not trying to upset Dad. I just need a better explanation.

Dad sighs heavily then brushes hair out of my face. "I've failed again." He says. "That's what has kept me away from you for so long—being reminded of my failure. And that's what has me working so hard at my marriage now. I'm afraid of failing my new wife."

Personally, I can't see how Corrine would expect Dad to be faithful after he cheated on Mom with her for so long. But I see where Dad is coming from.

He leans closer to me. "I don't deserve your forgiveness, Bethany. But being with you again makes me realize how badly I want it."

I'd been forgiving Dad over and over since I'd started seeing Eric. If he had apologized like this before it would have made everything so much easier. But then I wouldn't have grown as much as I have. And I wouldn't have gotten to know Eric as well. Of this, I'm thankful.

I reach out to take Dad's hand. "I forgive you."

I've never seen my Dad cry before. Even when he had announced his affair and resignation, it had been with a controlled demeanor. But now he's laughing and crying all at once. He leans over and gives me a hug that crushes me and crinkles the paper covering the cushion of the exam table.

He sits back down and a rush of words come pouring out. "I'm sorry. For everything. I felt so bad about Trinity's wedding that I couldn't even enjoy my cruise. Finally Corrine got me to tell her what was bugging me. You should have heard the earful she gave me. She wouldn't let me fly home to Montana with her. I got a separate flight to Boise straight from Los Angeles."

I laugh in surprise. "You didn't tell Corrine about the wedding?" And here I'd thought the woman was being an evil stepmother by not letting Dad attend.

Dad shakes his head humbly. "I'm so afraid to mess up that I don't even suggest anything I'm worried will upset her."

He's like a beaten puppy. For the first time since the affair I feel sorry for him. "Is that why you didn't come out for Christmas either? It was your decision and not hers?"

Dad makes a helpless face. "Guilty." Then his expression becomes concerned. "I hope you didn't ever get mad at Corrine about that. She's on your side."

Now *I'm* feeling guilty. And not just for hating Corrine, but for becoming Corrine. "Actually, it's been harder for me to forgive her than it has been to forgive you."

Dad runs his hands over his face. "We both messed up, honey. I'm not going to give you any excuses. We didn't make the right choice. But I want to *make* it right."

I fiddle with adjusting the ice pack. Before tonight I might not have been able to forgive Corrine. "I understand," I say softly.

Dad continues. "We didn't plan to get involved in the first place. It started out as ministry."

I think of Eric's sermon. Then I just think of Eric. "An innocent disaster."

"Exactly. That's a good way to put it." Dad's face scrunches up. "Where have I heard that before?"

"My pastor," I answer.

Dad's eyes look toward the corner of the ceiling while he thinks. They widen as he looks back at me. "You're right!"

"Eric told me that he was the first person you confessed to." My chest feels constricted.

Dad's head tilts to one side. "He's been a good friend to you, hasn't he?"

That's all it takes. I try to prevent the tears, but my nose starts to run, giving me away. "I'm in love with him."

I think of all the times I couldn't forgive Dad for letting himself get into the situation I'm in and all the times that Eric has convinced me to forgive him. Falling for Eric could be the very thing that brings my family back together. That is if my dad doesn't judge me in return. If he doesn't get mad at me the way Mom did.

Dad's dark eyes become as still as my heartbeat. "Does he know?"

My abrupt laugh surprises me. How can I laugh at such a serious problem? It must be the meds. Or maybe it's the ridiculously insane situation I'm in. What else can I do but laugh? My laughter bubbles into hyperventilating causing Dad to scoot to the edge of his seat. The noise coming from my mouth finally subsides. "I told him tonight," I whimper.

The wrinkles in Dad's forehead are deeper than I ever remember them being. "What did he say?"

I wonder what Dad hopes he said. Daddies are supposed to be fiercely protective when it comes to their daughter's love life. But from his own experiences he might want me to back off the way Corrine didn't. I open my mouth to answer the question but don't know what to say. Um... "I don't think he said anything. He was quieter than he's ever been."

Dad sits up straight. "Oh, honey."

I'm worried that a lecture is coming—that he thinks I've gotten my hopes up. "I wasn't planning to tell Eric. Honest. I cancelled my counseling session last night and explained everything to his fiancée. When I said goodbye to him tonight..." I pause and look down at my hands, remembering the beautiful wedding band that was on Laurel's ring finger and thinking about the band that Eric will give Brooke. "That was for good."

Dad shakes his head a little as he listens to me talk. "I had no idea." He reads the story behind my eyes. "That took a lot of courage for you to do."

Maybe it's the compassion in my dad's voice. Or the respect. But the undeserved compliment reopens the wound. "It wasn't what I wanted to do!" I'm a sinner not a saint. "I'm not any better than you, Daddy."

Mom's comment echoes through my mind. *The sins of the father...*

"Honey, honey," Dad soothes me only the way a father can. He wraps both my hands in his. "Nobody is better than anybody else. We're all sinners. But, what you did today..." He traps my chin between two fingers and tilts it up so I have to look into his eyes. "What you did today was a self-sacrifice. That's Christ-like, baby. I couldn't be prouder of you."

Christ-like? How about humiliating? Pathetic? Desperate? "Then why do I feel so bad?"

Dad's lips spread into an almost smile. "All patients feel bad when they come to the emergency room." Then as if hearing how corny his joke really is, he adds, "I could quote you a couple scripture verses to answer that question, or I could live the scripture and just love on you."

I'm feeling more loved than I have in a long time. "I love you, Dad," I say. And unlike my earlier experience today, the man I say this to says it back.

Chapter 46

Dad and I enter the church. It's beautiful—everything Grace Chapel is not. Stained glass windows, a pipe organ, and pews. I never would have expected Brooke to go for traditional, though I think it fits Eric just fine.

"Hold on, honey," Dad says. "I've got to find Christian and give him this boutonniere." My dumb brother got his rose at the rehearsal dinner last night but then forgot to put it on his tux this morning.

"Okay." We head back toward the Sunday school classrooms where the wedding party is getting ready.

Dad's been a lifesaver this week. If it weren't for him I wouldn't have come to the wedding. Though I'm not sure why I'm here. I do have this fantasy that Eric sees me, calls off the wedding, and we start our new life together by taking all the catered food to the homeless shelter downtown, but in reality I guess I just want to show that I'm happy Eric's happy. I haven't spoken to him at all, but Dee Dee relayed the message from Brooke that I was still invited. Just not as a bridesmaid.

Scenes from the movie *My Best Friend's Wedding* haunt me. I bawled when I watched it the first time, and that was before I knew Eric. This week I've been watching movies like *The Sound of Music*—you know, movies that turn out well for "the other woman."

Just as Dad and I are about to turn from the reception room into a side hallway we hear a crash from behind. I whirl around to see one side of the punch table collapse to the ground and the punch fountain sliding toward the carpet. Before I can react, an army of men in monkey suits (as Christian calls them) race past to do battle with the beverage display. Dad rushes away as well.

315

I watch in amazement for a moment then look around for the hidden camera. Am I going to be on the next episode of "The Real Wedding Crashers?" No cameras—just a very well-groomed groom. If I were a talent scout I would hire him on the spot to star in the next James Bond movie.

Eric's jacket is unbuttoned and his hands are in his pockets. He's obviously not going to worry about the revolt of the refreshments. Nope. He walks my way and it feels like he's moving in slow motion.

"Hi," I hobble back a step. I want to tell him how handsome he looks, but I'll leave that up to Brooke to inform him.

Eric's eyes ricochet back and forth between mine. I would almost rather have him ignore me. But that might be just as painful.

"I'm glad you came," he says.

I look down at my crutches.

"I've been thinking a lot about you."

Why? Why is he doing this to me? I'm sure he hasn't been thinking about me as much as I've been thinking about him.

Eric waits for me to look up. "I want to thank you."

Now my eyes lift above him to the ceiling and I give a slight shake of my head. What does he have to thank me for?

"Thank you for going to Brooke first when you realized how you felt about me."

I don't want to talk about this. Alright, I made a fool of myself. Let's forget about it. Or let Eric forget about it. I never will.

Eric looks past me at all the commotion still taking place, making me feel like I'm in the eye of the storm. He turns back.

"I told you before that every marriage is only thirty seconds from disaster. That could have been me."

My arms lock against my crutches pushing my spine up straighter. What was he saying?

"You're very attractive, Bethany."

The toes of my right foot curl in the peep-toe of my pump. The cast on my other foot keeps those toes from curling, but they try anyway.

"I enjoyed your company. I was flattered by all the attention you gave me." He shrugs. "I discounted it by telling myself that you treat everybody that way."

I tilt my head and try to listen objectively, without showing my longing. The man is getting married today.

"If you hadn't told me that you talked to Brooke first, I wouldn't have been thinking about her. I would have been thinking about me and what felt right at the time. I would have done something I would regret for the rest of my life."

I take a deep breath and catch a hint of his familiar aftershave—a heady concoction when mixed with visions of Eric and me involved in an innocent disaster. "Would it have really been so bad?" I ask quietly. I'm not trying to steal him. It's too late for that. I just want to keep believing that the attraction was not all in my imagination.

One side of Eric's lips curl up. "You don't want to start a relationship with a guy who can justify cheating. You deserve better than that."

He put it so nicely—makes himself sound like the jerk, not the other way around. And he almost makes me think that there is somebody else out there for me. I give a little chuckle at what an amazing counselor he is. "I should thank you too, Eric. Thanks for giving me the courage to consider the possibility of marriage in my future...and to forgive my dad for his past. I judged him prematurely."

The gang of groomsmen have accomplished their mission and trickle back toward us, laughing and joking. Christian wraps his arm around Eric's neck in an overfriendly/needy hug.

"I'll join you guys in a minute," Eric says smoothly.

Christian tries to smile at me before walking off. I watch him quietly join the other guys. He's become this humble man that I almost don't recognize. He's not as fun as when he's putting on a show, but he's more real. And that's going to make his comedy club as empowering as it is entertaining.

I turn back to Eric, wondering what else he has to say. I'm amazed that he's opened up to me so much already. But I'm sure everything he's telling me he's already said to Brooke. He's that kind of guy. I tune in for the conclusion of our relationship, but Dad appears beside me.

"Sir," Eric addresses him with the utmost respect, even after knowing what he knows. "I need to finish up one last counseling session with your daughter. If you don't mind, I'll send her out to sit with you in the sanctuary when we're finished."

Dad looks at me, and I'm sure I'm looking a little lost. He waits for me to nod before leaving us alone.

If I weren't hanging onto my crutches for stability right now, I would be wringing my fingers together in expectancy. Does Eric have more feedback for me? He's been so sensitive up till now. Was he just warming up to let me have it?

"Counseling?" I ask uncertainly.

Eric's eyes revert back to mine. "I was thinking of what you said to me about how I worry too much about the opinion of others."

Oh no. That had not been my finest moment. I'd attacked Eric out of frustration. "I didn't mean…"

"You were right."

I was? I rock back on my heels—not easy in a cast.

"So I'm keeping the house."

I picture a big red bow on the front door when Eric carries Brooke over the threshold. Tears spring into my eyes, knowing that I had something to do with it, even though I wish it were me going home with Eric for good. "Good," is all I can think to say.

"Yeah." Eric's easy smile disappears and he studies me with intensity. "But it made me realize that judgmental people are a trigger for you."

I feel my eyebrows scrunch together. I'd never thought about it that way. "I guess so."

Eric continues, "And whenever there is a trigger, there is an experience that created it. What do you think your experience would have been?"

318

I shake my head as if jostling my thoughts. When have I been judged? A mental timeline runs through my mind like tickertape and jolts to stop on the moment two years ago when Dad announced his affair at church. My mouth opens. "Dad," I say gustily.

Eric nods as if he knew this all along. "I thought so. And may I suggest that the reason this has affected you so much is because you judged yourself even harder?"

Eric did it again. He made the complexities of my life seem so simple. Hadn't I just said that I judged Dad prematurely? And I judged Mom for her boob job and Brooke for her blabber mouth and Christian for his porn addiction and Star for not being the perfect mother and Dee Dee for her abortion.

At the hospital the other night I realized that I'm not any better than my father, but the truth is that I'm not any better than any of them. We all do the best we know how to. As Christians we should love each other, not judge each other. When we see somebody else's blind spot we need to point it out with love and encouragement. That's what accountability is all about.

I'd like to say that I finally get it. But I'm sure I have a lot more to learn.

"What do I do now?" And how will I do it without Eric?

"You've made some huge steps in forgiving your father. But now you need to forgive the congregation. And I think the best way for you to do that is go back to Living Faith."

That's something I wouldn't have thought of on my own. But because Eric believes I can do it, I'm going to try.

"Hey Eric! Hey Bethany!" Mick's energetic voice bellows at us from a distance. I look over my shoulder to see him trotting our way from the lobby.

My eyes meet Eric's again and I think I spy a little twinkle. "And I'm guessing that Mick will be changing churches with you," he says.

Chapter 47

Mick gives Eric some high-five-guy-slap then hands him car keys. "You should see your truck," he says.

Eric chuckles. It's a charming sound. "I'd rather not."

Mick smiles at me, and I feel embarrassed for him.

Eric nods at both of us before heading back to the Sunday school classroom where the groomsmen are getting ready. I watch him go, wondering when I'll see him next after the wedding.

When you're heart aches with pain, it is hard to imagine life without it. It's so much easier just to feel sorry for yourself.

"So," Mick gives me his full attention. "I've got to join the wedding party, but do you wanna come see the Corvette I'm loaning the bride and groom first? None of the other groomsmen know, so they decorated the wrong ride."

"Okay." I'm not going to lead him on. But I don't want to hurt his feelings either.

I hobble along next to the big guy, going so slowly I get passed by an old lady headed to the gift table.

"Too bad about your ankle," Mick says.

If he only knew.

He continues. "I'm sure Brooke was disappointed you couldn't be in the wedding."

I grunt. "It worked out." Unlike the wedding Mick had planned with his former fiancée. I'm ashamed all over again.

"Well if you weren't all banged up I'd invite you snowboarding. I go almost every weekend."

A guffaw escapes me. The mental picture of Mick on a snowboard is very similar to that of the goons chasing Granny in the animated movie *Hoodwinked*.

Mick looks me up and down as a challenge. "Don't tell me you don't snowboard."

"I've never tried it," I admit.

Now it's Mick's turn to guffaw. "We've got to do something about that."

He grabs a handful of pastel M & Ms from a side table. I wonder who brought them...Brooke or Eric? Or maybe Eric's mom. "Do you want some?" Mick offers.

I can already taste the satisfying chocolate. But it's only a memory, just like all my time spent munching on Eric's office couch, and finding the candy in my Christmas stocking, and stuffing my face at the New Year's party so I didn't have to talk. It's like I was self-medicating. But now I don't need them anymore.

"No thanks." I smile in confidence. I'm going to be fine.

Mick holds the door for me as we step outside into the blustery weather. It's freezing, but beautiful. Eric and Brooke will get some amazing wedding pictures in the snow. A sigh escapes my lips.

Mick thinks it's because I love his car. "Nice, huh? I'll give you a ride sometime."

The car is pretty—sleek and cherry red. But when I look up at Mick, his face gets redder. The thing is, I know just how he feels. Only I feel it for Eric.

I give a small smile. "Mick, I've learned that there are no such things as accidents. And it's no accident that you are here with me right now. I really need a friend."

Mick looks hesitantly happy. I gave him the "friends" speech, but at the same time I told him that I'm glad he's here.

Love at first sight it's not. But then, wouldn't love at first sight be based on feelings, not fact?

If ever Mick stood a chance with me, it's now. Not because I'm lonely, not because I've decided that I want to get married, but because I'm not going to judge him and because I'm going to live my life looking for the value.

He holds out his hand. "Friends?"

There is a lot of value in a good friend. I accept his offer. We shake. "Just friends." For now.

Turn the page for an exciting preview of

Shake It Up

the second book in the
Body and Soul Series
by Angela Ruth Strong

Available Summer 2013

Chapter One

The music transitions to a slower beat for the cool down, and I try to slow my motor mouth as well. I already talk a lot as it is, but since the OCD instructor came to take my Body Jam class, I've really been putting on a show. It's not that I think Paige is a better aerobics instructor than me, but she does seem to be in the running for instructor of the year, and I'd really like to win that award twice in a row.

Instead of cue the next move verbally, I point down toward my hips and demonstrate the hip circle. It's all about attitude, baby.

Paige's circles are just a little too big. She obviously doesn't have a dance background, but she's gotten certified in everything from spinning to step to kickboxing, so I know Body Jam is next. She lives and breathes Group X (a.k.a. group exercise), and the Gold's Gym members love her even though she's not authentic.

I demonstrate a shimmy forward then backwards. My favorite students Martin and Zia get it, but Paige has some kind of Jane Fonda bounce going on. She misses the idea of flava—that's "flavor" without an R at the end. She's always dancing at breakout level, like she's here for the workout and not the self-expression.

One final deep breath in...strike a pose...music fades. "You all rock!" I encourage through my headset microphone. They didn't all rock, but they feel like they rocked, and that's what matters. "If you have any questions about a move, come up and let me help you out. Hope to see you next week!"

Class sizes always drop in the summer, but I still love teaching. There's just more energy in the room when the sun is still shining at eight-thirty in the evening. And we've got a great view of Boise's barren mountains from the windows in our Park Center location. There's nowhere else I'd rather be right now. Not even back in Hollywood.

"Star!" Martin hurries over. He's a little guy. Little in height, anyway. He makes his living as a lawyer, but you'd never know it from the skullcap he's got covering his balding head at the moment. In the aerobics studio he's all funk—except when he's obsessing about getting things right. "Star, on that hop-cross-hop move, do I plant my whole foot or just dig my heel into the floor?" He demonstrates both versions.

I hop-cross-hop as well. "I do the heel dig," I say.

"Okay. Heel dig."

I imagine he's making a mental note of it. Heaven forbid he leave out the heel dig next time.

Martin looks over his shoulder. "That's cool that Paige came to your class," he says.

I follow his gaze. The OCD instructor is at the back of the room mopping her face with a towel. I hope she's sore tomorrow.

"She's got a lot of energy," I say. The truth is, I think she's a spy for my boss. I've never gotten in trouble from her tattling, but I know others who have.

Martin pops his knuckles. He does this a lot, and I wonder what kind of reaction it gets him when he's at trial. "Is she going to start teaching Body Jam?"

Now why would he want to know that? "You'll have to ask Paige." I wave as Zia walks over to join us.

"Alright." Martin's thoughts have already left me. "Great class today, by the way."

I know he means it, but the questions about Paige outweigh the compliment. I ignore the fact that he's trotting over to talk to another instructor and give Zia my brightest smile. The girl inspires me. She's as wide as Martin is tall, and she has to take lots of breaks during class to catch her breath, but when she moves to the music you can see the enjoyment on her face.

"What's up, gorgeous?" I ask.

"Oh." She blushes at the compliment. She's probably not been called gorgeous much in her life, but I mean it. "I... uh...wanted to tell you that I won't be coming to class for a few weeks."

I untangle the headset from my ear. "You okay?"

"Yeah." She looks down. "I love your class, Star, and I usually don't let the lyrics to your music bother me, but you have a new song that makes me uncomfortable."

Huh. Now I'm wishing there was something wrong with her and not my music. I try to think back over the CD I just played. It was perfect for the choreography. "What song are you talking about?"

Zia scrunches up her pudgy face. "It was the one that said 'I lead a sinful life'." Her eyes dart away. "I don't feel right dancing to music like that."

I stare in surprise. Other classes have had complaints about songs like Highway to Hell, but Body Jammers seem to be more accepting of lyrics. I mean, it's not like we're singing them.

"I'm sorry, Zia," I offer. "I hadn't thought about it that way. But..." here I steal from my sister's newfound religious babble, "aren't we all sinners?"

Zia's thick shoulders twitch in what might be a shrug. "Yes. But it sounds like the song is glorifying that kind of lifestyle."

Dang. I sigh. "Well, I'll be doing this routine for the rest of the month. I hope you'll come back when I start incorporating the older stuff again."

I'm not responsible for the music selection. Every three months I get a Body Jam CD and DVD. I do the new stuff for a month then mix up the routines until the next release arrives. A lot of it is sexual (as my mom pointed out, spelling it so my daughter didn't understand) and there have even been a few curse words sprinkled in here and there, though I usually grunt loud enough in the appropriate places so those can't be heard. Of all the songs that would chase away gym members, I didn't think this would be the one.

"I want to come back," Zia replies, but she sounds hesitant.

I don't know what else to say. Zia was always my biggest fan. "Okay. Have a great summer."

I watch as she lumbers toward Martin and Paige. Robbie is talking to them, as well. I roll my eyes and turn to lock up the stereo.

See, Robbie is my boss. So not only is Martin losing interest in me and Zia is dropping out of my class, but now Paige's probably critiquing my every move to the fitness manager... My music was too loud. And I didn't face the class the entire time—I turned around while teaching the spin so that we were all going the same direction. Oh, I also ran in at the last second before Body Jam was supposed to start because the clock in the childcare was slow.

But that shouldn't matter. Robbie is my neighbor and I got him the job here, so he better not try to lecture me. I slide my gaze back to where they are talking. Besides, if I know Robbie, he's more interested in asking Paige out than talking business.

Robbie catches my glance and nods as if he expected me to be looking at him. If he weren't so cocky he'd be cute. Tall and trim, African-American like me, with teasing dark eyes and a contagious smile. I can't help smiling back, so I add a head shake to let him know I don't approve of his flirtatiousness.

I toss my tune belt and headset battery into my gym bag and head for the door. Robbie leaves Paige and her new fan club to join me.

"Star Light, Star bright. First Star I see tonight."

Did I mention that my adopted parent's knowingly gave me the name Star Light when I joined the family? This is not the first time I've been teased.

"Reciting a nursery rhyme doesn't count as spouting a sonnet on the romance scale," I inform Robbie.

Robbie grabs at his heart as if I've wounded him. He grunts in mock pain. "Believe me, you would know if I was going for romance. I'm just playing with you."

From his own lips—he's a player.

"So?" I ask. "What negative things did Paige have to say about my class?" Hopefully Zia didn't mention the music lyrics. My stomach knots as I think about my last conversation.

Robbie smirks. "Paige said your class was incredible."

"Really?" My stomach begins to untwist. To have Paige's approval is almost up there with instructor of the year. "She said that?"

"Yep." Robbie and I walk past the cardio equipment lining the 2nd story balcony and head down concrete stairs into the heart of the gym—the weight room. "Though she is concerned about your soda consumption."

And there it is. I should have known. "Caffeine keeps me going. And it's not that bad. Some gyms even offer shots of espresso during spin classes." I used to teach at the cutting edge Crunch Fitness in L.A. where the trend was started.

Robbie makes a sucking noise with his mouth, an it's-not-okay-sucking-noise. "Espresso doesn't have all the sugar and carbonation." He's got a point. "Remember when Paul the personal trainer was fired for smoking in the parking lot?"

"Give me a break." Cigarette's have warning labels and are illegal for minors. There's a huge difference between cigarettes and soda.

Robbie continues with me past the juice bar toward the childcare. "You're only here for two classes a week, Star. Think you could survive for a couple hours without drinking pop? You know, set a good example for the members seeking to improve their health and fitness?"

I open the half-door leading to the cubby closet. Robbie follows. I open the second half door leading into a play-room that smells like graham crackers. Robbie follows.

"Okay, Robbie. I will keep my beverage of choice off the premises." Or maybe I could smuggle it in. I think I have a black Nike water bottle at home.

"Great."

I scan the room for Jennica. She's not climbing on the huge plastic fire engine or coloring at the art table. Oh, there she is—dancing and singing with The Wiggles on T.V. That's my girl. Not The Wiggles part, but the dancing and singing.

"Jennica!" I call while signing her out on the childcare log.

Jennica twirls around. She takes three huge frog leaps toward me then crosses the rest of the distance doing a penguin waddle. Oh to be three years old again.

I swoop her up and brush her cheek with kisses. "Hey, baby." She smells faintly of the coconut oil that holds her hair in cornrows. I used to hate that smell when I got my hair done, but now it reminds me of her. Anyway, I got all my hair chopped off, so I don't use the gunk anymore.

"Hi Jennica," Robbie holds up a fist. "Pound it," he says. She knocks her toddler-sized knuckles with his. Yes, Robbie charms women of all ages.

I set Jennica down so she can grab her bunny, and I can carry my gym bag. The three of us troop out. I shoot Robbie a suspicious glance. "Did you send Paige in to spy on my class?"

Robbie's eyebrows arch high. He's perfected the innocent look. "No. I think she's just planning to take the Body Jam training—get certified—since she's becoming a master trainer and all."

I stop in my tracks. Jennica keeps going, but happily backtracks and starts walking circles around me when she realizes I'm not moving anymore. "She's going to be a master trainer? She's only been teaching for a year."

Master trainers are the best of the best. They travel the world, training other instructors. Paige wouldn't be a Body Jam master trainer—she'd probably do step trainings—but I've thought about applying. I would love to motivate and inspire. To birth a new generation of fitness teachers. The only thing that has kept me back is the hours. I'd be gone two to three weekends a month. And I already have trouble getting childcare for Jennica as it is.

Robbie pauses with me. He leans up against the railing that separates the walkway from the weight floor. "Paige has got what it takes," he says.

He's right, and I don't like it. And I don't like the fact that he's the one telling me. I start walking again. "So did you ask her out? Is that why you came up to the aerobics studio?" Okay, I'm being petty. But I don't want to talk about Paige's step aerobics skills anymore.

Robbie laughs. It's not a chuckle this time. He's either surprised by my question or he enjoys irking me. We reach the set of glass double doors at the exit. Robbie holds one opens so Jennica and I can walk into the sunshine. It doesn't really cool off at night in Boise in the summer—makes for a fantastic Fourth of July.

"Actually..." Robbie joins us on the sidewalk. I stay put. It would be silly for him to walk all the way to my SUV with me. I'll just let him say what he has to say. "I went upstairs to ask you out," he says.

Ugh. I roll my head back on my neck. We've been through this before. "You know I don't date."

"Really? I thought Martin was your boyfriend."

I don't reply. His joke was old the first time he told it.

Robbie laughs anyway. "I know, I know. That Dr. Laura thing." Robbie waves his hand as if he could wipe away Dr. Laura's advice for single parents to stay single, thus creating a secure environment for their children. "It's not a date. I just happened to get VIP tickets from Josh for a concert at The Knitting Factory, and I knew you would enjoy it."

Josh is the CEO for Gold's Gym. The Knitting Factory is a concert house. And the VIP room is for members only. "Who's playing?"

Robbie's eyes twinkle. He knows he's peaked my interest. "David Crowder Band. Have you heard of them?"

"No." I love new bands, though. "When is it?"

"Tomorrow night."

Jennica tugs at my hand. She doesn't need anything. She just wants to go.

I will play Candy Land with her and read her a bedtime story. Maybe I'll even let her sleep in my bed so we can snuggle in the morning before breakfast. I think all this first, so I don't feel guilty about planning to ask my sister to watch Jennica tomorrow night. I haven't been to a concert in forever.

"It's not a date?" I double check.

Robbie lifts his shoulders in a casual shrug. "Not unless you want it to be."

He's relentless. "Just say no, Robbie."

"No." He says the word, but I'm not sure if he's saying no, it's not a date or no, he won't just say no.

"Alright." What have I got to lose?

www.ingramcontent.com/pod-product-compliance
Lightning Source LLC
Chambersburg PA
CBHW051953240626
47153CB00005B/1744